ALSO BY JILL EISENSTADT

From Rockaway

KISS OUT

KISS OUT

JILL EISENSTADT

ALFRED A. KNOPF   NEW YORK   1991

THIS IS A BORZOI BOOK
PUBLISHED BY ALFRED A. KNOPF, INC.

Library of Congress
Cataloging-in-Publication Data

Eisenstadt, Jill, [date]
  Kiss out / Jill Eisenstadt. — 1st ed.
    p. cm.
  ISBN 0-394-58230-6
PS3555.I844K57   1991
813'.54—dc20   90-52958   CIP

Manufactured in the United States of America
First Edition

*For Marv, Barb, Jeff, Deb, Steve,
and in memory of Sam*

One must not become attached to animals: they do not last long enough. Or to men: they last too long.

Anonymous

CONTENTS

KISS OUT

1

THE BIG CATCH

"SHE'S REALLY, really rich. . . . Besides, I love her."

So it's not just a rumor. Sam Lubin *is* getting married, and soon.

"You would have to go ruin a perfectly good night." Oscar Arm searches for the waitress, because it's useless—he'll never be able to keep two dozen steamers down now. And it's stupid too—his only thought is to smush Sam's face in the sawdust.

Lil's Fish Fry Palace has sawdust ankle deep, varnished rope trim on the tables and on the driftwood bar, a stuffed, airbrushed marlin, divers' helmets in hanging dinghies; each lamp is actually a dead, gutted sea urchin.

The waitress wears a plastic abalone-shell name tag: RONNIE. "No way," she informs Oscar, as she collects Sam's cigarette butts in her apron. "Once the order goes in, that's it; policy." She stoops to avoid the droopy fishnet that threatens her hair mold. Like an ice cream scoop. Definitely not a do from Chester's, the Arm family's beauty parlor; the only beauty parlor in Sidehill, Queens.

Oscar assesses: not a style that "works with her." Is it an outer-borough creation? And if so, which borough? Has she been stripped, dyed, blow-dried, permed, set, cellophaned? For how much? To last how long? Fred would know.

"Where *is* Fred?" Though he's Oscar's *identical* twin, Fred alone possesses those conceptual talents. "Fred isn't late, ever." He's never professionally handled a pair of shears, yet Fred can look at any head of hair and promptly determine its potential best cut. "You did invite Fred . . . ?" Fred, who grouches, "Just looking at *some* people's coifs can be *physically* painful." Wait till he gets a load of Ronnie. "So . . . Where is he?"

"Busy," says Sam. His hair is blackish, abundant, borderline frizzy, side-parted and kept under control only through infrequent washing. "Anyway, I think this is good as a permutation. You and me. Two's company."

"No candlelight?" Permutation?

"Later, some a the other guys are comin down to toast me. Maybe Fred'll show for that. . . . *What? Arm! What* are you lookin at?"

Ronnie's still standing around, intrigued.

"Lemme talk to Lil. I'll cancel the order myself," says Oscar.

This starts Ronnie sneezing. Six in a row, setting free the whole apronful of Sam's cigarette ends.

"Tsk on you, Osc," says Sam, thumbing through the menu. "Poor Lil's out there right now clammin for your chow. What'd ya do, forget your wallet again? Just a minute ago you were starvola. *Hey!* Did I even get to tellin you about Claire's *private* stream? I am serious. This chick's got trouts swimming around her backyard. Reality. Yo! *What is with that look?*"

"You're really not kidding," Oscar says, busying himself with the connect-the-dots menu puzzle. He'd been so certain the engagement was hearsay. He digs the lines in with the butter knife, hard. Also, he'd somehow gotten the retard idea that Sam was buying tonight, that Sam had invited him here for a big ha ha: Sidehill, the neighborhood that can't so much as gossip efficiently. Oscar accidentally slices right through the paper. Marrying off, of all people, *Sam,* c'mon.

Not even Louette believed it. Said she was just passing the word, in case. And she always seems to believe rumors that Oscar's cheating on her.

But Sam confirms it again. "I am not kiddin'. Matrimony. Hitched. Now quit askin; I'm bored a this."

Oscar is vaguely disappointed to see the dot-to-dot reveal a clown and not a fisherman.

He met Claire once, months ago. And would've examined her more thoroughly had he known she'd be Sam's *wife*-to-be. What he recalls best: Her bald dad, who had a head-smoothing tic. Her hair—non-color brown-yellow, save a chlorine-greenish cast (what are heated indoor/outdoor pools to a girl with her own trout stream?). Her front teeth—more specifically, the huge space between them. And an offensive boa constrictor handbag.

Not that Oscar had any bleeding-heart attacks over it, hardened as he is by the daily atrocities he confronts at his job managing the PetMart or learns of from *Disease Profiles*— required reading for the Ornithology II course he takes, and takes very seriously, through the mail from LION (the Long Island Organization of Naturalists). In fact, if Oscar had to make the choice—despite long-standing Sierra Club, Humane Society, Jacques Cousteau, World Wildlife Fund, and Save Our Shores memberships—he'd prefer being a handbag any day, a wallet, a condom-carrying case, you name it, over someone's pet Bauble or Puddin', or Jonquil. Every reason for living save food anticipation bred clean out of you.

"All right already!" Sam fakes a yawn. "Rerun! Rerun!" To Oscar's frequently voiced dismay, Sam remains a loyal pet owner. "My girl Nancy reduces stress, lowers my blood pressure, and will one day make me a superior dad; it's proven." Poodle owner, no less. "Yes, thanks to that love pup, I can eat all the butter and angus steak I care to." Who refers to his dog as his girlfriend. Often. Or did. "I *am* a little worried how they'll get along . . . Claire and Nance. I mean, Nancy doesn't get all worked up like she used to with Judy. Remember how every—"

"Look," Oscar says. "I only met this girl once, but . . ." Claire insisted Oscar Arm was not a real name, then went on to mention how she'd recently created a seven-foot penny roll "from scratch." "Do you call this meaningful work, Sam? Just answer, how can you go and marry such a person? I don't get it."

Oscar's searching, he truly is, scrutinizing Sam's face for some sort of explanation. But all he sees are mistakes. The wrecked cars, kissed hockey sticks, bar fights, sprinkler-head run-ins. Scars that Oscar (and Fred) have personally witnessed being born. Even those faint little white neck blemishes, a result of Sam attacking his chicken pox with a hairbrush—how long ago?

The trio—Sam (long-standing go between/get between), Fred, and Oscar—has begun its dissolve.

"You're shaking," Sam says. "You're takin this worse than my father did. He's downed a whole bottle of asprins in two days. Ravin pissed at Peaches for sort of givin me the idea. If Claire won't turn Jewish, he'll ruin his stomach lining."

"Whatayamean *sort of* giving you the idea?" Oscar asks. Sam's mother, Peaches, a combination of pushy two-hundred-fifty-pound clotheshorse and youth-obsessed R & B drummer for the Lubin family band, The Bouncetones, has never had just *sort of* an idea in all her life. "Stop. Forget it. I don't think I care to hear any more right now."

"Keep out of Chester's, in that case. Or wear your earplugs," Sam says, crossing his eyes; a new habit. It highlights the divot between his eyebrows, that scar the result of a flying lunchroom spoon years ago. "And stay outta the pool hall. And DoNuTs! And off the bus stops and—"

"Now Louette's going to nag me to marry her too."

"Why don't you?"

"Will *you* marry me, Ronnie?" The waitress has arrived with Sam's angus steak. "I'd like two Jameson's with ice, please," says Oscar.

"I don't want that," Sam says.

"It isn't for you."

"I'm married," Ronnie says to Oscar. "But I'll think about it. . . . Naah, gotta pass, but thanks. I got your clams eighty-sixed. *Since* you looked so god-awful depressed about em." She adds, "Congratulations," to Sam. "The next table told me."

Naturally, all three of them look over to the next table, where two elderly shrunken heads (scarce and transparent hair) eat pie and nod. Sam nods back.

"How about that? True love in this day and age!" Ronnie blares, extra heartily for the assumed-to-be hearing impaired and directly into Oscar's ear as she's leaning over his lap to straighten a framed, cracked Alaskan king crab.

"Truuue, and *safe*," Sam croons in his extraordinary voice. A deep, plush baritone; he could entrance just singing the specials off the blackboard. "Truuue, and—"

Safe? It's a nightmare. From where Oscar sits he has a good view of a whole wall of black-and-white photographs. Fishermen in rubber hip boots heave-hoing up the Big Catch. As if happiness *is that* and nothing to get so worked up about.

"True love, my ass," Oscar says. Sam's freshly peeled thumb callous flutters down, one piece, into the black ashtray. Amazing how the fingerprint comes right off with it. "So . . . what's next? Are you going to finally make your move, quit The Bouncetones? Go solo?" Sam's sister, Lynn, has already defected (the Partridgesque lifestyle bringing on a latent nervous condition, or so rumor has it) for marriage, for Maryland, for an entry-level job in *banking*. Bleh. "Maybe start writing some of your own material? True love songs?"

"Who says?" Sam snaps, apparently panicked at the mere suggestion of anything original being expected of him. "I'm thinkin The Tones'll play the fund-raiser." How he refers to his wedding. "That is, if it's OK with Claire."

"Without a singer? I don't know. The little Mrs. might feel gypped." It's got to be the voice she fell for. Hooks all the females, that voice. Even Ronnie is reeled in. Still hanging around, her unpleasantly slouching breasts point in different directions but breathe down, up, down, in unison. "I really wish I could get those drinks," Oscar hints.

One of the ancients at the next table has gotten something

in her eye. She cranks at her friend, "I can get it out myself, thank you." Her voice is hellaciously grainy.

"You know, Claire could very well wind up sounding like that," Oscar warns Sam. "After a coupla years, when she graduates into her real personality; you'll see. The upper-arm flab appears—"

"Betcha"—Ronnie shakes her head at the pie people—"it's that darn sawdust."

Sam just winks, sucking his fingertips one by one—each guitar-callused, dripping with steak sauce. "She's only eighteen, Osc."

"Say what?"

"Sawdust, I'm pos." Ronnie trudges off to offer a tissue and advice. Oscar hears her explaining, "Stuff gets in everywhere. My hair, shoes, pocketbook. You should see my bed. Like sleepin in a lumberyard. My husband says ta me, 'Ronnie,' he says . . ."

"You heard. One. Eight."

"If you stop to consider how much sawdust that's been actually ingested in this place . . ."

"Eighteen?"

"Eighteen."

"I could prolly get workman's comp . . ."

"What's the catch? Eighteen? Is she pregnant? Is she Catholic? Doesn't she notice you're ugly?"

Sam sniggers and picks some yellowish crud off his form-fitting Mets jersey. All his shirts are too tight. He likes to think he's muscular. "Well, since you asked . . . Don't go tellin the world, but . . . I shouldn't be divulging this, but we're buddies, aren't we? Get ready, Osc—I got myself a real live virgin this time!" A sort of hobby of Sam's. "Which means virgin parts, which means—well, you know what it means. . . ."

"I do?"

"AIDS-free."

"You mean—"

But now Ronnie's back with the Jameson. Just when they were getting somewhere. Oscar downs the shots—one swallow apiece—and orders a third. Partly to blur Sam, now complaining he's been "scammed of a toast," his due. Partly to get rid of this leech of a waitress. Either she really, really likes them or she's heavily chumming for the big tip.

"Anything else tonight?" Ronnie asks. "Tissues? Asprin? Advice?"

So she's just another gossipmonger. If Oscar cared, he could probably get the dirt on the entire Fish Fry staff, from Lil herself all the ladder down to the kid who stuffs the little cardboard cups with inedible coleslaw. Fortunately, humans aren't Oscar's animal of interest.

Ronnie folds her arms into a disappointed humph. "I don't think I made a joke."

Sam is laughing, laughing, laughing his gravelly Eh huh. Drops that trained voice down to uncharted depths to wail, "Baby, baby. You want some a my meat?" Eh huh, eh huh. He holds up a forkful of wet-looking gristle. Oscar is amused despite being appalled. Ronnie's response is another sneeze eruption.

"Now you've contaminated his steak," Oscar tells her.

"It's that darn sawdust again," says Sam. "It's always that darn sawdust."

"God bless," call the pie people.

Though still gazing at the meat, Ronnie asks Oscar why he looks so familiar. A stock question only a touch less idiotic than "What are you thinking?"

"Cause there's two of him walking the planet. Doubled odds," Sam takes it upon himself to explain. "Replicas. Like, see how his leg's jiggling? Well, if you can picture this, right now there's a corresponding jiggling leg elsewheres. Woman, you should watch the two of em eat sometime! They rock back and forth to beat—"

"But he's not eating," Ronnie whines. "I got the clams canceled."

"I heard *some*one call a waitress, I'm sure." Oscar makes a face till Ronnie catches on, duuuh, shrugs, and walks off.

"You hurt that one deeply, guy," says Sam. He looks greasy and happy and too large (sideways) for the booth. Chewing.

Oscar notices that Sam's taken to wearing his class ring.

That he *has* a class ring. It pings gratingly on the plate edge whenever he switches fork and knife to cut.

"I hope Nancy's all right tied up outside," says Sam. The guy can't stop talking for more than three bites. "Whataya-think?" Can't not mention Nancy for more than six. "I just feel terrible leaving her like—*Wouldya stop that?!*"

"Stop what?" says Oscar.

"Lookin at me like that."

"Like what?"

"Like you're suddenly this true love expert. Whataya know about it?"

"I have my theories."

"Yeah, bein betrothed to Fred, you would. Look, you're jealous. OK, we relate; just control it. Nancy's jealous too, I can tell. . . . Remember how she'd get herself all worked up and charge Judy, always humpin Judy's leg, peein on—"

"True love," says Oscar.

"Soon as Claire shows, though, whoosh, she's outta there, whinin and snarlin and sulkin under the table."

"Come up for air, Sam. Please. Try. One attempt to convey to me really why you need to marry this girl? *Please?*"

Sam nods slightly, with appropriate solemnity, downs his entire glass of water *and* Oscar's, then straightens his already noteworthy posture and pushes his plate aside and folds his hands in front him and belches. Commanding belch. He repeats, as if rehearsed:

"She's really, really rich. . . . Besides, I love her."

So OSCAR leaves him to the steak (Sam *would* order steak in a seafood place) and Ronnie, the huge tanks of lobsters on death row, plastic seagulls, the check, good, the check, but forgets his allotted mint toothpick and—he realizes as he stands beside his once sunshine-yellow Toyota—his jacket, denim. It has taken Oscar four years to get it to a perfect state of worn-in-ness. Even so, not worth going back for. Nothing is.

Still light out. The time of year when you're still surprised it's still light out. The air gets that sensual feel before summer turns it restless. Even here in Sidehill, where huge jets fly low at all hours, spring gets in. Even in front of Lil's Fish Fry Palace, the air smells different. All of which only heightens Oscar's irritation. It should be raining mud when he's this disillusioned. At the very least, dark.

Nancy yaps, of course. What are poodles for? She strains at her leash and yaps and sits and stands and sits and yaps, attached to an expired meter in front of Sam's van. Sam has trained her to *Sit!* whenever she sees a car, so even the relatively light flow of traffic on this strip of Sidehill Avenue has her zanily sitting, standing, sitting, standing.

The poodle bark is a truly unbearable racket. Particularly after six hours of the PetMart's truly unbearable racket, led by Memo—the high-decibel parrot prodigy—polishing his jackhammer imitation picked up from the new construction site across the street from the shop. Oscar needs Nancy's yapping, after Sam's news, on top of Ronnie's questions, like he needs a parade.

He ducks into his car to get away, get going. But where to go on a night like this? On a night like this, if he were younger, there'd be a street corner to claim. A case of Bud tins stashed in the bushes. Constant packs of girl/women roaming past on display. And not because *watching* is, nowadays, all safe sex permits, but because maybe watching was, in those days, all you *felt* like doing. Just watching the way the girls walked past and didn't quite lift their feet enough, causing that subtle wriggle, or lifted them too much, a flounce under, through the streetlamp spotlight—bright, squeaky hair haloed, outline of front-closing bras, slight glint of root beer lip gloss.

Yes, now, on a night like this, Oscar's options are more limited: Fred—except he still lives at home. Louette—that would mean confirming the marriage gossip. The pool hall—ditto, yet a possibility. His apartment—too skanky (yesterday he found mushrooms growing in the couch). Or the library—no way.

Maybe he'll let the car go where it chooses. On its own, though, the car will only idle indecisively. It's *his* car, after all.

Streamlined body but lame pickup. No rust yet but failing brakes, shot shocks, fairly messy inside, and nearing empty. Yellow.

Oscar would be eating steamers if it hadn't been for Sam's news. And knowing Sam, he's probably right now hitting on Ronnie. For old times' sake. Last licks before the big M. *Mar*riage. *Mistake.* More scars for his collection. The worst kind—invisible scars like his parents, Peaches and Sid, have—you get from marrying someone you don't love, because you need a drummer (or so the rumor goes). Because she's really, really rich and diseaseproof (or so goes Sam's excuse). And *those* scars you can't go flaunting at parties. They endure till death death death do you . . . realize, Sam?

Unable to come out and say any of this in Lil's, Oscar brought up The Bouncetones to insinuate. An idiotic idea. Think next time. Think how generous Sid Lubin (and Sam, by association) was, is. The old man who let the whole rowdy crew of them, fifteen-year-old goons, loose in his basement amongst all that costly, highly damageable professional music equipment. Nutty Sid, why? Generous Sid, how come? To teach them all those good, good walkin blues.

Sid Lubin knew how unlikely it was that his son's friends would ever again find anything requiring so little practice that yielded such enormous results. Godsend of the frustrated adolescent, the single twelve-bar progression can be jammed on indefinitely, incessantly, and always sound totally cool. The fact that the neighbors complained only helped convince their sorry crew that like all true artists they were misunderstood.

By high school Oscar and Fred had lost interest in favor of juggling. But some of the other guys started a band, Dinner and the Talk, which did a few copies decently ("Stairway to Heaven," "Dust in the Wind") and a few original numbers with ripped-off tunes well enough to get them hired for parties and in bars around Sidehill.

Which got them girls. The girls would point—which one do *you* like?—and dance up close to the stage, never a real stage. When the band took a break, the girls'd hang out, asking,

Which one is Dinner? Do you need a back-up singer? Wanna dance? I got tickets to Yes at the Garden Friday, interested?— smiling, stroking the instruments, even, since there's nothing like a teenage guy who knows how to *do* something besides solid geometry, play quarters, fix a fan belt, and since Sam especially knew what to do. Pick out one in particular to baste with those long, dark, liquidy glances whenever he broke into a true love song—like, I sat up all night writing this one for you, babe—inevitably getting the chick squirming and mush-eyed. The girls who intentionally came to see them were like the girls you hear on any pop radio station, screaming, *Noooo! I can't believe it! I won?! Ohmygod!! I get the T-shirt!? Ohmygod this is not happening to me!* or just a throaty, *Hey, I'd like to request Aerosmith, "Big Ten Inch," for Rick.*

Oscar downshifts with little time to spare before the yellow light turns red. He hasn't thought about any of this in a very long time, and wonders if Sam misses it. Not the music (though Sam did once have a torrid aspiration for rock 'n' roll glory) or, god forbid, high school, but the way it all felt so . . . knowable then. What was expected of you. What .you expected. Sam at center stage, playing star. Sam, bolstered by a freak gene, the incredibly lush and enigmatic vocal cords—his only truly stellar feature (still, one more than anyone else had)—recognized years earlier when he was chosen to do the God voice-overs in each and every Hebrew school production.

Stopped at the red light, Oscar chances to see a five-dollar bill lying in the empty next lane and debates whether or not to get out and retrieve it. Every one of his decisions seems to have this quality lately: small enough to be meaningless but too big to ignore.

IN KEEPING WITH the theory that a person's regular hangouts serve the same function as bird roosts, Oscar winds up at the pool hall. He draws eighty-six, a very far-off number, then wanders over toward the phone to call Fred. Patience, he tells himself.

What Oscar likes about the place isn't even pool so much—

his game neither improves nor worsens—but the hall: its huge-ness, its dimness. The only time he gets to spend in a huge, dim space. And the reassurance that he'll never outgrow it, never start feeling at home and then be too old. The way it goes with those street corners, certain bars, all schools. The way it went with Sam's basement.

"You study in the pool hall?" Mom asks when she answers the phone like he dreaded.

"No, in the car . . . Nothing . . . School's good." Mom's count-ing on him to become the family's first professional—a mail-order ornithologist. "Yes. Give me Fred. . . . Then wake him; he's faking. I saw him at DoNuTs! this morning. . . . No, no-thing's wrong, Ma. No . . . *noth*ing."

"You don't sound nothing," Mom argues, but eventually she agrees to put Fred on.

While he waits, Oscar tries sign-languaging Hairy Leroy to toss over a bag of chips, but elicits only a wave from the guy. Leroy tends bar and hands out balls and calls "Sixty-nine . . . Sixty-nine" over the mike and turns on lights—his duties. He's not required to act as a waiter.

The pool hall's crowded, as always. In the afternoon, with Chi-nese kids learning capitalism. A couple of them cut school early to grab up all the table numbers so whoever comes in after three is stuck having to pay them off to play. And when they leave at dinnertime, it's the old men who enter. The heavies, in ones, each carrying his own stick in a fancy calf-leather case, creating the hush that means money riding, watch and watch out. Till now, around nine, ten, when it's yuppie turnover.

"Rise and issue forth!" Oscar tells Fred in response to a loud sigh in lieu of hello.

"I'm flu-ridden."

"An airing sounds about right, then."

"What are you doing there that you can't come here?" Fred asks after he's already committed himself to coming but be-fore he hangs up. No byes.

"My car brought me," Oscar says into dial tone.

Leroy calls "Seventy-seven" over the loudspeaker. "Seventy-seven."

A good person, Leroy, if distant, with dated middle part, sideburns, heart-shaped face and attitude. Oscar gives him a discount on cat food for the many strays he feeds and old clothes for the needy mortals he sustains on chips and soda, stale machine nuts, cigarettes.

Oscar wants chips, badly, but not enough to risk losing his seat. Two old guys—well, one old, one middle—linger at the nearest table, shooting a final short rack for fun. Old tells crude jokes, using his pool stick as a prop. This causes Middle to take his eye off the shot, banking the orange five slightly left so that it's intercepted by the caroming cue ball and spun off course. Kiss out.

"Damn it, George. You too funny."

George has a full head of dandruffy, used-looking steel wool. "Didya hear about the gal who had her left side removed? She's all right now!"

"Then again . . ." Middle has a horseshoe fringe of hair around baldness. What the future holds in store for Oscar's dad. ". . . funny's relative."

It's the kind of dopey language joke Fred uses in his street act or sets to music to sing in his wobbly way with a banjo. No musical genius, Fred, but—

"Relatives are funny," says George.

Out of all the guys who started off in the Lubin basement, Sam's the only one who turned into a real musician. The Lubin Family—as The Bouncetones are commonly called—is primarily a swing band and does well despite an ever changing brass section, also despite an overbearing Peaches. Sam gets to travel around some, playing guitar, keyboards, singing all those old numbers "with feeling." Gets to meet all these new women with money. Write off his van and—

Fred.

"Fred." He looks worse than Oscar feels. He looks exactly four minutes younger than Oscar. Only pale right now and in possession of certain clothes (tonight white corduroy overalls) that Oscar would never wear. Also missing a fingertip (casualty of juggling) and—the biggest difference—beardless. Oscar's one great claim to fame is that he's never shaved, ever. But for all that, he's grown only one measly tuft like a carpet ball, which everyone hates, most of all women. Louette once tried shaving it off him mid-nap.

"The suspense is putting me to sleep," Fred says. "This better be good or else real bad." He grabs Oscar's number ticket. "It must be! You spaced, ninster! I heard him call eighty-nine as I came in."

Oscar jumps up to fight for his table, but just as quickly slumps back down. "I started thinking."

"I see, you got me here to celebrate."

"About the old days."

"What old days? We're twenty-six."

"You sure don't look it."

The way Fred slowly bends his lankiness into sitting position reminds Oscar of Uncle Hersh with his hemorrhoids. The unclasped overall buckles clang against the hard blue seat.

"I know." Fred hugs himself.

"Sam's getting married," Oscar states. His stomach gurgles like a bent hose.

"Is that what you got me out of my deathbed for? Don't you know I've already heard that rumble?"

"Fact."

"Yeah, right."

"It's true."

"True fact? For Sam to even consider marriage she'd need to be a clinically unsullied porno centerfold or some megarich illegal alien."

"That's not funny." Oscar's boss, Vladimir, recently married a Swedish alien for five hundred dollars cash.

"Funny is relative."

"And she's really, really rich, Claire is, apparently."

"Who's Claire?"

"This girl Sam met two minutes ago."

"Short? All one length?"

"That's Judy."

"Pageboy?"

"Sue. No, no. Listen, I don't think you ever saw this one. Wings, Fred, she's got wings. Remember wings?"

"Don't insult my intelligence."

"Point is, he's really doing it. We just had dinner—well, I didn't have dinner, but still."

"What in hell are you talking about?" Fred's shivering. Stringy voice and hair and body.

"Sam. He *is* engaged."

"He's a better bullshitter than he was before is what he is if you believe him."

"He's about to become a husband. I'm certain."

"But why!?"

"That's exactly what I said."

Oscar and Fred lapse into one of their mutual viewing sessions. Dad's all-time favorite "my children" anecdote involves their discovery of mirrors (when two or three years old), how Oscar kept mistaking his reflection for Fred and vice versa.

The twin sets of eyes, which can't decide one color to turn—blue, green, gray, depending on shirts and skies, moods, each other, ailments—are set, ever so slightly, too far apart. Oscar once read that this signifies a criminal-to-be.

Tonight Fred's eyes are a lightless milky blue with veiny red streaks. Red, white, and blue, huge pupils. He cackles at the idea—marriage. Where other small boys insist they'll one day wed mom, Oscar and Fred planned to marry each other. Harmless kid notion. But around the beauty parlor, they've never stopped being ribbed for it. Fred and Osc, engaged forever.

It is a good one. They can recognize that. And Fred's laughter is as contagious as his flu must be. But Oscar resists it, glares down at his sneakers, held together with silver duct tape, keeps his mouth corners clamped.

"Do I have a fever?" Fred is still chuckling as he makes Oscar compare forehead heat. But Oscar's hands sweat, one of them inky from the forgotten, balled-up number ticket.

"Can't tell. Anyway, sick is relative. No excuse for standing us up at Lil's."

"Lil's?"

"Didn't Sam . . . ? Oh, of course."

"Lil's when?"

"He didn't even invite you, did he?"

"Whatayamean of course?"

"The liar."

"He's compulsive, I told you. Bet he's not really even getting hitched."

"He *is*, Fred! He *is*, OK! So what! You're not! Forget it!" Oscar scares himself with the outburst, but Fred, who seems oblivious, just eyes George and hacks away.

"Look at the horseshoe fringe on that guy," Fred manages to gasp. "Dire."

Don't you think I already noticed? Oscar doesn't bother saying. Nor, *Yes, I know, we both know it's what Dad's headed for.* Some moments, like now, their alikeness just riles him. Make that some days. Starting right at breakfast this morning.

DoNuTs! on Sidehill. Oscar arrived to find Fred had already ordered blueberry pancakes for the both of them.

What gave him the right?

"The fact that you wanted them," Fred reasoned.

True, Oscar wanted them, but as a matter of principle, to make Fred grasp the violation, he went ahead and changed the order to waffles. Oscar forced himself to eat waffles when he really wanted pancakes.

Some days, like today—when too many people on the street appear to share the same haircut (close-layered and a little puffy on top) yet each individual head makes it look so incredibly, frighteningly different; and when Vladimir has ordered him to scour the city to try and sell defective hamster tubing, or stay late training pit bull pups to chew through thrift-store couches; and when the headlines say Leg Flies 100 Feet from Body; and when Fred comes down with the flu, which means Oscar's just destined for it; and when Sam announces he's get-

ting married for the Wrong Reasons—the mere fact that Oscar
has to be human at all nettles him.

"TRY AND gladden thyself, brother," Fred encourages Oscar
outside. "At least Sam's not reborn, enlisting, or dead. All more
likely."

"But that's the thing. Why *is* he doing it? Don't say *love*,
Fred. Sam wouldn't call his old man on his birthday."

"Oh, he's just showing off; you know Sam."

"She's no great shakes. I saw her."

"Not showing her off—showing off. He always has to be first,
that's all. First to get a dirt bike, suspended, bar mitzvahed,
laid, and into college, which about covers it, I suppose. He
never even cared about being short, since it meant he got to
be first in line."

"Beautiful; he'll get the first divorce. He's too old for this
sleaziness, Fred. He's almost—"

"Young, you mean. He's too young."

"Not at all. You can be young and sleazy. But when you're
an adult and sleazy, you're nothing but a sleazy adult, see?"

"What's it to you what he is?"

"What's it to you what's it to me?"

Gridlock.

"Nothing," Fred says, phlegmy.

They agree to agree. For now. Without the help of Sam, their
usual arbitrator/instigator, they come to their own semi-
understanding. For once. Who needs him? They have buckets
of other friends. For sure. They have each other. For now, all
that matters is that Oscar gets his jacket back.

2

UNIVERSAL SIGNALS

CLAIRE YAWNS. Across and against the vast lawn, purple flowers look two-dimensional. Yellow ones, shy. It bugs her that she can't name most of the flowers. When she yawns her jaw clicks.

"I hope that is no indication of your sentiments regarding this . . . this . . ." Dad smooths his very pale bald head. Gets so nervous, Claire thinks, he forgets his hair's gone. The pink flowers look painted on by a four-year-old. She yawns again; click.

Though it's only the two of them on the patio, ten or so chairs have been brought out and dusted, arranged as if an invisible council were convening to vote on Claire's engagement to Sam Lubin.

> *PROS*
> Bottomless voice
> Charm
> Good posture
> Even-keeled so far
> Mildly practical

"I woke up as soon as I got to sleep," Claire says. "Now you're yawning too? Remind me to bust that mystery—how yawns catch."

"Will do." Claire's dad always takes her seriously. "It has something to do with sympathy, I'm sure of it." Always looks serious too—thick black mustache, matching mono-brow.

"Now, there's a lead. Soon as they hand over my Nobel, we'll buy us a blowtorch and split it. Fair?" Deciding one of those flowers out there needs a lapel, Claire rises. The white ones look wearable. She will try to walk there backward.

> *CONS*
> His mother
> She hardly knows him
> His poodle
> She's too young
> His father insists she convert to Judaism
> She's a virgin
> His customized van

Walking backward, Claire trips over a chaise, then catches herself saying "I'm sorry" to it. To lawn furniture.

"See what good manners you taught me?"

Her father is staring at the crescent-shaped pool.

"Get Sam to clean it for you."

His lips tuck into a thin line, deliberating.

"Nothing ever happens to me," Claire finally said to him this morning. No fear of sounding spoiled; it's a fact that she is. "We've gone clear across everywhere, and nothing even happened."

"That's why you want to get married?"

"Partly."

Really, she wants to swim. She's passing the pool now, backward.

Thinking ahead does not come naturally to Claire. At the moment Sam proposed, *then* she'd wanted to get married. When Dad suggested an alternative—more school—*then* she panicked. What she heard in her father's voice: a good college for a good job in case it isn't a good marriage and so after the children grow up you'll have something fulfilling to go back to before grandchildren (if you're lucky) fill that place before death.

She'd rather marry someone she doesn't like. She'd rather watch the gardener work. Collect things for projects like her seven-foot penny roll: 1,485 pennies. Seventeen pennies per inch. But mostly and always, she'd rather go swimming.

Claire crouches to stick her hand in the water, considers falling in, an on-purpose accident. If she mentions swimming, Dad'll remind her she just had lunch. Be careful of stomach cramps. The water's cold. And there's all kinds of debris floating around. Dad calls pool scum debris.

Claire sprints toward the garden and starts counting—third from the left—to make sure she rips up the very flower she'd chosen from across the lawn. It's these things that keep a person sane. Scrawny—the wind would've gotten it anyhow, but the root has come out too. What to do? Throw it back in the immaculate bed or keep it to remind herself how little delicacy she has?

"Where's the spark? Do I see a spark? A little friction?" Dad asked this morning while swallowing—he doesn't chew—his low-cholesterol melba-toast, Sweet'n Lowed–grapefruit, and decaf breakfast. The same "bird food" Claire's been eating since she began trying to lose weight. "I've been over you two with my electron microscope, and frankly, nope, nada, can't see it, dear."

The warning didn't bother Claire as much—when Sam sings, everyone in earshot sparks: fact—as the lack of fatherly recall. When I was about to get married, such and such. Your mother and I . . . In those days . . . Or regular advice, or hugs. What she expected, she's not even sure.

In the two years since her mother died, Claire's father hasn't mentioned his wife once, or once stopped thinking of her. It's obvious.

That Claire has been relegated to the job of family spokesperson remains, ironically, unspoken. How it happened, ironically, unarticulable. Claire started answering when he wouldn't, and it stuck, she'd guess. And it stinks. When people ask—in tender tones disguising curiosity—Claire says her mother choked. When people inquire further—in tender tones disguising nosiness—Claire says steak. When people out-and-out pry—without trying to disguise it—filet mignon, OK? She gagged on a tough wad of beef flesh and fatty gristle at a garden club luncheon; satisfied?

The size of a rubber eraser.

But all those things, though true, are a lie too, are the circumstances rather than the cause of Claire's mother's death at forty-five because . . .

She did not bring her hands to her neck in the universal signal for *choking*. Did not grab someone, pound the table, rip open her shirt buttons, turn bright colors, tip over her chair. She did nothing to save herself except sit in silence and strangle while a sun porch crammed with Heimlich-capable women (or so they all claim now) discussed, who knows, landscaping goldfish ponds, repotting ginkgo trees. What Claire's mother died of was plain old embarrassment.

The flower's mouth shivers as Claire pushes it through Dad's buttonhole. White flower to match white shirt, white awning, the yellowish whites of his dull, money-colored eyes, directly above his heart, which the doctor says "murmurs." A misleadingly gentle sound, murmurs, intended for wind, babies, water, not body parts, not her dad's overburdened vital organ.

His legs cross, uncross, cross. Cue-stick legs lost in big wrinkly trousers.

"The verdict?" Claire wonders aloud. "Well, Dad?" If he says not to marry Sam, she probably won't. One part loyalty, one part respect for his wisdom, two parts plain indifference. "Hmmm?" Claire has taken to walking around on her hands and humming. As she does this it comes in—softly, without flourish, unforeseen—the verdict: "It's your life."

Mine? What's that supposed to mean? Since when? As she lets her body flip over and right itself, feet down, what Claire is most aware of is her mouth's independent gibbering. Some nonsense about rabbit stew for Easter, not funny. Worse, chocolate Easter egg soufflé. Permeating the moment is the odor of

skunk, which Claire and her dad both love, even though it usually signifies that an animal has been flattened under car
wheels.

After Stella Allswell, her mother, made that fateful choice—
losing her life to save face—Claire's father, Arthur, pulled
Claire out of high school and dragged her all around Europe,
Africa, the Middle and Far Easts. Not only was Claire cut off
from friends, plans, interests (with the exception of swimming), but she never replaced them with new ones. Just tem-
porary hobbies—the radio, collecting junk, reading, and now
that they're back home in New Jersey, waking early to watch
the gardener work without a shirt on, glowing.

It starts in her bedroom, the west end of the house, and
when he moves out of that frame, she follows him. Room to
room. Window to window. She watches him mow the lawn,
bend over to plant or weed, diligently trim hedges, put out
birdseed, fertilize. Afterward, Claire sometimes returns to the
starting point and masturbates, but more often she just stands
there and thinks, thinking—What skills do I have besides packing a neat suitcase, boarding planes, ordering overpriced meals
that Dad only pokes at? None of my clothes fit right since I
began eating for both of us, starved by sadness. And she's left
with that weird tired boredom feeling, like having mono.

Claire had mono three times in two years. Athens. Tangier.
Austria somewhere.

Late-day shadows begin to stretch and bend on the lawn.
Your life? Though Claire could never admit it aloud, Sam is
really no different from Russ (her made-up name for the gardener), except tangible. Except *hers.* Because didn't Sam, out
of a whole retirement party full of possibilities, lock into *her,*
Claire, when he sang "Chances Are," dark eyes never straying
from *hers.* "Chances are I weaaaar a silly grinnnn, the moment
youuuuu waaaalk into vieeeew . . ." By the time he introduced
himself as Sam—"We're The Bouncetones, if you ever need a
little music"—Lubin, she already felt as if he'd kissed her.

"Just listen to that," even Dad said. "Now, there's a voice
that makes one take notice. Excellent." With his eyes closed.

Dad! And when Claire agreed, blushing, he added, "A voice with pull. One of a kind. I told you this wouldn't be a total loss." Claire had made a fuss over how she hadn't wanted to attend some farty retirement party where she'd have to stand around dressed up and be pitied. For having no more mother. For having her whole life in front of her. For having gotten slightly chunky on two years of rich international cuisine.

But now her father's smoothing his head again, looking toward the hand-cut stone wall, its little weathered wooden gate, then up at the sun, clouds, or airplanes. Once, on a beach in Spain, a bird managed to crap on him without his knowledge. Claire, unable to say a thing, spent an excruciating afternoon praying he wouldn't smooth his head and find out that way.

"Say something else, Dad, please."

"Like what?"

"Anything."

"We need new screens in the den."

"What you want, then."

"New screens."

"Really want, I mean."

"A gin and tonic, my pet, but I'm afraid it's too early."

"You won't let me live with him, so what can I do?"

"You're eighteen. You can live as you please. I only want you to be happy."

Eighteen is annoying, anticlimactic. An illusion of choice. Claire doesn't even have a driver's license. Has to carry a passport around with her. To top it off, once you wait your entire life to be eighteen, the everything age gets moved up to twenty-one.

"Don't think of it like I'm leaving *you*." Claire can't help picturing him all alone in the already monstrously empty house. "What can I do?"

"Decide."

A joke? A new tactic? Trick? Up till now her toughest decisions have been what clothes to wear to a bullfight, what to drink before dinner, whether to take aspirin, Advil, Nuprin, or Tylenol.

"Do you think I'm getting crusty?" Dad asks, suddenly jumping to his feet to perform two deep knee bends. Earnestly. "All right." Then he nods at the flower, as if noticing it for the first time. "This they call a paper-white narcissus. Want a bite?"

CLAIRE TRIES ON outfits for her double date.
White pants. Blue cotton V-neck sweater. Too summery.
Black pants. Diamond-patterned button-down. Macho.
Beige rayon dress. Boring and ripped.
With blue cotton V-neck sweater. Just bagginess.
White pants again. Flowered skirt. Aloha.
Red pleated skirt. Secretarial. No shoes go.
Yellow jumpsuit. Pukey. With blue cotton V-neck sweater. Pukey.
The doorbell rings. A song so lengthy and elaborate, you can reach the foyer from anywhere in the huge house before the chimes even stop.
"It's Sam!" Dad calls up, as if anyone else ever visits, besides Grandma Lillian, who comes once or twice a year. "Sam's here! . . . Claire?"
Claire is standing in her underwear. Momentarily sidetracked, she looks at earrings.
"What's he wearing?" she calls back, pulling on the original outfit. White pants. Blue cotton V-neck sweater. Too summery.

"DON'T YOU look summery?" Dad says.
Claire has looked in a number of locations before finding them in the living room. Is Sam aware of the honor? He kisses her hand now—real or mock gentleman? Both of the men have stood up, drinks rattling, to greet her.
"Oh," she chirps. Then, testing her voice, "Does the lady get a cocktail too?" Not unshrill, but better. She feels as she imagines it must feel to really, really want a cigarette.
"We're sort of late," Sam says. "Share mine."

Tastes like mouthwash with a twist. She hands it back. Rather, she chases after him to hand it back. His perfectly faded denim jacket is tied loosely around his neck the way models wear them, yechy. He seems unable to stand still. Strides heavily across the living room, where everything is off white, highly breakable, long lost under a ubiquitous layer of dust. Stops to admire things Claire has never noticed: lamps and wood grain, pictures and table feet, an ornate letter opener. Though Claire suspects Sam really wants a cigarette and is secretly hunting an ashtray, he does seem to know an awful lot about wood grain. To the point of boring even Dad. Not easy.

"You look Italian," Dad tells Sam.

What sort of response is he after? Yes, I've been told that. (By Claire.) Am I really that hairy? (Hairier.) Jews and Italians are known to pal out. Or the real response—a moment of soundless discomfort as the sun sets through the dirt-streaked picture window.

Dad looks at his watch and asks Sam, "What time do you have? You two make sure and have some fun for me." He's always the most dismal when he attempts chipper.

We'll try. Yes. Thanks. Thanks. Sam's face looks like it's put on too tight. He licks his teeth. Claire should speak—Dad's smoothing his head again—help this thing along.

But "Lately, I'm not in any of my dreams" is all that'll come. "I keep having all these dreams without myself in them. Isn't that a crack-up? That's a crack-up, isn't it?"

The two men just stare at her and gulp at their Scope.

THEY GO TO the movies. Recent Oldies Nite—half price. *Ordinary People.* A stadium-size multiplex in Queens; startling.

"Used to be a duplex," Sam explains. "But it kept undergoing mitosis. After 'Quad' they gave up renaming it."

A ten-minute walk from the car just to get to the ticket line. Twenty overlapping movies on one floor. Video games and pinball in the lobby. You can find any kind of candy, ice cream, juice, sandwich, cappuccino, espresso; water fountains in three sizes, including handicapped. In the bathroom: weigh yourself, have your blood pressure, cholesterol, biorhythm checked, buy from a machine: makeup, birth control, and those plastic bubble capsules filled with parachute men, gold-painted trinkets, Super Balls. Best of all (Claire can't wait to tell Dad this), along the walls leading to the theaters: Art for sale—ugly sad-faced clowns on velvet, paint-by-numberish rainbows, touched-up photographs of beach sunsets with silhouette lovers, all framed, all $15.99. Before the movie, a short is shown explaining how to get yourself out of the parking lot.

Not surprisingly, they haven't been able to find Sam's friends, and so they sit alone near the back, where Sam can smoke. All that trouble deciding what to wear, and now they're sitting in the dark. Eating Milk Duds. Inevitably, there'll be stains on Claire's white pants.

They hold hands. Sam's fingernails are longer than hers (guitar picks). They hold elbows. No, Sam holds *her* elbow, cupping it like a breast. He says he likes its pointiness. You do? He says, Milk Duds are always stale. Hmmm. He went to a shrink himself once, just to see. Really? When his old girlfriend Judy "went wild" on him. I see. Movie theaters should have double armrests. Yes.

So far all she's gleaned from the movie is that the whole family is very upset, particularly Timothy Hutton, who can pull off looking puzzled, sexy, irked all at once but is incapable of ordinariness.

"His knapsack's pretty ordinary," Sam says. "I have the same one."

"What do you suppose he's carrying around in there all the time?"

"His problems. . . . that or his brother's carcass. Finely diced in Mary Tyler Moore's Cuisinart. How's that for a twist and a half?"

The lady behind them coughs, says "Youse two shut up" into their necks. Sam coughs back at her and runs the empty Milk Duds box slowly along the inside of Claire's thigh.

AFTER THE CREDITS, which Sam insists on sitting through, they find his friend Oscar buying popcorn. *After* the movie.

"Line was too long before. *Whoa, my jacket—you got it. Thanks!* Hello, Claire. 'Member me? How does being fiancéed feel? Secure?"

Claire doesn't know whether she should be offended. Sam warned her that Oscar is touchy. About the engagement for one, but about lots of things, Sam says, all the time—dogs in clothes, defense spending, certain phrases that make him crazy, such as "the whole kit and caboodle." This Sam attributes to Oscar's twindom. "Like being half of someone else, half of *Fred*. A nice guy but no genius. A mostly confused guy, still living at home, having his underwear ironed."

Claire's not convinced. Oscar's appearance is, if anything, solid. A body that moves uncarefully—the popcorn sails. Popcorn and hair compete for puffiest, yellowest. He's biting the cardboard tub to zip his sweatshirt. Fine, Claire thinks. With the kind of tallness that looks tall only in comparison—next to Sam. Very fine, Claire decides, a marvel, except for that disconcerting beard puff, which she actually first thought was fake and taped on crooked.

It occurs to Claire that she's been staring at Oscar. He and Sam are staring at her staring at him.

"Where's your friend?" she asks, semi-normally.

Oscar gestures toward an elf girl beating her fists on a Video Trivia machine. She's wearing a neon-green miniskirt *and* knickers and two black shirts. Claire wonders whether American styles have changed that much or it's just Queens, or just Louette. No one else in the lobby looks quite so . . . graphic.

"Louette!" Sam yells. "Stop! Come meet my future." Zapping Claire with a chill right through.

The girl gives the machine one final kick with the heel of her red high-top (her other shoe's blue), then turns with an unexpected grace, bony, kittenish; it reminds Claire, inexplicably, of Europe.

"You must be the bride-to-be. Cheers. Did you ever dream Mary Tyler Moore would turn into such a bitch? . . ."

"Claire's not in her dreams," Sam offers.

". . . Like I told Osc, we should've seen *Demon Seed*, where the woman gets raped by a computer. Or that other one"— referring to a poster on the wall—"*Programmed to Kill.* Like what is going on here, right? Pick your type—tall dark handsome Mac or all-American blond IBM? It gets harder and harder to know everything these days; you always need a bigger disk. Like I told Osc, it . . ."

". . . YOU MEAN you've never considered cosmetic bonding?" Louette's amazed and amazing, still talking when they reach the car. "I could easily refer you—" Sam interrupts to suggest pool next. Louette grumbles, "No-o-o, I wanna go dance or eat lo mein." Then, apologizing for the mood swing, she pleads, "PMS." With a weary only-*we*-girls-know-what-*that*-entails smile, she's rolling a small rock back and forth beneath her sneaker. Two pairs of blue socks over blue stockings.

Standing next to her, Claire feels alien and fat in her white pants, and young, very. Pieces of glass and aluminum sparkle in the dark.

Oscar makes the decision to play pool. His bumper sticker says, I (heart) MY GRANDKIDS.

White pants gleam embarrassingly in the dark. Claire makes the decision to buy her wedding dress a size small. Her plan: eat only raw, cold food till she shrinks into it.

Sam makes the decision to go in Oscar's car, thus volunteering his friend for Designated Driver.

Louette's hoop earrings swing in their limited arc. Her decision: get married before all her friends divorce.

CLAIRE WIPES UP at pool, to unanimous astonishment. Even Oscar's impressed, though feigning cool.

Sam taunts him. "Do I know how to pick 'em or do I know . . ." Which Claire, mentally measuring at what angle to hit the six, hears as if from a far distance, like a faint, strenuous holler through a terrible connection. There's too much to take in. She's never been to a pool hall. Are they all like this? Cavernous, echoey, but not cool like you'd imagine an echoey cavernous place to be. Hot; in fact, steamy. Nor does Claire feel dwarfed by the high ceilings, but rather larger than ever, ponderous as she attempts to maneuver her body and line up the shot. The green six is lodged near-hopelessly up against the cushion.

Oscar chants, "Sam's marrying a hustler." His voice sounds thin in the general din of sighs, chatter, balls being broken up, racked up, swallowed, occasionally flipped up and off the perfect green lawns of felt—twenty to forty strong, arranged in rows, and doused, each one, in an individualized puddle of orangish lamplight—to crack against the concrete floor and roll. The total noise effect is that of someone dropping drawers of silverware on carpet in the next room.

"Sam's marrying a hustler / He really, really loves her."

Claire's hands tremble. Making a firm bridge—impossible. The six needs only the slightest tap. She bends forward at the hips, conscious of a mild but complex odor mix beneath the beer, must, mothballishness. Get it over with, she tells herself, shoot. And does. Forgetting to keep her head in line. The cue balls taps the six to the pocket's edge, where both balls hesitate, then fall in. Scratch.

"At long last!" Oscar says. "Someone else gets a chance. That was a stunning performance nevertheless, my dear. Bravo." He passes his bottle of Jameson's, grudgingly—a kid told to share. Sam finally had to tell him, Share.

Louette has already taken her turn and missed. She sulks. "I suck at this worse than bowling. I quit. Maybe it's movie lag." Prancing off to try her luck at grabbing stuffed animals out of a plexiglass box with huge mechanical tongs. Strange.

Movies grouch her out, Oscar explains. She's so short she's

got to sit on coats or her legs or him to see. He doesn't say, Engagement announcements don't agree with her too well either.

"How bout being my best man?" Sam asks. He's feeling his cheeks—for stubble? *He's* short too, for a guy. Compact, scarred up, shiny.

"Fourballinthefarleftpocket," Oscar calls.

A poor choice. The four looks deceivingly simple. There must be two, three more likely shots. Meaning he's not paying attention? Likes playing dangerously? Both? When the wrong ball drops into the right pocket, he seems unsurprised.

"Well," Sam says. "How about it?"

Claire knows it'd be good manners to disappear. To the bathroom? Phone booth? Candy machine? Louette? The stuffed animals come in many grotesquely vibrant colors.

"Do we have to talk about this?" Oscar wants to know.

Sam closes his eyes, showing off those heavy lashes. "Of course," he says.

"Now?"

Claire can't resist staying.

"What's the diff? Just answer."

"Later."

"The eager beaver gets the worm."

"Later." Now glaring at Claire. "Think."

"Think now or forever hold your bladder."

"Later. I'm calling Fred. Forgot I told him I'd—"

"Ask his permission first? Tie his shoelaces? I'd just love to have a tape of your mind, Armpit. No, make that plural—*pits*. You two are worse than *married;* you're grafted." Sam shouts at Oscar's retreating back. "Hey, don't forget, *I've* seen the flip side. *I was there!* These clones, Claire, they fight way dirtier then your average singular person, lemme tellya from first hand. They'd be grabbin on to each other's *faces* and *squeeezin* like oooh. If it wasn't for me, there were a few times they'da really . . . But we used to have fun with em too, standing around and placin bets on the outcome." Snort. "Oh, he forgets, but I don't. *I was always there.*"

Claire smears a line of chalk on her white pants into a blurry, lopsided heart and tries to fit C+S inside but can't. Mushbrain, she thinks. You should have done the heart second.

And, Oscar hates you or the idea of you, or the idea of you with Sam. This is clear. He has a twin, Fred, who'll also hate you, and a girlfriend, Louette, who might hate you or might just have PMS. This is complex. You had better lie low. This is definitely no rousing start.

When Oscar returns, Louette's on his arm, stuffed-animal-less, saying, "Get a grip. You look like you're about to have a bloody-nose attack. I won't milk ya for any more quarters, promise. Besides, tonight I'm the one with the ego sweats. A girl's entitled."

"Go," Oscar commands Claire, and after a second of paranoiac eye-bulge, she realizes he means the game.

"How'd you get so good anyway, Claire?" Louette wonders aloud. In the dusky light, her hair looks blue and solid.

"Spent a lot of time in hotel gamerooms abroad."

"A-broad," repeats Louette.

"Abroad." Sam, too, testing it. "Abroad."

Oscar chimes in, sarcastic, "Abroad. How very tiresome. Dinky Europe and all that, yawn. Abroad."

Claire cannot read him. There is nothing more depressing than a hotel gameroom.

"I mean, it was fine, I guess." This seems to be what they want to hear. "Except all I had was bratty twelve-year-olds to play with. With curfews."

Louette looks confused. "Twelve-year-olds?" It occurs to Claire that the three of them can't so much as form a picture of it.

"There's also a billiard room in her house in New Jersey," Sam adds, offhandish, when actually he'd been completely astounded by it—wood grain again. Spent a whole afternoon just touching stuff—the long oak table, row of maple sticks in their handmade teak cabinet with its special chalk drawer, the long-out-of-use servant button. He even lay down to put his cheek to the floor. Claire had liked watching him be so careful about it, demure almost. Tongue dangling. A kid on his best behavior. But now he sounds cocky, like it's *his* house.

"I should be getting home, Sam."

Louette perks up. "Let's go for the ride."

Oscar hugs her from behind, neck nuzzling. "They want to be alone, Lou." Feet-shuffling till Claire deciphers . . .

"Oh, sure, you're welcome to come." Why is she being nice to *him?*

"They are not." Sam stamps his foot. "We want to be alone. . . . Now, what you gonna be, amigo? Best man or coat check guy?"

"He's *my* best man." Louette giggles, stretching her arms back over Oscar's neck. "All the others, they're junk." She makes sounds in her throat to acknowledge Oscar's hands, massaging her shoulder blades.

"Lou here's just like a cat that drools when you pet it," Oscar says.

"Yes, Mr. Peebles." She's uninsulted. "Please don't stop, Mr. Pee—"

"And *you?*" Oscar suddenly asks Claire, looking somewhere above her eyes—her hair? Is it greasy? Is it sticking up? What? "Any pets?"

"No. I'm afraid. I don't know much about them. See, we—"

"Don't worry," Louette reassures. "We been goin out close on six months and I just the other night found out Saint Bernards don't really carry whiskey in casks."

"They don't?" Sam asks.

"There was a horse once. John," Claire thinks to relate. "My mom named it John for John F. Kennedy. But that doesn't really count. I mean, he—"

"Was just a horse." Oscar seems to be smirking.

"Died. He's dead."

Sam informs them that New Jersey is "horse country."

IN THE CAR, no, van, Claire is afraid again. Sam will want to have sex. In the van. It's the latest addition to her long list of fears, whose highlights include crowds, choking, math, public speaking, and death.

But sex is something different. It's only a matter of time till Sam discovers she's a virgin. Or maybe he knows and likes the idea. A rarity. She keeps telling him, Wait, you won't be sorry. A scary promise to be making. What if she's no good in bed? What *is* good in bed? Waiting for a bed to be good in. Instead of an old van filled with music stands, half-chewed Milk-Bones. Instead of Sam's shabby mattress full of burn holes and stains. A bloody nose, he claims. Sure.

He's fiddling with the radio. "You never know anymore. What's a song, what's a commercial. There should be laws."

Claire says she'd rather hear *him* sing. Would he? Please, please?

"You don't need to beg *me*."

"Sam the Ham."

"You got it, darlin'." He launches right into "I Can't Give You Anything but Love." A conscious choice? A song he sings regularly with The Bouncetones. " 'I can't give you anything but love, baby / That's the only thing I've plenty of, baby . . .' " He makes the instrumental sounds way back in his throat, oversized Adam's apple sliding and vibrating, and taps out the rhythm very lightly on the steering column with his class ring. Binghamton '83. " 'Gee, I'd like to see you lookin swell, baby / Diamond bracelets Woolworth's doesn't sell, baby / Till that lucky day you know darn well, baby / I can't give you anything but love. . . . ' "

He brings Claire's head down onto his chest. She can hear his voice in there, low, low, primordial. Emanating through his jacket and into her ear like an ice sliver warming, melting down from her head, throat, shoulders through the chest, arms, lingering for a moment in her belly before leaking lower, lower. The way surfacing after a dive can be, a renewal, everything clear, tingly.

" 'I'll be there to getchoo in a taxi, honey . . .' "

Marriage seems all right while he's singing. A fuzzy comfortable brownishness, like his eyes.

Sam stops short at a stop sign, and Claire's head knocks against the steering wheel. Still he keeps on singing, now rubbing her head and singing. Claire feels soberized. Sits up. Takes a look out the window.

" 'Now, baby, don't be late / We wanna be there when the band starts playing . . .' "

On the side of the road is a crushed red plastic toy, lit up by their headlights for a few seconds as they pass. A wind-up doll? Truck? Train? She cannot, will not let it get to her. Beach pail? Squeaky bath animal? Stop.

" 'Remember when we get there, honey . . .' " Sam steers with his wrist dangling rhythmically over the top of the wheel.

How does a toy end up on a highway? Is some kid right now missing it? Sam taps out the beat on the dash with his class ring. Claire's mother used to sing "Those Were the Days" in the car sometimes. The only song she sang—and not very tunefully—in Claire's recollection.

"Thank you, ladies and gents," Sam's saying, the song over now. "You've been one fan-tastic audience."

"I have," Claire agrees. Her head stings. She's spacey.

"Don't think I forgot the ring, the ring, the ring," Sam sings to the tune of "Row, Row, Row Your Boat." He must have noticed Claire noticing his.

"What ring?"

"Engagement, silly. I owe you, don't lemme forget it." He turns onto the exit ramp without signaling. "I'm planning to weld it on to you." Stroking the crevice between her pinkie and ring finger, he asks, "Ticklish?"

"No. And it's not like that."

"What's not like what?"

"Like owe." Because he must be figuring she owes him too. Sex.

On the winding road toward her house, Sam unrolls the window, humming. Says, "Check this out," and all of a sudden turns off the headlights. Darkness. "This is the sort of activity you have to look forward to in college."

"Who said I'm going to coll"—Claire feels as if she just swallowed that ice cube again, whole—"ege."

"Isn't it weird?"

Lights again. His hair is all fluffed up on one side.

But since Claire has not answered, he repeats the feat, longer. Not even looking at the road this time but at her, to determine—what? Is she frightened? Yeah. Impressed? If it'll stop this. Turned on? No, no, no. Her throat constricts. Her teeth grind. She can't seem to find her tongue anywhere.

"Wheee!" Sam screams, on his private roller coaster ride. Big trees lean, threatening to puncture the windshield. "Isn't it weird?" he asks a second time. "At the controls of something outta control. Sometimes, I dunno, it's like a craving. . . ."

Claire slams on invisible brakes. She's horrified, perplexed. He's twenty-six. He's demented. The road twirls. Behind, under, in front of them, simultaneously. Claire keeps squeezing the door handle as if that'll help. Unstoppable gunk rises up in waves; it's—

Lights. Action. Puke.

Sam woohoos, panting giddily until he catches a whiff. "What is that smell? God." A splash of half-digested Milk Duds and lo mein. Unfortunately, it missed hitting him. Fortunately, it missed her too. She has twisted around to retch, courteously, on the backseat. "Intense, huh?"

"You could say that," Claire manages to utter. A very funny noise. Like car wheels spinning futilely in a snowbank.

"You all right?"

"Alive." Her legs jerk involuntarily.

"My fault. I didn't know you were a carsick-type. If I'da known . . . Look, don't worry about that back there, I'll just hose. . . . Nancy's always whizzin here. A shampoo and creme rinse is way overdue." He punches open the glove compartment for gum to offer her, smooths her hair, which feels nice despite . . . "Really, you all right? I am sorry, really. I'll pull over."

"Home."

"See, like I'm memorizing the way, though. Shows commitment, doesn't it? Next time I'll find it blindfolded." Hah. "I ever tell you how I spent a whole weekend blindfolded?"

"Why?" He's not even fazed by their near death.

"To see what it'd be like. I wrote a paper for school on the experience."

"What *was* it like?"

"A hassle," Sam says. "Basically." But then he goes on about the paper's "many merits," how the teacher was always "citin it in class discussion and all."

Claire can't follow. Though Sam drives slowly now and talks as slowly as he drives and cranks all the windows open for air, her heart still pounds at its previous clip, ferocious, perhaps anticipating the next adventure scene. Almost Sex.

Claire is an Almost Sex expert. And not just with Sam. In high school (another world). In Christopher Sneeb's basement on a hanging wicker chair. In France (very almost), with a non-English-, non-French-speaking Swede named Stephan. In England, where she'd sneak out late to kiss (the name escapes her), a timid, eager busboy who called it "gumming." All that Almost Sex supplemented, of course, by the imaginary kind. Men on the street or in book jacket photographs, blackjack dealers, pilots, and Russ. Muscle Russ, the lone shirtless gardener.

Loneliness should head Claire's list of fears, but she puts it near the bottom for being so cliché, so long-standing, so vaporous. Loneliness is followed by Siamese cats, loud voices (Louette goes in that category), cellulite, and, lastly, for some reason, Pee-wee Herman.

SAM'S HANDS are in her white pants. Claire's hands are in his; he's slippery. Hugging, Claire watches Sam's keys swing from the ignition. A low tug makes her want to continue—should she? She shivers slightly when he licks the space behind her ear. Can real sex be *that* much different from Almost? She kisses the line of hair that climbs to Sam's belly button. An outie. Curiosity mounting on her way back down, with so many varying pressures to test. Can it really fit? Inside *me?* A big thing like that?

His hands slide, rough-callused. Wind picks up gravel from the driveway.

Well, Louette's tiny and she manages; the whole world manages. That's it—the Actress. Louette reminds her of the tired, important-looking Italian actress Claire once saw her father kiss. And really kiss.

Sam has got her pinned in a half-lying position on the roomy plastic van seat and is rubbing against her. His tongue, dryish, flicks across her chest. His class ring is cold, sharp somehow in her armpit. That does it.

"No," Claire says, trying hard for a serious *no* that won't sound like yes. Not easy. He's not the least bit discouraged. He's stretching out her blue cotton V-neck sweater with his head.

"No." This time more barklike. This time pushing him away.

"Why do you keep teasing me? We're engaged, right?" Sam moves faster on top of her, faster. Seems he's given up on the real stuff. And faster.

"Isn't anything sacred?" Claire asks, feeling supremely stupid for it. Sam's breathing goes into double time, hoarse.

"This," he squeaks. His hand, running through her hair, is stopped by a knot. He doesn't let go, and so Claire is in pain as, pulling her hair, he comes on her sweater, the van seat, the edge of Oscar's denim jacket. She concentrates on not being disgusted. (There's so much of it!) On the brown plastic mat beneath her feet. Everything's sticky.

"I just don't get it," Sam says, recovering. Angry? Ashamed? She can't tell. "Don't you want me?" Movie line. A whiskey, chocolate-smelling whisper. Claire thinks, Not really, not now anyway, and says, "Well, yeah, but . . ."

"But? But what? I'm listening." He isn't looking at her, though.

"Not in my parents' driveway."

Sam leans on the window. One side of his hair is still puffed, stuck up like that. It occurs to Claire that she's also somewhere seen the headlight game on screen.

"I'm sorry," she tells him. "It's just gotta be—"

"Sacred?" Sam groans. "Doll, you are settin yourself up for one whopping letdown."

Maybe he can tell she's a virgin, after all. Maybe he's comparing her to his old girl, Judy, and deciding he prefers the "went wild" style.

"Well." Claire adjusts her clothing—wet spots, chalk dust, her own brown hairs. "Bet I smell like sex." Almost Sex. She eyes the house. "Bet my dad's up."

"Is that it? Dad forbid? Is that what all this virtue's about? Daddy?"

"Shut up." Claire opens the door. "Goodbye, I guess. And I take it back about being sorry. I'm not."

"Well, I am," Sam says. "Sorry."

"I'm sure."

"I'm sure."

"Well, I'm not."

He starts up the engine. Lights a cigarette and stares at his feet. So wide the leather sides of his shoes are cracking. Claire sits with the door hanging open and bites her lip. With the car light on, Sam's scars really show up. She likes them, usually. They mean he's done things. But now she wonders. *What things* has he done? The thin lines crisscross and arc over fat ones. Sam is tapping his ring again, loud now, to no song and in no particular time.

Claire wants to tell him to zip his pants, but can't. To tell him wait, you won't be sorry, but can't. Instead she says, "Are we still getting married?"

DAD'S UP.

Claire walks right in and starts yelling. "*So I still have a curfew? Is that what this is? You treat me like a toddler. I can't stand it. I can't take it. Are you going to lecture me now on proper behavior for a young lady? Spare me. There's no such thing. I don't want to hear it. I don't want you waiting up and worrying every time I go out. I'm fine. I'm fine. I'm always fine!"*

"You'll pull something," Dad says, at the edge of his chair. The chair with indentations that fit his body. "Relax."

"And don't say that."

"What?"

"Relax. Don't tell me to relax, ever."

"Deal. Just sit. Please, Clara."

She obeys. It's the Clara that does it. Her real name, and until now used only by her mother; not used at all for two whole years. But she sits on the floor away from him, in a corner, Indian style, rocking.

"Begin at the beginning," Dad says, scratching his thick black mustache.

"I don't know what you mean."

"You're upset."

"I'm fine. I said I'm fine, and I am."

"Rotten date?"

"No."

"I think so."

"So think so."

"Stop rocking, please. You're making me dizzy." Claire obeys and lies down on her stomach to hide the jism stain on her sweater. "And you're a little sloshed, I see. So let's have another. We'll talk."

Claire is not sloshed, even a little. This is Dad's excuse to have one himself. The carpet is bone-color and scratchy.

"Why is it always this way? You're all understanding during talks"—i.e., when he's drinking. "Then you go back."

"Back where?"

Back to not saying anything for days at a time. "And I hate that word 'sloshed.' Back to sulking and sleeping in your clothes. In your chair." She stares up at a simple aqua glass vase, simple, aqua, in her own house. It is not the vaguest bit familiar.

"That drink?" Dad offers, standing.

"Chocolate milk, please."

"Sure?"

"You can trust me, Dad, I swear it."

LATER, Dad admits he was sitting up for her because he couldn't sleep. Because he couldn't wait to tell her his idea: an engagement party! When was the last time we entertained? And for a second Claire almost thinks he'll blurt it: Two years, since *she* died. But he says, "I was telling Sam earlier that we might have some connections. Possibly we can arrange some commercial work, voice-overs or—"

"We can? You told him that? Tonight?"

Something seems to have happened to Dad; he's grinning. A lift in the shoulders.

"Yes, we had quite a nice little chat." Lowering his voice—Sam imitation?—he adds, "Man to man." A full-fledged joke.

"And—lemme guess—then he asked you to be his best man." They hadn't looked all that chummy to her in the living room.

Now Claire and her father lounge in the kitchen, a more reassuring spot. A lot more living goes on in here. Unlike the living room, the kitchen is human scale. Unlike a simple aqua vase in an enormous space—the many enormous spaces choked with neglect and dust, nicey-nice.

Since returning from their travels, they haven't bothered to call in any outside help (except for Russ and an occasional plumber). The vigilance necessary to maintain a house this size is in neither of their natures and anyway seems totally beside the point now. Funny, how fast old ideas of decorum can go once "what the neighbors think" proves fatal.

In the kitchen, Claire knows the name of the flowers on the wallpaper. Her mother once told her. Sweat pea. Delicate like her mother, with a lot of little folds—yellow, white, purple, pink. Her mother always made a big deal about *enunciating*. Sweet. Pea.

Guilt-y. Diet's shot. Milk Duds, popcorn, whiskey, lo mein, and three chocolate milks. Or is it Sam? Not having sex with him. Or is it the things she doesn't remember that her mother told her?

Dad's acting . . . "effervescent" is probably the word he'd use. He begins making a party list in the margins of the yellow pages. "Erratic" is the word she'd choose, concerned as always about his heartbeats. But even his old bathrobe looks changed—redder, or better-fitting. Claire's afraid to let herself imagine this, but—well, it's possible—he's behaving the way he used to Before.

Dad asks, "So what'll it be? Shall we have hors d'oeuvres? I need *input*." He gestures *input* with his drink in the air. A sort of crossing-guard Go signal.

"Balloons!" This she doesn't have to think about. "To stand up on our chests from static electricity." Dad's tickled. He actually puts his feet up on the table. Claire'd forgotten all about that. How he'd always put his feet up on the kitchen table Before.

"A fellow to make balloon dachshunds and giraffes?" Dad suggests, and they both wail "No-o-o!" together and try to think up other long, tubular animals.

"Lemon meringue pie too, lots," Claire says, smiling at his veiny ankle, at his velvet slippers, which her mother embroidered his initials on for Christmas. Two years ago. Claire thinks, Screw the diet. I could eat an entire lemon meringue pie right now.

"And escargots?" Dad asks. "I've been having a hankering." He writes it down before she answers. He's bouncing his feet. "And . . ."

What if he's got a fever? That's it. What if his sorry old heart has started murmuring again and he's not better, he's worse? He's pushed aside his gin and tonic to finish off her chocolate milk.

If this is a dream, Claire thinks, at least I'm in it. I'm sitting in the kitchen in the dream, wearing my white pants, yawning, saying, "That's all I can think of. Except can we use those champagne glasses?"

"Which? We've got cabinets and cabinets of crystal."

In the dream, Claire is not scared to say, "The ones Mom liked too much to use. Etched. Long. Whataya call it? Fluted?" And Dad doesn't even look away at the word "Mom," because in the dream he's the new way, which is really his old way but seems new after two protracted years.

"Why, certainly, madame." He bows, exposing the tip of his head. A couple of lumps that Claire, being shorter, doesn't see too often.

"Maybe The Bouncetones'll play," she says. "You should have heard Sam serenade me tonight." She likes Sam when she remembers his singing. "He's one grievous driver, though." She despises him when she remembers the fool headlight game. Likes and despises herself both for the Almost Sex.

"Only if they let us pay them," Dad says. "A bounteous fee. Which reminds me—guest list. Ask Sam to make one."

Claire nods. "I sure don't know anyone." Not feeling sorry for herself, just stating a fact.

Dad sticks out his lower lip in commiseration. Too slender a lip to make an effective pout. "What ever happened to your high school buddies?" he asks. "That Laura, and whatshername down the road . . . the Dufour girl . . . Prudence?"

"Close. Constance."

"Her too."

It's as if he has forgotten all about their big disappearing act, as if he never watched Claire mail all those postcards (the first year). Like throwing bits of colored paper into a void, since there was no place where she could tell her friends to write back.

She doesn't bother saying any of this, but instead describes the parts of her night she can comfortably divulge. Multiplex mostly. The pool hall—she really showed them. Oscar Arm—remember meeting him once? What a name. A personality strange enough to fit it. And Louette, with the mannerisms of that Italian actress. You know. Began with an *S?* Here Claire's really pushing it.

"Ah," Dad says, planting his feet back on the ground. Damn,

she's blown it; he'll be smoothing his head again any—. No? A smile? A smile. "Uh huh, Sophia, sure." A little flustered, even. "Not Loren, of course, but now *there* was a woman with resources." Which one? "Hey, whataya say *we* shoot some pool, girl? If you don't mind my rust."

"Not at all." Claire minds only still being called girl. She brushes her nose past his. Eskimo kiss, another of those things they did Before. She flaps her eyelashes against his cheek. Butterfly kiss. Eager to graduate to Woman with Resources.

"Clara?" Dad asks. Just her name, but hearing it once more, tonight and in that form, from that mouth, with one of his magnificent pauses following, she tenses for something major: favor to be done, confession, gushing emotional climax.

"What is it?" Still close up to his face, she sees his skin is flaking off in places. Big pieces too. Stress.

"Tell me," Dad says. "What's Queens like?"

3

BEST INTERESTS

FRED DOES JUGGLING, sleight of hand, acrobatics, and some not so hot banjo-playing on the street. His parents are edgy. His parents let him know they're edgy without actually saying it. They say, "*Oscar* is doing well in his LION studies and at the PetMart. Oscar's always done well; even when he hit that bumpy spot"—they caught him getting the neighbor's dog stoned and immediately sent him to a psychiatrist—"he got through it, a natural go-getter, Oscar." Entrepreneur is more like it: he was dealing pot to all the kids in Sidehill. "You see, Fred, the thing is, Oscar has interests."

It's useless to try and explain that he has interests, too, only they don't happen to be all that lucrative yet. Or how confused Oscar really is. Just because he's got a job, a hole to crash in, and a Ph.D. on the way one day, maybe, is no reason not to worry; Fred worries about Oscar. Oscar hates (or at least doesn't communicate well with) humans except Fred, hasn't made a new friend except Louette since forever, seems to exist in this constant state of botheration over waste-of-time problems: why policemen don't wear sneakers, why he never sees any *baby* pigeons, how to clean a grater without shredding the sponge. Oscar was the kid who always asked, Would you rather be blind or deaf? a sad genius or a happy idiot? Endlessly pondering every last variable until, exhausted and still undecided, he'd wind himself up in some new dilemma—say, infinity.

Fred's more practical. But his first few attempts to make some real cash (OTB, lottery, Atlantic City) fell through, so he's decided to make a greater effort juggling. Eight in the morning he's on the bus to the 7 train to the 1 train to Columbus Circle. To *his* corner.

It's hard. Either too hot or too cold. People stop, not really to watch but to stall before the office. Bums heckle. Kids give away the secrets to his tricks. He gets ripped off, lonely, drowned out by traffic. No one admires a guy who smiles all day long.

WITH ONE LEG wrapped around his head, Fred hops animatedly on the other—his Stretchman routine.

It's tough competing with so many hot dog, sock, and drug vendors, not to mention Mr. Chris Columbus himself, marble and five stories high. Also tough projecting at a major intersection, over electric amps and ghetto blasters—with his head jammed into his chest. But in the old, old days, the 1970s, when Fred and Osc (aka Ored and Fosc) were a duo, teenagers, it was not this way. The twin gimmick was a sure thing. Or so it seems now. Make the skeptics see double, then hit them up for twice the cash.

"Those of you with bills please feel free to push your way to the front." For all the chaos about, there's only a few people actually loitering near Fred. An albino woman with long, cottony braids—three of them—and her scruffy, regularly colored kid *on a leash*. Also about is the one-armed Indian, envy of all the neighborhood homeless for his carpeted refrigerator box inside the park's fenced lagoon area. "Line forms here. Remember, guilt can be a terrrrible thing."

After Oscar bailed out, Fred had taken on Tommy Eako as a partner, which wasn't the same but had its good moments. They didn't fight like Ored and Fosc—viciously, sometimes mid-performance, and without Sam nearby to referee. Fred and

Tommy worked obsessively on their routines: juggling fire, juggling knives, juggling on stilts or with no hands—just Ping-Pong balls with their mouths. They worked birthday parties and bar mitzvahs (sometimes in tandem with The Bounce-tones), hospitals and schools, prisons, Renaissance fairs, department stores, anywhere, anytime. They worked so often Fred got good enough to audition for Clown College; Tommy, to get in.

"*Sex!*" Fred continues, six years later. He yells, "Look! A fight!" He's at the desperate-to-rouse-*some*-attention-already point, from the fleeting businesspersons, perplexed tourists, socializing dogs and masters, cats in baby carriages, Sam. Sam? "Hey, Sam!"

Sam's standing near the park entrance. His legs are so hairy you can't see any skin. He's wearing *leather shorts* and biting—eeee, *chewing*—a double red Popsicle. As he begins to make his way toward Fred, he head snuggles poodle Nancy, who sticks out from the top of an unzipped knapsack.

"Not another step, buddy, till you cough up some moola, hear?"

"Good Pesach to you too, Dutch. Or are you supposed to be Bavarian? Don't you know pretzels are *leavened* bread? Let's see your Mr. Matzoh."

Fred, grateful for the reminder of Passover—he should probably call Oscar and extend the courtesy—nonetheless says, "Kindly stop dripping your Popsicle in my collection hat." The way of certain friendships, this—fond, nonstop abuse.

Sam's unloading a bunch of pennies into the top hat. "Now I know where to get rid of these." His tongue looks diseased from the Popsicle. "Since Claire's finished her seven-foot penny roll." He scratches at his bluish five o'clock shadow, appearing dwarfed by the massive Hitachi billboard beyond. It reads 3:02:13. Fred supposes *he* should shave (he can get away with shaving only triannually). There'll be guests at the house. Uncle Hersh and Aunt Mary from Miami. Maybe Elijah.

"Ya know, Pretzel, one day your face is gonna freeze like that, then your body. You'll start sprouting salt."

"Why is it," Fred asks, unraveling himself, "that as soon as you put on shorts your personality changes?"

He feels good and elasticized after Stretchman, and glad for an excuse to stop, pack up—juggling pins, torches, rings, banjo, gorilla head.

The one-armed Indian comes closer to the pile of stuff and breathes his gloomy blessing upon it. "Objects are the ultimate martyrs." Then he leaves.

Fred just *has to* do something to rev up his act; it's tired. The coins in the cap are all stuck together from sugar now.

But: "Behold! Manna!" A dollar flutters down at Fred from the sky. He looks up to find that his patron is none other than Kid-on-a-Leash. "Ah, the wisdom of children." Kids always like Sam.

"Can I try on your head?" asks the little guy, enraptured with the gorilla mask.

"Can I try on your head?" mimics albino woman, enraptured with Sam. Women always like Sam. The ends of her braids are fastened with trash twists.

THEY GO to Barney's. Sam "needs" to look at tuxes, needs to see "how the other half dresses."

"In billions and billions of ties," Fred concludes, awed by the selection. He's distressed knowing he'll probably have to wear one to the seder tonight. "Only a masochist could've invented this . . . noose." He hopes he can stop himself from the juvenile whine: "But *Oscar's* not wearing one." Now, Sam, on the other hand, he's a different species. He spends his own money on ties and is right now singling out a hideous *ascot*, blue with one big pink flamingo.

"I think that's inappropriate for a wedding, son," Fred tells him as a way in to the topic. Oscar's apparently ready to boycott the whole affair. "Have you thought of renting out Chester's for the ceremony? You could give all the guests electrolysis as party favors."

"Fab," Sam says. Fred isn't sure whether he means the idea

or the tie. Sam holds the ascot to his neck and checks his reflection. Thick, stubbly neck stretching up in its proud, faintly reptilian way, and a chin that looks the same from every angle—scarred. "I'm thinking—ya know—for the engagement party." He doesn't seem to be asking for a second opinion. "Don't panic, your invites are in the mail. Gold writing, lots of fancy loops. Texture. My mother's even framin hers." He bows at three-quarter angle to include Fred's image in the mirror. "Frederick! Come quick while the bubbly's still chilled. Old chap? A toast! The BYOB days are over. Wait'll you see her . . ."

"Yeah, maybe," Fred says. "But I'm not wearing any *ascot*— I don't care if she's Miss Subways." The declaration of apathy only enhances his interest. "Is she coming to your seder?" The idea: He could casually stop by and finally eyewitness this New Jersey treasure.

"Naah. She's got somethin goin with her old man. They're a tight pair; she doesn't like leavin him. You know."

"Not really."

"The Jewish stuff freaks her out pretty majorly too, I think. Since my dad tried converting her and all." Sam laughs. Once. Loud.

"So Sid's really into—"

"Not anymore. It's Peaches who's the *involved* one." Then Sam does something Fred's never seen. He starts picking his ear with a car key.

"My Aunt Mary's a Christian fundamentalist," Fred says. "She even wears a crucifix to our house on Passover. It's quite the democratic scene."

"I don't think Claire's Christian," Sam says, examining the key. "I don't think she's anything."

"ONCE I SAW this Hungarian performer"—Fred grabs a blazer off the rack and throws it over his shoulders to demonstrate— "whose whole act consisted of tying himself up in a straitjacket and threatening to stay tied up until he collected seven bucks. Believe it or not, there were these Hasidic guys standing around, squeezing nickels out by the dozen for him, seriously concerned."

Sam holds the sleeves of the jacket behind Fred's back, tight, and they're laughing and trying to shush yap-a-pup Nancy when it hits Fred—Oscar saw that Hungarian performer, not me. Oscar's experience, not mine! Oscar.

"Remember that guy Seth, Shlomo, what was his name? That Hasidic guy in high school?"

"Uh huh," Fred says, still privately shocked. He had pictured every detail of the Hungarian's act. Now he's equally disturbed by Sam's reference to the Hasidic kid Shlomo. The guy asked them to smoke pot with him, so they did, after which, sideburn ringlets and all, Shlomo went straight into the lunchroom and stabbed some girl with a pair of scissors.

"That was *biz*-arre," Sam says. "Oscar went cuckoo."

"He did not," Fred says. But he did. Affected, characteristically, most by the particulars. For instance, that they were lefty scissors. Oscar's left-handed but not Fred. Identical twins in the strictest sense—mirror images. "He just—"

"*Is* cuckoo." Sam claps Fred on the shoulder. "So talk to him, will ya? Convince him to be my best man. He'll listen to you. Same genetic makeup and all."

"What'd you say to him anyway?"

"Whatayamean? I said, 'Would you be my best—' "

"What else? In Lil's? To get him so worked up?"

Fred decides not to bring up how Sam lied about having invited Fred. Sam obviously had not wanted Fred to be there.

No answer. Sam sings, " 'She'll be comin round the mountain when she *comes* ...' " while Fred rubs crossed arms, goose-bumpy from the air-conditioning, or in response to the murderous stare of a ruthlessly stylish Wall Streeter, flipping through snakeskin wallets.

They haven't even found the tuxes yet. Every staircase seems to lead back to the room they just left. Full of suits and ties, socks and ties, hats, cologne, ties, robes, ties, tie clips. Looking around, Fred realizes how unskilled most men are at shopping. How they try to cover up the fact that they're wandering helplessly by pretending they're rushed, late for important meetings. Pathetic, really. They'll buy the first thing a salesperson happens to suggest; five of them in the same color, agreeing to the accessories, cufflinks, suspenders, belts, anything to get out of here for some air.

And then you see the women. Not even jockstraps intimidate them. They know just what their men should wear and why, and how to find it. Check labels, assemble outfits, consider coloring, seasons, occasions, what's packable, affordable, washable, enduring. Fred thinks he know their secret: women don't merely touch everything, they *feel* it.

"What's she like?" he asks Sam in the shoes section.

"Who?"

"C'mon."

"Miss Subways, Lady Liberty, The Girl Next Door, all rolled into—"

"C'mon."

"Claire, she's very . . . Claire is . . . open for interpretation."

"So interpret."

"She's brutal, Fred."

"How?"

"Sultry, willful . . . she's full of—"

"Oh, no."

"That's right—fear. Yet fearless. Succulent yet deadly, a-swim in a broth of beef stock and money market medleys. That is to say, untamed, wholesome, young . . . *tip-top o' the food chain.*"

"Better," Fred says. "You're warming up." But when he tries reconciling Sam's contradictory list with Oscar's short and merciless one—wings, pool finesse, tooth gap—still no credible image is forth-gelling.

"Trousers should shiver on the shoe but not break," Sam prescribes.

"Ya know, Oscar thinks—"

"*Does* Oscar think without you to wind him up? Or is he the winder? I used to think . . . Whose wedding is this? I mean, what does Oscar care?" This has evidently been building for a while. "Oscar seems to think that whatever he thinks makes some big difference."

Fred begins juggling dress shoes. Sam's size—nine triple E. "He just cares, OK?"

"Well, people don't want to be cared about that way. You can tell him that for me. People don't want to be cared about so ... *carefully*." Sam moves his knapsack to the front and rests it against his chest, where he can hug it. Hug Nancy, that is. Scratch Nancy's head, which gets him an appreciative lick on the chin.

Fred flings the shoes higher, letting them cartwheel down to the lowest possible point before snapping them up again, and faster, again, till the blur happens, a dark arc. The tip of Fred's left index finger, print and all, once got wicked off by a falling machete (occupational hazard), but the digit works just as well without it.

"In any case. Like, I know I can count on *you*, Fred. If Osc cops out, you'll back me up as best man, right? Yo!"

The shoe drops, ricocheting first off the salesman's foot (tapping annoyance—no pets allowed), then veering off to upset a handkerchief display, finally landing laces to the carpet, only to be foot-scooped and armpit-caught again by Fred. He grins mightily. He says, "Lucky I'm not a nuclear technician."

FRED SAYS, "Lucky I'm not a nuclear technician," again at home, after purposely fumbling a toilet paper roll. This in order to try the line out on Oscar, who shrugs. So Fred juggles on, never give up, four rolls. Instead of dropping, this time he lets one hit the low attic room ceiling. "Just an illusion, folks!" Again, Oscar shrugs. So five rolls Fred tosses, then kicks at airborne. "My famous crashing 747 trick!" Oscar shrugs. Dated. So what the hell, six, let's go for it, six rolls and the brass egg paperweight. This time one roll falls without Fred's help. "Equipment failure! Well? Equipment failure? Is that funny?"

"Marginally." Inside the closet, Oscar shrugs again.

"And what are *we* looking for?" Childhood objects soar out at Fred. Holy toesocks. Half this stuff Fred hasn't thought about in . . . ?

But Oscar picks through as if he's doing inventory. He claims to have a mental catalog of all of it except . . . "What'd ya do with that old steel-string guitar, the Silvertone?"

"Hocked it to buy you a thumb pick," Fred says, brimming to tell Oscar how he believes it now—Sam marrying for money. But, in Fred's judgment, for his mother, Peaches, too, not to mention for Claire's prize hymen, which, in Sam's own words (failing to take gynecology into account), remains "untouched by human hands." And then there's the job offer—understudy best man. Fred'd like to discuss that. To lighten things up, Fred thought he might throw in a description of that alarming flamingo ascot, but—

Already Oscar's fingernails are chomped as far down as they'll go, and something about the way he looks—sitting there in the heap of closet junk, in a pair of stiffly new, too-big-for-him Levi's, wearing *a tie* (Oscar?), spooked or wired-seeming, a little sad, demanding to know what happened to that Silvertone—causes Fred to hesitate. He sighs, "Try behind the dresser." Fred braces himself for the inevitable twelve-bar blues à la Sid Lubin's basement—site of many a fun marathon jam session, first kiss, Super Bowl Sunday.

Fred gingerly wades through camp plaques and string art, an abandoned ant farm, slipping on Matchbox cars, kicking up mitts, bongs, whole fortresses of board games, a tiny glittery green Super Ball, Lite Brite, a mess of capless dried-up Magic Markers. Things familiar *and* remote. A stack of yellowing Archie comics brings up the issue of "Old Betty and Veronica, who," Oscar insists, "are exactly the same person except for the hair color."

"*I* know." Fred is beginning to suspect that his brother is keeping secrets.

Oscar kneels on the bed and points his downy chin toward some more memorabilia. A stack of love letters on girlish bordered stationery—lilac, tissuey, addressed to *The Arm Twins,* both, from, on yeah, *her*. Horrendous shag. Harelip. Joanne O'Leary. *Dear Oscar, Dear Fred, Hi. How are you?* Each letter begins identically. *The weather here is hot.* And proceeds with some variation on *You are the foxiest guys in 7th grade and nice,* which Oscar sings now—without bothering to tune the Silvertone—in a forced deep, wavy parody of Sam. There's a tag still attached to the back of his new pants.

"Oh Joaaanne O'Harelip / You maaake me flip . . ."

Fred bangs out the beat on the night table, which is marred by dozens of water rings and the black gummy remains of Wackypack stickers.

"Your kisses may be crooked / But you still are good-looked. / I'm your man, Joanne, yip, Joanne Harelip."

A brief instrumental segment, while Oscar thinks up more lyrics. Fred returns to his juggling practice, attempting three Hot Wheels and G.I. Joe.

"But can't you see, honey harelip / Love in threes ain't my trip / O Joaaanne I can't staaand—"

"Who's Joanne?" asks a woman's voice moments before Louette appears in the doorway. She has a new florescent-orange butch chop.

"Pixieish, OK, good instinct, but . . . too much sideburn action." Far as Fred's concerned.

"Did I ask you?" Louette attempts to hide her hair with her hands.

"Color's putrid," Fred adds without intending.

Here he was about to get going with Oscar, when Louette has to barge in with her eyesore do and—

"Joanne who?" she wants to know. Jealousy.

Opening his hands mid-toss as if describing the length of something or performing a benediction, Fred quick-submits, "Gust of gravity!" for approval. But Oscar's too busy watching the toys fall.

ON ALL PREVIOUS VISITS, Great-Uncle Hersh has brought them gifts of nail file kits. On this night, he doesn't even wait till his coat's off. Doesn't ring the bell or yoo-hoo. Materializes, rather—the largest thing in the kitchen all year. Heavy dandruff fallout on the shoulders of his black coat. He's shouting—really shouting—"*Yellow! Yellow!*" Fred likes to think one greeting for each twin.

What Great-Uncle Hersh calls a hug is encirclement, both brothers smushed in together against him—smell of closets (he probably doesn't need the coat in Miami), of hair tonic (with which his few remaining strands have been strategically arranged), and of that miscellaneous other (just plain oldness?). Uncle Hersh was always old, and his coat was always an old man's coat.

As for Aunt Mary, she's a woman you'd call well-preserved, handsome, spry, all those compliments that can easily double as insults. Her annual contribution—mashed potatoes and one dry noisy cheek peck apiece. "Mr. Oscar" she calls Oscar. Fred gets stuck with "Sad Sacks." "Mr. Lester" she calls Lester. Charlotte, "an absolute vision."

"And look at you," Mom bubbles back. "That skin and your figure."

Mary also possesses the kind of aloofness which many people take for an indication of Serious Thinking in Progress, and a related talent for making any chair automatically her throne. Yet more prized still (by this family anyhow) is her thick hair. The color of steam. Timeless. Swirl, dip, tuck, always. Seamless. No evidence of pin or clip to hold it up. Magic. Not a flyaway, stray, or split end. Ever.

Next to Mary, Hersh tends to look like a sloppy cartoon. But there's no humor in the sight of someone who really seems to be struggling against *gusts of gravity*. And liquor. And losing. Hersh.

When Oscar introduces Louette, the old man's whole face crumples. He stares at the twins' unopened nail file kits, confused, counting. One short. He seems to be willing another kit to grow in Louette's palm. Disappointed he can't make it materialize, he asks of her blazing hair, "*What happened?*" and reaches out to touch the stubby, varnished, electrified tips.

Really, Fred and Oscar assure him, it's no problem. She can have one of theirs; they'll share. But Hersh vetoes that idea. "A man's got to keep his hands nice." His own fingers, scrubbed ruddy, parched like the rest of him, have gone so skeletal he's begun wearing his wedding band around his thumb.

The twins say, "Thank you, Uncle Hersh," and unzip the little leather cases, well aware that inside they'll find four miniature metal utensils. The nail file, the pointy tool for cleaning, the blunt cuticle pusher, and a scissor way too small to get your fingers through. Louette scale, actually.

She's truly agog, Fred thinks, having had her hairdo probed so, and envious, probably, of the intense pink that Hersh's scalp, face, and neck achieve. After spending all morning trying to get her hair that very shade (the nerve! after all the freebies Dad's let her have at Chester's, serves her right!), to wind up with this lifeguard-orange beacon. Fred never did trust her. *Her* nails, Louette informs them, must be kept clipped short since they're constantly rooting around inside people's mouths.

"Oooh." Mom effuses over the gifts. "Ohhh. Hmmm. Lookit that!" She pushes up her also brand-new overlarge, overlemony perm. "*Clev*er . . . My . . . *Hand*y." She's never seen anything so darling.

"Since last year," Dad mouths mischievously, bouncing in place behind her. His hair, one dusty swoop like a hurricane on a weather map, circles an ever-enlarging now dollar-size bald spot. His shirt, predinner, is already spotty from some sauce; typical. His impatience mounts as the Virtues of the Portable Nail Kit are reviewed in full, till he interrupts, urging Hersh, "Sit. Take your coat off. Consider parking awhile." Slipping into Yinglish, "You wanna cup coffee maybe?"

"Scotch," Hersh bellows, limping toward the nearest chair. He's got an ancient wound (war?) and can't bend one of his knees too well.

Already seated, with the neatly foil-covered glass casserole of potatoes in her lap, Mary distractedly picks white nubs from her sweater. Her spine, as stiffly regal as the rest of her, stays an inch from the chair back at all times. Her legs are crossed at the ankles only. Her chin is permanently raised at a slight tilt, as if she were eternally about to have her picture taken.

"Sco-otch?" A two-syllable whine. "Neat I want. Ya hear me, Lester? *Neat.* Always forgets, he . . ." Hersh trails off momentarily as he lowers himself, coat and all, gradually into sitting mode.

"Me too," Oscar says. "I'll have a glass." He's just now noticed the tag sticking up from his Levi's. The paper part rips off easily enough, but the staples give him trouble.

"Me too," Louette says too. "Thank you."

And Fred, "Me three." Over Mom's protests.

"It's so early, it's too early. I have hot spiced cider all set to serve." Mom purposely doesn't mention how Hersh gets loaded every year. Every morning, maybe, in Miami. How if he'd married Jewish, no offense, he'd likely be overeating instead. "Lemme fix you a cup, just—"

"I schlepp two and a half hours on a plane for lukewarm apple juice?" Hersh crabs at her. Then, apparently soothed by the sudden shimmying of Louette's plastic skeleton earrings, he falls silent.

"But it's delicious," Mom insists. "Taste?" She thrusts a cup of cider in Hersh's face. His jaw clamps defiantly. A kid refusing medicine.

"Something smells wonderful," Louette says, abruptly self-conscious under Fred's stare—his objective. "I'll bet it's that cider." Sucking up to the potential mother-in-law, no doubt.

"Sco-otch." Hersh kicks at a linoleum square showing its first signs of edge-curling.

"Well, it's a holiday, isn't it?" Dad asks, gently. "Who's to say what's early." He marches off in his springy way—heel up, step, heel up, step—for the Scotch. Shot elastic on his socks reveals chapped and hairy ankles.

"Go bang your head against the wall," Mom complains into her cider. Her shoulders bunch into a shrug and stay that way. She fiddles with her heart locket. Bad omen.

Though her "for nice" jewelry and "a real heirloom," it was bought in a store. She swears she's been meaning to replace the photo but never has. Can't decide who deserves the honor (a sour reflection on Dad). As she whisks the locket along its chain, it makes a tiny unbearable zipper sound.

"Stop that!" Fred snaps. He cannot stand it.

Mom frowns. What Dad always says is true: she *does* look prettier angry. Cheeks hollow, lips puff, dark eyes scan the room, wide, glittery, slow.

"Leave her alone." Oscar to the rescue. Mom's and/or Louette's.

Because Hersh wants an answer *now!* "What's wrong with your hair, miss?" He leans his bulkiness over to cop another feel. "You one of them whatchamacallits? Uh . . ."

"MTV people." Mom supplies the word he may or may not be looking for. "All the kids are into that now."

Low blow. Louette's twenty-nine.

"No," she says, not even insulted. "I just like looking goofy. Sort of how Fred is with his street act."

Low blow. Fred does not aim for any such thing! "Oh"—he is insulted—"she's just lucky she didn't burn a hole in her scalp with that crap."

"Just an experiment," Louette snarls.

"She learned her lesson," says Dad. Too lenient.

"I keep up," says Hersh. "We get the trades still. I see what goes on."

"I don't even have MTV," says Louette.

"Are you bragging or complaining?" asks Fred.

"I'm no relic." Hersh looks down at his chest as if to convince himself.

"He used to own a beauty parlor too," Oscar explains.

"That's a *salon*, son, thank you. And not 'as well.' It was better!" He lifts Mary's long, thin, motionless hand off her lap and kisses it. "High-class establishment we had. On Fifth Avenue, where all the stars came." He's beginning to rant. "Bette Davis, a regular customer. All the stars. Don't you go letting

Lester tell you otherwise. Beauty parlor! He's got the brains of a knish, that one. Always has. I taught him everything he knows and then some. And then more. Right, Mare? Tell em!"

"OK." Mary pats his bad leg. "OK."

"True enough," Dad adds, returning with a dust-coated bottle of Scotch. Fred imagines how he must have been as a child with that silly walk-bounce. Probably played a mean leapfrog.

"All the stars?" Louette asks. She's toying with her skirt hem. Green mini with a fruit-and-vegetable pattern.

Dad places a tray, with the bottle and glasses on it, dangerously close to the table edge. He says, "Coiffure," just for the sound of it, and, "It is a shame all the things Hersh taught me that I never get to use nowadays. Some real doozies. Chignon Bob, Coquette Bob . . ."

"Shingle Bob," Hersh continues. "Ultramannish Bob!" He slaps the table in delight. He's got his drink. He's got his favorite topic going. Heaven.

"Don't forget the Personality Bob," Mary joins in. "Or the New Moon Bob."

"I have better," Dad says. For some reason, he's smashing up the ice with a letter opener. "OK, ready? Remember the Andalusian Swirl?"

"Is this for real?" Oscar asks, and, "What's your hair called, Mary?" he studies the swirl, dip, tuck at closer range. "I bet Fred could do that."

"I call it a French Knot. Modified," she says proudly, accepting a Scotch from dad.

Even though she is generally unknowable and refuses to let him live down the fact that as a kid he loathed getting his hair cut (Sad Sacks), Fred likes Mary. A woman recovering gracefully from having been beautiful. He himself, however, would be more inclined to call her hairstyle a "Boy Scout Knot. Feminized."

"But what stars specifically?" asks Louette, having accepted cider and Scotch both but guzzling the Scotch first—one swallow, like a shot.

You can tell Oscar's embarrassed by it, since she's not. He tries to change the subject, remarking that feathers develop almost identically to hair. "They're just skin cells that specialize. Why hair anyway? I've been wondering." That's Oscar for you. "Feathers are more manageable, equally attractive, cleaner. Even better, why not scales we'd simply shed? Like structured dandruff."

Dull, Fred doesn't tell him. But Hersh does. "Dull." He even yawns and says, "What ifs, what ifs. What ifs never made me a penny. How much you makin now?"

"Now? Not that much now, but—"

"Eh! Spare me the cockamamy excuses. When I was your age, I had worked all the way up to own a shop on Fifth Avenue."

Even duller. Fred catches Hersh's yawn and watches a cinnamon stick float in the cider. He goes back to feeling sorry for Mom. She puts so much thought into a small touch like cinnamon and then completely overlooks the larger inappropriateness—who drinks hot cider in April? And she spends hours in the living room with the vacuum, cloth, air freshener, before stripping the couches of their plastic slipcovers, all for what? Every year the guests wind up congregated in the kitchen: mud-streaked floors, food-splattered counters, garbage odor, vertical mazes of magazines filled with sweepstake entry forms. Mom's personal weakness.

Win $10,000 worth of groceries or this diamond-and-sapphire "Tiara Royale." Information about each contest Mom enters (any she's eligible for) is tacked tidily to the corkboard beside the phone. She's never hit a jackpot so far, but failure only feeds the fever to embark on some Journey for Two in the Romantic Altitudes. Or win Lotto and get your face plastered all over the subway.

There are worse habits. Fred observes his freckly mother stomping irritably around the island of stove-counter-oven, poking, stirring, tasting—ah, yawning too—in turn. A flustered and wobbly sight on the high red pumps, and with a run in her stockings she doesn't know about. Could be she's jealous of Mary for still being in love with the man she married. And him with her. But . . .

Hersh loves his wife inordinately, it seems, to all distraction, he'll tell you, against all obstacles; he's proved it. For this love, he was booted from synagogue and family. His own mother, he heard, sat shiva as if he were truly dead, all seven days. Bad enough he married a Gentile, but to wed one with the name of *Mary* . . . god forbid.

And how poor they were, oy vey, in those days; so wretched.

"Poor as skimmed piss," Mary testifies.

"Starting off with nothing, less than nothing, not even a hairbrush between us, a pair of scissors we had, an old comb, and penniless. Began cutting hair at home like my lousy father and his lousy father before him. Working, slaving, working. Every night I'd come home and say up to the ceiling, 'God!'—because God was not the one who disowned me—'God,' I'd say, 'I know one day you'll provide, but can't you provide a little something to tide us over while we're waiting for you to provide?' And He heard, He must have, because things did improve—not overnight, mind you, but in installments like. Ten years down the line we were doing custom hairstyles for—"

"Who?" Louette's refrain. Even Fred's getting curious now. Who else besides?

"Bette Davis was a regular in Nolas. This wasn't no chop shop, sweetie."

" 'Salon' spelled backward," Lester throws in. Fred can see Louette's face working it out.

"Appointments weeks in advance . . . A first-name basis with everyone who—"

"Not everyone," Mary says, but you can't sober Hersh once he gets going.

Three Scotches; the blur starts in. They've got to listen to him go on *again* about the backstage passes they had "coming out of their ears," the secrets they were entrusted with ("only your hairdresser knows"), the autographed photos they have back in Miami to this day, framed and hanging. "Priceless, I'm telling you. You could offer me one billion smackeroos, I wouldn't sell. Nope! No! Never!" He holds up his hands as if they were all throwing cash at him.

"Well, then," Mom says, from her own conversation. "At least have some dip. Soak up the poisons." She offers guacamole and a bowl of gleaming vegetables. Guacamole and cider? For Passover?

"What stars?" Louette whimpers. "Please? Whose autograph?"

ON ALL OTHER NIGHTS, Dad sits in the den with two TVs and a radio. HBO or VCR for movies on the big set. The portable Sony for talk shows and sitcoms. Periodically, he scans the AM/FM dials for ball game scores and news highlights. None of this stops him from holding a conversation, should you walk in and desire one. Otherwise, there's the crossword to be done *in pen* while he pedals the Lifecycle (wearing his silver plastic sweatsuit), or "hair ideas" to dictate into his tape deck.

So tonight, when everyone's seated around the table and Dad whips out "something contemporary"—*The Animated Haggadah,* a video seder from Tru-Food—nobody's surprised.

Except Louette: "What's a Haggadah? That Jewish dance?"

Hersh: "Whataya wasting money on that schlock for? We have books, no?"

Mary: "I saw something similar just recently—*Visit the Louvre on your VCR* What-all will they think of next?"

Oscar: "Visit Tru-Food on your VCR."

Fred: "How ya gonna get the TV and VCR into the dining room?"

But Mom, notorious for getting suddenly religious on holidays—she was "very active in the temple" before meeting Dad—becomes positively combative. "This is the end-all, Lester!"—who has answered Fred's question by sliding a luggage pulley into view. "I've had it!" The vein in her temple throbs in tempo with her clenching, unclenching jaw. "You do this to spite me, don't you? You enjoy seeing me like this." She's more than just frowning now; her eyebrows jut to form a ledge. She yanks at her upper arms as if to pull the skin off. "If you do *not* get that *trash* out of my house by the count of *three* . . ."

"One," Mom says, queasily. The counting threat. She's used it as a motivational technique for purposes ranging from homework to chores. (Fred and Oscar's chores often included some vague indignity like having to wash two dozen pink beautician aprons.) But at some point early on came the discovery that when she gets to three *nothing happens.*

Oscar helps Dad wheel in the TV. The two of them have donned Mr. Coffee filters as yarmulkes.

"You would do this to me," says Mom.

The fact is, Dad thought she'd like a video seder. The root of their biggest problem: Dad never has a clue what it is Mom wants. After twenty-eight years, he still consistently gives her things she has to return.

"It's cute; give it a look-see." Dad rushes to hook up the VCR, while Mom darts around in her toppling heels, handing out to everyone—no, flinging—copies of the Deluxe Edition of the Maxwell House Haggadah. A race.

"Well, no shortage of reference materials," Fred says, leafing through the little book.

Nuggets of learning, says its inner flap, *gleaned from our teachers, have been unobtrusively incorporated in the translation.*

"Get those ridiculous coffee things off your heads," Mom says. "This is a holiday, not a three-ring circus."

Under the table, Oscar deposits an extra filter on Fred's lap and whispers, "One size fits all drips."

"Don't I get one?" Louette fake-complains.

"Hold your horses, Char," Dad says, continuing Mom's circus allusion. He flicks on the TV. "Remember: stress bad, stress bad. Fiber good. Fish oil."

"You've gone too far, Lester."

"Fish oil isn't kosher," Fred asks, "is it?"

Mom fumes. "On Thanksgiving, he brings home a video of a log burning!"

The new translations herein offered are suffused with meaning for the tragic and heroic experiences of our people, Fred reads.

Hersh holds up a hand to refuse the coffee filter Oscar's offering him.

"The question is, will one idiotic log burn for two hours? Yes. One log. Two hours."

"We sell video aquariums like that at the PetMart," says Oscar. "Dogs too. Running around in sunny yards. We also sell yarmulkes for dogs, believe it or not, with little embroidered gold Jewish stars. Actual Jews buy them. Kosher pet food too—regular and special Passover kosher. You'd be surprised."

"From that he makes a living?" Hersh asks the tablecloth in dismay.

"Nothing could surprise me anymore, Osc." Mom gazes woefully at the host of TV Passover, a John Madden look-alike with the voice of Marlin Perkins.

"Oh, yeah?" Dad grabs her from behind and swings her up, shrieking, into the air. "No surprises? Oh, yeah?" He distributes little kisses up and down Mom's inner arm.

"Whatayamean *actual* Jews?" says Hersh.

"Lamb shank," lilts TV man, touching the symbolic slab of meat. Then the video cuts to a Claymation of Jews in ancient Egypt.

"Is John Madden Jewish?" asks Fred.

The Claymation Jews are dark-skinned, with big noses, even Moses, though he's depicted as considerably taller and broader-shouldered than the others. With dimples.

"It's a cute idea, right? Isn't it a cute idea?" Dad pleads, holding Mom aloft. Her expression, the only response, is a harsh one: *I'd be an actual Jew if it wasn't for marrying you and your hair career.* "Say it's a cute idea, or you'll have to eat your dinner up here."

"It's sort of cute," Louette concedes.

"Thata girl. Now you, Charl—say it, sugar."

"It's meshugge," Hersh says for her. "Books we have already."

"Turn it off, Fred," Mom bursts out, plucking off Dad's coffee filter to Frisbee. Her wristy girl-throw is so pathetic, Fred takes pity and obeys.

"Turn it on, Osc," Dad says, laughing. Again, misinterpreting her. He thinks this is a game. "Hey, what'd ya do that for?" He frowns at his discarded paper yarmulke. "I need it to cover my bald spot; it's chilly."

Oscar turns the TV back on.

Fred, off. Oscar, on. Fred, off. Until Mom keenly mentions that dinner is "drying out" and orders a compromise. Just the picture, no sound.

Mary speaks up then to say they have a VCR in Miami, still in its box. The instruction manual is a video she has no way of knowing how to play without an instruction manual.

"So that's what these little books are for?" Louette asks. She nevertheless uses the Haggadah as a fan.

First cup of wine. Hold it! Stand up. Mom forgot to take the annual picture. Not the group shot, but the photo of her table setting. The sort of thing that ticks off Oscar maximally.

"Who ever looks at all these pictures she takes of plates? It's worse than the nature slides of their trip cross-country." Oscar's pacing, squeezing his beard in two fists. "She should put one in her heart locket."

"Don't call her *she*," Fred says. The staples still sticking out of Oscar's Levi's are beginning to bug him. "What's your problem?"

And your girlfriend's. Louette is turning up the volume on the video.

And Hersh's. He's drifting out of the kitchen with his coat still on, carrying the Scotch bottle, no glass.

And Mary's. She's pale to the illumination point, but somehow sober seeming, even though she matches her husband swallow for swallow.

And Dad's. He's bouncing, bouncing, and opens a fresh squabble by announcing he's going to hide the *afikomen* matzoh now to save time. "While she fusses over her table snap-shot."

"Don't call her *she*," Oscar mocks.

Mom steadies the camera.

"You've got flair," Mary tells her. "I'm always saying to Hersh, 'That Charlotte has real panache.' "

"With panache she's loaded," says Lester.

"I'm serious. My reverend, Reverend Osbin"—Mary's faith healer—"emphasizes the importance of—"

"What?" The twins both ask. Jinx.

"Thank god for good old Ozzy," Hersh teases. "He Band-Aids her soul just beauti—"

"You shush up, old man," says Mary, sitting down at the table mid-picture.

A gorgeous table, Fred thinks, and worthy of being immor-talized on film. This is where Mom's efforts shine. Yellow mon-ster tulips vibrate against red linen—Red Sea. Carrots set out in a Star of David pattern, gravy boat shaped like Noah's ark (wrong time period, but who's keeping track), the napkin rings homemade out of leftover leopardskin curtain fabric.

It is this "important napkin jewelry" that Oscar's now fo-cused on. He removes a ring and adds it to Louette's mass of colored plastic wrist bangles.

Fred collects the butter knives to juggle. Might as well en-tertain the hungry while we wait. He begins exhibiting the knives' illusory sharpness, smashing a carrot down on one. Antique antic. A broom could "cut" a carrot as easily.

"Please," Mom says, "watch what you're doing." But she might also mean Hersh, who obeys, watching himself sway, splashing Scotch onto the dining room tiles, unconsciously humming the TV Haggadah theme song—a mournful lite-rock ballad.

It gives tasteful Mary a "torrential headache." But, face in her hands, she refuses and re-refuses aspirin on fundamental-ist principles. "The Lord heals."

"But your faith healer?" Fred, Oscar, *and* Lester ask in var-ious ways. "Where does he come in? What does he do?"

"The Reverend heals *through* the Lord."

"Are you sure?" Mom looks physically ill. "Tylenol?"

Mary re-re-refuses. But not to worry, she assures them. "I'm tough as a boiled owl."

Second cup. Another false alarm. You have to hold the glass up and replace it, untouched. Dad pours a glass for Elijah, the prophet who never died, poor guy. You have to open the door for him; he's too weak from all that living.

"They haven't done any of that on the video yet," Louette says, suddenly a seder expert. "But they did mention that Elijah is a harbinger of the Messiah."

A fact Fred pretends to have known. How come he never knew that? Perhaps the result of getting stoned before Hebrew school.

"Do you pour wine for your guests before they arrive?" This is the route Oscar's questioning takes. "Why don't we see if he shows first." And, "Wouldn't someone alive this long want something a little stronger?" From anyone else this would seem humorous, but Oscar's hectic, sucked-in look discourages laughter.

"Yes, yes. Kid's got a point," Hersh agrees. Then, in an unusual burst of energy, he decides to remove the coat. "But a touch of the jumbles as well, mmm hmm, uh uh, no good." The mysterious diagnosis is concurrent with a flurry of dry flakes that rain from Hersh's chest, arms, neck, even eyebrows. Dad goes ahead and plows through the blessing.

Why is this night different from all other nights? Fred, the youngest by those four crucial minutes, gets to ask the Four Questions. There's only that one question, actually, but four answers. Luckily the Hagaddah has the Hebrew all written out phonetically.

"*Ma nish-ta-naw ha-lai-law ha-zeh mee-kawl ha-lay-los?*" Fred recites in his Queens accent. "Because we eat matzoh." He notices Oscar's tie. "And bitter herbs." It's knotted wrong. "We dip parsley in salt water twice." He's all choked up, ironed, seething. "And recline." And remote.

"Why not skip ahead," Dad says, anticipating Mom's objection and proposing a vote. The nays—Charlotte, sure enough, and Mary (polite). The yeas—Dad, Hersh, Oscar, Fred. Louette abstains—boredom or diplomacy.

"But this is the best part," Mom insists. "This is the story."

"She'd read the book cover to cover if we let her." Dad volunteers. "Fred? Give us a summary, then."

"Me?"

"Go ahead. Tell the gist."

"Do it, bro." Oscar lights up. "Sing for ya suppa. You're the oral-interpretation star." He flicks matzoh shards at Fred's nose.

"That's special Smearna matzoh," Mom whines.

Fred knows Oscar knows that Fred considers himself a good talker. Oscar's caught him more than once delivering impromptu Academy Award acceptance speeches before the mirror.

"The Jews," Fred begins, "were slaves in Egypt. Because the pharaoh was a real dick . . . tator. He rarely fed them. Always whipped them. Had them chained up by the ankles and wrists. The living conditions were intensely foul and unlivable. Basically, the brute broke their balls in every—"

"Fred!" Mom says.

"Alliteration," Oscar allows.

"—every way his limited imagination could dream up. And the Jews, forced to lug around marble and build pyramids or sewage systems, whatever, roads, had a lot of time to gripe to God about this hor-rendous state of affairs, which they did regularly to no avail until da dada daaa! *Moses shows.*" Fred imagines, not the Claymation version, but the real Hollywood thing, Charlton Heston. "A very charismatic guy who knows how to loosen God up some, get him chatting." After Charlton has his rendezvous with the Almighty, he returns with this bushy beard and big gray pompadour. "And, OK, God's kind of a tightwad—"

"Fred!" Mom says.

"—about divulging his name. Well, he was! But he did come out with that classic line that Popeye would steal centuries later, *'I am what I am.'* And he came through in the clutch with the plagues. *My* fave. Too bad the movie only skims it. But anyway, fun ahead, you all get to dribble wine on the tablecloth as a lesson not to go partying over other people's misfortunes. *Ready,* are you? *Set . . . ?"*

"*Go!*" Louette finishes, rejuvenated by the idea of some vandalism. She still carries a gold metallic marker around everywhere in her purse.

"*Blood! Frogs! Vermin! Flies! Locusts!*" Fred's voice cracks with a genuine thrill. "*Murrain!*" Oscar tries to interrupt to tell how the frogs are always escaping in the PetMart, but interruption will not be tolerated just now. "*Boils! Hail!*" Hersh slings his wine around, dousing the tablecloth. "*Locusts! Darkness! And the slaying of the firstborn!*"

"Some nice God," murmurs Mary.

"Big shot," says Louette.

"And these nasty displays of what I'd have to call divine machismo got us outta there. Along with the Red Sea episode, which scientists say could have been a tidal phenomenon." Silence. So Fred tacks on, "The end." They all continue to look at him. After what seems a long while, he breaks down and asks, "Well, elders?" for approval, applause, coins. "Did I get it right or what?"

Split decision.

"More or less." From Mom.

"Less is more." Dad.

And, "Yes." Louette, consulting both Haggadahs—print and video. "I think so."

"I'M SO HUNGRY," Lester announces at the sight of Mom coming around the table with a tray of sliced meat, "I'd eat pancake syrup on a sponge. What is this? Beef? Chicken? Sacrificial lamb chops? Did it get darker in here, or are my eyes just dirty?"

"Shouldn't we worry?" Mom whispers, because Hersh has begun snoring. Plain worn out after having his gefilte fish tantrum.

"Texture's off." "Slimy." "It's store bought." All of which Mom patiently ignored, replacing the plate with a bowl of borscht she had prepared "special." Not that it made a whole lot of difference.

After only two spoonfuls, Hersh had begun drifting, sinking.

"Abusing his reclining privileges," Fred joked.

Soon Hersh's head met the tablecloth, and now one elbow rests comfortably in the soup.

"He's turning borscht," Mary reports with an unusual giggle, massaging her temples. He *is* turning borscht color (hot pink), if that's what she means.

"Shouldn't we worry?" Mom again.

Mary shakes her head no, and goes on psychically tending her headache.

"This concludes our Passout seder," Dad quips. "Could I have some ketchup, please, Charlotte?" Thus reinitiating the running ketchup spat.

"There's gravy."

"I want both."

"Shouldn't we open a window or something?" Fred asks. An attempt at diversion that fails.

"All day in the beauty parlor, and you people expect Julia Child."

"I am not you people," says Dad. "I am Lester, and I like ketchup."

"*We* are not you people," says Fred. "If I may speak for we."

"Certainly," says Oscar.

"You know I like ketchup," Lester continues. "Yet you refuse to let me have ketchup. Why? Is it a crime for a man to like ketchup?"

"He's turning ketchup," says Oscar.

"Get it yourself, then." Mom gives up.

"Fred?" says Dad. "Go."

"Oscar'll do it," says Fred.

No one moves.

"Would someone please get their old man some goddamn ketchup!"

The twins jolt to a stand, only to find Louette also on her feet beside them. Grin exchange—what the hell. Fred and Oscar direct *her* toward the ketchup.

"Such gentlemen." Dad snickers. "*I* never taught you that. Did *you*, Charl?" Trying to get a rise out of her. No go.

Throughout, Hersh has not stirred.

"Sit down and eat," Fred and Oscar have to keep telling their mother. "Sit. Eat. You're making us dizzy." But there's always one more thing to bring out from the kitchen. Some over-cooked gaseous broccoli. Diet soda. Serving tongs.

The video seder emcee suggests Tru-Food red grape juice as a wine alternative.

MARY CUTS her meat into itty-bitty bite-size units that she chews, thoroughly, down to nothing. On her pristine plate, no food group is allowed to make contact with another, and no gravy either—it might leak off the meat, taint a string bean, puddle up the carrots. No one has the heart to tell her she's got a wine mustache.

"Sublime smashed potatoes, as always," Fred compliments, as he goes about his ritual of eating them. Sculpt the peak with knife held flat. Indent volcano with spoon back. Ladle in some gravy. Fork for patterning. At last, slowly eat away till the lava runs down. "Yes."

"Thank you kindly." Hersh takes credit.

From the depths of his plate, Fred starts at the name "Lubin." Dad is saying he ran into Sid Lubin yesterday at Hardware and Pain—so called because of the sign's missing final *t*. Fred can see Oscar's face die a little with each word. ". . . Sid walks up and says to me—guess what? You won't believe. He says—"

"Sam's getting married?" Mom ventures.

"Yeah. How—"

"You don't tell me anything!"

"You knew already. Why didn't *you* tell *me*?"

"Well, I heard it. That doesn't mean I knew it. Why didn't *you* tell *me*?"

Oscar's leg shoots up, down, up, beneath the table.

"I am, if you'd just shut—So I says, 'Sidney,' I says, 'you sure you're talkin about *your* Sam? The kid who's had a new girl every other week since kindergarten? You're yankin my chain, Sid.' I was sure he was."

Oscar seems to have given up breathing.

"Apparently, he and Peaches were just as shocked as I was. Allswell's the name. Stinking rich and not Jewish. Allswell Cap N Gown. They've got some sort of monopoly going on East Coast graduations."

"Is that so?" Mom says, offended; always the last to hear everything. "Why, just last Wednesday," she complains, "Peaches was in for her usual, and she didn't breathe a word about Caps N Gowns. Not that she shut her trap for one minute about the engagement, mind you."

Fred would prefer ignorance of Peaches Lubin's "usual"—mustache bleach, wash and set, manicure, eyebrow tweeze, facial electrolysis session. But like it or not, he can rattle off the particulars of just about every "usual" in Sidehill. The sort of data he's convinced clogs up valuable brain space.

"You can cut that woman's schmaltz with a fork," Mom adds. "The way she goes on about—"

"So." Dad derails her from that track. Peaches is one of Mom's least favorite people. Their rivalry began more than twenty years ago, when Peaches apparently slammed the door in Mom's face for trying to collect charity money. "I was shaking," goes the story. "I was younger then than you kids are now. We had just moved here. I rode up there on my bicycle, then back home in tears." A poignant image, unlike: "So ... when will we hear wedding bells for *you* two lovebirds?"

Oscar's leg leaps high enough this time to bang the table and overturn both the gravy boat and Fred's wineglass. Oscar grips his steak knife, upright, homicidal style, and mops the mess with his sleeve.

"Beastly," Louette says, her mouth crammed end to end with broccoli. She's been scooping in food nonstop for the last twenty minutes. Seems panicky now, looking at Oscar (the bleeding gravy-wine stain) and then at Hersh (the thin line of spittle connecting his mouth to the tablecloth), and back to Oscar and back to Hersh again, Oscar, Hersh, Oscar, perhaps seeing some obscure correlation there.

"I expect I'll hear it from a customer when and if Osc pops the question," Mom kids, uncharacteristically. She's not all that gung ho on Louette. "Anyhow," she persists, "I think it's just terrific Sam's decided to grow up. Surprising, but terrific."

Once, after a weekend away—a weekend-long party the twins threw, with the house to themselves—Mom walked in and immediately spied a condom wrapper underneath the kitchen table. Sam's: the twins told the truth; they blamed it on him. This was in the olden days, when you weren't commended for such a thing.

"I'd love some grandkids of my own before I'm bedridden."

"Aw. Don't talk like that, Lester."

"She won't convert, though. Some people are hung up on that." An indirect jab at Mom. Dad actually likes Louette. A lot. Gives her those free haircuts, calls her "cute as a bug's ear." In return, she gets him a discount on dental work.

"Would you rather I marry a rich, intelligent, but disabled black Jew," Oscar asks, as he systematically mutilates his carrots, "or a poor stupid white-trash Protestant?"

"How wealthy *is* this girl exactly?" Mom tries, but, getting no response besides the clatter of Oscar's knife hitting his plate, goes on to speculate about the cap-and-gown business. "They must make a killing in June."

"Claire never graduated," Louette's pleased to disclose. "She told us herself; she's a dropout."

"You mean you met her?" Mom simply cannot contain herself. "Well, tell, tell . . . how, when? Is she sweet, attractive? What was she wearing? She lives where?"

"Beeswax, Beeslamp, Bee something, New Jersey. That's all I know except that she went all around Europe and plays pool like a guy. I liked her." Louette's opinion.

"Do we have to talk about this now?" Oscar says.

"What on earth is wrong with you tonight?"

"Sam asked Osc to be best man," Louette blabs.

"He *did?* . . . So what's so terrible? That's lovely." Mom pauses to think on the concept. "You could use the new suit, Oscar. There's a sale going on right now at—"

"No."

"Gray linen, I picture, some nice shoes . . . and enough already with that beard . . . Please, I'm pleading, shave? For *me?* For your poor mother."

"Forget it, Ma."

"Debutante Bob," says Hersh, in his sleep.

Pitiful.

And does anyone stop for one second to ask about Fred being best man? About Oscar being chosen and not Fred, when Fred would've probably said yes. No! And why should they? Just because the three of them have been friends—equals, Fred used to assume—since preschool doesn't mean anyone should give Fred's feelings a thought. And no one knows that Sam asked him too—to pinch-hit, as it were, if Oscar doesn't feel up to it.

"You know what they say," Dad says. "A wise man looking for a bride should take an ignoramus along to advise him."

"Who says this?" Oscar demands to know. "Meaning what?"

"He hasn't given Sam an answer yet." Louette just doesn't know when to stop.

"Well, why not? What are you afraid of?" asks Mom, astutely. It's exactly what Fred's been wondering. "Are you jealous? Or—"

Oscar's hand slams down, right on the plate, somehow jarring Mary, who yelps. Then, screaking his chair out, Oscar smiles; eerie. "I'm *going* to hunt for the matzoh."

"Aw, Fred," Mary says, calming, confusing them. "Little Sad Sacks."

The third cup makes Louette's nose bleed. Mom ushers her off to the bathroom, saying she might as well just throw out the tablecloth now. Hersh's mouth begins moving in small bursts, as if he's dreaming of sucking on a nut.

"What *do* you think he's dreaming?" Fred asks Mary and Dad, the only ones left. Dad shrugs, goes on eating. Mary pushes crumbs around the tablecloth. Her swirl, dip, tuck is still intact, perfect, but Mary's clearly woozy. Are she and Hersh some kind of alcoholic team? Psyche Knot—another hairdo Fred once heard of but cannot picture. Is it true that alcoholics don't dream?

After so much chaos, the minuscule click of the video (going into automatic rewind) is what finally wakes Hersh. "Just in time," for the *third cup.*

A DRIZZLE starts up. Dad sends Fred out to check the car windows. A one-car driveway, so Oscar's Toyota sticks out into the street. It's not drizzling; it's raining. Warm rain, though.

It's fortunate the windows on the station wagon are already closed, because they're remote control and Fred has forgotten the key. Inside, all Dad's gadgets stand by—thermometer, compass, CB, fuzzbuster, phone, books on tape. Plus a year's worth of bridge tokens, plus deodorizer, plus the latest brainstorm, displayed on the back windshield: printed decals that say, CHESTER'S. WHERE BEAUTY IS BOTH AN ART AND A SCIENCE. SINCE 1955. A lie. Fred's sure it was '57. And, NOW WE'RE UNISEX! An exaggeration. No normal guy'd be caught dead getting his hair done in a beauty parlor. Dad's sure to slap one on Oscar's car.

Did he call it? On Oscar's car, the sticker. Glow-in-the-dark gold—he'll love this—looks even brighter compared with the faded I (heart) MY GRANDKIDS. All four windows are open. Seats already damp, accentuating the regular stink: dog food, moldy gym clothes, Louette. Or so Fred imagines as he leans in to look at the scrap of paper on the driver's seat. In Oscar's big, messy script: "the 'yawning reflex' theory, recently advanced, that parrots will yawn when scratched between the base of the upper beak and the ear opening if—"

"Aah!" Fred is startled to find Oscar lying on the backseat. Wet seats. "You could've given me a heart attack." Fred sits, slams the door. "Is this where you suspect Dad hid the *afikomen?* In your glove compartment?"

"Shhh," Oscar says. "I'm studying."

Fred obeys. Facing forward, he clutches the steering wheel and pretends this is his car, that he's driving to his own home in his own car. Maybe if he got some standard job, he's thinking, just temporarily, just until some money started accumulating . . . when he spots, among the car garbage—soda bottles, newspapers, vinyl dog toys—*Louette's diaphragm.* At least he assumes it belongs to her. Lying in plain, icky view on the floor. Its vaginal rubber color matches Chester's hairdresser-smock pink.

"I've heard of parrots living eighty years," Oscar is telling Fred.

Fred decides that as long as he's daydreaming, he might as well stick a girl in the frame. A girl plainer than Louette. Brown hair, perhaps, a Susan or Jennifer who wears sweaters. But then again, nothing too regular, nothing cornball or dumpy. He envisions Louette's micro nose, one feature he wouldn't shun. Ideal nose, in fact (when not gushing blood), and a complement to the admittedly charming wee earlobes (when not decorated with skeletons).

"Don't elbows look like brains?"

Fred shifts around, to catch Oscar actually using Hersh's

nail kit. The filing sound gives Fred the heebie-jeebies even worse than Mom's scraping locket. "What is it, Oscar?"

"When exactly did Sam turn slime?"

"He did? I don't get it." Mostly what Fred doesn't get is how it's possible that he doesn't get it. "At all."

"WHAT'S THAT?" Louette's voice floats down to them in the foyer.

"Elijah," Hersh whispers.

"No, really."

"It's *him.*"

"Who's there?" Louette calls out, frightened. And without speaking, both Fred and Oscar crouch down out of the light. At the top of the stairs, Louette holds a long banner of toilet paper to her face. She's trying to lean her head back *and* look down at the door. Hersh towers over her, laughing, one arm around Mary's waist, the other touching Louette's hair. He is three times the size of Louette.

You left your diaphragm in the car, Fred thinks of calling out, but he isn't sure how Oscar would take it, not to mention Mary, the faith-healed fundamentalist. Besides, Louette isn't really that bad. Oscar once told him she could will her nose to bleed.

"Don't you want any of our crappy wine, Elijah?" Hersh bellows down.

"If it's *him,*" Louette says, as if it were entirely possible, "I'm mortified."

No ONE can find the matzoh, so Dad gives two clues. "Kitchen and above your waist." Whoever locates it first can demand ransom cash. But Louette's indisposed by her nose, which needs to be pointing up at the kitchen ceiling. Oscar's not even trying. The adult adults aren't supposed to look. So it's only a matter of time for Fred, not much fun.

"Why does Mom hang up all these plates and rugs? Functional objects." Oscar is mind-reading Fred, thought for thought.

Uncommon but not rare. Reassuring rather than scary. Plates and rugs are about the only things Fred sees above the waist. "Because," he speculates happily, "to borrow a phrase from a one-armed Indian man, 'Objects are the ultimate martyrs.' "

"Did I ever tell you about the jazz experiment I was in, in college?" asks Oscar.

"Yeah."

"Where I had to get up in front of hundreds of people, think of the saddest thing that ever happened to me, then take a bite of matzoh?"

"Yeah."

"What did you think of?" Louette asks, from behind her tissue-wrapped nose.

"You."

"Hey," Fred says. "Let's find this *afikomen* before the roaches do."

"Yah." Oscar tackles Fred and wrestles him to the floor. In the process, the staples from his new Levi's finally pop loose and shoot across the room—a distraction that gives Oscar the opportunity to clamp his leg firmly around Fred's middle, tight, right where all that food's digesting.

"I'll puke on you."

Louette, standing above them, dangles her reams of bloody t.p. and giggle-squeals, "Cut it out, Osc."

He's bending Fred's arm to wrap him in a headlock and pushing his chin up, back, rough now.

Underdog Fred has to throw elbows to get free, then they're rolling soundlessly across the linoleum, rolling without even grunting—the floor sticky where something (Scotch, most likely) spilled—squeezing leg on leg, arm on leg, leg on leg on arm. Louette's gone or quiet. Oscar is shoving Fred's head into his own stomach. Fist action is about to break out when Fred catches a glimpse of the matzoh, shoved up behind a framed picture over the sink. The two of them in miniature kelly-green corduroy overalls flanking a photography studio's wishing well. Once again Fred's caught off guard, trying to call *"Time"*—whoa, Oscar's slamming him up against the cabinets—*"out!"* Fred sees no stars but dozens of Oscar's tiny nose blackheads. He wonders, Do I have those? He wonders, Is this a real fight or not?

4

TEXTURE THIS

THERE WAS ALMOST a divorce over what to name the beauty parlor. Charlotte and Lester Arm celebrated their grand opening with the window still blank. They argued. In that first month, summer 1957, they had two, maybe three customers and a huge debt, growing worse. Finally, forced to compromise, they decided to join names. Chester's.

"A cop out," Oscar says every time his parents tell *that* story. He and Fred call the place Chesty's, a comment on the clientele (the regulars, that is—more than a hundred now, weekly). The *rubber grandmoms* (buzzwords in the Arm-twin idiom) who devote entire wash-and-set mornings to complaints and gossip, whole dryer-helmeted afternoons to gossip and complaints: Husband's been inarticulate for thirty years or out in the toolshed all weekend, or over god-knows-where since god-knows-when with Murray and god-only-knows who else. Bowling. Shooting pool. Fishing, can you believe? Sam's marrying a rich shiksa. Corns and bunions. Sure, with Peaches' blessing. Better fish you can buy in Waldbaum's, gutted. Bone spurs and liver spots. A virgin, no less; she knows from nothing. Low-sodium, low-calorie, low-fat, low-cholesterol diets, what Dr. Horowitz said about tests. *This* I need, yet? Never has been a secret who wears the pants in *that* family, who wears the mustache. Terrible. The neighborhood's changed; you can hardly recognize. You want terrible? *You* schlepp out to White Plains on the wrong day for a sale. And their children . . . why don't their children ever call? Why aren't their children having children? If it rains tonight their collective hair will droop and fall.

Once in a while, you'll see a small Debbie or Jill dragged in, screaming. Sit still. Sit up. Sit quiet. Now, *she* has the face for bangs. Lookit that. Look at you, Miss Lizzy Tish, so grown up, having her hair done in the beauuuty parlor. If that doesn't work, there's always bribery—stale candy that needs to be peeled off the paper it's wrapped in, shiny blue barrettes shaped like cats or pianos. Or threats: You turn off those tear ducts, young lady or . . .

Even worse is what a boy endures, the all-out psychic trauma *this* boy—raspberry blond, spindly, big-footed—endures. Having lost the good fight to keep his Mets cap on, he must bravely witness its confiscation. *This place is for girls, Ma.* Swallow, swallow. He must never, ever, no matter what, cry.

Oscar stands under the beauty parlor's landmark sycamore, shouldering an African gray parrot and watching through the window, on which Dad has added "Since 1955" under CHES-TER'S, and a little pink swirl maybe meant to be a tulip. The improvement renews Oscar's optimism, necessary to any sales pitch.

Picture this: Exotica beauty! A live parrot your trademark! Chester's gets a whole new aura, a jungle motif, with indoor trees and misters. Tropical music. Hell, go all the way, spring for the juice bar; with all the nonstop dieting in this joint, the concept'll fly. Which reminds me, for my parents, a can't-beat-it price on this authentic import from PetMart (where Oscar is paid on a part-commission/part-salary-part-Vladimir-whim basis), insider price, honest.

The idea just came to him. After his healthy morning rage, healthier than usual—Oscar tore the bell down from the PetMart door—it just flooded his head: *Get rid of the goddamn bird already.* Grays, with their well-known talent as mimics, fetch a good price, impress people. *Put in some effort. How difficult can it be?* Grays imitate not only words and phrases but whatever they happen to hear—sirens, coughing, phones, babies crying, construction work, bells ringing, ringing, ringing—pushing Oscar toward new depths of discomfort, new heights of preposterous brainstorming, as in: (1.) Ask the construction crew to keep it down, please. (2.) Break into the store after hours to perform a mysterious vocal-cordectomy(?). (3.) Sell the bird to the beauty parlor.

Oscar figures: In high school I could sell a pound of pot on my lunch hour, no sweat. Why not a single parrot now? Oscar figures: Bring the animal along. If there's one thing selling drugs teaches, it's that people want to see exactly what they're buying. Oscar figures; Today. Right now. Because it's either me or Memo.

That's the bird's name.

But ten minutes Oscar's lost already, distracted by this bowl cut in progress. The big-footed boy is afraid Sandrine's scissors are getting too close. His ears are going to stick out. She's completely uncovering both ears. The kid *liked* his hair fine before and never wanted to come here in the first place, even if he does get to eat at McDonald's afterward. Unfortunately, the kid is way too young to even begin appreciating the many toothsome vulgarities of Sandrine.

Sandrine once had top billing in Oscar's adolescent wet dreams. The way she'd dance around—"I'm engaged"—in fuzzy sweaters to whatever music happened to be heading the charts, giggling, wiping sculpting gel off her hand onto the tight seat of her skirt, always with a hip thrust out *in that way*, always licking her lips, slow-ly. Hence the station Dad's assigned her, near the window. Free advertising.

More than a decade (and three husbands) later, Sandrine still won't wear a bra, and so the mammoth tits swing now in the poor kid's neck. "My, you're dashing," she's likely saying, or, "So tell me, what grade? Fourth? Fifth? Have a girlfriend? Natural waves like these? *Wasted* on a boy." Also something to the effect of "Call me up in fifteen years, sweet cheeks."

Sweet Cheeks was her name for Oscar and Fred—both big

blushers—bad enough before someone from school got hold of it. *Sweet Cheeks*, woo woo, here they come, the Arm fairies. The Arm fairies from the beauuuty parlor, woo woo, on top of that other bit—First comes lo-o-ove, then comes marriage—that escaped about Oscar and Fred vowing to stay together, always, in holy matrimony! Not to mention the curl-yanking. A double curse being blond. A triple curse being dressed alike, cute, matching outfits, often Hanukkah or birthday gifts from the rubber grandmoms, often featuring auxiliary doodads like beaded belts and bolo ties. Sure, Mom made sure they knew she adored them, she wouldn't trade them in "even for daughters I could gussy up." But *pretty poo*, went the taunts regardless. You wanna be my squeeze? Oops, forgot, already taken.

Jerry Gooch down the block might have had it hard, with his dad the proud owner of a garbage barge. And Sam too, with his mother, Peaches, a two-hundred-pound drummer. But the twins' experience was uniquely hellish, worse even perhaps than that of Oscar's co-worker Marci, who grew up over her father's funeral parlor. This could explain Fred's resistance to his obvious calling (obvious at least to everyone but him): hair. It could also explain the puzzling backed-up feeling Oscar gets each and every time he enters Chester's. Call it déjà vu, call it natural trepidation, but it's probably just the perm-chemical stink—thioglycolates.

Once through the door, Oscar realizes instantly: *big mistake.* It's Wednesday. Peaches Lubin gets her usual on Wednesday. Not even a bird as skilled as Memo can reproduce the greeting Peaches emits as she pops out at Oscar from under the first dryer bonnet like some Halloween jack-in-the-box monstrosity—green facial cream, wire curlers, rolls upon rolls of recently massaged flesh loaded into blue jeans, size . . . uncharted. The poor parrot can only scream.

"Oeeeaaach!"

Peaches outshrills the bird, a feat.

And not only is it Wednesday. It's the last Wednesday of the month. Oscar has disrupted the tail end of Charlotte's Makeup Workshop for the Blind. Mom's idea of community service.

This is not the time to try and sell parrots.

The sightless women flinch at all the noise and jerk their dogs' leashes close. The Seeing Eye German shepherds and Labs growl their meaty, obedient growls. Cosmetics smear up, down, across, and into every facial orifice. Sandrine's little-boy victim finally and totally erupts.

"Hold it!" Mom's arms shoot up straight, seemingly kept on only by the pink smock. Her incredibly skinny neck by the matching scarf. Her mouth by lipstick. "Hold on!"

How wrong *is* staring at blind people, since they don't know you're staring? Not that Oscar is staring. He just feels as though he is, since he's purposely not. Exaggerating the situation, Charlotte's workshop is held in the back of the shop, where the floor is raised by a few steps, a natural stage, ideal for staring.

Oscar shushes the bird with seeds. Sandrine shushes the kid with stale candy. Four out of five blind women shush their dogs with treats high in beta-carotene. Peaches shushes herself, but you can't count on that to last.

"Will you all please forgive the disturbance?" Mom says, taking on her telephone singsong, and looking, but not staring, at the blind women.

Sure they will, sure, they nod—brunettes all. The dogs whine softly, suspicious. "What happened?" one woman asks affably. Another jokes, "Madge stop by for a soak in Palmolive?" A third calls for makeup remover and "Emergency cotton balls!" Good sports all. It depresses Oscar.

"It's my son! Hi, hon!" Mom calls down, keeping the lilt intact. "What's new and different? My son has come over to . . . What's up, sweetie? Didyaeat?"

"He wants something," mumbles Peaches, quite audibly.

Shaky Bea, the floor sweeper, rushes to Oscar's defense. "What? He can't come for a pleasant visit with his mother?" Bea, one of those unrelated relatives the Arm family tried to make a bona fide aunt by tacking on that prefix when Oscar and Fred were kids.

"I'm simply de-tecting the signs is all. Bout time you ladies get hip to it." Peaches fancies herself as really in tune. "Now, *my* Sam . . . Why, Oscar hasn't even congratulated me yet."

Peaches, Oscar thinks, like most obese people, only sees herself from the neck up.

"*My* Sam's engaged," she's announcing, for the sake of the Sightless. "To the young heiress Claire J. Allswell." Her nose rises incrementally, as if attached to a string from heaven. "And I should think kudos *are* in order for the mother-in-law-to-be." Naturally, all the Sightful have already gnawed the subject clean through. "It's not every day that the Lubins *and* The Bouncetones, mind you, join forces with such a prosperous—"

"Kudos?" Oscar ponders as he tries to remain calm, if nothing else, for Memo. The bird fluffs up his feathers, whistles brief, sharp, nervous notes. "I really don't follow."

Peaches just eyeballs the bird with an expression that belies true disgust, and pants, "Go! Back!" Perhaps it's the way two of the parrot's toes point forward, two back. Or the fleshy cylindrical tongue. "Get that thing—what *is* that?—away from me." She's curled into a semi-fetal position, nostrils flared, blue mascara-encrusted lashes brutally clashing with the green face. "Is it real?"

"What kinda question . . . ? *He's* blinking, isn't he?" Memo's whitish bare skin circles pale-yellow eyes. Almost congenial when his mouth is shut. But this is no time for congenial. Dazzle the ladies, big guy, don't frighten 'em. "Are *you* real?"

Sandrine titters.

"I don't have to answer that," Peaches says, one hand rooting through her purse. Then, lighting a menthol 100, she says, "All I care is that it's sterile."

"Boil it," Sandrine suggests. "It's probably a delicacy somewhere."

"Yes!" Oscar gets excited. "It was. Rome. They imported too many as pets and chowed down the surplus."

Peaches tsks. "Germs."

Which gives Shaky Bea a thought. "Lice rinse you could try."

A sincere offer of help. She's a veritable, if sad, legend around Chester's. After twenty-five years spent sweeping up hair clumps, hunchbacked and shrunken. Now she's cooing, "Hello, birdy, hi! Dirty birdy. Over here." Delighted.

"They're cleaner than you people," Oscar doesn't mean to say.

"But look at those teeny-weeny beady eyes." Peaches fake-shivers.

Oscar looks instead at Bea. "How are you feeling?" She's not only been sweeping hair clumps for a quarter century but been doing it in front of all these mirrors. Bad enough to get wrinkly, misshapen, sluggish, elderly, but to watch it all happen: heartbreaking.

"Elegant." They hardly even let her wash hair anymore, she's so shaky. "Imagining a beauty parlor bird."

How'd she know? She always could read him ten times better than Mom. Used to keep an eye on him and Fred, after school, Saturdays, vacations, used to provide a new story to explain her nickname each time they asked. She got frostbite in the Swiss Alps, where she was a princess once. She held a friend's hand so hard something popped. She got scared. She saw a monster in her Frigidaire and hasn't stopped shaking since. Or God himself sent down the affliction as punishment for the time she gave her Aunt Ruth the finger.

"I thought he might improve the decor," Oscar admits.

"The decor! Oh!" Bea sniffs dramatically, teasing. "I see." Even her nose hairs are starting to gray, to shake. Had they not been so tactful, the adults might have found out the disorder's source at the start. Now, too late, they hardly wonder anymore—who with the shakes would choose to work in a beauty parlor?—and they feel sorry for her, though she's probably the highest-paid hair-clump sweeper in Queens, with ten sick days and two paid vacations a year. "The decor, huh?" Bea pulls the towel from her shoulder and swipes at Oscar, locker-room style, a mild flirtation. Lately, she seems kind of embarrassed that he and Fred have grown up.

"What's all this decor nonsense?" Mom calls down, impatiently. "Wallpaper we tried. It peels with all these dryers. . . . Come, Oscar, meet my group."

This launches Peaches into a description of *her* community service work—so as not to be upstaged by Charlotte—"raising money for AIDS." The Bouncetones will be giving free concerts come summer.

There's a new one. But before Oscar can rip into Peaches, Mom calls, "Where's my hug?" kiss-kissing the air but making her displeasure known to Oscar with her forehead. Customer service, her highest law. Customers first. Customers beautiful. Customers always right. Customers treated regally *even* when they're Peaches Lubin. All of this Mom says with her forehead.

Oscar tries to be optimistic. But the sudden silence as he strides through the vast, pink, triangular room—central boutique/make-over station and dozing receptionist at its apex—makes him aware of his cheeks' sweetening, on fire. All the rubber grandmoms under dryer bonnets are grim-lipped, mute. The mute and the blind. Oscar's sneaker squeaks as he mounts the three small steps to the dais.

"Down! Down, boy!" The Seeing Eye dogs have gone sniffbonkers. They strain their snouts toward Oscar, struggling to get a whiff of rabbit, newt, mealworm, tiny mammal in heat, or whatever odor combination Oscar has carried over from the PetMart.

"Where's Dad?" Oscar pushes through the dogs. Oddly, they ignore the bird, who's taking a snooze, balanced on one scaled silver leg.

"Getting Danish. Why? You don't want to chat with your old mother?"

"Sure, it's just . . . I'm on my lunch hour."

"Good, you'll stay for Danish." Mom takes Oscar's hand. "This is my other son, not to be confused with the one who you once met," she says, by way of introduction.

"Join us," says the smileyest of the blind women, either Eleanor, Jean, Ronnie (no, not the waitress), Stepha, or Louise.

She's doing fairly well with the makeup, except for a little Raspberry Picnic lipstick running up into her nostril area.

"Forgive me," Mom apologizes. "I haven't quite learned the dogs' names yet . . . or the parrot's."

"They call these birds grays. For obvious reasons." Whoops! Not obvious to these ladies. Strike one. Two of the women, here only for "cheek work," are wearing dark glasses. "I mean Africa." Oscar sinks deeper. "African grays." As if that makes any sense, as if Africa were gray. Should he, Oscar wonders, change his opening to *Texture this?* "Memo is his given name."

Just don't stare, whatever happens. Say, "Hello, ladies," and hope the bird will take the cue. No go. Just don't go pondering blindness. How, for instance, these women have to take Charlotte's word for what colors to wear, what colors are *their* colors, what colors *are*. At least five different grays in Memo's feathers alone! Paling upward toward the head, which keeps moving slightly, even as he naps, moving slowly back and forth, as constantly as one of the blind ladies' heads.

The dogs settle down. Clean animals, good-looking. As far from a pit bull as Claire is from Sam. As far from a toy poodle as a human being. "Hello, ladieees." Oscar tries again to wake the stubborn bird, who's probably pretending to sleep to spite Oscar for tearing down his favorite bell. "You'll see. He'll get going. Just a kid . . . shy."

The real kid meanwhile is squirming to get a look. He has total faith the parrot will speak.

"Hello-o-o. C'mon, Memo, say—"

"Is Lester *baking* that Danish?" Peaches gripes, waddling over and plopping herself down at one of the manicure tables. "He's been getting that Danish for going on half an hour." She proceeds to twirl the nail polish carousel, faster, faster, faster. "Can you do me, Char. Or . . . ?" Peaches gallops her claws across the table surface.

"Certainly." Mom's gracious, seething. "As soon as I'm finished up here . . ." Then, to the blind crowd, "But you still haven't said a proper hi to my handsome"—she winces on handsome—"son."

"Fred," says one of the two women wearing dark glasses. The main head swiveler. Base makeup in her eyebrows.

"That's the other one," says the other one. She with fancier frames, designer, red. "You don't listen."

"I don't listen and I don't see." Base in her eyebrows and blush on her teeth. "So shoot me."

"Excuse." Peaches is tapping her wire curlers—ping, ping. "I'm in a rush." Ping. "I'm up to my ears in wedding here—"

Mom says, "Did I mention how my Oscar studies ornithology? A very difficult science." She never stops with this.

"Can we touch?" asks black glasses.

"Why not?" Mom answers for Oscar. "But don't say I didn't warn you when you come across that shmata of a beard he's got." She never stops with that either.

"By the way, mazel tov to you, Peaches," says the smiley blind lady. "My own son, he's married ten years. Three beautiful grandkids." She rifles through her purse. For pictures? A blind woman!

"Let Eleanor touch, Osc," Mom commands.

"But they're all gonna wanna touch then," jokes another sightless woman, the dogless one. Ronnie—Oscar's fairly sure—the pretty, dogless one. She doesn't need any makeup.

"Go on." Mom nudges Oscar. So what else can he do but pass his face around along with the cotton balls. They *do* all want to touch him, his face. They say, "Mmm," and "Oh," probing the skin. Some fingers slender, some veiny or compact, squat. All with subtly differing pressures. "What cheekbones!" Smiley exclaims.

"His mother's mouth," says Black Glasses, very thorough in scanning Oscar's features.

"He looks exactly like the other one, Fred." Pretty Ronnie laughs, as if a joke were being played on her. "Sly." Faintly blush-faced. "My type." She has by far the lightest (ticklish) stroke but mysteriously icy fingertips.

None of them have the slightest interest in touching the bird. But haircut kid does.

"CAREFUL NOW . . ." A tiny budgie can inflict a painful chomp; a macaw can take off an entire finger. A gray somewhere in between. "Don't worry." Oscar removes an orange from his windbreaker pocket. "Take this and—"

"He certainly will not!" says the kids' mother, appalled. She's wearing a tennis outfit the shape and color of a pineapple. "You certainly will not!"

"Hat," the kid says. Up close, he seems strangely devoid of eyelashes.

Sandrine protests. She hasn't had a chance to perform the postoperatives—brushing away stray hairs, combing the do one more time, holding up the mirror so he can see how the back looks—as if a little kid like this cared. The boy howls and chases Oscar around till Mother Tennis unsheathes her fiberglass racket to brandish. "It's OK, thank you very much, miss. . . ." She sizes Sandrine up before tipping.

"Hat," the kid repeats.

A dimwit? Retards and blind people? What a day!

"Hat." The kid speaks up yet a third time, once he's finally got his Mets cap back and has emphatically shoved it down on his head. "Hat."

Oscar tries to console him. "Hair hell, isn't it?" But the child hides behind his mom—a coward too?—continuing to peek out at the parrot from there. Oscar's disappointed. Last chance: "I'll bet you pitch a wicked curve ball."

The kid shakes his head, cringing.

"Well, then, all I can tellya is go home, chill awhile. Later on, what you do, you get some PB and J from the fridge and rub it all around in your scalp, see, like this." Oscar mimes. "I guarantee you'll be one hundred percent in no time." Which naturally does not please Pineapple Mom one iota. She nearly snaps the kid's wrist as she yanks him out the door.

Enter Dad with Danish. "Osc!" he calls. There's a bloody speck of toilet paper stuck on his chin. "Have some Danish!" He runs over to stick his face up close to Memo's hooked beak.

"Does he speak, Dr. Dolittle?" Dad wrinkles his very large, brown, and deeply lined brow. Oscar suspects he's snuck over to Bronze God tanning salon again.

"Finally!" Mom says, now speed-wrapping Peaches' chubby fingers. She presses on the silk with Krazy Glue and white powder. Beauty voodoo.

"Mmm," Peaches says. "Smell that. Delish . . ."

"Polly want a Danish?" Dad laughs. He wears a baseball cap too. Make that a basketball cap—St. John's Red Men. It covers his bald spot.

The bird stretches, making little bunched fists that open and close like a child gesturing bye-bye.

"Awww," Bea says.

"Awww," Dad says.

"Awww," Sandrine says.

Memo wants the orange. "Say 'I love you, Lester,' " Oscar begs. "C'mon." Useless. "In the store, this guy blables nonstop, but here, well . . . Just wait'll the phone rings. He likes the phone."

Dad holds up and shakes the white paper Danish bag. "Grossberger's prune. Known to loosen the most stubborn tongues."

Unfortunately, Oscar explains, parrots don't relate to reward/punishment the way us humans do but mimic only by association. "I gotta be goin anyway." He'll have to try this on a day that's not Wednesday. When the stars are in better places or whatever. "As it is, I'm really severely late."

"Late, shmate." Dad doesn't want to hear it. "Who buys pets in the afternoon?"

"Maybe you do," Oscar says. Giving it a go, what the hey. If anyone'll consider an innovation such as parrot decor, it's Dad. "I was thinking . . . This place could use some sprucing. A make-over, to borrow a phrase from your own profession." Oscar follows his father over to the Mr. Coffee machine. "A whole new image, if you will."

"Hmmm," Dad says, suddenly darting over to Peaches' head

as if it were something he left to burn in the oven. He starts frantically undoing the curlers. "Since you've been so kind as to share that vision . . ." Plastic curlers work better, but wire are faster. "Come by Sunday. We'll start with the back rooms. Scraping and repainting."

"That feels *wonder*ful." Peaches moans. "A little lower. Down, left."

"What I mean," says Oscar, "what I was suggesting . . . maybe something a little more . . . atmospheric. Say, a jungle motif . . . Birds, say."

"Atmospheric? Can you check that coffee, Osc?"

Amaretto decaf, bleh.

Dad's got a comb and brush in one hand. In the other, a palmful of Peaches' hair (predictably Peach Frosty on top of every other color in the catalog). "Restaurants have atmospheric, Osc." His mouth is crammed with Danish.

"I told him no wallpaper. Remember how it peeled with all—"

"Who said anything about wallpaper, Ma? Parrots."

"I think a little wallpaper would be charming," Peaches butts in. "Anyway, birds carry disease."

"Final offer: Buy Memo, I'll throw in a year's worth of feed free."

"Are you nuts?" asks Sandrine, eyeing the Danish. "I thought you were joking."

"We got enough squawkin in here," says Bea. So much for Oscar's ally.

Even Latvia, the waxer, takes a rare break from jangling her trillion metal bracelets to opine, "The problem with pets, they excrete."

Dad agrees, vigorously. "In college I had some, same problem. *Shit.* The Shit Problem, we called it." Laughing, Dad uses his Danish for a pointer. "You gotta feed birds too, remember." As if he were talking some whiny youngster out of getting his first pet.

Never. Oscar has never, will never want another living being to boss around and own and name and walk and pet once and forget about.

"How bout stuffed ones?" Dad winks for punctuation. He's a big winker, chameleon-eyed like his sons but with festive speckles mixed in the iris. "We can stuff a few customers too."

"That's disgusting, Lester."

"I know a guy who does freeze-dry," Oscar offers. His boss, Vladimir, in fact. "I know. . . ." A new tack. "What you're looking for are canaries . . . Gorgeous singers . . . The patrons'll throng."

Mom hoots. *"Thronging* we have plenty. I got a one o'clock wax waiting right now." She gestures with her chin toward the waiting area. One o'clock's face is serene, composed. Oscar tries to imagine how her expression will change as bubbling wax gets basted on her inner thighs. God.

"Waxing already? In May?" asks Peaches. She's chosen Mauve Rapture for her polish, raw meat color.

"I wax all year round," says Sandrine.

"As you should," confirms Latvia, the waxer, wiping her hands on her huge Romanian rump. "Otherwise . . . bad." Depending on who she's addressing, how tired she is, etc., Latvia's accent can sound more foreign than Vladimir's or more local than Mom's. Variations on Eastern European with an NYC outer-borough spin.

"I shave," Peaches discloses. "I have a low tolerance for pain." Then, just as Mom takes one giant bite, "How many calories you calculate are in that Danish, Char?" Evil.

"Pain is good for you," Lester tells her.

But Peaches isn't done harassing Mom. "A moment on your lips but a lifetime on your hips." She should know. Pushing maximum density, as Sam himself has often joked. Critical mass.

"Since when did you have parrots in college?" Oscar asks, not about to believe any story he hasn't heard his father tell before.

"Pain is only a perception." Zen Sandrine. Her first husband was a shiatsu masseur.

"A parakeet. He turned out to be a deaf-mute who stank to high heaven."

Sandrine's second, it so happens, was a deaf Vietnam-vet photographer.

"I bought him all those learn-to-speak records, but it was useless."

The PetMart sells similar recordings, mostly on cassettes and CDs now. But they're for parrots, not parakeets. Memo has gone through them all and far, too far, beyond. Not that any of these people would be able to guess.

"I'll train them myself." Why beat this thing to death? Oscar's obsession with follow-through. Maybe it's Sam's problem as well. Maybe he asked for Claire's hand in a lust spasm and has too much integrity to renege now. Doubtful. "I'll teach them barbershop quartets in four-part harmony. Or how to dance the hustle."

"Can you do that?" Bea asks, serious.

"I once saw this really creepy movie about a parrot," says Sandrine. Her third husband was a tree surgeon. "This one gets a curse on him back in the darkest jungle, so when he gets to the pet store, he's possessed and—"

"Enough," Mom insists. "No birds. It's final. We do not even own a dog. Forget it."

"Just think about it, would you?" Oscar pleads. "Just give it a think?"

Nobody answers him.

"Hello? We're leaving now. Bye."

"Adiós," Memo squawks, finally but too late. A greeting he picked up from the most recent PetMart arrivals—three yellow-cheeked Amazon parrots. But nobody at Chester's is even remotely impressed. Not one head so much as looks up.

It's really rilesome. "Hey, Dad," Oscar vents. "What's with this window sham? Chesty's didn't open in fifty-five, and you know it."

"And you know it," Memo repeats as Oscar closes the door behind him. "You know it, you know it, and you know it."

It's a bratty thing to have said. In front of customers too.

Fifty-five, fifty-seven—who cares? Regretful, Oscar kicks a run-over New Coke can toward the PetMart. Lester must; otherwise, why bother lying about it? Thought he'd round the numbers off backward, by fives? And was Mom a conspirator in the sign hoax? Oscar will never know.

The inscrutability of couples, all of them: not just the un-thinkables, like Sam and Claire, but his own parents, the Un-seeing and their dogs, the pilot and co-, single dads and their daughters, best friends. It continually astounds him. For to Oscar, only he and Fred will ever make real team sense—the genetic way.

Already an hour late and his shoulder stings, and now the damn parrot won't shut up: "And you know it! And you know it!" But still Oscar stands in the street, determined to kick the can up over a stubborn curb.

OSCAR WAS recently promoted to manager of the PetMart by default. The former manager, Stan, bought dozens of huskies to breed and retired to California. "The oranges taste like oranges," he writes in his postcards. "The women taste like oranges." Etc. Besides all that vitamin C, there's real water to swim in at sunset (orange), unlike at the Y, where god knows what kind of microscopic life forms circulate. And in California the disasters are natural, whereas here in Queens, in the PetMart, disaster means the frogs have escaped. Which they have in Oscar's absence, two biggies having wound up in some woman's pocketbook. A purely human error, possibly his.

There are frogs perched atop the cash register. Frogs hopping across counters and hiding behind shelf stock. Frogs lost in corner dust, sad, far-off, a-croaking. Frogs being chewed on as dog bones and swallowed whole by snakes and scratch-pawed to death as cat toys. Everywhere underfoot (already one messy shoe casualty) and overhead (deep frying in the light fixtures), frogs.

The woman, apparently, has threatened to sue; Vladimir, to dock Oscar's pay and make him clean out the cat cages, all

twenty, starting now, after he collects all these frogs. For late-
ness, Vlad says, for absconding with my parrot, you worthless,
unreliable nincompoop. Or something in Russian along those
lines.

Nothing like a little chaos to perk a guy up. Oscar is actually
sort of enjoying this. "Managers do not clean cages," he as-
serts, grabbing a pooper scooper to use as a frog shovel. "Get
Marci to do it. She looks bored."

Marci smiles at Oscar, revealing her chipped eyetooth (sort
of sexy). Then she agrees to clean the cages, no fight.

Just the right amount of curviness on her. Her snug turquoise sand-blasted jeans have manufactured bleach spots and
lots of intriguing zippers. Oscar'd really be interested if she
weren't so obedient, alarmingly so. An ideal hypnotism subject. Tell her Strangle the boss and she'd grab a leash. Not
such a bad idea, come to think of it.

Vladimir's a compulsive whiner. On amphetamines Oscar
couldn't work fast enough to please him. "To you the frogs
hop back in themselves, as if?" is a typical linguistic construction for Vladimir. He takes a small jumping step backward—
feet the size of Oscar's hands—to illustrate.

"I'm hoping Marci'll do a Pied Piperess for us," Oscar says
as he gently tugs on her ponytail. Staticky clean. Long, glossy
black. Oscar alerts her whenever it needs a trim, and Marci,
naturally, listens.

"Gotcha." Marci's method of entrapment: she accidentally
lets loose the frog in hand whenever she bends down to pick
up another, resulting in what seems an endless series of caresses. The girl is not stupid or timid or particularly ambitious. Why, then, such a slave brain? Somehow Oscar
associates it with the crucifix necklace she's always chewing
on, and the chipped eyetooth. A reminder of Louette that makes
it unlikely Oscar will one day haul off and kiss her.

Oscar goes on watching till Marci eventually gives up, moves
on to cat cage duty. Despite frighteningly long nails—triple the
length of Peaches' and unpainted—Marci has a way of making
even rubber gloves look stylish. "You should've seen that lady,

Osc. I-rate. Hollering how she was having a coronary, her bag was Gucci, her—Look, Oscar! Scat Cat caught another ribit." Marci's word for frog. This sort of stuff really excites her.

Marci has a name for each individual animal. No one else can keep track. She should really have been the one made manager, only Vladimir was overly impressed by Oscar's ornithology studies. The old man only made it to the Russian equivalent of tenth grade, a fact he's alternately proud and abashed about.

"Oh, yeah, Osc," Marci adds. "You got some phone calls. Sam—"

"If he calls again, I'm out."

"Why?"

"He's engaged."

"Who is he?"

"Schlock, with a poodle and an awful mother. I know he'll never return my denim jacket, my favorite jacket." Oscar forgot to ask for it back the other night. "An old friend."

"Oh," Marci says. "Also your girlfriend, twice." Marci holds her thumb and pointer finger about a quarter inch apart. "She sounded *this* big."

"What's that mean? Louette, you mean?"

"I don't know. She said tell him his girlfriend."

Oscar sighs heavily. Mostly, but not totally, for Marci's benefit.

"Now we become answering services?" Vladimir asks. He wears big, square, plastic glasses and two pens behind one ear. "Maybe an idea is have you go on long vacation like Stan to Mexico."

"Would you quit worrying," Oscar tells him. "The frog woman won't sue." He winces as Vladimir spits into a fish tank. Serpae tetras, which look like tiny colored flags. "Even if she does take you to court, she won't get a thing except maybe a new purse; no big deal. Besides, Stan went to California."

"Lemme tell you about no big deal."

But Oscar can see it vividly on his own: Vladimir standing there in shock, wailing, "Do something!" while Marci gathers, drops, handfuls of frogs, kissing each of their filmy green heads in case there's a possible prince among them.

"Where *did* you go?" Marci wants to know. "With Memo."

"He needed a new hair—"

"For what do I pay you!?" Vladimir interrupts. His squat little fingers flutter down to womanish hips, and he claps a dust cloud out of his knit pants. Oscar, spotting a stray frog near Marci's foot, feels the charity to leave it. They're pretty much rounded up now. "You need out of my hair," says Vlad, his usual gruff self but smiling, sort of. "I have option plan for you, Oscar."

"Oh?"

"You would like from me"—Vlad's voice is actually sunny almost—"free vacation?"

"Wha?" Unheard of!

"To see your jungle roostings in the Yucatán . . ."

"Oh." This is one of Oscar's longtime fantasies.

"I know a man there."

"Oh?"

"And you will bring me back birds for breeding then. Big cash. And you will feel so largely better. Also more."

"Ohhh." Oscar comprehends at last.

When the phone rings, Memo rings. When a siren whines by, Memo whines in place. In between, Memo practices his new sentence: "You know it! You know it!" until the jackhammer operators return from lunch break and the bird not only throbs and whistles but says, "Nice ass." Says, "Baby. Baby. Fuckin A. Fuckin incredible."

Vladimir encourages it. Marci appears indifferent.

Oscar plugs his ears and buries the phone in a drawer. Then, removing a clipboard from a wall hook, he sets off down the long back aisle toward the warehouse. He's trying to envision the Yucatán lushness, roosts of Technicolor parrots, and himself tiptoeing up to them, when—

The phone—no, Memo, showing off his already modified imitation of the phone ringing. It sounds like a phone ringing from inside a drawer. Ringing again. "You know it."

THE WAREHOUSE is enormous, a little chilly with zoo smell. Did Stan really make his money smuggling? Were the huskies a cover? Buying hot animals is one of Vlad's many sleazy business practices, but actually hiring people—Stan?!—to go get them? Possible. PetMart is a nationwide chain, but Vladimir's franchise, the New York branch, is more a pet outlet, supplying retailers all over the metropolitan area. Oscar hasn't the time to note where the animals are coming from, so busy is he worrying about getting them where they're going. Could Stan have smuggled?

Oscar picks up the phone to return Louette's call and finds Marci already on it. He has to resist eavesdropping, not easy. ". . . early supper," Oscar hears Marci say. "Something light . . ." And suddenly realizing he hasn't eaten all day (no Danish, nothing), he blurts, "Let's have a goldfish fry" into the receiver before hanging up. Punchy.

Sometimes, when he's all alone in the shop, Oscar'll let his beard-scrap dangle into one of the tanks just to see what'll happen. What happens is the fish swim up to check if it's eatable, then treat it like just another uprooted plastic plant. But as Oscar has learned repeatedly in school, if you only try once it is not an experiment.

The silliness extends, as Oscar is struck with the notion of training Memo to say, "For a good time, call . . ." with Peaches' or, better yet, Claire's home phone number. Just then Vladimir appears in the doorway to let Oscar know the smuggling proposition was no joke.

"Think of it till Monday. We rush." And "Don't get talking in front of other peoples please. . . . Ten thousand dollars, Oscar, we can have for one scarlet macaw. Ten thousand dollars. Unless you maybe have coward feet?" So speaks King of the World, as Vladimir has ofttimes informed Oscar his name translates. The most common name in all of Russia. Imagine, a whole country populated with Kings of the World.

It is in fact the King of the PetMart who has offered Vladimir this opportunity to offer Oscar this opportunity. Or so Oscar deduces from Vladimir's ramble. Seems the big-shot owner and president—Ernie T. Ducklander, Esq., whose titanic pompadour and childish signature Oscar has seen in numerous employee newsletters over his seven years of PetMart service—wants to do Vlad a favor of some kind, so impressed was he on a recent visit to the Russian's newest entrepreneurial venture, a pit bull breeding and training farm in upstate New York. Big boss's idea: do the same for exotic birds on the same land, "quintuple" their profits.

"I'm speechless," Oscar says, aware of the oxymoron only after he's drifted back to his rounds. He strolls from sea horses to box turtles (illegal in N.Y. but not in N.J.). Why me? Oscar can't stop wondering, and loses count of the salamanders. Why was I chosen? He mistakenly records in the gerbils column the dozen hamsters (like pink erasers) born while his head was turned.

Only when he gets to the aviaries does Oscar stop to really look at the new arrivals, three beautiful yellow-cheeked Amazons, earnestly launching off their perches for flight. Immediately they plummet, immediately launch again and plummet, launch, plummet.

Their wing feathers have been clipped in Guatemala or Honduras or Ecuador, wherever they were trapped and dealt. A pretty routine barbarism. Done well, it cripples the parrot for a year or so, until the feather stumps fall out and new ones grow in. Done poorly, it cripples them permanently. Done, as with these parrots, neither well nor poorly, there's simply no telling.

Of course Marci's already christened them all. Oscar remembers only Lila, for the bird with the lilac crown feathers; a golden-eyed starlet in what looks like a lime gown, scarlet silk scarf around her forehead. These parrots won't mate with just any bird, and almost never in captivity.

"So what about that? How *are* you gonna get the birds to

mate while pit bulls run around trying to devour them all day?'' Oscar asks. But Vladimir's vanished.

The birds take off, drop straight out of the air, take off, drop, take off—as hopeful as a bunch of blind ladies applying makeup.

5

DOUBLE HAPPINESS
EMERGENCY

CLAIRE'S MOM is in a mausoleum. Her mom's mom's in the kitchen. With new blue hair, a lap full of knitting, a beer on the table, as well as cards, toffee, a biography of Liberace, and a family-size squeeze bottle of piña colada–scented hand cream, she looks all set for a day of waiting in an airport.

But it's the engagement party she means to sit out. Stubbornly. Comfortably.

"I'm sorry, I'm sorry," Claire apologizes. "I just couldn't deal with visiting a cemetery *today*. Don't be angry, OK? I'm sorry."

"Angry, no." Lillian's extremely meager eyebrows slide toward each other, crunching up the skin in between. "Disappointed, yes. There's a difference." Lillian taps the poker deck for emphasis. "Your mother deserves some remembrance at these milestones."

"I remember her." Claire remembers she had those same eyebrows, but her mother's were employed mostly for joketelling or (on a "milestone" like this) to convey mounting hysteria. Last-minute party jitters never failed to undo the woman. One brow curling up, she'd say: "Get useful, Clara. Cut flowers. Check if there's back-up t.p." One brow curling down: "A little mascara won't kill you, surely." Both brows up: "Think I talk because I like the sound of my own voice? Why are you loitering? Go!" Both brows down: "No toothpicks? Clara, get over here! No toothpicks!" One up, one down—watch out: "What time is it? Oh god, I'm not dressed. Are you dressed? You're not going to wear *that*, are you? Who's in charge of this baked brie?"—currently puckering into globules and dribbling through the oven racks. "Chairs! Hangers! Arthur?!" Her voice shrillifying up to levels only dogs can hear, or so Dad would tease, sending Mom's eyebrows into total neurotic abandon. "You're underfoot, Clara. I'm warning you. You're in my hair. . . . Get out of this kitchen or you'll regret it; I mean it." And meaning it. It isn't true at all what people say—that you remember only nice things about dead people.

The missed cemetery visit is not Claire's sole affront. Her grandmother sees the entire engagement bash, due to commence within the hour, as nothing short of mutiny.

She wasn't consulted in the menu-planning. "Escargots, champagne, and lemon meringue? My lord, we'll all retch."

Certain maternal relatives have been left off the guest list. "Just because you can't picture them, dear, doesn't mean they don't love you."

Claire has refused to wear that "darling" dress that Lillian bought her—like a bedspread with armholes.

All pointing to the underlying real crime—Sam himself, "the unknown." (Marriage itself—"the unpredictable"; Claire's mother's recent death, "the unexpected.")

"Remember her or remorse," Grandma Lillian warns, expertly shuffling the deck of cards. "Sack that memory for particulars while they're still fresh, and you'll always—"

Through the window, the faint chaos of a string quartet tuning up sounds urgent or fanciful, depending. Claire wonders, What, then, was the point of all that time spent traveling around to forget, only to come home and remember?

Whenever Grandma Lillian visits, she takes control of the entire household. This was true even when Mom was alive. Somehow, she is victor in all arguments, pool and poker champ, winner in most every sports bet—Lillian's special forte. And how she loves to collect, loves to rub it in; she cackles. Her late husband used to openly admit that she was the "man of the family." In this respect nothing like Mom but, maybe, a tiny bit like Claire. In spirit.

Never would Grandma Lillian have given *her* life to save face in front of some "pinch-assed garden club."

Lillian's own cemetery excursions usually begin with a cathartic rant-a-thon. "Happy now? You were always a grabby kid, Stella. Now look what you went and did, fool!" And wind up full of sobbed "I didn't mean it, baby"s. "My baby, my baby."

Mom could do this fancy shuffling too—tossing the card piles in and out of each other, Slinky like, or pressing down with her thumbs for that satisfying crunch. Grandma Lillian must have taught her. Claire's about to beg, "Teach me too," when the old woman begins laying down a solitaire hand on the Liberace book. The placement of each card is given such a seemingly reverential dose of thought that not only is Claire unable to interrupt but, captivated by the ritual, she imagines her own future is there in her grandmother's hands.

"Do you love him?" A simple enough inquiry, but it brings Claire to her feet.

Look, I'm a virgin; I can't be too accurate on the L subject. Seriously *blank*ing, or the opposite, a tangent flood: the string quartet, the gardener, what shoes to wear—pumps'll sink into the lawn, but flats'll make her look fat. There were two Liberace TV life stories, one authorized, one un-, and Claire saw both of them. And she once saw a girl her age in a diner wearing red nail polish eat a ketchup sandwich. And the girl's mother was asking, "Who you gonna marry? Doctorlawyer-indianchief?" Claire says, "Um. Sam?"

"Your slip is hanging out," Grandma Lillian reads in the cards. "Fix your slip."

THE SKY in New Jersey is bigger than the sky in Queens, and the grass seems an alien green. "For all I know, could be some newfangled Astroturf that smells when you scratch it," says Sam. Nancy claws at the lawn without penalty. It is strewn with clusters of balloons, hundreds. It is bordered by color-coded flower beds, deluxe. But the Allswell heaven and Allswell earth are only brief stops along Sam's "five-cent" tour, which features lake, stream, pool and pond, greenhouse, main house (library, projection, and billiard rooms), cottage, barn, stables, tennis courts, *archery*, all complete with corresponding paraphernalia. The boat bellies even read HELP in case of capsize.

"You sound like some sleazy real estate guy," Oscar says, because Sam seems oblivious to how neglected the place really looks, excepting these flower beds, of course, and the lawn. Must be the labor of some awfully gung ho gardener.

"Imagine the football possibilities," Sam suggests, noticing Oscar's interest.

"Yah. Midget pet *is* the ideal punting size." Oscar can't help it. Nancy's giving him that itchy foot he gets around small dogs that yap at every damn bird, squirrel, rustling bush, or balloon.

Sam is wearing a weird, queeny, hairdresserish scarf thing.

"It's an ascot." Sam pushes his chest out, the better to show off the flamingo print.

When Nancy's not barking she's peeing. Not something you'd notice—her legs being only two inches off the ground—unless your sock started feeling damp. "Sam! Can't you . . ."

"Real estate, pal." Sam's hands pan. Hair crawls out of his cuffs onto his wrists. "You're standin on solid gold."

"Sedate this animal now, or we'll be playing tackle."

"What is *with* you?" asks Sam.

Maybe it's the sight of such a beefy guy (in mind *and* body) with a dainty dog like Nancy. Maybe Oscar's just been "in pets" too long. Maybe the fight he had with Louette is finally *it*. Maybe he just cannot stand seeing his oldest friend trade his life in for *ascots*.

"My mother's polluted," is what Sam finally says, after his tour has come full circle, after he's collected his nickel, after three exaggerated, unnecessary sighs. "She wants to dance with you."

Two women in identical pink dresses.

"What a coincidence! We're *twins.*"

"So it seems. Twins. Well. Isn't that a riot."

Claire squelches a giggle in her napkin. One of the Bobbseys is Sam's mom, Peaches, and she's twice, almost three times the size of the other, Mrs. . . .

"Fashion tourney?" The muffled voice belongs to a girl approaching Claire. Chipped eyetooth and shiny, complicated black braid.

"So it seems. Twins," Claire says, mimicking Peaches' completely deadpan mock attempt at being a good sport. The girl joins Claire in giggling into a napkin. The napkins are monogrammed with the words SAM AND CLARA and the date in slender gold script.

"An uncanny coincidence!" says the girl, still laughing. She captures the I'm-certain-I-must-have-purchased-mine-first tone well. "Seems we've worn the same nose today." A remark that's doubly amusing seeing as it's true; the girl's nose actually does have a small diamond-shaped bump like Claire's own (like Lillian's). A funny girl. Soon she and Claire are at that point of perpetual motion where they're laughing just because they're laughing. Without even knowing each other; more a wonder than wonderful.

"Marci," the girl ekes out, between waves. "I work . . . the PetMart . . . Oscar."

"Oh." That name. It sobers Claire right up. And when Oscar's face appears in front of her, any remaining good cheer fast evaporates. What's *he* doing here? The napkin is already reduced to a tiny wad in Claire's fist.

"Fred." Fred and Claire shake hands. He's beardless, of course, with a roundish chin that might just be what Oscar's hiding.

"I was hoping—well . . ." Marci observes Fred. Her gaze, intense. Grandma Lillian'd call it "sheep eyes," but to Claire it's more like piranha jaw. "Maybe I could be introduced?"

"Allow me," says Fred, reddening. Unless he's really Oscar, shaved. "Fred, Marci, Marci, Fred, Claire, Marci, Marci, Claire, Claire, Fred, Fred, Claire." In one breath. Then he pulls a napkin from his mouth and makes it vanish up his sleeve. Slick. "Insanely glad to meet all of you."

He is, too. After hearing so much about her, after having her built up (by Sam) and played down (by Oscar), here she is—live. Hair effervescent, with odd green shimmerings. Equally bewitching is Marci's head—quality stuff, like mink, and a lot of it. Why has Oscar not once mentioned this prize? Either he slept with her (and it was boring) behind Louette's back, or he's still trying not to.

Girls. Their dresses in the breezes wind around their legs like flags, or are swept up, revealing just enough skin to get your attention before they flutter teasingly back down. Fred revels in each detail, the difference in knees, sun glinting in the arm hairs, respective teeth irregularities—Claire's gap, Marci's pointy broken tooth. Watching them together, Fred even envies them some. How easily two girls at a party—strangers—can talk and laugh and get along.

". . . a hideous dress anyhow," Claire's saying. "Garish." Puckered—what is it?—crepe? Strapless, with an overkill of ruffles and a jagged hem. Vaguely harlequin.

Both of the women in pink swear on their husbands' *lives* that this has never happened before. They seem to be more amiable now that the initial shock has passed, commiserating almost.

"With *this* kooky dress, who'd expect it?"

"Just my luck. I tell you I was practically out the door in a silk blend. Chartreuse."

"It's simply humiliating."

"I'm returning it."

"I'm burning it."

"I'm giving it to rummage."

All of which is humorous to Claire only in a panicky will-this-happen-to-me? sort of way. Not turning up in a duplicate dress, but having it matter so. With age, with marriage. Her own mom would undoubtedly have reacted like these women, possibly worse. Perhaps it's inevitable.

When Fred smiles, the sides of his head crease. Claire can't help liking that, his head. Not a bad-looking body either. Tall but less bumbling than Oscar, sleeker. "The bottom line," Fred joins in. "Who got the better bargain."

"Oh, no," Claire assures him. "Not Mrs. Doody anyway—the third Mrs. Doody, by the way. My mom used to play golf at her house. She's so rich she'd hate to have paid less. Make her look cheap."

"The real question here," speculates Marci, "seems to be who's wearing the larger size." Plain to see, even if Mrs. Doody is no beanpole. In addition, Peaches wins hands down at pounding the champagne. Blimpiest, tipsiest, hiccupiest.

Diet! Diet! Claire's checklist of reminders: Hold in that stomach; futile. Stand tall, smile. Check the ever creeping slip. Claire's own dress, flesh-colored, feels stapled on at the waist. Her self-consciousness breaking out now like a rash, she smooths, smooths her napkin. With her ring finger, traces the SAM AND CLARA monogram, again and again. Its gold script no longer looks so elegant and grown-up, but tacky now and *too final*, as in "Do you love him?"

"They think *they've* got problems," Fred says. "Imagine going around with someone else's face your whole life." He immediately regrets the comment. It's dangerous and wrong to use the truth for light party conversation.

Ever since Passover, Oscar's made Fred feel a traitor for not more strongly disapproving of the wedding and, by extension, of Claire. But what Oscar earmarked "wings" are, to Fred's eye, merely bangs in that awkward mid-growing-out phase, indicating the noble quality of being able to recognize and rectify one's mistakes. Claire does not, no way, have the face for bangs.

Mrs. Doody announces she's going to "sneak" home and change, now that it's been discovered, on top of everything else, that both women have had their shoes dyed to match. Crisis.

"How does it feel?" Marci asks Claire, spearing a balloon with her pump heel. "All this commotion over *you*, all these people here because of *you*, to salute *you*?"

Her voice is familiar from phone calls to the PetMart, Fred realizes. She must be Oscar's date. Now that he and Louette have had a big tiff—something about mascara and a toaster oven.

"Like walking beside my shoes," Claire answers, referring to a saying she heard in Paris, "and still getting blisters."

Claire's voice is familiar too, Fred realizes, and her eyes, from daydreams he plans on having.

ON SAM'S INSISTENCE, Oscar "samples" the escargots. Tastes like the sauce it's in—brown. Across the grass, they watch Peaches drowning her sorrows (and the pink dress) in yet more champagne.

"Luckily," Sam says, "she got it at Loehmann's."

Oscar recalls the Halloween when Charlotte costumed him and Fred as "two peas in a pod" and literally *sewed* them together; torture. Yet along came Sam (eight or nine years old at the time), begging to be sewn in too. Part of a phase, short-lived, in which Sam became obsessed with being the twins' other, their triplet; absolutely clueless as to what special brand of nightmare it is to be identical. Despite himself, Oscar feels genuinely sympathetic toward Peaches in her duplicate-dress fix. He might even dance with her. Well, maybe not *dance*, but—

"I could eat em for breakfast, lunch, dinner, and snack time." Sam's bragging about the escargots, though he doesn't seem to be actually eating any. "We should invest. Look at this. Bite-size, portable, comes naturally in its own container. All the basic McNugget requirements, fulfilled."

"Money," Oscar reminds him. "Snails are pricey. From imported dirt, I'm sure." Even the napkins here are engraved.

"I'll be swimming in it, once Peaches gets—I mean, once I'm married and all."

"Why doesn't she divorce Sid and marry the father? It'd be easier."

"Shhh. Don't put it in her head."

"Do you love her?"

"She's my mother."

"Not her."

"Sure. Yo, you been rethinkin my best-man offer?"

Oscar taps the spiral shell, experimentally. Look at yourself, you gutless son-of-a-bitch. Stop looking at that stupid tie. Listen to yourself, you dronerrr. Stop listening to your mother. Grow up and sit down and think for a goddamn change. But instead Oscar hears himself say, "Snails are hermaphrodites."

Sam's puzzled. "Hermaphrodites? Like self sex? Safe sex?" Sam's preoccupation. "Hey, where's your drink, pal?" Two hours into the party, and Oscar hasn't touched a glass. "Teetotaling? This must be way worse than even I thought."

"You mean rethought?"

"What?"

"Whatayamean *you?*"

"Not me."

"Whatayamean *than even I thought?*"

"What?"

With exchanges like that, Oscar doesn't need a drink. Or really does. The snails, though, are growing on him.

"Ya know, I finally bought a ring," Sam says, changing the subject. "I got both rings now. Choked up this diamond-studded band from some dead relation. Both of em diamond too; two for the price of one."

"Yeah. Cool." Oscar scans the yard for the snail guy. Time for a refill.

"It's an investment, I figure." Sam goes on as if to convince himself. "You put out for the ring so hopefully you can sidestep the prenuptial agreement." Again, a plan that smacks of Peaches. "Wait'll Claire sees this rock, though. I'm talkin froth at the mouth. I can't wait."

Oscar's appetite vanishes with the image of Claire frothing.

"So, like, my Mr. Very Best Man, why dontcha just cut the shit and say'll you do it, guy?"

"Because, *pal*, doing it *is* the shit."

FRED'S BEEN TRICKED. Formal wear, he's discovered, aims to subdue men into background Muzak against which women and their pink dresses can shine. Here he'd been expecting an identity bloom with adulthood, free choice—and what changes? Now he and Oscar have to dress not only like each other but like every other male in the world as well.

No wonder Sam goes in for grotesque flamingo accessories, Fred thinks forgivingly as he's swallowed up by a passing balloon cluster—reds, yellows, blues, purples, whites. Balloons by the hundreds. Who blew them all up? Balloons skim the ultra-green lawn, gently bob around folding chairs, brush past skirt hems, sidle up against Claire's calf—mesmerizing Fred, leaving him easy prey for Peaches.

She is slinking toward him—as much as a two-hundred-pound woman can slink—in that pink jester dress. "Kiss-kiss for Auntie Peaches." Champagne and Bloody Mary breath. She bats big false eyelashes. Shouts, "Dance with me, handsome," at an embarrassing volume. "Let's do the dizzy rounds, big boy." Fred wishes she'd watch where she's waving that cigarette. Not even a real cigarette but one of those smelly feminine cigars, special for the occasion, *designer*—Yves Saint Laurent.

Fred spins around in desperation to whisper-ask the girls whether "this constitutes harassment." He thinks he sees Marci wink.

But Peaches, getting a solid grip on Fred's biceps with her long purple claws, whips him close and begins tangoing to the string quartet's waltz.

"For a guy whose life is music"—she shakes her head toward her husband, Sid, the bandleader, happily assembling his trombone to warm up for The Bouncetones' set—"Sid sure lacks the rhythm. . . . His body type, I think; too white." Fred always liked Sid. Sid's OK. "Not that the high blood pressure helps. Saturated fats, I'm telling you. They build up and bam, you're clogged. . . . Ah, but youth is carefree, yes?" She's acting as if she's in some old Hollywood movie about rich people on a big lawn.

Under numerous layers of pancake makeup, Peaches' upper lip sweats beige.

JERRY GOOCH holds his champagne glass in a fist and holds it against his flat forehead. "The string unit," he says, "seriously needs a drummer." In high school Gooch himself played traps for their band, Dinner and the Talk. It is an experience that left him with a nervous air-drumming habit and his nickname, Deja Vu (D.J.), for getting jokes fifteen minutes after they've been told.

The rest of the former band members have been invited too, and they stand around in one clump, guzzling "classy stuff, Heinies and Shivers" (Heinekens and Chivas). Except Eliot Horowitz, who nurses his peptic ulcer with warm Coke. Except Oscar, who pretends with club soda, lime, and a swizzle stick.

Oscar's sick of having to explain why he's not drinking—that is, trying to explain that if he could explain, he'd *be* drinking.

"Which one's the little woman?"

"Are there bees here in Beeslink?"

"I'm missing Monster Car Crash at Nassau Coliseum for this."

"What'll ya give me if I eat one of them slugs?"

"You know, where those giant tractors drag things through the mud."

"What'll ya give me if I eat one of them slugs?"

"Where's Brooke Shields? Isn't Brooke a Jersey virgin?"

"Hail that tray with the social lubricants."

"All the babes here look undercooked."

"Gimme a substance, I'll abuse it."

"Stewed Peaches."

"Yo, Osc, I think your jacket is chirping."

The chicks! Oscar has spaced. This morning at the PetMart, he slipped two chicks inside his blazer pocket for engagement gifts. And they're still breathing. "I should turn myself in to the ASPCA." But no one's the slightest bit interested in Oscar's sort of chicks. Having spotted Fred dancing with Peaches, the guys howl and ape.

Oscar should *do* something. If not defend his brother, then at least join in. But goofing off with these dunces, trashing Fred, seems just another way of spoofing himself.

HIS BALD HEAD shellacked with sweat and sun, tie loosened, Claire's dad grips the metal awning rail with one hand. With the other, he waves his white silk handkerchief. Surrender.

"To the engagees"—his eyes are closed—"Sam and Clara." He kicks at the grass. "To Hymen, the god of marriage." Did he look that up in some tourist guide to Greece? "Adam and Eve!" An attempt to put the Jewish guests at ease? "To yoke-mates, consorts, one bone, one flesh!" What? "The sacred nuptial knot." This seems totally out of character, almost glib. "To happiness, double happiness." Double Happiness!? That's the local Chinese restaurant. "OK." Dad waves off the guests, most of whom have just begun listening. "Go back to yourselves. Finito." Then he smooths his head, very rapidly, once.

Applause. Claire wonders about the etiquette involved. If they're clapping for Dad, should she join in? If for her and Sam, should she bow, nod, go find him?

"Glad to have ya aboard," Sid Lubin says, stepping up to Claire and hugging her. Aboard? He's the closest thing there is to a stick figure in three dimensions.

Claire says, "Thanks." Claire thinks, Lubin. For the first time, she mulls over the name. Might this man be expecting that she'll take it on? Claire Marie Lubin. No chance.

Claire's dizzyish. Dad's bone/flesh toast gave her the creeps. She's been laid open to stares galore by that Hymen allusion; awful. More than anything, she's hungry, having half starved all week for this dress that is still too tight, really. And starting to sway a little now, sway a little more, Claire grabs at the first thing . . . Louette.

"Whoa. Claire." Louette with brown hair. White gloves. Cigar. "What is it?" Her dress has this big hard-to-look-at bull's-eye on it. "Whatsamatter?"

"Oh . . . I don't know. I keep getting boiling then freezing then boiling."

"Looks like you're in for a real rocky menopause."

"Yeah."

"No, Claire, that's a joke."

"Is this a good party?" Not exactly what Claire wants to ask, but related somehow.

"In Queens you know a party's good if the law shows."

"Really?"

"No; that's a joke too. You OK? I just came up to see if maybe you wanna go to the beach next weekend."

"Me?"

"Youuu and only youuu . . .," Sam sings, whooshing up from behind Claire, lifting her aloft. He ducks from her shoe, which flies off—finesse. He kisses the backs of Claire's knees, ticklish. He picks up the speed, whirling and whirling her, singing.

It *is* cooler up here; that's something. Claire has a rare aerial view of Louette gawking up at her, and of Sid, who says, "He takes after his mother, I tell you."

Air rushes up Claire's skirt. A crowd forms. Peaches, Oscar, Constance Dufour (Claire's only old acquaintance to respond to the invitation), a guy with a flat forehead and massive chest, plus Sam's poodle, Nancy, twirling and jumping like some berserk toy too tightly wound.

"Please put me down!" The last thing Claire really wants. It's been so long since anyone's carried her, forever since she's felt this weightless, safe . . . cherishable. "Put me down now!" she says, because she figures it's what's expected of her.

But Sam obeys.

Back on her feet, Claire watches the lawn spin and ripple. Sam sinks his face into her neck. Claire loves that. Tangly black eyelashes tickle. Sam whispers, "Is there some convenient broom closet I could ravish you in?" and "I have surprises—a jumbo one for later on, a small one for right—" *Ow!* His teeth clench down on her neck. "Wow, you're supposed to say. Not Ow." And Sam pulls out an orchid—purple white, a wrist corsage, gaudy, yes, but the very kind Claire never got to wear at the prom she never went to. She loves that too.

OSCAR PRESENTS the chicks to the honorary couple, but Louette distracts him. Brown hair for a change, interesting. Long white gloves, charm bracelet, cigar—c'mon. "What're you doing here?" After she chased him around her apartment trying to put mascara on him. "Loony?"

She's smug. The only way she'll acknowledge him is by not acknowledging him. She called him names too—homophobic—then threw a toaster at him.

"Do I get an answer?"

In her own good time. Oscar must first wait out the gracious dental hygienist smile, mock-bored eye-rolling, a drag on the foul cigar, before "So how's ever little thing with you, darling?" Sugary as a DoNuTs! cruller. "If you're so hot to know, I received a personal invite. Isn't that right, Claire?"

Claire nods imperceptibly.

"Is this a prank?" Sam asks, cupping his hands in front of him to indicate that Oscar should toss him a bird. "What am I supposed to do with this? Chicken salad?" Then, to Louette, "Dig the hair."

"Why, thank you."

Claire echoes these same words to Flathead, who hands back her shoe. Then to Oscar, giving over the second chick. Reaching for it, Claire half anticipates that Oscar will retract his hand at the last minute, snigger. But the transfer could not be more gentle. The yellow fluff, scratchy-clawed, light. An observation Sam seems to have made as well. Volleying his own bird back and forth between his palms, he's asking, "Fred ever juggle these babies?"

"You'll hurt him!" Claire blurts. "They're so—" Ready to say "soft" when Louette substitutes:

"Yellow. Like this." She points with her cigar—Oscar, chick, Oscar—though there's really only a minor similarity. Oscar's hair, coarse waves that fuzz out in balls at the ends, has more and darker shades. No comparison.

"Is it a him, the chick?" Claire asks, which somehow earns smiles from Oscar. A novel sight, if not entirely unfamiliar thanks to Fred.

"Sam and Claire, meet Clam and Square!" Oscar thought up thispun in the car, but only now thought to apply it to the chicks.

It gets a few chuckles anyway. Most of all, from a blond girl in green sequins who has disconcertingly pert tits.

Peaches says, "Isn't that clever, Sid?" Sid fixes her smudged lipstick with his index finger. That's *real* love, Oscar figures.

"Watch out they don't shit on you," Green Sequins warns like a definite pet owner. Oscar'd guess rabbits. Rabbits, a canary, or some similar cute thing she regrets having fallen for and purchased on a whim. Her bustline has Sam completely goggle-eyed, jaw-hung.

Claire's certain she's hallucinating. No way would Sam have the nerve to be so blatant. At our engagement party? No. With Constance Dufour, no less.

This is the girl who wrapped herself naked in the American flag for the ninth-grade yearbook photo.

"I get it," Flathead says. "Sam and Claire. Clam and Square!"

Oscar and Sam scoff at him, but before long they're trading riffs. "Ham and Pear." "Man and Underwear." "Damn this Car." Almost as if they've found an alternative way to curse at each other. "Cram and Tear."

"WHAT'S WITH your hair?"

"It's my real color, stupid," Louette says. Shock. After months of sleeping with her, Oscar's never noticed.

"How did you two meet?" Claire asks, seriously wondering. Also: Do you love each other?

None of your business, thinks Oscar.

"On the seven train," says Louette. "Picture that, in the middle of August in the subway, like real romantic."

"Texture that," Oscar adds, incoherently.

"I've never been in the subway," says Claire.

Oscar remembers every detail of how they met. It was rush time, as he prefers to call rush hour. After all, there are crowds on the subway from five to two, from three to ten.

"And?" Fred asks, resentful that he's never heard this story before. But not about to show it. He watches a group of party guests playing musical chaise longues. Green Sequins moves as if she were naked and oiled.

"I was hangover-thirsty that morning. In a bad way," Oscar says. Painfully tired. He slept standing up, woke with the sensation his leg was on fire.

"I was in a train fire once," Fred reminds Oscar. "Remem—"

Just coffee. The paper cup of coffee he'd been holding had tilted and dripped burning liquid all down one pant leg. When he had then got a seat, Oscar went right out again, even dreamed something. The train gently cruised past his stop.

"How come your trains gently cruise and mine lurch and squeak and catch fire?" Fred's tormented with the thought that Oscar is keeping secrets. Slept with Marci? And? *He* doesn't have any.

Oscar revived for the second time to find himself resting on a stranger's shoulder. And so met Louette. "I didn't have the heart to wake you." A scrawnyish redhead (he assumed a real redhead at the time) with mini ears beneath a queer spotted hat. She said, "You looked so beat, and your pants are all stained." And Oscar feigned the flu to blow off work and go have his teeth cleaned.

"How come," Fred asks, "all the women *I* meet on the train are blind, deaf, non-English-speaking cripples threatening to blare saxophones in my face if I don't pay up?"

But Oscar is not amused. Maybe he's feeling sorry he ever met Louette.

Guiding Fred out of earshot, Oscar informs him, "I'm going to Mexico to smuggle parrots." Matter-of-fact. "Wanna come?" Fred doesn't believe him. "You look like you swallowed gum." Until now, Fred has always known whether to believe Oscar. "Vlad's made me an unturndownable offer." Fred's beginning to believe. "And you're coming with me."

"Because you had an argument with Louette?" Does he love her, is that it? What does any of this have to do with how they met?

"What?"

And, "Did you make up?"

"Please do not mention makeup."

But Fred is not amused. Maybe he's feeling sorry for himself.

DOUBLE HAPPINESS emergency. Claire rushes to the kitchen. "Right again, Grandma. I don't know the first thing about throwing a party. Everyone's starving and leaving. . . . Except Peaches Lubin. She's throwing up."

Claire deposits the two chicks in the sink while she dials. "What should I order?" Chicken is out.

"How about something fulfilling?"

"Spare ribs? What do you think?"

Lillian thinks it's a riot. Her droopy cheeks and upper arm folds wobble when she laughs, her s's whistle when she teases, "Miss Hoity-Toity," which Claire interprets as the equivalent of an affectionate spanking. It's not Claire's fault that all the money comes on Dad's side—Allswell Cap N Gown. All the death, on Mom's.

Claire orders a hundred and twenty-five egg rolls and one of every item on the menu. You can do that. Then she transfers the chicks to a salad bowl and carries them over to the table. Cheapest ploy she can think of. But it works. Her grandmother's eyes, two nailheads, look down at the baby creatures and shine right up wet—instant love.

"You'll learn," Lillian tells the birds. "You're young yet."

No more escargots. But Oscar has kept his last little red plastic spear and, so armed, heads for the kitchen to hunt down any possible extras. He knows the way from Sam's tour—if you go through the driveway, there's a separate *servants'* entrance.

"Whatchawant?" An old lady's in there. Blue hair and scary lack of eyebrows.

"Uh, a tissue." It's the first thing that comes to mind. And it reminds him of Louette again. She'll probably auto-bleed the minute Oscar decides to break up with her. A minute ago.

"Violà," the woman says, pulling a tissue out of her sleeve with a knitting needle.

Weird. She's got enough to occupy her here for weeks. Book. Cards. Chicks in the salad bowl. TV tuned to the Knick-Celtic game. Fake-blowing his nose, Oscar leans to catch the score.

"What are you looking at?" Lillian asks, pushing her hair up. "It's real. Dyed, but real hair."

"Sure," Oscar says. That reminds him of Louette too. She had to have her hair *dyed* its real color. "I can tell. Our dad owns a salon." Salon? It just slipped out.

"Really?" This perks her up. "Well, why didntcha do something with Claire's—"

Wings? Oscar doesn't supply. "I only met her a few weeks ago."

"You one a Caruso's friends?"

"Sam?"

"Who else?"

"You don't like him?"

"Do you?"

"You'd make one spectacular cruise ship director," Fred calls after Sam, who's off to do his "obligatory mingling."

Claire says she's just grateful that *someone's* willing; she certainly doesn't want to or know how to or want to know how to. Besides, her feet hurt. Her dad's even worse, she says, pointing him out. He's standing alone, on the patio's edge, squeezing his elbows.

"Our dad's the other way," Fred confides, conscious of the "our"—it never sounds quite right. "He used to embarrass me all the time." *Me* sounds even clunkier. "Talking to every stranger on the street, telling waitresses their eyes are 'beauty-full.' "

Neither of them is too nimble with small talk, nor cares, so they go on watching Claire's dad. That is, Fred watches Claire go on watching her dad, deciding she isn't the way Oscar or Sam or even Louette made her out to be. She's striking. Semi-shy, but direct. A beautiful neck. A long, stately neck of a neck.

With one lurid hickey interruption.

Claire hands Fred her half-full champagne glass—"Hold this a sec?"—and a gift wrapped in shiny blue paper.

"What is it?"

"I don't know. I don't even know the person who gave it to me. To tell you the truth—" Claire interrupts herself, crouching to curse out her sandals. Glorified thongs, really. Gold. They collect pebbles, she tells Fred, they slip off, trip her, blister the sides of her pinkie toes.

"What a grownup, though," Fred's still marveling. "To get a gift and not straightaway rip it open." Absentmindedly, he's drained Claire's champagne and begun to juggle—glass, gift, glass, in one hand. Looking down at Claire's scalp, he fights the bizarre desire to follow her zigzagging part with his fingertip.

Her hair, besides the green sheen, is the color of the lightly toasted whole-wheat slice Fred ritually jams down his throat en route to the bus to the subway to the city.

If Fred took up Dad's running offer of a job at Chesty's, he could nix the commute altogether, sleep late, run fingertips down parts to his heart's content.

Naah.

The gift falls heavily compared to the glass. Fred's just dying to know what it is, about to insist, when Claire stands up and gasps.

"Whatsamatter?"

"You're juggling Waterford crystal?"

It sounds like a question, so Fred stops, checks for some sort of label.

"No! I mean . . ." Claire laughs, refreshed. "Forget it." She does not bother squelching these laughs in a napkin. "Please just keep going, please," It looks effortless. The only strain occurs on his shirt's shoulder seams. Broad shoulders. "How do you do that?" It baffles her how people can all *do* things.

"Your shoes still hurting?" Fred asks.

"What?"

"The shoes."

"You sure?" But Claire's already unstrapping. Eager to feel the grass on her soles.

Fred bows, accepting the sandals. "What do we have? Something *old*" (nodding at the glass), "something *new*" (shoes), "something . . ." Uh oh, what's *borrowed?*

"The gift!" Claire shrieks. "You're borrowing it from me! It's new *and* borrowed!"

"All right." Fred's touched by her enthusiasm. "Let's review. Something old, something newish, something borrowed, and"—launching the shiny blue box—"something bluish!"

Claire jumps up and down, attracting an audience. That ruins it. That makes it work. People start trying to hand Fred their shoes and plates, beer bottles, cigar butts. One lady even wants him to take her purse. But Sam's the magician now; Claire vanishes inside his hug. And Fred becomes the audience. His hands, limp.

"Stop by Columbus Circle," he tells everyone. "Any day of the week." Angry for some reason. Angry but smiling. Fred the juggler. A pathetic thing to be, and freshly strange to him. Now that he's tasted the difference. Juggling for something vs. juggling for someone. "Stop looking at me. Please."

"I SEE you've changed your tie," the old woman in the kitchen says to Oscar. "You spill something?"

"No." He only owns one tie. "You must've seen my twin, Fred."

"Lillian." Her hand is pinker and softer than the tissue that Oscar just fake-used.

"Hello," he says. "Oscar Arm."

"Sit." Lillian yanks out a chair so hard it screams, then she vigorously pats the seat. Oscar wonders if she's lonely.

"All right." He wonders if he's lonely.

"You like hoops, Fred?"

"Osc—"

"Good. We'll have us a wager. My late husband, Francis, may he rest in peace, used to bet me into so much debt, by the playoffs I'd have to take in typing. But shorthand goes a tall foot. It's what I keep telling Clara. Act like a person. Some honest work, an aptitude, instead of this malarkey. Aaach, I'm wasting your time. I'll give ya New York and three and a half."

"*You* know the betting line?"

Triangulation of the area where eyebrows usually are. "Does the Pope wear a beanie?" Lillian howls. "Did Liberace like jewelry?"

CLAIRE'S DANCING with Sam. It's easy with him. Doesn't matter that she's never learned how. With Sam, all you have to do is Raggedy Ann relax—he showed Claire that the first time they met—and you're there before you know it, sweeping across, around, coasting. The less grounded the better. Sensations Claire associates with sex—in her good scenario. Close. Awash.

They swing past a lawn chair that's been flipped over, crunched. A pair of black silk pumps is carelessly balanced on

its curved spine. Marci's. She's barefoot, talking with Fred.
Don't start juggling for *her* too, Claire thinks, as Sam probes
her ear with his tongue. "Please don't."

"I've got a surprise for youuu," Sam whispers. Claire is less
interested in what it is than in whether he realizes he already
informed her of this, *more than twice.*

"Do you love me?" Claire's sorry a millisecond after it's
out.

Of course Sam says, "Of course." Of course he'll ask her the
same. But he doesn't. Claire waits and he doesn't. An offense.
A relief. If he had, she'd be forced to answer. She'd maybe
know the answer.

"How can you tell," Claire asks, "if we haven't had sex or a
fight yet?"

LILLIAN FEEDS the chicks snails. "This morning, Fred, I woke
up, felt like I'd grown a tooth."

"Oscar," Oscar says. "Oscar Arm. Excuse me, but I don't
know if escargot is the best food for baby birds."

"They're eating 'em, aren't they? They could be eating 'em
in trees just as easy."

Oscar decides not to get into the fact that chickens don't
climb trees or fly.

"Claire ordered Chink food."

Which reminds Oscar he's hungry. That he came in here for
food once upon a time.

"Fact of life," Lillian says. "Boys are always hungry. Girls
are always eating." Then she starts oinking at the TV. "That
Mr. Bird is in hog heaven again. Oink. Oink. Why do I like this
team anyway?"

"They're white and they win?" Oscar guesses. "Or used
to." In the short time he's been sitting here, Lillian's trashed
blacks, Jews, gays (Liberace), Chinese, and rich people. But
Oscar likes her. As long as she's prejudiced *in general*, he
doesn't mind. "Sometimes," he tells her, "I wake up and can't
find my arm."

MARCI OFFERS to share with Fred half a tuna sandwich left over from lunch. They walk across the lawn toward Oscar's car. Along the way Marci picks up party trash and stuffs it in her bag; quaint. She flatters Fred, or thinks she does, by calling him "the man with a thousand arms" and "the merry, juggling Oscar." Though barefoot, Marci walks very carefully, as if she's afraid she'll damage the grass.

"Are you drunk?" she asks Fred.

"I don't know."

"Cause I figure if you are, I am."

"How's that?" Fred's edgy, and not sure why. He's got to move somehow. Preferably Stretchman, but that might freak her out too much. A couple of handsprings, then; cheerier.

And lo and behold, she's doing them too. Blur of long legs, flash of red striped underwear. And when they pass the pool the two of them walk the edge, tempting each other to push and be pushed in by accident on purpose. They refrain. It'd be like kissing too soon and missing the best part: almost kissing.

Marci dips a foot in the water. "That was nice of you, Freddy." She's calling him Freddy already. "To dance with that lady. Really sweet."

"Peaches?" there goes his face, pinkening. "It's sweet of you to say it was sweet of me," Fred tells Marci. Going from pink to red. Was that even a sentence? The very reason he should stop performing. He'll never make it on coordination alone. He needs poise, voice, authority, a little more schmaltz, a lot more arrogance. Whatever it is Sam has Fred needs.

MASSAGING his left breast, Mr. Allswell looks lost in his own kitchen. As he moves across the room, he gives the impression of someone rushing slowly, or there being something very seriously wrong with him.

"Lie down," Lillian says. "Gimme that cigar."

Mr. Allswell removes some pills from a cabinet and swallows them. No water. He leans on the counter for a while, heaving.

"Lie down," Lillian repeats, this time like an admonishment. "Or at least sit, Arthur."

Arthur listens, and carefully makes his way to the table. Awful khaki complexion clashing with his sunburned pate and thick black eyebrows.

Oscar pulls out a chair, saying, "Mr. Allswell?" and helps take off his jacket. It startles Oscar to hear the two squeaks that is the man asking, "What quarter?" of the basketball game. It pains him to see the man struggle to grin at an emphatic two-handed Ewing jam but be not quite able to get the face muscles together to do it. But everything's fine, Mr. Allswell calmly assures Oscar, he's fine, just heartache, happens all the time. And then he notices the chicks. "Oh." He picks up a chick from the bowl and does the most eccentric thing yet. He drops the bird down his shirt.

"Gimme that cigar," Lillian says again, leaning over to pluck it from Mr. Allswell's breast pocket. "You shouldn't be smoking, you know that." She proceeds to light it for herself.

Louette would like this woman, Oscar thinks. And maybe Louette is good for me, after all, or at least better than nothing. Oscar remembers nothing, and Louette's definitely better.

"The poor thing," Lillian says, peeking down Mr. Allswell's shirt. Unclear whether she means the man's heart or the chick. "Fred here brought them for Clara."

"Oscar," Oscar says, though he knows it's useless.

"Isn't that thoughtful? Arthur? Arthur? . . ."

But Mr. Allswell refuses to answer while his eyes are leaking.

IT'S PARTLY MARCI. Graceful without being fragile, unlike Louette. Sexy in an unthreatening way, unlike Green Sequins. Unengaged, unlike Claire. Fred isn't going to delude himself. It's partly Marci, but it's mostly horniness.

"Kind of damp and squashed," Marci apologizes, frowning at the tuna sandwich. "So's the banana."

"Fine with me." Banana too? Lucky day.

"Take it all."

"No."

"Please."

"No."

"I don't want it, really; it's smelly."

Fred wonders whether he should want it, then. But not only is he horny, he's starved. Twin feelings, but not identical.

They sit on the roof of Oscar's faded yellow Toyota. Hercules is Marci's name for it. The shabbiest car in the driveway, excepting Louette's VW with its broken side mirror. Roach Coach is Marci's name for *it*. She proceeds like this down the row of vehicles, extemporaneously dubbing them "Princess" (the pink 124 Sports Spider convertible) and "Hidalgo" (a station wagon), while Fred scarfs the soggy white-bread-and-mayo-with-tuna-flecks, bypassing his taste buds as much as possible. "Crispus . . . Software." Better than personalized license plates, Fred tells Marci's hair, which he'd like nothing better than to hide beneath.

When all the automobiles have been given names, Marci entertains him with imitations. Edward G. Robinson's opening line in *Little Caesar:* "Coffee and spaghetti for two, please!" Memo, a big-mouth parrot from the PetMart: "You know it! *Squawk.* You know it!" Carmen Miranda: dancing on the car hood, with the banana kept beautifully balanced on her head.

A phone rings inside the house. The harbinger of the Chinese food truck! Double Happiness, truly. The truck honks and crunches up the gravel drive. Then Marci's face is closing in on him for a—yes, yes—*kiss out.*

She is slanting up her eyes Orientally with her pinkies.

THE PHONE'S RINGING. Then the doorbell starts its endless chime. Dad spills his heart medicine onto the counter.

Grandma Lillian reclines with her feet up on the table, sucking a cigar, hollering at Larry Bird on the TV, and trying to teach Oscar how to knit. Claire rushes for the door. The chicks are peeping wildly.

Garlicky food smell competes with the phone for most overbearing. Cigar smoke next. The Chinese food delivery man's short with her. Claire needs money. The phone goes on. How ill is Dad? The Chinese food man wears a puka shell necklace. Sam comes in, jovial but broke; figures; and with *Constance*; figures. Constance shuffles around, her green sequins aglitter, as if she's anxious to get rid of Sam.

Am I marrying a boring guy? Claire wonders. Does Constance think I'm marrying a boring guy?

The urge to push something in the girl's face reminds Claire of the thirty lemon meringue pies on standby. But is there anyone left outside? Did Fred leave? The Chinese food man cracks his knuckles, miffed, and the phone is still ringing, ringing.

"Pick it up already if it bothers you so much." Grandma Lillian mind-reads.

"Hello?" Heavy breathing. That's all Claire needs. "Who is this?" Sam, walking jauntily over, clasps her from behind. "Get off me. . . . Who is this? . . . Get off me; go eat. . . ." A stopped-up male voice asks for "Arms? . . . Either one, please."

"Excuse—"

"Oscar or Fred. Emergency."

LESTER'S CALLING himself "your father" signifies Trouble. His voice, soft and loud, breaks every other word. Shaken.

Aunt Mary's had a stroke.

What?

We always thought if it was anyone, it'd be Hersh, but—

Where are you?

Mary's had a stroke in the matinee. *Cats.*

We're on our way.

No hospital . . . She won't go.

Where's Mom? How's Mom?

She was like my mom when I was young; she was just—

Just hold on, I mean hang up, so we can get—

No one knew she wasn't part of the play, Osc. No one knew not to watch.

IN THE DRIVEWAY, Fred and Marci hold hands, greasy from spare ribs. Brush knees. Whisper. They look neither away nor at one another. Seeing them together like this, Oscar's stumped how to feel. Glad for Fred? Wary of Marci? Jealous . . . of which one? Seeing him, the two of them disengage, but unhurriedly.

Oscar sputters the news and tells them to "Get in the car." Marci, apologetic as usual, says she left her shoes on the patio.

"Go get them."

"Do you want me to get a ride home from someone else? I—"

"Stop sniveling," Oscar snaps. Then softly, "Take your time." He has the feeling they'll be sitting a lot once they get home anyhow. Sitting around and looking at each other and looking at Mary looking at Hersh drinking himself worse and/or looking out the window for a sign from the Lord as to whether He'll be healing her, as she obviously avidly believes. Wouldn't she go the hospital otherwise? Wouldn't she do like a normal dying person?

"I'm sorry," says Fred with his Sad Sacks face on.

"Me too. She—"

"No, I mean to you."

"For Marci?"

"She was your date."

"Me too."

Fred says, "We don't know her."

"I know."

They saw Mary only once or twice a year. They saw her this very morning all dolled up and departing for brunch at the Russian Tea Room, to be followed by the matinee. Springlike New York City day.

The Chinese man—who finally paid him?—rushes from the

house and climbs into his van but does not start the engine. Instead he reaches across the seat for a wad of tinfoil, which turns out to contain half a bagel, lox, cream cheese, which he nibbles on—unhungrily, dreamily, with the door hanging open, fixing his eyes outward on the exotic balloon-adorned landscape.

"I'm hungry," Oscar says. "How can I be hungry now? I'm a shit."

"I'm horny," Fred says. "That's worse."

They both want to cry but only sort of, and can't anyway in front of each other. In this light, the swimming pool looks almost mystical.

TRUCE. Claire and Lillian are breaking open fortune cookies, so far fifty or so, to find—the best? the truest? To take their minds off—

A SOFT ANSWER TURNETH AWAY WRATH.

Do you love him? What if I did? Who wants to end up like Dad, upstairs resting? What if I didn't? What about safe sex, self-doubt, loneliness-quenching. Look at Liberace. Look at—

HOW YOU LOOK DEPENDS ON WHERE YOU GO.

What if I don't know? Mr. Doody's on wife number three, and he's alive. He's happy. Is he happy?

WHAT YOU THINK CAN'T HAPPEN WON'T.

"That was a very nice boy, that Fred," Grandma Lillian says. "But I burned him on the game." Heh heh.

"Whatsamatter?" The question of the hour, of the day. But only Lillian has faith that there's a *right* answer.

THE MORE ONE KNOWS THE LESS ONE BELIEVES.

6

THIRTEEN LIES

"So I thought, Well, what would Dear Abby say?" Louette tells Claire, with her face sunk in the closet. Topic: Oscar and their "star-crossed affair."

But compared to Dear Abby, who's Claire to offer advice on Love Matters? She could hardly pick out which suit to wear to the beach, spent the entire morning determining that the blue one-piece with the crisscrossed back looked, not exactly great, but better than her other choices—barring emergency shopping, which she actually considered. The last thing she expected was to walk in on the same scene in Queens: Louette nude, wet-toenailed, cartoon-viewing, and now flinging bikini parts over her bony shoulder, one by one. "I love him, I love him not, I love him—"

I should try that—I love him, I love him not—thinks Claire, flicking an ant off her wrist. Common methods—her feelings—haven't exactly been the most accurate guide lately. She's still not even sure whether she *likes* Sam. A tickle on her calf, turns up a second ant.

As Louette chants on, Claire begins to notice more and more of the insects, including a real fatty vigorously paddling for survival in a pool of white quick-drying polish on Louette's big left toe.

"Ohhh . . . Uhhh . . ."

"I could try reading the configurations that my suits make as they land on the rug. I Ching–like." Louette hasn't noticed the ants yet.

"Oh, Lou . . ."

"Huh?" Louette raises her feet up onto the coffee table, settling in for the "My Little Pony" cartoon, humming the theme song and *still* not noticing. Claire spots the tell-tale double-dotted line: ant thruway. It runs around the closet wall and flows out toward a sticky half-moon spill on the kitchenette linoleum.

"Louette. You've got—"

"Aberrant behavior, I know. I'm turning thirty any second, I know, I know. But *you* try peering into people's mouths all week, you'd get hooked on 'My Little Pony' too. Six months' worth of coffee, tea, wine, tobacco, sugar-abuse residue these people save up just for me. Not to mention whatever fresh animal flesh is stuck between their molars from lunch. Uhhh. I'm telling you, there's really nothing better than 'My Little Pony' to reaffirm the fact that I'm doing absolutely nothing. Yea, Saturday! Gimme . . . Ants?!" Louette perceives the one stuck on her toenail and issues a wrenching sinus bleat. She lunges for the tissue box, but alas, the polish has hardened. The unlucky bug is encased in Precious Snowflake No. 6. "Errrech."

"Eeech," Claire agrees, and resolves to be of help to Louette, who's now frantically hopping across the room—as if the dead ant affected her walking abilities—to where a Mickey Mouse phone sits alone, in a little thronelike alcove.

"Ever been to Puerto Rico?" Louette asks, trembly-voiced. She dials, the offending foot stretched as far from the rest of her as is physically possible. "I don't even have any nail polish remover."

"No," Claire says to Puerto Rico. She enters the little kitchenette in search of a sponge, cleanser. "No?" to the nail polish remover. Claire offers to run to a drugstore for some. "Traps too? I could get? Why not get . . . ?"

"You sound just like Oscar."

So Claire drops the subject, drops to her knees, hikes up her blue sundress, and confronts the sticky insect mecca. The puddle looks to be dried grapefruit juice, a spill the shape of Puerto Rico. (Not really.) One of the few places she and Dad never hit. Puerto Rico and Queens. What shape *is* Puerto Rico? What would Dad make of Queens and this place, Louette's place, a cross between some kind of pop shrine—Jesus tablecloth, light-up Elvis-bust bookends—and the inside of I Dream of Jeannie's bottle: fuchsia couches, fluffy lavender fake-fur rugs, deep-purple satin pillows, enormous scarf canopies of the most transparent pale-pink silk.

He'd be amused. Mom, appalled. Grandma Lillian, giddy over the array of accessories: paper bowls heaped with bright, cheap jewelry, oddly shaped glittery hats and belts on pegs, ornate parasols with silver animal-head handles, and delicate lace gloves stored in seemingly bottomless worn leather trunks smelling of potpourri. Although Claire could probably guess the reaction of just about everyone she knows (granted that's only a measly four or five people), she is completely unable to form any clear impression of her own. Like the dreams she keeps having—no role for her anywhere.

"Ants!" Louette is yelling into the phone. "Black! Crawly! Ants!" As if volume alone will translate. She turns to Claire. "How's your Spanish?"

"I speak it OK." The ants die on the sponge or attach themselves to Claire's bracelet and forearms.

"Well, why didn't ya say so?"

"You asked about Puerto—"

Louette's hand flies up to signal silence as she obviously tries to absorb whatever's being said on the other end. Then, exhaling loudly, she says, "That is not my problem, Mr. Gutierrez. I'm entitled to extermination in my lease. . . . What? . . . What?"

Incomprehensible how anyone can sustain a serious conversation while speaking into a Mickey Mouse phone, let alone how anyone can slam down those big happy ears in anger. And if that hadn't killed Claire's giggle mid-breath, Louette's huff into the kitchenette would have. That intimate sound—open, close, open—of refrigerator-door suction—reminds Claire of her own horrible habit: standing in front of an open refrigerator, eating.

"They're living in the phone," Louette says, finally taking out, not lemon meringue pie, pasta, bread, ice cream, but two ripe tomatoes. "I caught 'em crawling out of Mickey's hearing canals just now." She bites into a tomato as if it were an apple, ignoring the pulpy seed slop—ants'll love it—that slides down her inner arm and plop-plops onto the tiles. A singular image. Naked girl standing beside an open window—yellow light— and in front of the fridge—blue light—with a red tomato and with Precious Snowflake No. 6, white toenails, in a cramped lime-green kitchenette. "You speak Spanish," Louette says flatly, a statement.

Claire wishes her hostess would get dressed already. And cannot help noticing that her pubic and head hair match now that she's gone back to her original color, if it is her original color—plain brown. Possible that she dyes her body hair too.

"What about the ants?" Claire asks. The broken screens at her house in New Jersey only let in an occasional wasp.

"For complaints, he doesn't speak English. I should have let you deal."

"Do you feel"—Claire's so used to being asked herself, it sounds funny being the asker—"OK?"

"Actually, my nose itches," Louette says, wiggling it. "It seems that every time I have my hands full, my nose decides to itch." She looks down at the two tomatoes she's holding, as if she doesn't know how they got there, and then just whips the half-eaten one out the open window—to the sheer delight of neighborhood kids, who stop mid-game. Drop Hands and Run.

"Whoa." And Claire always thought herself impulsive.

The kids drop hands and circle the tiny messy heart splat. "Yo, Lou-ette!" they call up. "Hey, Lou-ette! Whazat?!" And other unhearables due to passing planes and clamorous Sundae Fun construction.

"That's better. I feel much better now." Louette touches her nose, then checks her fingers, smiles. "No blood."

"Good." Claire's mildly horrified. She recalls how Sam said Louette can will her nose to bleed.

"It's biodegradable," Louette rationalizes, and extends the second tomato out to Claire. "Like to try?"

Well . . . "Why not?"

They watch it hit the brick wall opposite, then plummet the eight floors to the pavement.

"See the PetMart?" Louette points.

"I see Sundae Fun," Claire says, hungry.

"I wonder if he's in there."

"I see Hardware and Pain."

"Should I look?"

"Sure."

"Really?"

"Well . . ." Claire's mom used to say pursuing men was "crude and common." A statement that hadn't carried much weight at the time; but now, well. "I see Video Maniac and Meat Palace." The authority of begin dead; it's something.

"What do you do when a fire breaks out? Drop hands and run."

Louette shrugs and goes back to bathing suit wading. She'd look great in all twenty; that's not the problem.

"Oscar thinks . . . oh, forget it." That's the problem. They will never get to the beach, at this rate. "Which suit? You pick."

Mismatched tops and bottoms? Claire suggests in hopes of speeding the action, but by Louette's nonresponse quickly learns that mismatched tops and bottoms were the in thing two years or more ago, which might as well be one hundred.

No matter. Louette could "pull it off," "fill it out," "get away with it." All daunting concepts to Claire, implying that mysterious ability *to deal.*

"I know! We'll go to Chester's for bikini waxes, my treat." Louette makes it sound like going to Sundae Fun for banana splits. Hot wax, hot fudge. She snaps off the TV. "Ya know, Oscar says the reason cartoons start at noon now is cause all the kids on drugs can't get up. Oscar—"

"Get counseling," Claire blurts. "That's what Dear Abby would say."

STUFFING PARROTS into suitcases is out of the question. But falsified permits are risky and would entail weeks of quarantine: Customs. Pricey too; reservations need to be booked months in advance and, thanks to a new export ban on *all* wildlife, can be made now only in the name of Science.

"No!" Oscar objects before Vladimir has the chance to unhook his mouth from a liverwurst sandwich and *dare* suggest that they scam his ornithology adviser into unknowingly helping them smuggle parrots. "Never!"

Oscar has already arranged to get school credit, though. Pick a research thesis title was the gist of his adviser's advice. "Say, 'Roosting Habits in Tropical Rain Forest Zones,' 'Incubation and Rearing of Toucan Young,' 'Parrot Fish Hydrodynamics.' "

Vladimir sits on a crate filled with Security Britches (chastity belts for female dogs in heat), cupping the sandwich. His plan—send Oscar to Cancún, where he will rent a car, drive fifty or so miles to Playa Alguna, and meet a Mr. Fernando Jamón. Big, blond, blue-eyed Mexican. Runs the dive shop. "Him you miss cannot no way in hell." He knows where macaws are, how to trap them; he has boat for transport. "Zip zip Miami." Vladimir takes a sloppy bite, chews with his mouth open. Then, "Science. A very good idea. Perhaps—"

"*No*. Think again!"

Oscar's yelling sets off an entire warehouse of barks and squeals, squeaks, clicks, jabberings, all sounding faint next to the unbearable screech of the parrots. The bandleader, Memo, has recently added to his repertoire the Aldo Tate campaign slogans. Also plane roar.

"Wind's wrong I can't think nothing," Vladimir says. When

the wind's wrong—that's blowing northwest—the planes take off from La Guardia right into Sidehill. "Shhh." Vlad makes a three-quarter turn away on his crate, covering his sandwich with his entire body.

"Shhh," Oscar mimics, checking on the yellow-cheeks. In this short time, the birds have actually compensated quite nicely for their clipped wings, taking advantage of the great hinge that allows their bills to function like a third foot in climbing; adaptation.

"No worries," Vladimir assures from his throne. "I pray for it. You bring birds for me. We have big cash."

Oscar cannot even laugh. "I appreciate that you don't want to *bore* me with technicalities, but there are a few obstacles I'd like to dis—"

"Pleh," Vlad says. Russian for nonsense or nonsense for nonsense or the universal language for liverwurst stuck in gullet. "Let me tell you of obstacles. . . ." He pauses, Oscar thinks, to recharge before launching into his usual spiel about how good life is in the U.S. of A. "You no appreciate meat?" (Liverwurst? Afraid not.) "The oranges you juggle, my people have killed for." (You can have it.) "When I was small child I had to sleep always in the bed with five brothers." (Oscar and Fred slept in the same bed too.) "Obstacle you see if your eye takes off from the goal."

Ah, a new cliché; Oscar was waiting for just this sort of conclusion. "That's lovely, thank you. Except the *goal*"—Oscar mimics Vladimir's accent, which makes the word sound like *ghoul*—"happens to be a felony"—he makes this up—"and you better believe that if I'm caught, I'm naming—"

"Soon," Vladimir says, unfazed, "you would enjoy being partners."

"Dangling a new carrot, I see? Interesting."

"Carrot? I not familiar with this expression." Vladimir gets up and cranks open the big warehouse door.

"Aldo Tate! Vote Aldo Tate!" Memo squawks. "Vote! Aldo Tate! You know it! You know it!"

"Said simple, go or be fire." Vlad makes it plain. Not only

does he squirrel his sandwiches, but he hasn't the common decency to turn around while urinating—right outside the warehouse now, where the trucks unload. As if staking the territory.

Perfume/chemical/burnt-hair waft-blast as you enter. Pink. Vast. Immediate mirror-mirror-on-the-wall attack, except worse. The mirror frames are pink too, and vast too. Mirrors hang on every available surface. With the blow-dryer hiss, woman shrill, radio, phones, and running faucets, the noise level competes with the street. Claire fears that if she doesn't keep alert, she could wind up radically altered.

"This way," Louette explains, smoothing down her eyebrows. "If I run into Oscar *here*, it'll be an accident." Her confidence is apparently boosting as Claire's plunges. This is nothing at all like Sundae Fun.

"There is no place like this place anywhere near this place," Louette says, waving with her visor at a hairdresser who's wearing leather pants. "Sandrine, hey!"

"It's very pink," Claire can't help noticing over and over. She's already goose-bumpy from the industrial-strength air-conditioning. Near the magazines, one unit is dripping in time to the radio. Pink speakers too; pink floors, chairs, brushes, smocks, dryers, sinks; pink skin. Like strawberry ice cream. "How bout we go for some double cones instead?"

"No," says Louette. "He *might* show. Anyhow, it's just rip-rip and we're done."

"We don't even have appointments," Claire tries, her voice involuntarily rising to a screech.

"Lester'll slip us in," Louette guarantees. "Lester, at least, is one Arm that loves me." She ushers Claire toward the magazines, then flits off to "Good morning" the room, even though it's afternoon and the beach hours are dwindling.

With her back turned, Louette—short hair, narrow hips, orange gym shorts—could pass for a young boy, but she's voicing a womanly complaint. "Walked right by that raucous construction site without generating a single whistle!" She peers into a mirror as if for an explanation.

"What are we gonna do with the Lou-Loon here?" asks a lady whose hair is twisted into individual tinfoil pouches. "The way she carries on . . . Her worst enemy couldn't wish on her what she thinks up herself."

"*Personally,*" says the hairdresser in leather pants, "I think those jackhammer savages are kinda sexy." She looks whistled at, hourly. Thirty-eightish, massively Jazzercised; she's having difficulty wedging her tip, a single bill, into a very snug back pocket.

"If I was *you,*" Louette tells Sandrine, cryptically, "I'd think so too." She passes out little spools of dental floss.

"God bless," says the first recipient, who has red paste swirled on her head like frosting. "One mitzvah leads to another." She suggests that Louette join Hadassah.

"Can't meet any men in Hadassah," Sandrine disagrees, as if she's already tried it.

"Mitzvah?" Louette's stuck on the word. Claire too. "Is that like a Danish?" Louette demonstrates the proper flossing technique: side to side, a "scooping" motion.

"Charlotte's workshop. Now, there's a mitzvah if I ever saw," Red Paste says.

Voices lower. "How *does* the woman do it? Makeup for blind people. Uh."

"Ask me. Those girls could use a hairdo workshop too. The way they come in, some of them, you—"

"Ida!"

"What's so terrible? If god forbid something should happen where *I* . . . I'd hope my friends would tell me—"

"What, Ida? Go have a body wave?"

From the corner of her eye, Claire witnesses a woman slowly moving her sweater to cover the magazine in her lap, looking around on all sides, then starting to tear something out, tearing just a little bit at a time, then looking up again, tearing, looking, looking, tearing.

"Is it our business what those poor women do?"

"All I can tell you, *I* wouldn't be caught gallivanting around wearing lipstick if god forbid—"

"We'll see."

"Why shouldn't they fix themselves up?" Louette asks. "We can still look at them even if—"

Claire tries to read a magazine. But she has no way of discerning whether the list of "ins and outs" for '91 are a joke or not.

Sushi's out (parasites). Venison, in (home cooking). But where do you find venison in Queens? Food as fashion.

Lace is in. Leather, out. Sorry, Sandrine.

Temporal Mandibular Joint Syndrome (aka clench-jaw) is in. Obsessive-compulsive disorder, out. Illness as fashion.

Sex is out too, in favor of talking about it. And breasts are decidedly back, in a big way.

A flash bulletin booms through the parlor's unfortunately excellent acoustics.

"She's Sam Lubin's Fiancée?" Sam Lubin's fiancée in the flesh! Alert the press.

Claire's an instant celebrity.

"Over there! I see." Red Paste points. "Under the sign by the magazines."

Jolting upright, the woman illicitly tearing one of the magazines freezes. "My luncheon! . . . Marinades . . . The board of trustees . . . I needed the recipe, OK? So have my head!"

"Goy . . . Peaches . . . teenybopper . . . dead."

The truth is, Claire feels flattered to be gossiped about. If nothing else, it takes the mind off hot wax between the legs. And almost makes Claire want to get her hair cut. Just to join in. To be *let in* the circle of women—lazy, animated, cotton balls between the toes, every lap occupied with shopping lists and checkbooks, crewelwork and food-drive particulars, crosswords, yarn, floss, tissues—energetically waiting together as each in-progress hairdo ticks to its own clock. Talking, ticking, talking. Enviable, the way they talk with Louette and *to* her, *at* her, and *on* her behalf. They all have a remedy for her "ant situation," or a kind word about how the natural hair color "positively lights up her face," or a giggle for the White-Out she lies about having used on her toenails: "That's our Loony-ette." Studying them all, Claire catches herself reinventing her mother.

GLANCING UP from the outline of a watch on his wrist, Fred sees—is that Claire? What's *she* doing *here?* His arm automatically reaches up to press his hair down (these damn mirrors). He notices again Claire's fine head, or is it neck, yes, neck, or is it the harmonious manner in which the two are connected? Tiptoeing up behind her, he remembers what he . . .

"Uh!" Claire jumps. Fred. She thought he was a fly. "Oh. Hi." A fly in her ear. But it's a half-dollar that he's pulled from behind it.

"Don't you use Q-Tips?" Fred bows, extending the coin out to Claire, palm up, dignified.

His face is pink too, but darker than the room pink. Its features are delicate, precise, inappropriate to the nimbus hair. An incredibly springy yellow jumble, almost wiglike.

"I haven't seen one of these in I don't know how long," Claire says about the half-dollar. "What is it? Kennedy?" Naming faces on money, a game she used to play with Mom. A rich kid's game, it occurs to her.

"It's yours," Fred says, not mentioning how he found the coin this morning when he smashed open a very old piggy bank—originally a mutual (twin) fund. He is *that* broke. Hence this job at Chesty's.

"Well, I appreciate it. Thanks . . . thanks a lot," Claire says. The words "thanks" and "sorry" make up half her vocabulary these days. She begins to balance the coin on her nose, its small, flat diamond bump.

"Attractive." Fred's take, and true. The effort involved in keeping the coin still turns Claire's eyebrows to tildes. Plush brows, dark, contrasting with the fair, odd, greenish hair. Tragic if she's here to have them waxed, plucked, (mis)shaped, electrolysized. "Please no." Not that he'd be surprised.

"What?" The half-dollar drops off Claire's royal-blue sun-dressed lap. She could swear she just saw his eyes change color—brown to green. Possible? "Please no, what?" and then "Please no what?" doesn't sound like English, and Claire starts to laugh and Fred too.

She watches the pink of his face deepen to burgundy. The laughter's getting attention now—Sam's fiancée with the owner's son in hysterics?

Sandrine, patrolling the two of them, blow-dries a single strand of hair to pieces, no doubt conjuring all sorts of misinformation to feed to the ladies later.

"Is he off center or . . . ?" The man asking, Claire is 99 percent sure, is Lester Arm. The same eyes as his son's, though Claire, struck with shyness, can't quite get her own to meet them directly.

"Hi," Claire plunges in, focusing instead on the stained wide-collared shirt and badly fitting, shoulder-padded dark blazer.

"If it isn't Herman Munster," Fred howls. "All ya need's a coupla bolts in your neck."

"Howdaya like that?" Mr. Arm grins powerfully, bouncing on the balls of his feet. "I pay him to abuse me."

Claire likes him at once. Except for the tan—too tan for June—and the faint eye bags, Lester's the picture of the twinkly huggable strapping galoot of a TV dad who works hard and eats sensibly and maybe can't always manage to match his socks but tries (they're both in the brown range). In contrast to her own father—the impeccably dressed, misty-eyed, gin-and-tonic-swilling Cap N Gown exec who cannot seem to do so much as boil an egg—Lester Arm is, well, positively wholesome.

"I see you're a swimmer." Lester starts to lift up a clump of Claire's thoroughly chlorinated split ends to examine, when Louette charges up, stops short, gasps tinily, lets her head droop.

It's obvious that she has confused Fred for Oscar. Even she. Spooky.

Fred stops mid-laugh.

"Lester," Louette says, regaining speech, beating him to introductions. "This here is—"

"Ah, yes, the waxing virgin."

"Dad!" Fred says.

"Fred!" Dad says.

"Louette!" Claire says.

"Claire!" Louette says.

Lester Arm offers "the VIPs" all services on the house. If only he were twenty years younger.

ON A WHIM, Oscar buys expensive amber-tinted Ray-Bans on the way home from the PetMart. And red gym shorts, and Scotch for Hersh—a misdeed, but it'll be the last time. And three chickens—a good deed. He plans on making the old man eat. And gum for the plane, three flavors, all sugary, in defiance of Louette's dental hygiene sensibility.

Inside his messy apartment, Oscar trips over the defective hamster tubing he lied to Vlad he'd try and huckster, and sails onto the bed to attempt a nap.

But the toilet flushes by itself. It does that. Oscar's apartment is modestly haunted: every so often an object will propel itself off a shelf; the stereo breaks down by playing faster and faster. There are pressures building up everywhere that we humans know nothing about. The plumbing barks.

There is no way he'll sleep. Too sunny, highlighting every molecule of dinge in the room. The dust swirls pirouette. The sink looks infected. People with sunny apartments have to clean more: fact. People in sunny countries?

Sunglasses help. Sunglass first aid. This is how the world was meant to look. A world with some juice left. Louette would be particularly fond of the Ray-Bans, but she'd only get around to wearing them once before they vanished, along with all Oscar's good things—shirts, tapes, even pillowcases—into that swirling vortex of *her closet*, which overflows continuously yet somehow never with any of *his* stuff. *His* stuff it just sucks in and digests.

It's enough to make him call her. Vibrate those Mickey Mouse ears. Demand at least his blender back. Or, if she truly bewitches him, knock her flat: lucky day—get ready for a trip to the Yuc with your fav fun guy. . . .

Louette's machine picks up. "I want you"—her special machine voice: more responsible sounding but less upbeat than her usual melodious chatter—"if you're an exterminator." So she's got ants again. Oscar keeps telling her to buy boric acid and traps, but she will not hear of it.

"That stuff's not childproof."

"You don't have children."

"But I want some."

"So."

So he hangs up.

LATVIA, the waxer, has hardly any lips or hair, an oblong head, and loud silver bracelets all the way up both arms. "I know," she tells Claire, "You're scared spitless." Then, "Strip." Then, "Lie down—move down, not *up*—do you know up from down, miss?" She stirs the vat of boiling wax ominously and hums from her throat. Latvian folk tunes? Claire makes a fist around the half-dollar that Fred pulled from her ear.

"That was bikini and half-leg?"

"No. Just—"

"Eyebrow and leg?"

"No. I—"

"Well, I'm not no mind reader, hon. Whatcha want?" She must have immigrated to this country at a young enough age to lose her accent. "Hurry up now; goo's congealin."

"Bikini," Claire manages.

"No stomach? . . . If I were you . . . It's dreadful." Latvia traces the line of hair from crotch to navel with a long fingernail, metal arms jangling.

"Well, OK." Claire braces herself by biting the hand that squeezes the coin, as Latvia smears hot wax onto the insides of her thighs with a small wooden paddle. Next she applies a cloth, as if to wipe up the wax, when *rip*, no warning, *rip rip*. Louette's terminology and very accurate. *Rip rip.* But it isn't near over yet.

"Stop the shaking," Latvia says. "It'll be through one, two, five." Though she breaks to exhibit the cloth with Claire's woolly hairs laminated under caramel-colored gunk. "See this? Dreadful."

"Yes." Scared spitless.

Rip rip rip rip. Eight in a row. Is this like an initiation? Don't count. Claire digs her nails into the fist she's biting, clutching the half-dollar. Raw meat for thighs.

"By the way, congratulations."

"For remaining conscious?"

Latvia ignores the crack. "I do Peaches regular." She sniffs, rattling those bracelets. Defending her technique with credentials. "I've done Peaches for years." Claire senses even more zest in the next series of rippings. *Ripping.* For distraction, she indulges in hating this woman, irrationally but totally. It does help. To think, people pay for this. Louette pays.

"The more you come—sit still—it won't hurt so much," Latvia explains by way of apology. Latvia *is* a country, isn't it? Add that to the list of places she and Dad never went to. Puerto Rico, Queens, Latvia. "Hold on." The grand finale includes a behind-the-eyelids light show. Dull throbbing red swamp pricked with white sparkles. Coin stuck to her palm. Add Latvia to the list of places she and Dad are never going to.

"WHAT WAS *she* doing *here?*" Peaches asks, post–electrolysis and hairwash. That is, blemished and dripping out from under her badly fastened towel turban (Fred's still learning). She leaves a trail from Fred's sink to Dad's souped-up chair—gold-leafed, sheepskin-upholstered, Christmas-light-trimmed, and even license-plated CHESTER'S. "What was *she* doing *here?* . . . If any of youse breathed a word about . . . later . . ."

No, no, all the ladies attest, ever fearful of the wrath of Peaches. Not a syllable. Our lips were Velcroed.

"Word of what?" Fred asks. The bachelor party? Is Peaches in on that too? Or has she something else planned, something she needs sprucing up for? "What are *you* doing here?" Besides having wire needles with volts inserted into your chin follicles. "It's not Wednesday."

"I'm feeling transitional." Peaches addresses Dad, not Fred. A sliver embarrassed after that "magical" dance she and Fred shared? "I've decided to go the distance." Donning the paper apron herself, she manages to squeeze into Dad's chair in one motion. "I've had it up to here with this blah wash-and-set business. See what I'm sayin?" As her hands leap up to the wet hair, Peaches' neck and triceps drummer muscles positively bulge. "It's perm time. Listen up, Les. I'm talking the whole kit and caboodle. I don't wan any discussion." She lights a cigarette with a match from Lil's Fish Fry Palace. "So just hurry and *do me.*"

"You got it, babe," Dad croaks, winking at Fred and pulling the towel off Peaches' head dramatically. "Ta daaa! Is to die for or what? The all-time rock 'n' roll mama." He swivels the back of the chair.

"Oh, Lester, you—"

"Aren't you supposed to test for allergic reactions?" Fred asks. "Latvia said before perms . . ."

"Well, theoretically . . ."

"And what is *he* doing here?" Peaches shrews. She's much nicer drunk.

"He's in training to be me," Lester tells her, and then whispers to Fred, "Yes, certain chemical combinations can, well, very occasionally cause . . ."

"Scalp burns and rashes. Blisters, brittle split ends, hives. Latvia says she's seen rollers baked onto people's heads if—"

"Watch how I comb her," Lester interrupts. "See, Fred, *up* like this you comb, *up.*"

"I know how to comb hair, Dad. But shouldn't—"

"You're a real green salad." Sandrine interferes. She's blow-drying a priest! He came in off the street, demanding a "stylish cut." "We've had like maybe three adverse reactions in—what is it?—four, five years now." Maybe he's the faith healer Mary express-ordered from Miami. "Waste a time, if you ask me."

"Happens." Latvia disagrees. She's taking yet another coffee break.

"Eh." Unconcerned, Peaches giggles at Father Hairdo or at the sensation of having the perm solution dabbed on her elbow's inner fold. "I cry whenever I get my hair done anyhow. I don't know why."

Fred's not convinced. "But if you don't test, and then—"

"Look." Dad shrugs, perturbed. "It's not fatal. Twenty-four hours, we'll know."

"The last time I got permed it smelled like kitty litter for weeks," reports Sandrine's next appointment from the sidelines. A *tousled* auburnette with exposed black roots.

"Air conditioner's leaking again!" Shaky Bea announces. "Looks toxic."

"It is," Fred says. "Latvia—"

"This is fascinating." Peaches sighs. "But wouldya step on it, please. I'm tryin to be spontaneous here."

"Yes, ma'am." Dad's relief shows in his springy bounce-in-place. He quickly douses Peaches' head with the perm solution, then throws a pair of rubber gloves at Fred. "Peel those eyeballs!" He mushes the gunk around in Peaches' hair. "Ya watchin?"

"Watchin, Dad."

"OK. Concentrate. Stay cool now. I'm walking ya through."

Fred can hardly bring himself to sink his hands into Peaches' frothing scalp, and when he does, Latvia's right away instructing.

"Work it in."

But the activity seems so intimate.

"Use some muscle."

But the smell is ghastly, maskworthy.

Dad's encouraging. "Doin fine, son. Now for technique—rolling and timing." Lester grabs two limp stalks of hair. "Choose your weapon." Fred does. Like a soggy strip of gray felt, not exactly a turn-on. "Not too large a strand, now. Use an end paper—prevents crushing." Then they wind the locks onto the rollers and clip. "Rustproof clips only . . . *roll in the direction of the curl you want* . . . and you got it, that's it, yeah, that's good, yeah, he's a natural, look at that, he's . . ."

"Do it, Fred!" Sandrine whoops. The priest is busy examining his cuticles. "But closer together! You don't want the curls to look separated."

Even Bea has to have her say. "Avoid the eyes. We wouldn't want her to wind up in Charlotte's workshop."

"What?" Peaches gurgles.

Fred tries to conjure up more appealing heads, old girlfriends' heads, with some difficulty. It's been a while. He can't remember ever even washing a girl's hair. And he'd remember.

"Alternate directions every roller row for body waves," Dad goes on just as Fred starts to get an image. Claire's soft comma curls at the sides of her—"Hello? Fred?" Then there's Marci's fantastic all-over-the-place black mop he could—"Hey, Fred, what'd I just tell you?"

"For an alternate body—"

"This is my head you're talking about," says Peaches.

"Done." Dad smiles. "Two hands are faster than one. Hit the dryers, woman."

"Four than two, you mean," Bea says. "Four hands."

"Perm virgin no more." Peaches unwads herself from the chair.

"Let the curls cool before brushing her out," Dad instructs. "And remember not to—"

"I've got errands," Fred says, fed up. "Can I?"

"*I've* got errands," Dad says. "*May* you?"

Pause. Dad's leaving to Mary-sit, evidently.

"Fred's going to the store for me?" Sandrine asks, coy. She requests tampons—right in front of the priest!—and honey-lemon cough drops.

"You don't have a cough."

"I like chewing them." She's furiously shaking a can of Final Net.

"And who's gonna finish me off?" Peaches panics. Now that

she's stepped down, Dad's covering up his chair with a special pink tarp. "Some apprentice." She tsks at Fred. "I certainly hope you're a more reliable best man."

Sandrine perks up. "Best man?"

Bea snarls, "*I'll* finish you off."

"None of that," the priest says, jumping out of the line of hairspray. "That'd be vanity."

ROCKAWAY BEACH. At a red light, a mangy kid on a bike sidles up to Louette's car. "Wanna space?"

"What?"

"Need a space?"

Newfangled drug lingo? "Space?"

"Duuuh, parkin space."

"Yeah."

"Ten bucks an hour."

"Steep."

"Ya want it or what?"

"Where?"

"Ya want it or what?"

"Yeah."

So they follow the bike, a brand-new off-white girl's Raleigh, to the parking space, which turns out to be right on the beach block in front of a brick two-family house with a rusted-out porch swing on the lawn. Louette says she'll give him two dollars, and the kid cracks up. "Let's be real here," he says. "This is ninety-one."

"Where's your mom?" Claire asks.

"Dead."

"Dad?"

"Not home."

"I'd like to say hi to him later."

"Awright, four bucks; half now, half later."

"Deal." They walk away looking as if they just got off horses—the waxing—and Louette turns back to tell the kid, "You're gonna go places."

And he mouths, "Yeah—sucker—in—your—car."

"You too," Louette tells Claire, an afterthought.

The beach is closed.

"Fungus," the lifeguard says apologetically. "Closed due to fungus."

"Whatayamean fungus?"

"Like athlete's foot, I guess."

"We get medical waste in New Jersey," Claire says. "Never stopped me."

"If the beach is closed," Louette asks the lifeguard, "what are you doin here?"

"Tellin you the beach is closed. I got two more hours."

He's sort of rugged good-looking except for a nose that appears to lack necessary cartilage.

"Can we sit on it?" Claire asks.

"It's a free country." He seems to be around fifteen and growing younger.

"I mean is the fungus in the sand or water?"

"Duuuh." Maybe he and the kid are in cahoots. Maybe the lifeguard gets a cut of the parking-space action.

"That brat," Louette says. "He'll probably steal my hubcaps." She yanks off her shorts on the spot, then her shirt, her sandals. "I'm not one to turn down any free vitamin D." The black string bikini she eventually decided upon makes the lifeguard literally sway.

"So what'll happen if I go swimming?" Claire asks, conscious of her buttocks itchy-sealed together from wax. You think Latvia's bad, Louette told her, never, never go to an Asian. Those women don't have any hair; they don't even know how it feels.

CHICO CAN'T FUCK I KNOW, says the low beach wall in white paint.

"Where you people from anyways?" asks the lifeguard.

"France," Louette lies. She's in the midst of campsite assemblage. "Paris, France." An astounding array of beach paraphernalia emerges from the one bag: towels, radio, reflector, two paperbacks—*Romeo and Juliet* and a how-to, *Men Who Love Women Who Hate Men Who Love Men.* Lotion is absent, wine coolers abundant. "We're stewardesses, see."

"No shit?" He believes it. Taller already. "You sure speak good English."

Claire hoists herself onto the wall for an improved view of the water. Sudsy.

"Is this the Atlantic or the Pacific?" Louette asks, pushing it.

"Duuuh," Claire says. Sudsy but tempting. How bad could it be? "What's with this fungus anyway? What is it?"

"Se-wage." He enunciates carefully for the benefit of foreigners and even translates. "Ya know, *sew*-age."

Well, why not. "I'd rather swim in a clean dirty place than a dirty clean place any day."

And so Claire finds herself sprinting down to the water before she's even made up her mind to run, wet before she's thought to swim, only then realizing her dress is still on and ballooning. When she twirls, a small current of the foamy water, gray water, warm for June water, encircles her. When she traps pockets of it in her skirt lap, the blue hem bobs like some feathery sea thing. Splash echoes. Invisible fungus. Louette doesn't know what she's missing. Swimming.

THE WIND'S WRONG. A jet screams overhead. Fred can see the yellow of taxis reflected on the brushed-aluminum plane belly and fantasizes about flying to Mexico with Oscar tomorrow morning. But, No, he already flat out said. "No. I cannot just go off to the tropics. I've got plans and debts and a real job now. No."

"You're coming," Oscar commanded, bullying any chance of it away.

"*No.*"

It *is* unthinkable, though—Oscar smuggling parrots out of a steamy, poisonous jungle via boat, plane, car, while staving off all manner of exotic illness and foreign-languaged danger, intrigue, romance. An adventure more suited to . . . no one Fred knows, except . . . Claire?

They're still rebuilding the dinky curb in front of Sundae Fun. Fred pauses to consider how much money the dozen unionized overtime guys and a cement mixer, taking their time, will make today. The construction, adding its bass-line throb to the plane drum rumble, ice cream bells, car horn section, and kid squeak arpeggios, a layered and excessive racket, seems somehow to quiet itself when two gorgeous women with Walkmans on jog by *shout*ing a conversation about how the wind's wrong.

A flier slices across Fred's neck, nasty. ALDO TATE FOR CITY COUNCIL lettered above a picture of a bland and battered-looking too-smiley face.

"Who's this?" Fred asks.

"Me," the guy says, extending his hand.

"Ah." Though he honestly cannot see any resemblance between this person and this person's picture—the real-life version has a severe pair of muttonchops—Fred shakes once, firmly. The man's hand is hot but not at all sweaty. Fred's own is still slightly chemical-odored from Peaches' perm. "*Aldo Tate for a great City Council,*" a second, red-eared fellow belts through a megaphone. "*Aldo Tate for a great city.*"

"*There's* an issue for you, Aldo. Noise pollution." But Fred says this in a friendly way, because if anyone knows how tough selling yourself on the street is, it's Fred. The guy has it hard enough already with that yellow teeth film and misleading campaign photo.

Another plane. Fred imagines Oscar aboard, slowly eating his meager allotment of foil-packed nuts. He is going, going. The plane looks about to smash right into the elementary school—these things do happen—but banks left at the last possible moment toward his parents' house, where Mary's lying half paralyzed and waiting, stubbornly waiting, for Dr. God to appear, or, her second choice, that faith healer from Miami. Everyone assumed Hersh'd kick first, most of all Hersh himself. Not that he couldn't still pull it off, at the rate he's drinking. Fred should make him eat something, some nuts at least.

At the door to the PetMart, Fred delays to watch the plane ascend, veer on a right slant, turn into a glint, and vanish. In the window are a pair of black rabbits, madly humping.

"VLADIMIR WILL ONLY listen to Frank, Bing, or Perry," Marci yells over the music. Sinatra singing "L.A. Is My Lady." "Loud."

"Not a bad fish-watching number," Fred says, kneeling by his favorite specimen, a monster parallelogram with contour-map markings—green, yellow, blue, black.

"That's Sheila," Marci tells Fred, pushing her hip out, nodding. She's been arranging Wee Wee Pads in a most precarious-looking pyramid. "Ninety-nine ninety-nine. You got good taste." Her breasts warp and hide some of the lettering on her T-shirt. T-A-P, it reads on first glance, but closer examination reveals an advertisement—RENT-A-PET. An actual service—but on Marci, it's more suggestive. No bra.

"Where's Osc?" Fred asks.

"Well." Marci hesitates, fumbling a Wee Wee Pad. "Not out to lunch but not exactly *in* either." Whatever that means. But, "Hang around. Fish get to know you by your footfalls."

A furry hand grabs Fred's shoulder then. Vladimir. "And why are you doing here?!" sets off a gray parrot squawking— "Get to work, get to work"—which starts the dogs barking, the fish freaking.

Fred points to his shaven chin. "I'm not him." He smiles, though. Always smile. "Release me, please, thank you."

Vladimir raises his milky eyeballs, like, What a major nuisance this all is, life. He tramps off, but not before reprimanding Marci for mispricing the Herbal Flea Collars. And would she please "make silence on this godlydamn Memo bird!" Bad mood.

"Look, um," Fred says, perusing the Cat Snacks and trying to decide what message to leave Oscar. How best to persuade him to attend Sam's bachelor party tonight? Marci follows Fred up and down the aisles. The Cat Snacks come in Italian, Hollywood, or Yuppie style. "Um . . ." And there's cat pâté.

"Shhh, Memo," Marci coos. The bird hangs its head down from the perch, still "Get to work"ing. The only uncaged creature in the place, excepting humans.

"Wanna see me feed the snakeheads?" Marci asks. And taking silence for a yes, she wheels over the tall ladder, simultaneously grabbing a net and changing the radio station. Coordinated. Fred remembers her fine handsprings. "This is a real treat," Marci readies him. "Yum-yum."

The parrot halts mid-round—"Get to"—and looks right at Fred, motionless, then slowly spreads his crimson tail feathers. He burps once and bends over to rattle his food dish. In it sits a Wiffle ball, regulation size.

"I know," Marci says. "You be the customer and I'll be the saleslady."

A little kinky, Fred thinks, but what the hell.

"All right, you come in and ask for goldfish and snakeheads."

Fred obeys, actually leaving the store and, for realism, reentering with a limp and a British accent. "Miss? I'd like to purchase some fish, please."

Marci titters. "Aggressive or nonaggressive, sir? Is your tank . . . ?"

"Um." He's not quite sure of his lines here. "Do I look like the aggressive type?"

She moves on. "Now, which fish did you have in mind?"

"An Oscar. No, no, no. I'll take fancy goldfish and snakeheads."

"That spells gobble-gobble," Marci says. "Allow me to demonstrate." She nets a large bulbous-eyed goldfish and dumps it in with the snakeheads. Small, striped eel-like demons. In less than an instant, Goldy's eyeballs have been plucked out and the snakeheads are moving in to fight over the body.

"Don't feel bad," Marci says. "Anyhow, fancy goldfish dirty the tank. You don't want that."

"Certainly not," Fred agrees, slightly queasy, but still in character.

"Something else interest you?" Marci raises one eyebrow flirtatiously and glows down from her ladder at Fred. "Sir?"

CLAIRE DISCOVERS a sandbar, where tiny waves beach her, twenty yards from shore. Water knee-deep and sun-glittered. Superb view. The beach, resolved from individual sand grits into one soft, curved, pinkish mass, is like an arm, on which Louette and the lifeguard are only small thumbs, fiddling.

Claire waves at them to signal Come on in. She'd like to show them this, her sandbar, with the dead, purply-veined jellyfish, her dress, with its funny L-shaped tear in the armpit, the boats in the distance, like fishtank or bathtub toys bobbing backward on a string. But they don't see her, or else see her and, fungus phobic, resist. Claire is astonished to come across the half-dollar, still safely tucked in her dress pocket.

I love him, I love him not. That's one con she forgot—Sam can't swim very well. Claire had tried telling Louette earlier in the car: Sam can't swim at all. Plain English. But Louette had gotten all daffy, winky, as if "Sam can't swim" were some kind of euphemism. Anything but.

"AND SEVENTEEN PERCENT of all Americans would throw their pets off a cliff for one million dollars, you know that?" Marci asks. But Fred hears, "You want me?" He's daydreaming. Marci pendulums her precious blue-black woosh of hair. "*Do* you have any pets?" The hair is like a pet—tame, nuzzleable, alive. "A real tank?" sounds like "Your place or mine?" Fred is sure he's not imagining it. Oscar would lend them his apartment. Even if he and Fred have not been getting along lately, they're still brothers, aren't they? Twins! He's sure Oscar would not turn down an offer like this himself. Fred even considers lying, You bet I have a tank; love it! He could rush across town and buy one from a competitor right now. But

Marci's already switched to extolling her own thirty-five-gallon saltwater aquarium. Colored lights, real coral, glow-in-the-dark tropical plastic plants, Burbling Skull and Treasure Hunt with Greek Urn, the works. "You should really see it sometime."

"When?" Burbling Skull.

"Slows your pulse too." Dig. "You know it."

"You know it," Memo repeats. "You know it."

"I need it," Fred says, ablush. Remember: She's asking *you* out.

"Would you . . . ?" Yes. As he settles into the idea, Fred likes it more and more, and leans back to let the tanks work on him. "What I'm trying to say is . . ." Let her finish. He's never been propositioned before. It's excruciating. ". . . ask, I mean, is maybe if some weekend . . ." You can do it, you can—"Do you think you might do . . ." Choke it up, beautiful. "When you're not busy or anything . . ." He really should rescue her, but— "If you are, I totally understand . . ." This is more fun than watching a kid trying to wriggle his way out of a haircut. "It's just I figured you being around and—well . . ." Every fidget and squint makes his ego do another cartwheel. "I figured, like some Saturday . . ." Today! Now! Tonight! He'd gladly forfeit Sam's bachelor party. It'd make Oscar happy to boot. *C'mon.* "I might as well come right out and ask . . . right?" Marci starts to tuck, untuck, tuck her T-shirt.

"Righto." Fred's already setting the scene. She'll have her hair down and eyebrows up. Dinner for two by aquarium light. And afterward—

"This is the thing, OK."

This *is* the thing. "OK."

"The tank's really heavy. I know it's presumptuous of me. I go through this every time it needs cleaning; I know. But you can't imagine what a drag it is." What is she saying? "It's terrible of me to ask you, I know. It's a humongous favor when we're practically strangers and . . . but . . ." Each added word like a fresh injection. Chump.

And the zoo responds. Squawking: Back up! Back up! We do too know each other. Barking: Manual labor!? Me? Do I look like one of those construction dudes out there? Shrieking: But I wanted to go swimming in your hair. Purring: Poor, poor Fred.

Animals are in such a constant state of sensual thrill . . . and fear, it's weird. Fred stares down at those damn rabbits, humping the day away.

"Course, usually Oscar does it with me, but he's like leaving tomorrow."

"Yeah," says Fred. "No prob." I'd love to get a hernia lifting your thirty-five gallons of salt water. So Oscar "usually does it" with her, is that it? Animals want whatever toy's not theirs. Oscar's already blazed this trail. For almost sure. "That is unless I go with him . . . I might be." This part just pops out on its own.

"I'll pay you, naturally." Getting worse. And the smell in here—god, it's suffocating. How can anybody work in here? Even Chesty's isn't this bad. "I *expect* to pay you."

Got the message, snakehead. "Gotta go now."

"I'll call and we'll . . ."

Vacuum gravel together; swell.

"GET UP, woman! Rise!" Hersh shouts, much as Oscar imagines the faith healer will, as he tugs on Mary's delicate nightgown sleeve. Bawling, Hersh looks the ghastly same as always—borscht complexion and like a man smeared, no clear outlines left. There is no way for Oscar to get through to Hersh short of luring him out of the room with the bottle.

"Why were you shouting at her?" Oscar's shouting at Hersh. Walking backward down the stairs with his great-uncle stumbling toward him (the bottle), Oscar feels as if *he's* the bombed, helpless one. "Tell me."

But no words are forthcoming until the bottle's safely his and drained a good inch and a half, and then it's Flutidub or Shlubeebib or maybe still no words, just the sound of the old man's butt hitting the kitchen floor.

"Eeee," Oscar says, afraid, annoyed. Hersh eyes the black-

and-white-checked linoleum as if *it* attacked *him*. "Are you hurt?" Oscar asks, guilty for being annoyed, ashamed for being afraid, horrified in general. He pictures Mary's eyes, which can no longer move from side to side only vertically now. Up to God or down to Hersh. Quite a contrast. "And what's wrong with our furniture?" Oscar slides the *Sidehill Tattler* off the nearest chair and pats the seat. "Do me a favor, sit and drink out of a glass like a—" Shit! Oscar sounds to himself exactly like Charlotte. Not the first time.

The old man reaches forward—an exertion for a body so bloated and wet with whiskey-reeking sweat—to pick up the newspaper. But the white-haired knuckles slide right by, in favor of a square of floor whose edge is beginning to curl. The tips of Hersh's fingers, hesitant, test the linoleum, then flinch back, then test it again, as solemn and tense as an expert bomb defuser, braced for that expected but unpredictable blast.

"Wood!" Hersh erupts. Eureka. "Loook. Wood!" Monosyllabic, but speaking at least. The two men regard the discovery for a few moments in silence while they visualize—or at least Oscar does—the new kitchen floor. Planks of thick oak(?), stripped, sanded, waxed, and buffed to splendiferous luminescence.

"Why *did* you yell at her?" Oscar asks again, and watches Hersh's face labor. Nope. Close, though, very nearly. "Will you eat chicken?" That gets a sort of response. Throat click. "I'll take that for a yes." So inspired, Oscar even consults a cookbook index—*The Rapture of Eating*—under Chicken. "Would Mr. Hersh Israel Arm prefer his chicken livers with beef, tongue, or bacon appetizers? Just raise your hand or hold up a finger for whatever strikes your fancy. Chicken en casserole? No? Tetrazzini or cacciatore? Chicken corn balls? Hawaiian, lemon, cheddar chicken? How about with yoghurt—spelled yog-*hurt*."

But Hersh isn't listening. He's ripping up the whole damn floor.

"THE AVERAGE Japanese worker takes fifteen minutes for lunch," Sandrine tells Charlotte by way of ratting on Fred, who's late. "But your son's coffee break alone ran an hour and—"

"Heard!" Mom yells. Sandrine and Fred follow her across the room toward Mr. Coffee. They both gasp when Charlotte falters, sigh when she automatically rights herself again—a graceful three-part diagonal sashay movement. "OK."

Fred's first thought: Mary's finally died. But no, if that were the case, Mom wouldn't be here. Mary's still alive; that's what's wrung her out. At wits' end trying to get Hersh to sign the consent for Mary to be taken to a hospital. She is dying in their house, and she's not even related.

None of the rubber grandmoms or employees (not even Sandrine) know about Mary's stroke, though they would all (especially Sandrine) relish hearing every gruesome detail. How Mary drools and sweats, and needs a bedpan, and hardly ever blinks anymore, for instance.

"Frankly, Charlotte," Sandrine drones on, "I don't think it's OK. Wanda Crantz is a steady customer. *Was*, I mean, before Fred stood her up. This is—"

But Mom is no longer listening. Fred'd be relieved if she were. He'd prefer getting docked pay, even slapped, to her current expression—no expression. As if she just backed up over kittens but the ordeal hasn't sunk in yet.

"Far be it for me to say how you should run your beauty parlor," Sandrine rattles on.

"Why don't you take lunch yourself now, Drine." Mom cuts her off. "Lunchtime," she emphasizes by gazing toward the door. And "Get me tea, Fred. No, stay here. Talk to me. I must look a wreck." Even Sandrine can detect the high anxiety level when Mom begins to search her purse for a hand mirror. *Here*, in Mirror City. Not to mention asking for tea while drinking coffee.

"Where're my tampons?" Sandrine whines. She's not giving up so fast. Fred throws the box at her.

"You look fine, Ma," Fred tries. Her hair is lopsided, half puffed, but any hairstyle can look on purpose in this place and/or if you're able to carry it off. Which she can. Also, her sweater's inside out, but that's nothing a smock can't hide.

"Talk," Mom commands.

"What is it?"

"That air conditioner's leaking again."

"What is it, Ma?"

"I've had it."

"What?"

"Reasoning with drunks; it's ludicrous." Maybe she will yell at Fred after all. He and Oscar have been buying the bottles for Hersh. "Do I need this? In my house when people have strokes, they see a doctor. That's the way I was brought up. No evangelist people traipsing through my house. To think . . . What am I supposed to say to the Friedans and the Gershoffs?" Next-door neighbors, either side.

"Why do you have to tell the Friedans and the Gershoffs any—"

"There's a limit, Fred," Mom says that word, "limit," like "death," and starts to sob but real quietly and without moving too much. The neighbors. Her problems are not to be *news* for her clientele to chew on.

"Honey-lemon cough drop?" Fred offers moronically, watching his mother weep and holding out the box, helpless. Exactly how he and Oscar felt when they started buying Hersh the liquor. A hug? Fred tries that next but is shooed away.

"I start to think the craziest things. Maybe Jesus can hear her, only not in my house, a Jewish house. Maybe we could get the police to physically force her to go to the hospital? Isn't there some kinda law? Or get a doctor to dress up as . . . I just don't need this. Then, on my way over here, right on Junction, what do I see but the most beautiful boy, Osc—"

"Fred."

"Like a cherub, this kid. He has purple flowers under his

arm and a shopping bag *full*, bursting with gifts, and he's whistling, with his hair parted all neat and clean and good-smelling, just combed, ya know?"

"I know," Fred says, not really knowing and not liking the way Mom clutches her sweater, at the heart. Despite all her efforts toward discretion, she and Fred may as well have a spotlight on them. Every eye in the place is fastened on Charlotte's throbbing head vein.

But at least she's got the brassy coif figured out (pushed into place) now, got the smock on now, applying lipstick. "You don't need to tell me, I look homely as a mud fence. Run and get me a Lotto?"

"You don't look anything like a mud fence." Not that Fred's ever seen one. In Queens? "You have as much chance of winning Lotto if you play or if you don't."

"Let's not split hairs, dear."

THE PARKING-SPACE KID makes a big fuss about how Claire must be contaminated if she swam in that guck. "Put the money on the ground," he tells her. "I gotta go get my rubber gloves."

"He's evil," Louette says, already in the car.

"He's impressed," the lifeguard says, holding open the door for Claire. "I'm telling you."

That he's lost is what only Claire comprehends. The kid's mom is d-e-a-d. He's lonely.

"Well," the lifeguard says, "bon jour." He blushes wildly as he distributes a quick, slobbery kiss on each of Claire's cheeks and informs the kid, "That's European."

"That's AIDS."

"Jesus," says Louette. "Let's get gone."

"Now you're contaminated too," the kid continues.

"Yes," Claire says. "Thanks." There's that word again. Only marginally better than "Sorry." It seems too late to ask the lifeguard's name and too mean not to.

"Wouldya get in?" Louette says, starting to back out. Claire complies. And then, "All set?" Louette drives off as if she's late to meet someone she's mad at.

SAM. Sitting on his parents' front stoop with American cheese on white bread, a can of Budweiser, comic new crew cut. "This is a setup," Claire says.

"No," Louette swears.

Nancy's gone insane. A whimpering blur of fur bounding up, down, up, down, up, down the brick stairs, then back and forth, back and forth across Sam, up, down, up, down, up the flagstone. This is definitely a setup. Upsetting.

"No." Louette crosses her heart. "I just thought we'd drop by." Why? Why wouldn't she ask Claire whether it was all right?

Because it's not all right. Claire's shocked by how not all right it is. The minute she's out of the car she feels an urge to kick Sam. And Nancy. Tell him his haircut is stupid-looking. Kick Nancy again and run.

Sam yodels. "Mmm. Bathing beauties a-callin." He hugs Claire's knees, so she has no choice but to crouch. Claire holds the lucky half-dollar in her dress pocket—not about to lose it now, after she mouth-held it, swimming all that way back from the sandbar. Sam slides a piece of her fungus-crusted hair behind her ear, but it pops back out. "Salty." He retucks. It pops. Tuck, pop, tuck.

"Hey, you hit Chester's today too?" Louette asks.

"I don't go to any beauty parlor," Sam says. "This is my own work." Twisting about to model his head. It looks like a Stooge cut if Moe used mousse. "Cut it with my own two hands."

"And a carrot peeler?" Louette asks, vying with the planes and poodle to be heard.

"It's the football coach look," Sam says. "No combing, no washing. I just wipe it off with a rag."

"Sexy," Louette hoots.

"You gotta relieve yourself, Lou?" Sam points toward the open door. Really subtle.

"Oh, yeah," Louette says. "Guess I do . . . after the car trip . . . as long as it's all right."

No, it is not all right!

Sam moves in for Claire's elbow, one of his favorite courtship activities. He palms it. His face gets the look it had the night he proposed—in her pool, naked—and he reaches under her dress to snap at the blue bathing suit. "Surprises," he whispers. Surprises again. "Surprises I got like you won't believe."

"I won't?"

Then Sam kisses her, which *is* sort of nice until Claire notices the segment of cheese lodged in his teeth. "Surprises, surprises." He sticks his pointer finger through the rip in her dress armpit and wiggles it so she has to giggle despite a creeping repulsion she feels and the ferocious cold of his class ring.

"Well, I have a surprise for you too," Claire surprises herself by saying, between painful breaths. "I'm not marrying you." Just like that, she's decided. Love him not.

But since Claire's giggling, Sam thinks it's a joke. It's not. She shoves him off to prove it. He insists it's a joke. No; sorry (that word again). It is no joke. Still, Sam persists. It's just *got* to be. But he's noticeably wilting now. He of the famous posture. We'll talk.

Go ahead, she says. Talk.

Tomorrow.

Tomorrow?

You'll see.

I did.

The fluffy toy poodle's head twists toward whoever the speaker is, as if actually following the exchange and its meaning. Love him not.

Sam hugs Claire again, as if she were a stuffed animal, which is how a hug should be. One of the things she liked about him. Sam knows how to give a proper hug. A good hard hug without getting smothery. Next, he insists Claire take a bite of his sandwich and waltzes her around some on the stoop; fun. And though he calls her Sweets and does too much "I love you"ing, he does it humming, in *his* voice—the other thing she liked about him. For a moment it even occurs to Claire to wonder: Maybe I'm rash, chicken, too picky, maybe just cranky from the hot wax, hot sun, hot car, or—

"Stop. I'm serious." Claire ducks out of the embrace, backs down the steps, then, "I'm sorry." That word again. "I'm not going to marry you."

"Who else, then?" A joke? Sam takes out a portable aspirin tin. "Surprise!"

Cheese in his teeth. Claire's glad she hasn't fucked him. She hates surprises. Fucking is exactly what it would have been.

An engagement ring! White gold, square-stoned, on a tiny bed of cotton. Sam holds the open tin out to her like a discovery.

"Uh uh. No way," Claire stammers.

On cue, Peaches dances out the screen door. Industrial-size yellow kimono. Polaroid cocked, aimed. Chopsticks sticking in her hair, which is peach color, of course, but different today, curlier or taller. Around her neck squirm massive tangles of sun-zinging glass beads.

"Now, don't pose, kids. I want candid. . . . A little more visible this time with the ring, Sam. . . . A little more up, a little more . . . perfecto. *Ooh!* I got Nancy in too. Now one more . . ."

"Pardon me," Claire says, hiding her hands in her armpits. "But I—"

"Don't be shy, dear. Let Sam slip it—"

"I can't." But she already has.

"Adorable!" Peaches exclaims. "That's it, hold that, smile!"

The ring is too big, besides. The square diamond pebble flashes threateningly. "Fabulous," Peaches bellows. "Now wouldya mind if I steal her for a sec, Sam? I wanna show her my roses. Just us girls. Follow me, hon." Peaches joggles down the steps and back around toward the yard.

Claire takes the ring off and hands it back. But Sam won't take it. Claire thinks of the kid who made her put the money on the ground and does the same with the ring, careful to put it near where Sam's hand is resting on the stoop, so it won't get stepped on or thrown out with the beer can and sandwich crusts or gagged on by Nancy. Then Claire heads for the roses, her last duty, she figures, to explain to Peaches—

"Surprise!" A bridal shower. Claire's going to black out. She can feel each individual hair on her body, yet she's unable to focus on the square of lawn before her, gleaming with ribbons, women, food. And then everything gets brown around the borders, closing in on itself until Claire's sure she has fainted. No, she's being enveloped in Peaches' huge kimono, which does, strangely enough, smell of roses.

Sam? Sam is gone. "Of course," says a woman introduced as "your soon-to-be Aunt Paisy." "No men allowed." She winks lasciviously before turning her head back to Peaches. "She's cute, the goy."

"Now be nice," cautions a third lady, who's wearing a Mylar sweatsuit and high-heeled strapless sandals.

"Paisy? Nice?" Peaches howls. "If I live to be a hundred . . ."

Look sharp, Claire tells herself. The sensible thing to do here is to white-lie your way through and somehow out. How? Louette'll know. She'll forgive Louette if she knows. Where the hell is Louette? Claire scans the scattered and mismatched patio furniture. Dozens of people, but no one Claire knows or even recognizes—except a couple of ladies from the beauty parlor, who were, Claire realizes now, grooming for this, for her.

"Here she is? Well, lemme look. . . ." Claire's hand is seized, clasped, firmly pumped, by "Sam's sister Lynn," who drove all the way up—"and I *never* come home, believe me"—from Maryland, where she's just been promoted from bank teller to customer service representative. Lynn shares Sam's unabashed and authoritative baritone. ". . . yours truly, privy to the personal codes of every account in the branch!" And his hairy wrists. Lynn hands Claire a Bloody Mary. Just as Sam would. You drink what he drinks. Now that Claire has broken it off, she's surprised at how loathsome she finds him, her, them. "At first all that money was kinda dizzying, but after a while, believe me, it sinks in it's not yours. Ya lose interest." Lynn looks like him too. Sam with earrings.

CHICKEN SALAD, egg salad; tuna, macaroni, carrot, cabbage, beet salad; potato salad, potato pancakes, potato knishes; cherry blintzes, kasha varnishkes. Stuffed cabbage, stuffed mushrooms, stuffed derma. Herring, trout, white and gefilte fish, smoked salmon, smoked sable, smoked chicken, a twenty-pound turkey plus hot and cold cold cuts—tongue and pastrami, corned beef and roast beef. Not to mention the bread selection, cheese selection, beverages, and condiments. It thoroughly astounds Claire, distracts Claire, puts Claire's engagement party fare to shame.

"Escargots and Chinese food, god," Claire confides to her new friend, Cousin Sadie. The sun, lowering just behind Sadie's fine white orb of hair, turns it spun-sugarish. The very hairdo Grandma Lillian sported before going blue. How could Claire even have gone through with that party without having decided about Sam? And how can she be standing, chatting, eating, at this party, when she has?

"Champagne," Sadie adds. *Claire didn't even know Sadie was at her engagement party.* "I haven't giggled like that in a dog's age."

But Sadie is no giggler. Her brand of laugh is more a chuckle or a chortle or a chuh chuh. The enormous breasts jostle horizontally. How do you even begin to explain to such a nice person that Sam doesn't cut it, everything's called off, sorry to eat and run, but it's—

Delicious. Here in their element—green late-afternoon backyardness—the women radiate might, mirth, a soft, inexhaustible verve that knows only giving and more giving, and . . . they are accepting Claire into the fold, just as she wished for in the beauty parlor, earlier. Offering "mazel tov"s, roses, to wash, sew, iron, replace the ripped sundress. And watching her eat, rooting her on to eat, eat, the poor motherless shiksa; she hasn't even tried the salmon mold yet!

Sadie touches Claire's neck with two ultra-cool powdery fingertips, lovingly says, "Wallow, rest, have fun, savor this." An infinite, ominous pile of gifts waits in the near distance. "Listen to Sadie: don't waste your time worrying over what's to come tomorrow or in a year. You can't be sure what'll happen in the next five minutes."

Yes, Claire must do something *now,* in the next five minutes, but how? They're already steering her toward the lavender-ribboned chair next to Gift Mountain. "Who gave me that?" A plain, solid, low-to-the-ground wooden chair. To Claire, who grew up in a house full of dark, heavy, claw-footed, gold-leafed furniture, a simple chair like that, "It's magnificent."

"That old thing?" Sadie slaps her knee, "That's no gift . . . Paisy! Get her! *She* thought your old shower chair was for her, a present. Magnificent, yet." This causes Paisy to sputter up some salmon mold and shake her head and gurgle and tell Peaches, who roars in turn and tells it to a tall lady, who only grins but leans in to inform a fifth person, and so on. And so, dying privately, Claire has no thought but to flag down Lynn and request another Bloody Mary. Fraud. She is a fraud. She has a totally irrational yearning for that chair.

"Now I wanna hear everything about the cap and gown business," the tall lady swoops down to demand. She has a lipstick-covered birthmark on her mouth that Claire at first mistakes for a lingering scrap of lox. "I have three boys myself, which means—oh, I don't know—counting junior high . . ." Claire tries not to connect her own mother with food-on-the-face or meat-stuck-between-the-teeth people, but it's difficult. ". . . nine graduations, is it? Marvin, the oldest, won honors for his accordion play—"

"May I tear Claire away for one sec?" Louette to the rescue. It almost excuses the fact that she's showered, changed, fresh as the buffet, while Claire is still dirty, waxed, salted, fishy-fingered, and potentially fungus-contaminated.

"Thank you, thank you." This time it's warranted.

"For what? I haven't given it to you yet." Louette hands Claire a Barbie doll. Tropical Barbie in a wedding gown. "I had Ken in a tux, but Peaches said no men allowed."

"I'm not marrying Sam." The words work like a salve.

"You're not serious. You're just nervous, right? I've seen this look."

"I'm serious *and* nervous. I'm—"

"Ocher. Same shade you turned at your engagement party."

"It's off, Louette. I already told him."

"Oh. Yeah?"

"Yeah. *Oh.*"

"And *they* don't know?"

Claire moans.

And then Lynn's upon her with the drink she doesn't want anymore as soon as she sees what Lynn has—a bowl of chocolate ice cream. Close up, Lynn even has scars like Sam. Not as many, but still, if Claire didn't know better—and she doesn't—she might think the two of them were battered children or extremely clumsy people or . . . She is not going to start feeling sorry for Sam now.

"This one," Lynn says, more than happy to expound on any subject, but especially, it turns out, her scar history. "See? It makes a sort of cleft in my chin?" She's proud of them. "I was ridin my bike through the cemetery when I was like ten, singin 'Can't Buy Me Love,' when my bike just flipped and my head went smashin right into a headstone. For real." She's gloating. "Head into headstone." She's anywhere between twenty and forty. Married too.

Claire glances pleadingly at Louette. But just then Peaches rushes up to snap "the young people chatting" with her Polaroid. "Did you all get enough to eat?" She photographs the ravaged food next.

"Actually," Claire tells Lynn, "I was wondering where you got the ice cream."

"This?" Lynn's face lights up. "Have some, please!" She slides a spoonful into Claire's mouth before Claire can say—

Ohmygod. This isn't ice cream. Ohmygod.

"Should we have some music?" wonders Peaches. "I could put in the new Bouncetones demo."

Peaches is ignoring the fact that not only has Claire—"What *was* that?" Brown mushiness—gagged up on the lawn but her eyes are streaming tears.

"I just couldn't resist," Lynn explains, hysterical.

"Is it too warm out here?" Peaches continues.

"What, Ma, you're gonna adjust the temperature for us?"

"Lynn!" Peaches puffs. "I'm warning you. . . ." Wringing her kimono sleeves, flapping a little breeze up at Claire, not yet fully recuperated from the—

"Chopped liver," Lynn confesses, without any apologies other than "An acquired taste, what can I say?" She retreats into the house.

"That little . . ." Peaches shakes her new perm.

Bitch, Claire would like to supply. What did she do to deserve such a rotten trick? Posed with the ring, that's what. Promoted this lie.

"It's so warm. Isn't it warm?" Peaches rubs at her forehead. The skin there looks red, irritated. She seems to be developing a rash of some kind, scolding. "Claire? Now, I still haven't seen you try Paisy's mold." She wags her finger toward a milk-of-magnesia-colored, starfish-shaped blob.

"I'm full, thanks."

"We wouldn't want to insult Paisy, now, would—"

Yeah, yeah. "All right."

"Thatagirl . . . Mmm. Delish, isn't it? I might have a smidgen more myself."

"Excuse me, may I use the phone?" Claire asks. Last resort. Call Dad. No, call Grandma Lillian. She's one person who'll be glad to hear the news.

"Sam isn't home, if that's what you're scheming. You know the rules. No men allowed."

"But—"

"You like our little chair? Well, go rest your tuchus in it and start on the gifts. There's work ahead." Peaches scratches the inside of her elbow, which is bright pink and welting. Forehead, neck, inner arm, all really blooming now. She unslings her beads. "Go on."

"But there's something I have to tell—"

"Shhh. Believe me, the sweet nothings can wait. Give us old ladies a treat for once." Peaches shoves her two pointer fingers between her teeth and whistles. "Quiet!" Sam and Lynn did not inherit *her* voice. "Gift time!"

This announcement portends the arrival of glamorous Constance Dufour in the last of the sunlight, in long feather boa, breathless, apologetic. She had no time to wrap her offerings— Butterfly, the Walkman of Vibrators, and a Penis Pez dispenser. She has no time to stay.

OSCAR HEARS MOM at the side door. "Something's burning." Followed by the screen slamming and her high heels, ping-pong, ping-pong. Then Fred sneezes, ehhh-neghhh. Then pizza smell, heralding Dad with a pie. "Everything on it."

"None a that," Oscar says as they enter the kitchen, one by one. "Surprise. I'm making gourmet tonight."

"Not another carcass from the PetMart."

"One more joke, Lester, and I'll . . ." Mom threatens. "It's like an addiction with him." She hugs Oscar and takes off her sweater at the same time. Underneath, she still has on her pink work smock. "Hersh?" Mom asks sadly. "Wouldn't you rather sit on a chair?"

Fred crouches. "He can't tear up the floor from a chair."

"There's wood under there." Oscar points at the shredded linoleum. "Look."

But they all look at him.

"Something's burning," Mom repeats. As if she hadn't heard Oscar say he was cooking. Dad still hangs on to the pizza, in case he doesn't like the alternative.

"Yoghurt chicken," Oscar says brightly. "Mmm."

They all look at the floor.

"Oak." Hersh has spoken. Fred massages the thick, bent neck

till the old man grunts and uses his Scotch to brush the hand away.

They all look at the bottle.

"DEAL. I'LL GO." Oscar finally agrees to attend Sam's bachelor party, but not until they've sat down to eat. The twins are rocking and chewing in their usual unison, on a roll now. "And you'll come to Mexico."

"No," Fred says.

"Good," Mom says. She's already wrecked the collective appetite by breaking down and calling them all murderers. Hersh laughs. Copycats and murderers. She keeps insisting they *do something* about *her*. It's urgent. About the *situation*.

Dad suggests a toast. "To Oscar's research trip." But Mom refuses, pissed.

"To Sam's marriage?" Oscar refuses.

"To Fred, my new associate stylist." Fred refuses.

"To the moon, then; that's neutral. See that circle of red haze?" Hersh refuses.

"To yoghurt chicken." Everyone emphatically refuses.

THE FIRST wind-up cooking timer was easy. Boy do I need this! You have no idea how many dinners I would have burned. Claire imagines herself slaving over a stove for Sam. Ha! Also easy were the tablecloths, aprons, wicker paper-plate holders, and egg cups Claire unwrapped as if planning to use them all. The second timer, more of the same. It'll come in handy. Cooking two things at once—it's tricky. Thanks, really thanks. On the third, it got rough. Well . . . this is great, a backup! But upon opening the fourth, Claire simply loses it.

In the fading light, the women become purplish talking shapes with teeth and jewelry. "Aw, now." "Come now, don't cry." Touched. "Such feeling!" Lucky Sam. She should only use them in good health. What's so difficult? Everything's returnable, exchangeable, warrantied and guaranteed, god bless. Trade in a timer for a meat thermometer, but enjoy!

"A steamer/poacher/waffle iron/self-cleaning omelet pan!" Louette says, lying on her stomach, fisting up grass. She's the one who wants to get married; that's obvious. She hasn't had it that easy either, having to fend off all manner of question, from the personal: "Do you work out?" to the professional: "What does one do for bleeding gums?" to the plain old idiotic: "Are you husband-hunting too?"

"It's perfect," Claire hears herself say, zombied. But forging on. "I think it also makes cappuccino." This gets a few laughs. A ghost arm pushes a slice of lemon ring cake across the grass toward Claire's chair.

Of course everything will be sent back—all seven timers, the duck place mats and the three-speed juicer, the Mets coasters, His and Hers hand towels, the nightgown/peignoir set Peaches wore on her wedding night! and Lynn on hers! Good riddance! Apologies! Best wishes! No offense! Ah, your gift had the biggest bow and much more tape than the others, but . . . Thank you for the lovely cheese board; however . . . She'll return all of it through the mail, cowardly. She foot-pushes the cake away. It spooked her, just appearing like that, plateless and phosphorescent.

"It's ready to occur," Deja Vu Gooch proclaims. There's just one or two minor bachelor-partyish details to attend to yet, like "setting up the dog."

"Setting up the dog?" It sounds to Fred like one of their old Dinner and the Talk songs. Those burnt-out original tunes they used to only get away with playing at three A.M. when everyone was too drunk to notice. Such gems as "Combustible Rabbis" and "Tasty Good Girl."

"For the cake," D.J. explains, fake-straightening the bow tie silk-screened on the shirt he wears above swimming trunks. The backyard—Gooch's parents'—has a Doughboy overground tin-can pool that virtually ensured his childhood popularity.

"Cake?" Fred asks, and Gooch rushes off as if remembering he left the thing burning in the oven. From the other direction, Nancy bounds toward Fred, wearing a negligee—red with lacy black trim, wet dribble spots.

"What a scream, huh?" screams Gooch. The cake he's wheeling up on a dolly could never fit in any ordinary oven. "Grab her back legs, 'kay?"

Normally Fred would protest. Shoving a poodle inside a cake is inhumane. But this is just noodlehead Nancy, who looks like some little thing you'd pick off your sweater, who's been yapping forever, the sound of one of those plastic squeeze toys, and who's teeth, fairly major utensils, now pierce through the skin of Fred's hand. Nancy never did like Fred, because she never did like Oscar. Because Oscar never did like her. Mutual.

"Does Sam know about this?" Nancy thuds into the cake's inner cardboard bin, then lies there licking the air, getting her wind back.

"Yes and no," says Gooch. In other words, Sam suggested it but wants everyone to think he's surprised. Otherwise how did his dog get here?

"Yes or no."

"Sort of both."

Eliot Horowitz is less mysterious. He struts right up and states his position as foreman of the blow-job raffle. Five bucks, ten for twins. Eliot wears no shirt or shoes, just paisley suspenders to hold up stained old-man trousers and highlight his concave scrawniness.

"Oscar's not coming," Fred says, trying to sound matter-of-fact.

But Eliot won't hear of it. "Radio him on that ESP of yours, Fredhead. Tell him Eliot's got this feeling he's a winner to—"

"Can't you be useful?" D.J. snaps. "Blow up some dolls or pump the keg, something."

"I am trying to collect from the Arm man here, if ya don't mind!" Horowitz winces. His peptic ulcer is probably gurgling over again. "Ya into it or not?"

Fred will not admit to being into raffles for blow jobs or

blowing up dolls, whatever that means, but he gives Eliot the five bucks anyhow. Expecting that he'd be hit up for a donation, he weaseled an advance paycheck out of Dad.

"Jesus, Fred," Gooch says, as finicky as befits his title as new and improved best man. "Look. You're leanin on the fuckin cake. The whole side there's smushed."

"HEY, OSC!"

Fred turns, ready to play along, but there's "Tommy Eako!"—with a receding hairline, and what's left waxening. Fred hasn't seen this guy in two, maybe three years. Fellow street performer in the old days. Tommy was *the best*. Eventually went off to Barnum and Bailey Clown College, *the best* a street performer can hope for. Fred was rejected.

"Where's Fred?" Tommy asks. Fred is dejected. Eako, of all people, doesn't recognize him?

"Well," Tommy says. He's still got those same really red eyelids and the slight lisp that made his act unintentionally funny. "How you doin?"

"Fine. Fantastic."

"So where *is* Fred?"

"Oh, Mexico." Now Fred's a little offended for Oscar. Why isn't Tommy at all interested in Oscar?

"Mexico? What the hell for?"

"A divorce."

"Really?"

"No."

Tommy doesn't pursue it. He tells "Oscar" how he's been working summers on Fisherman's Wharf in "San Fran, man. You should get Fred to check it out." Hundred-dollar days. Hundred-fifty.

"What?" says Fred just like that, blah. At the moment, he hasn't got ten dollars in his bank account.

Tommy says, "Hey. You *are* Fred." He slaps Fred's thigh. The gesture smacks of rehearsed goofiness.

"Me?"

"Conned a con man, didya?" Among Tommy's most lucrative schemes, Fred remembers, was printing up official-looking deeds for moon real estate. Twenty bucks an acre. "How about that?"

"What makes you so sure?" Fred asks, not that curious.

"Your beer-drinking style. Right-handed. De-cidedly. And that missing fingertip."

Fred is looking down at his right hand as if expecting something new (besides Nancy's dental imprint) to be there, when Sam's car screeches up into the driveway. He thinks he's coming for a band meeting, Eliot says. Tell me another. What band?

D.J. wants everyone to hide. Where? I don't know. Bushes. Pool. In the house. Just hurry and vanish. Tommy laughs. C'mon, hurry.

"What is this, my Sweet Sixteen?" Sam says, when they all pop out. He doesn't even pretend to be surprised. He looks stoned, actually, and the box of DoNuTs! donuts under his arm confirms it. Glazed donuts are his fav munching food. Then there's cottonmouth which sends him hurrying right away toward the keg.

But a college buddy of his intercepts and says, "Where you think you're going, bro?" There are about ten of them. Binghamton frat dudes. All rude and too tall for their personalities. "Not so fast," one says to Sam, snapping *handcuffs* on him. "To the chains of matrimony! Yeh!" A cue for the others to chant, "Yeh! Yeh!" and break into fraternity babble—"We belong, we belong, sing along"—even Sam, smiling like a reborn imbecile as they tackle, strip, re-dress him in "Home of the Whopper" bikini briefs. Please.

Gooch is irate. Usurpers! This was not in the plans. *He's* the best man. *He's* in charge. But maybe D.J.'s just jealous and wishes he had planned this, because after a while he joins in too, screaming "Congratulations" and pouring whiskey all around, at the frat men and in Sam's newly chopped hair.

"A do to scare Godzilla." Tommy beats Fred to it.

It looks a lot like the one Fred did on his first try at Chester's last week—such a disaster that Dad offered to pay the customer.

Meanwhile, Eliot Horowitz, not at all fazed, seizes DoNuTs! donuts to snack on while watching the action. "Powdered donuts," he offers Fred. "A poor man's cocaine."

AND JUST WHEN Claire thought it was all over, she's let in on a tradition. Sandrine's been writing down Claire's response to each gift, and now she means to read them back aloud, a spoof on what Claire will be saying on her wedding night. " 'You don't know how much I need this' " and " 'Oooh, I know just where to put that.' " Sandrine's deep voice is raspy if not sexy. Cheap thrills for sweet old ladies. A watered-down geriatric Chippendales substitute. Lite smut.

The women holler, dig their heels into the lawn, squeal, lean back in their crunching lawn chairs, pant-yelp, and swat enormous jiggling thighs in spasms of hilarity. Peaches even whistles at intervals. Two fingers jammed between her lips; raunchy.

" 'How do you turn it on?' " reads Sandrine, throat-growling.

"How do you turn it off?" asks Lynn, getting laughs.

Meantime, Peaches aims and shoots and aims and shoots that Polaroid, determined to preserve in pictures Claire's most squirm-filled moments.

"This how we launch you into the world," Sadie says softly. "Sorry."

Peaches sings, "Yoo-hoo, Claire." Someone should really warn her about the worsening forehead rash. But Claire can't. Red, crusting blisters, horrific now, even in the hazy moonlight, oozing. "Say cheesy." The camera flash sticks on Claire's retina—a sensation like biting on tinfoil.

" 'Wow,' " reads Sandrine. 'It's, so-o-o *big!* Mmm mm!' "

OSCAR VOLUNTEERS to feed Mary this time. Broth. The room smells of urine—should he check her? It's terrible. Worse than terrible because though caved in, frightfully paralyzed, Mary is luminously pale, more regal than ever. A queen, propped up in a yellowing antique lace nightgown. The broth dribbles down her chin. Downstairs, a perpetual Mom and Dad sound track.

"... I'm full of it absolutely to the eyeballs, Charlotte...."

Mary's eyeballs move up and down, blink, up and down. I don't know this person, Oscar thinks, Fred had that right, but Hersh does. No matter how loaded he is, Hersh arranges Mary's hair every day in a swirl, dip, tuck, the way she likes it.

"You want it on your head, Lester? Fine. Let it be on *your* head."

Don't listen to them, Oscar tells Mary, in case she can hear. He's aware of the way the drapes move, like a young girl's skirt, and it reminds him of an awful story Marci told him today—a cat who hanged himself on a curtain pull. This he relates to Mary too, for something else to say. It should be added to the poster of HOUSEHOLD PET DANGERS Oscar once made for the store: heads getting stuck in jars, toilet bowl drownings, chocolate, and loose change. Not exactly cheery stuff but real.

Part of Mary's top lip is stuck on her teeth—should he fix it? Is she right now disintegrating in front of him? Should he be alarmed that she looks an awful lot like Curious George? Slight, slightening. As if Oscar could cover her with a tissue, so lost in the world, in the huge double bed that he and Fred once shared.

"Fred'll come with me to Mexico," Oscar finds himself asking Mary, "won't he?" He wants to shout at her when she doesn't answer. Wants to rock the bed when she won't answer again. Wants to shake her and shake her and scream, *Would you get up, just get up, would you?*

THERE'S A WAR ON between the guys who want to watch the Mets game (half the frat men, Sam, Eliot, and Tommy Eako) and the guys who want to watch the porno movies (Gooch, Sid, Eliot, and the other half of the frat men). Fred's torn.

D.J. says, "I dragged the stuff and rented the flick and set it up and . . ." In effect, It's my house; I'm in charge.

Sam says, "I'm the man of honor here." It's my party, and I'll cry if I wanna.

Eliot says, "I just don't understand why we can't all take turns."

No, not much has changed since the days of flaming marshmallow wars and spit fights. Instead of one-two-three shooting, they decide to flip a coin. Mets win. Instead of G.I. Joe, a Doughboy pool full of floating inflata-fuck Swedish teen dream dolls. Instead of seven minutes in heaven, it's marriage; that casual.

The cake starts barking. Fred imagines Sandrine popping out, but then realizes there's no way she could fit. "It's not dessert time yet," D.J. whispers hysterically. His carefully organized activity lineup does not accommodate such glitches as Sam, still handcuffed, hearing Nancy and strolling over to investigate.

Circling the cake, Sam seems truly perplexed. "Is that a dog in there?" Truly uncomfortable too. Sid has him freeze to have his snapshot taken lecherously licking at the frosting.

"Grin."

Fred wonders, vaguely, whether the thing's edible.

"I could swear that was Nancy's bark," Sam says.

Upon hearing her name, the poodle crashes up through the cardboard lid, attaching herself to Sam's wrist and thus getting whacked in the head with the handcuffs. Back she falls again, soundlessly, into the cake.

The whole thing takes maybe ten seconds, and in even less time there's a huddle around the mammoth dessert. Everyone peers down at the knocked-out poodle. She just lies there, all decked out in her luxuriant perfumed negligee, red bows in her hair.

"Nancy . . .," Sam wails, reaching out but inhibited by the handcuffs.

Gooch shrinks. "He's gonna fuckin kill me."

"Damn right I am. Who gave you permission to go puttin

Nancy inside a cake like some whore from Staten Island? She bit me! My own dog! Bit me! I'm fuckin bleedin here."

Which starts Eliot Horowitz screaming, "He's fuckin bleedin here. Whata we gonna do if she has rabies?"

Which gets Sam even more worked up. "Nancy doesn't have fuckin rabies, you dweeb. Now uncuff me before I bust ya head. What kinda party *is* this? I'm fuckin bleedin."

At which point the frat boy chorus gets in on the action with "Yeh yeh, what kinda fuckin party is this?" They refuse to produce keys for the handcuffs.

Horowitz insists, "It's not funny, you dweebs," which the frat boys don't like one bit, particularly from a sickly runt like Eliot. So they push him around a little until D.J. steps in and initiates a full-fledged brawl.

This is one aggressive tank.

IT TOOK forty-five minutes to leave, what with goodbyes and loading the car and more goodbyes and refusing the left-over cake, and a hundred unavoidable thank yous.

But Louette's the exhausted one. She lies on her crushed-velvet couch, reading *Romeo and Juliet,* with an ice pack on her head, every so often raising her chin to her drink (more ice, with tomato juice) or groaning about Oscar not calling for the seventh consecutive day. There is no point going on living, at least this weekend.

Louette reminds Claire of certain girls she knew in grade school who were allowed to wear makeup and spike heels. Kids of divorced parents mostly, at whose houses you could do any-thing, unsupervised, like eat ready-made bacon-onion dip, chips, and Coke for dinner in front of the TV; shave your legs; sneak looks at *Playboys* that Dad's hidden in hampers or un-derwear drawers, or hasn't hidden on coffee tables and in bathrooms; stay up all night setting fires in the backyard.

"How about we hock all this stuff and I go and get you an exterminator?" suggests Claire. The glacier of gifts sits center stage. An obstacle between Claire and the phone. She should call Dad, she has to call him, but she's worried about how he's going to take the news. He'll smooth his head and smooth his head and shake his head. "If your mother were alive . . ." He'll blame himself and retract whatever he said, right after having said it. Or insist on driving up now at three a.m. to "collect" her. Or, scariest scenario, drop the phone and have himself a heart attack.

"No wonder you were flirting with Malibu Ken," Louette says out of nowhere, her eyes still fastened to the paperback Shakespeare. "It's all clear to me now."

"The lifeguard?" Claire asks. "I felt sorry for him. He even asked if I'd be his pen pal. It could break—"

"It's cool. You don't have to get defensive."

"I just kept picturing him telling his mom all about these French stewardesses he met, while she makes him tomorrow's lunch, ya know."

"Don't be so naive, please. He'll tell his friends, not his mother, and he'll make most of it up." Louette's sunburn seems to have bloomed between the last time Claire looked and now. There's a jagged boundary where her bikini straps were apparently twisted. Louette, shutting the book with a sigh, pushes a thumb down on her calf to make a white circle swell on the skin there.

"Don't tell me you get tan too."

Too? Claire does—the way her mother also did—but says nothing. It occurs to her that Louette is jealous. But why? How? She doesn't know the half of it.

"I'm a virgin," Claire decides to announce. It isn't hard at all.

"Yeah." Yawning.

"Whatayamean yeah? You mean you . . . ? How do you . . . ?"

"Model that used nightgown and peignoir set for me, why not?" Sex is out; talking about it, in. But someone already told Louette. Sam, probably. Sam probably knew all along and told everybody all along.

"I'm sorry," Louette says, her turn this time. "I'm going to sleep a lousy person. It's not the first night." And softer, with the book to her lips, "Every time I read *Romeo and Juliet,* I keep hoping it's gonna end different."

"I BEEN ON the road twenny-fi years and part of it cruise stuff. When I was a young feller like you, that's all it was, cruises. . . . Back 'n' forth I been to Eur-*rope,* sevenny-fi trips. That's a lotta Dramamine."

Oscar doesn't have time to listen to Sid Lubin reminisce. To help Sid and company find Sam's handcuff key, supposedly lost in the grass during the scuffle. To even be here. But he's decided to make one last go at getting Fred to reconsider.

"You got some kinda eye problem?" Eliot Horowitz asks, pointing to Oscar's Ray Bans. It was ridiculous to think that he could remain incognito.

The party is loud and messy. There's cake strewn everywhere—in the pool, cake; on the poker table, cake.

"Don't eat it," warns Sid. "Frosting's got dog fur."

"What's wrong with Sam?" Not that Oscar cares, but the guy's leaning into the cake and bawling.

"Long time no friend." Tommy Eako! "Juggle some drinks with us, man. We thought you was already south a the border."

"I am. I mean, I can't stay long. How ya doin?"

Tommy's cue to start flapping . . . something about a Texan cowboy fire eater who had no teeth and thought that over time they'd been burned away but wasn't sure. "I tell ya that enlightening tale because . . ." Oscar waits. "Fred tipped me off your girl's in dental hygiene . . . Fascinating." He cracks up, blasted. Keech kee kee keech.

"Yeah." That's all Oscar can think to reply. Tommy's going nowhere, it's pretty clear; bleak. Tommy's too suspiciously enthusiastic about his life. The guy had his chance to get in the Barnum and Bailey Circus and blew it. So what's left? "Have you seen Fred?"

"Fred?" Oh ho. Kee kee keech. "He won the blow-job raffle! Quiche!"

"What?"

"He won the blow-job raffle! Quiche!"

"But gave it to Eliot," Fred himself says, suddenly appearing. He yanks at Oscar's sunglasses. "I get it. Smuggler profile."

Oscar glares. After that uncool remark, he is not at all sure that it's even safe to take Fred on this mission.

"Smuggling?" Tommy asks, *projecting*.

"No, no. Snuggling." Oscar saves himself. "With the girlfriend." Mustering a blush. Didn't even know he was capable.

"I don't get it."

"See," Fred says. "He doesn't get it. So chill out."

Oscar extricates himself, mumbling, "Beer . . . keg," and makes off in that general direction. But stopped en route by Sam's blubbering, truly dire, he takes one glance into the cake hollow and freaks.

"How could you people . . . Murderers!" The second accusation Fred's had in one night.

Watching his brother lift the motionless dog, Fred ponders the symmetry: I put Nancy in, he takes her out.

"You're an idiot," Oscar tells him. "I'm ashamed of your face."

"Oh?"

"We're taking her to the vet and going straight to the airport."

"We?"

"We can argue in the car."

"Is that an invitation?"

"Are you coming? Or not?"

Fred feels his face pulling. Yes. He guesses so, but then again . . . Oscar's gone.

A HALF MILE down Sidehill Avenue, Nancy stops breathing in the car. Screeching to the curb, Oscar pumps her chest, pinches her snout, angles her head up. Overwrought, he is actually sobbing now. He doesn't want responsibility for a dead poodle. The dog gets colder and colder.

Oscar can't cry over Mary. He can leave Mary to die and then break up over a negligeed poodle he's always hated. To top it off, this makes sense to him. And this makes him sick; he barely has time to get out of the car before puking up the yoghurt chicken. Walk. He starts walking, and walks around the block, carrying the dog, stopping every few paces to administer more CPR and breathing, walking, breathing. Respiration.

This is why I don't keep pets. They die. They eat, excrete, die, despite us. Or worse, *for* us.

Nancy's inert.

Oscar fast ducks into a pay phone for more emergency pet first aid, which luckily, he learned how to administer last year in a course at The New School. The neighborhood spies are no doubt at their windows, marking this down: Oscar Arm, half the twin set, son of Chester's owners, and manager of the PetMart, is giving mouth-to-mouth to Sam Lubin's poodle in a negligee in a phone booth in the middle of the night. Good heavens.

Pets don't gossip or rationalize their lives or get married, make money, smoke, Oscar has argued with many a pet lover. He has asked, Do you honestly believe a dog can tell the difference between rawhide fries and rawhide enchiladas?

Yes, they all say.

Because it's bad form to criticize pets. Pets are innocent. An example to us. An exalted us. Trust embodied. Friends. A life-affirming, non-fault-finding, spiritually enhancing Yes Yes Yes.

Nancy finally yaps to, licks her chops (she seems to like the cake taste), then quiets down, pooped. All right.

Oscar dials the Gooches' and waits out five rings, six rings, reading "Good girls go to heaven. Bad girls go everywhere else" scratched into the metal pay phone wall. Also, "Trust + Lust = True Love." He's about ready to hang up, when a girl answers— at a bachelor party?

She says, "What?"

"D.J. Gooch."

"No. Quiche."

"Give me D.J."

"Which one's he?"

"With the flat forehead."

The phone drops. Oscar can hear unidentifiable music. He checks Nancy's gums and teeth while he waits.

"Yup."

"D.J.? There's a rumor you killed a dog."

"Who is this?"

"Who do you think, skank?"

"Osc? You mean the vet said . . . ? Oh, Sam's gonna . . ."

"She didn't make it to the vet. I'm on Schwinn Avenue." Nancy snivels. Oscar inspects her nose leather next, which, like the footpads, should be smooth and tough yet pliable. The dog is in fine shape, considering.

"Well, Jesus, come back, then. Or keep going." His voice shakes. Not sorrow. Fear. Again, "Sam's gonna . . ."

"No."

"Whatayamean no? Whataya gonna do with a dead dog in Mexico?"

"I'm waiting right here for you to claim her."

"Aw, c'mon, man, there's a party goin on. We're having trouble again from those frat—"

Silence.

"Awright. Chill. I'll send Horowitz."

"Two fabulous weeks in the Bahamas." Sam tells Fred it's the honeymoon he's been planning for Claire. A surprise.

"Swell."

Sam's pacing and showing Fred the engagement diamond, a blur.

"Classy."

Sam's rubbing his sore wrists, finally unhandcuffed, and pushing his hair back and shrugging and smiling and shifting his feet and gripping Fred's biceps. Semi-frightening. Sam's yelling, "So how's it with you?" in a desperate sort of bleat. He's been physically restrained from taking Nancy to the vet himself by the frat guard and the enemy Sidehill gang, both. Caught in cross fire, you could say. He plops down on the grass. "I asked, so how's—"

"OK." But Fred's nauseated. In layers. From the top, the sour aftertaste of beer on yoghurt chicken on pizza. Mary's going. Oscar's gone. And Fred himself has nothing to look forward to now except his nine o'clock wash and set, cleaning Marci's fish tank, Sam's wedding.

"It was really nice of you to give Eliot that blow job." Sam's slurring.

Claire can't marry Sam, it now dawns on Fred. Oscar was right about that, even if for the wrong reasons.

"Fred? Lemme man-to-man a minute, hypothetical. If someone tells you No, do you hear No or do you hear Yes or do you hear maybe yes maybe no maybe maybe?"

"I give up. . . . Shhh. Look who's coming." Raffle whore. She's a colossal specimen, taller than Fred, wearing a white beaded dress, no undergarments, smoking.

"Ron," she's calling. "Ron."

"Listen-a-me, Fred. This is old Sam talkin serious."

Fred can't help thawing a little. This is old Sam talking serious. For all the guy's bullshit, his mercenary, lying, vaguely bigoted ways, he's still so . . . trusting. The way a kitten or a puppy can chew up all the furniture and then get this needy thing going in his eyes and voice to avoid being hit. What the girls eat up. What probably made Peaches fat.

"Ron." Quiche gyrates over to stroke Sam's hair.

She's followed by Gooch, made frantic by the mistake. "*Sam,* not Ron," he wails, "Jesus, whata we payin ya for?"

Quiche blows smoke down into Gooch's face. "Not my photojournal memory." She tries to bungle her way onto Sam's lap but doesn't exactly fit. Truly NBA size. Fred wouldn't be surprised if she cleared 6 foot 6.

"Look," Gooch says. "Forget it."

"Fine. I'll go home, then?"

"The night is young," Sam says thinly. His voice is failing him; unheard of.

"You wanna make an extra twenny?" asks Gooch.

"Suuure," Quiche says.

"Alls ya gotta do is go a few blocks from here, pick up a dog for me."

"No," Sam blurts. "Lemme go. Where is she? She's OK? Oh god, thank god." He kisses Quiche on the forehead.

"Hold it!" Gooch says, fighting with a frat galoot over the right to restrain Sam. The Binghamton contingent wants to treat Sam to a women's mud-wrestling contest. "Can ya just hold it a minute. I got a—"

"Did someone call for a coffin?" Sid Lubin appears, asking. He's clearly amused, laughing beer suds out his nose.

"Me, me!" Gooch's hand shoots up. "I told ya."

"There's a guy from Emerson's Funeral Parlor here with a coffin and hearse."

"My idea!" Gooch shrieks as if someone were trying to steal the credit.

"Brainstorm," Fred says to Tommy. Time to leave.

"You should see the grain on this thing, Sam." Sid tells his son. "Quality material. Cherrywood."

Eliot panics. "How much is this gonna cost?" He yanks the blow-job raffle money from his pocket and begins counting.

"For our Sam, carte blanche," D.J. crows, really full of himself now, tweaking Eliot's cheek and raising his plastic cup for a toast. "We shall all mourn the death of Bachelorhood together. Paint the town black. Die wild and free. Climb the highest telephone pole. Eat·Quiche and die."

Fred is not just going to throw up; he is going to throw up urgently, yoghurty chunks. Still, he's careful to avoid Sam's gray face below. Mouthing "Nancy."

CLAIRE DECIDES to ignore the knocking. It's Sam come to plead with her to change her mind, she's sure of it. But the knocking gets more intense, and Claire's afraid it'll wake Louette. Why can't she face him like an adult, yes, do it, do the mature thing for once. Yes.

"Thank god." It's Oscar.

"Thank god?" He looks like he's been jogging.

"I—Louette'll be glad."

"Can I come in?"

"Yeah. Oh. Sorry. I was just—" Claire smells vomit and steps back. "She's asleep."

"And how is the bride-to-be?" Oscar asks, noticing the heap of gifts. He looks too rushed to really be wanting an answer.

"Me?" Claire shrugs, gestures toward the bedroom, but Oscar's already on his way. Of course he knows the layout; these are normal people, lovers. He even knows to step over the ant stream, and when he closes the door behind him, it's like an old movie ending. Claire holds her breath for the reconciliation scene you don't get to see, tips her hat.

LOUETTE's fully dressed, and her futon is sheetless. Used floss on the night table; oh, priorities. It's five a.m. Oscar knows from the smell of donuts frying next door at DoNuTs! He has forty-five minutes to say goodbye, come with me, nothing. Miss nothing, he tells himself, easing loose Louette's sneaker laces. Get every detail. She's all zipped and buckled into some sort of toddler-like pastel shorts/overall contraption that looks as if it would take at least forty-five minutes to remove. Her legs are neat, sturdy, sure of themselves.

They dissolve him.

Oscar wants to lie down next to Louette, but she's sleeping diagonally, a bed hog. He wants to lick the insides of her wrists. Even though she flung a toaster at him. He wants to say, "Get up, sweetheart, and pack, we're going away," and for her to pop up and pull him down and tell him, "Never mind, I'll go as is." But it'd never be that way. She'd pop up maybe and pull him down maybe, but afterward there'd be a packing crisis—

clothes for a year and toiletries, accessories, not to mention the shopping and pistachio nut withdrawal Louette would experience once they got there. She'd nag him about sunscreen.

"Goodbye." Oscar caresses the space behind Louette's ear. That jolts her.

"Are you falling?" Oscar whispers. He tries not to move.

"No."

It's a delicate skill, tapping into her sleep talk. "Where are you?" He always feels a little fiendish doing it.

"At the opera."

And always a little shocked when it works. One time, he even got Fred over here for a demonstration, and Louette said, sleeptalking, "You smell like fresh bread from Brooklyn," which got the two of them cracking up, which woke her. She denied saying any such thing and threw them both out.

Louette always denies saying any such thing.

She often throws him out.

"What opera?" Oscar asks her now, holding his breath during the delay wherein she locates the nether voice. A weird, low, annoyed tone, completely absent from her waking speech.

"The *grand* opera."

He can't resist kissing her, on the bare hot-to-the-touch neck, making Louette jump up to an almost stand before tripping over her unlaced sneakers. She's going down, then recovers before going down with a funny hip jerk that lands her back on the bed instead.

"You shit," Louette moans. She was always a bad person to wake up. "Meany."

"Meany?" Oscar teases.

"Oh, go away, please, would you?" Louette's face is squashed against the mattress, bright pink. Looks like it stings. She hates pillows. "I said leave."

"I am."

"Good."

Oscar watches Louette's chest, rise, fall, rise. "Otherwise, Mrs. Lincoln," he says, "how did you like the show?"

"Open the window," Louette orders, crabby. But Oscar

obeys. There *is* a donut of red haze around the moon, like Dad said. "So. Where've you been?" She has to ask. A big hunk of pride to swallow, he can tell.

"Louette, I—"

"I wish—" She stops.

"You wish what?"

"I wish you were the person you sometimes are."

And what is he supposed to do with that?

CLAIRE KNOWS she shouldn't eavesdrop, but she can't help wondering. Is it going to end differently this time for Louette? She'd like to help, will it so, or, better, rewrite it happier, in indelible ink. But can't.

Instead Claire makes herself lie back on the couch and go to work on her own situation. She decides to do the brave thing. Talk to Dad face-to-face and not let him say one word till she's spelled out everything, including her intention to go back to school and get a job, both, and even her own place, eventually, and I'm sorry but there's nothing you can possibly say to change my mind, that's it. The spaces in between her toes itch. Maybe ants. The air smells like cake.

Finally, the bedroom door cracks open. Oscar. Carefully, somberly, he turns the knob till the latch makes that small, final click, and mutters, offhand, "If you need a ride out to Jersey . . ."

CLAIRE HOLDS her breath as they enter the Holland Tunnel, while Oscar allows his insides to scramble up with the radio. "Are you too cold or too hot or too anything?" he asks.

"No, thank you," Claire answers, politely, holding up the poodle lingerie. If only she knew her fiancé's dog nearly died wearing it.

Don't marry Sam, Oscar wants to say, because just now Claire looks so small sitting there, tentatively fingering the armpit hole in her sundress, fearful like, or at least lonesome.

Even those wings all of a sudden sort of touch Oscar. Salt-caked into waves, they look different, almost pretty. *I know Sam*, Oscar wants to tell her, *as the guy who used to have a booger collection on his headboard.*

Instead he sings, "Figaro, Figaro." And for lack of anything sayable asks, "Do you know opera? Grand opera?" A classy girl like her, you'd figure she might.

"Naah." Claire smiles. Teeth gap. "Opera singing makes you fat." Claire's pleased with herself when she hears him laughing—Fred's ringing exuberant yahaha yahaha.

As they emerge from the tunnel, Claire feels a yawn coming on and sticks her whole head out the window to make it a big one, satisfying. The warm air pushes into her face, whips her bangs all crazy, pulls out fake tears. A ring around the moon, her Mom always said, means rain.

And it's as if Claire just remembered, right here in the car, that she's young, she's a teenager, one day she'll say, "Yeah, I almost got married that time. Had a shower and everything." And she'll tell the whole story of Sam and Peaches and Louette, Oscar, Fred, and it'll seem sad and it'll seem hilarious and it'll seem very far away.

"Hey!" Claire pulls her head back in. "You missed my turnoff." Oscar's headed for Newark Airport. Yawning.

"Hello. Excuse me? Oscar? You missed my—" Then, again, that same question.

"How's your Spanish?"

7

SEX AND DEATH

"Sample me," Marci says. One large, friendly brown nipple juts out from a curtain of staticky hair.

Fred balks, coughs up beer foam. He stares at Marci's bare toes, obscenely stuffed into leather pumps with two-inch heels, the tops sprinkled with shaving stubble. Whatever happened to subtle come-ons like "Hi," like "Let's kiss," like no words at all—the best?

"Well?" Marci says in an unconvincing I-don't-have-all-day way. She gnaws at the cross on her necklace. "Whataya say, Freddy?"

What do you say? Don't call me that. Is a brief and not-guaranteed-to-be-pleasurable carnalrama worth the mandatory, awkward disease birth control checklist and the afterward weirdness of what do you owe me now?

Marci's hips roll, or lurch, advancing. No longer waiting for an answer, she's closing in, with a fierce nonsmile—ready or not, here I come. Oscar's apartment gets abundant sun but no cross-ventilation.

If this can't be what I want—something epic—Fred thinks, then at least let's make it a little bit like what I expected—something real, something tangible.

But the blue veins in Marci's breasts unnerve him. This would never happen to Oscar. If Marci shimmied up close to

Oscar (has she?), he'd laugh. He'd at least find a place to put down his beer. Not Fredhead, though; he's paralyzed, mute, electrified—the feel of ribs through his shirt—marveling as her nails skid down the back of his Levi's. He's overwhelmed—just who is sampling who here?

That word! It implies an appetizer-size portion, which simply will not be enough to appease him if Marci continues to run her tongue along his jawbone, lick his teeth; it isn't so-o-o bad. Have an open mind. Marci is sucking each of his fingers, one at a time, the missing-tip nub and all, thumb-lingering. She's leaving the other hand unsampled, crouching as she reaches—here she goes—for his fly.

It's been so long, too long. A lumbar tremble threatens Fred's muscle control. One wrong move and he'll . . . uncoil big time. In the eerie quiet he can hear some girl outside on the street, screaming, "Joeeey," crystalline, timeless. It's—

The doorbell. Like a conscience Fred wants to ignore. "Uh . . . uh . . . did you hear that?" His beer erupts, drips on Marci's head, and he's off balance, almost falling. *The doorbell.* I'm not here, Fred could say, and it would only be a half-lie.

"Stop! Someone's . . ." resorted to leaning on the bell now. "All right already! Who's there?" And then a slight coldness where Marci was.

"Louette, you goof. Lemme in."

"Not dressed!" Fred calls out. Levi's sit in a beer puddle around his ankles.

"So what's so special?" Louette says.

Marci stands, leaving Fred flushed, helpless. He has to ask her to put her shirt back on and waits out her deliberately drawn-out performance, button by button, the tucking, the smoothing, the blousing, while Louette, from outside, threatens, "If you don't open the door *now,* just forget ever getting your blender back."

"What's your problem?" Fred asks when he finally gets the door open, hoping to focus the attention away from any incriminating evidence: Marci. Beer. Hard-on encased in damp jeans.

"Oh, you," Louette says, bewildered but chipper. She brisks past Fred with her car keys and the blender, leaving the door ajar. "Sorry to barge." She obviously notices Marci and makes an effort not to look at her. Obviously feels better; she sports a cheerful new curry-yellow metallic beanie, striped knickers, summer boots, striped sunburn.

"Where's Osc? I've decided to throw pride to the—what's the expression?—and apologize. That is, unless he's already out picking up mall chicks."

Fred tries to look charmed, but when he leaps over Oscar's foyer-clogging hamster-tubing stockpile to close the door, his balls hurt, tender and congested.

"I had this deranged sort of nightmare," says Louette, "where I was just roaming the streets in bedroom slippers searching for him, and then I woke up incredibly thirsty, only no matter how much water I drank, it just kept tasting like my mouth."

"Vacation," Fred suggests. "Go join him." Now. Please. Before you screw up everything and let it spill about the apartment being Oscar's. If the hamster tubing hasn't already tipped Marci off. "Reunion in Mexico!"

Louette's glossy lower lip spasms out. "Mexico? What?"

Though Fred instantly grasps the situation, he's reluctant to believe that the rest of the borough could know Oscar's gone but not his own girlfriend. Man. That's what happens when you stop getting your hair done? You lose touch. Judging by Louette's eyes, though, she's lost way more.

She's dropped the blender. Oscar's downstairs neighbor bangs fast on his ceiling. After one small bounce, the appliance rests comfortably on its side, unscratched, intact. "Stooge," she says, kicking the base. Then more retaliation from below (sounds like a broomstick or one of those long metal police locks), which only makes Louette whack harder till the gasket comes loose. "I see," she says, stamping on it. "Good then, good, good . . ."

"It's near-indestructible," observes Marci, nodding with consumer approval.

When the phone starts ringing, Fred is sure it's the guy downstairs, wanting to verbalize his complaints.

". . . good, *good!*"

"Easy," Fred says. "I'm sure it'll all . . ." But why defend Oscar? The phone goes on and on. ". . . work out." Oscar's the one who's got the girl flipped out in love with him.

"Hah." Louette gives the blender one last wallop with her heel, which for some reason delights Marci into jumping up and down and enters the two of them into an all-out-evil, girl-eye stare-off. Worth not answering the phone to witness. Posed so, drenched in sun, adrenaline pumping, the women glow and hiss—gorgeous, horrible. In its way, it's a turn-on.

"You two remember each other, don't you?" Fred says. Wrong. Of course they do. Oscar brought Marci to the engagement party to make Louette jealous, which evidently worked. The glaring intensifies with every ring of the phone, and so does Fred's boner.

"The PetMart clerk," Louette says, monotone.

"That's me." Marci lifts her chin to throw Fred a wink, the nerve. If she dares call him Freddy with—

"This chick"—Louette's voice quivers—"bothers my sinuses." She drags a kitchen chair across to the sink area and, even standing atop it, must rise on tiptoe to reach the cabinet she's after. Inside is a whirling spice rack containing aspirin. Impressive. Louette knows more about Oscar's apartment than Fred does. Unforgivable.

Louette downs both pills right there on the chair without water, at once, macho. "That wench," she adds. She probably knows where Oscar hides the light bulbs too, the condoms. Probably she's privy to all sorts of secrets Fred's not.

"That's going too far." Marci fumbles for a comeback.

"Not you, peahead. Claire. My trusty friend Claire. *Got it?*"

"Who you callin a peahead?" Marci demands, but she's giggling.

"It's not funny!" Fred springs at Claire's name. Is this part of Oscar's little smear campaign? Louette enlisted to carry on ruining poor Claire's reputation? Soon Marci'll hate her for no reason too.

Already Marci's asking, "How rich is that girl, really, do you guys think?" Already forgiving Louette, it seems, wanting to gossip. "Millionairess? Is Cap N Gown like a monopoly or . . . ?"

"What'd she ever do to you?" Fred persists, puzzled as to why exactly he always finds himself defending that . . . acquaintance. "Huh?"

"Billionairess?" Marci continues, but it only heats Louette up more.

"Ran off with my boyfriend in the middle of the night is what! Left all her brand-new kitchenware in a heap on my floor to go off with my boyfriend. *And lied.*"

"Don't yell at Fred," Marci says. "Claire with Oscar?"

Outrageous. Oscar can't stand Claire. And, "Kitchenware? Does this have something to do with the blender?"

"Oh, clearly Lou-Lou's *puree*ing." Marci releasing her claws again. "As I'd be, were *my* dreamboat to flee to the tropics with an alluring young trillionairess." How fast the figure grows. How quickly Marci can become as catty as the next one.

"How'd you end up with her anyway?" Louette says to Fred, scratching back. "Oscar's leftovers."

"Sit down," Fred says.

"Mind your business."

"Stop it," Fred says. He must decipher this. "Shhh." What has Oscar gone and done this time?

"You're the one left over," Marci tells Louette.

"*Hush!*"

The phone begins ringing again and keeps ringing. Fred would like to throw the blender at it, then at Louette ("I'm leaving"), then at Marci ("Yes, do"). "I never even knew Oscar had a blender."

"He *did*," Louette says. "Past tense. It's mine. *Bye!* You can finish Fred's blow job now, Marci." The topper.

But nothing hurts worse than leftovers. And as usual, Fred's the one stuck with the *feelings:* the feeling that being here with

Marci has somehow double-crossed Lou, the feeling that it was he, not Oscar, who took off without telling her or asking her, with Claire. Really sorry. Reaching for Louette's hair with one hand and the ringing phone with the other—the acrobatics of it making his balls feel suspended on strings like pendulums swinging in opposite directions—Fred ends up with her hand and only the cord of the phone, wound around both their arms. "Don't worry. . . ."

Louette sighs, hiccups, consents. She leans over to kiss Fred's cheek and says, "I just wish you didn't have to look exactly like him."

"Me too." This time Fred means it.

MARY'S DEAD. You expect a sort of short-out to happen, but instead a bluster cranks up. Emotional smog and rude logistics. All of a sudden, everyone in the house is busy when the toupeed funeral parlor man appears. And lucky Fred is volunteered to show him to the Body.

His parents are just cowards, Fred consoles himself, children, anxious about death germs and haunted places. Well, big deal; he'll go. Can't be much worse than sitting down here watching Hersh rip up the newspaper, the whole Sunday *Times*, section by section, with his face spurting so the newsprint runs and turns his fingers black.

The bulbous man is inappropriately smiley and short-sleeved, toting a pocketbook. Already he's out of breath halfway up the stairs. How's *he* gonna lift a cadaver? His forehead looks as if someone took a bite out. Fred considers himself generally a good samaritan, but he has his limits, one of which is definitely carrying dead people. Not that he's scared of the Body, though it's the first he's ever seen. It's pretty straightforward, actually—just a rind lying there, looking a lot like it did when it contained Mary. But the idea of moving a stiff? What if he dropped it? It did once belong to someone he knew. That Mary has vacated, however, Fred has no doubt. A kind of revelation—you don't really have to die, because death makes you no longer you.

Mom and Dad and Hersh felt the relief too, they must have, coupled with that other solace—I'm still alive—though naturally no one will admit it. Hersh is too zoned even to realize. Dad's too preoccupied: "Details," the soothing concrete. Mom's busy being busy and self-righteous: If they'd only listened to her, they could have stopped it.

The Room, Fred finds, has been left dark, shades drawn, windows closed, a veritable simulated grave. Bracing himself, he hits the light switch, spook-chasing.

"But she's dead," the man says right away. His mouth hangs open, and Fred can see straight in, big, strong teeth and rough slab of tongue.

"Is that a joke?"

"No . . . no." The man backs up a step. His eyebrows give the sneaky impression that they can move horizontally. "No . . . not a bit." Gray eyebrows that don't match the flimsy blondish synthetic toupee, or the forehead hole, rusty stain color. When he crosses himself (three times—quick, then slow, then quick), Fred sees he's got blubbery arms, dimples in his elbows. The man does look truly pained, though, apart from his tenacious smirk.

"Well?" Fred isn't going to pick her up first.

The man walks to the bed—loose gray suit pants, striped track sneakers—and gets on his knees. Not the proper technique for corpse-lifting, is it?

"Kneel with me." The man holds down his eyelids with a thumb and a pointer finger.

Standard funeral parlor procedure? "I—I don't—um, I mean, I'm Jewish," is the most Fred can get out, in the midst of a minor but extremely disconcerting hallucination that Mary's pinkie finger has just moved a fraction to the right.

Fred feels hot then, mushy-boned, inescapably aware of the rotting smell and unsure whether he's about to gag, when the stranger rears up his dented head to ask, "Your blood?"

"Um, yeah, my aunt." That she's not technically a blood relative doesn't seem necessary to get into.

"My condolences." The man smiles again, but those eyebrows go off too, undermining him. As he rocks beside the bed, the man's shirt buttons strain, and the bulging canvas pocketbook pitches forward, backward, forward.

Fred's begun hurriedly opening the windows, wide as can be, but the smell is dense as ever. The door! Closed. Locked? Fred lunges for the door, struggles with the knob, panics.

He is totally wigging. Why'd I ever agree to this? His stomach yanks, bubbles. The smell. His balls ache faintly, unspent—when the door, thank god, pops open.

Just calm yourself, OK? OK, compose. No way did Mary's finger really move. Fred knows that; Fred knows the door was only stuck. Regardless, he bellows full blast down the stairs, "Dad! Get—up!—here!" Then he becomes perfectly still save his hands, cracking every last one of his knuckles.

"Here I am," Dad says. He's hiding behind a lowered voice.

"What's the problem?" Mom's hiding behind Dad.

"My Mary," says Hersh, too big to hide, shredding the *Book Review* and diving toward the foot of the bed, wretched.

The man gazes upward to take them all in and croons, "My heart is with you in this time of—"

"Then stop smiling," Fred bursts out, nerves shot. He spins around on both heels to make sure the door has not mysteriously closed again. "Who are you anyway?"

"Ah, son." A zealous lilt to the inflection. "Be not forgetful to entertain strangers." The faith healer! "For thereby some have entertained angels unawares." The faith healer, finally here (too late and just in time), armed with a pocketbook and mistaken for the funeral parlor man. Whoa.

Mom's gone berserk. "If you aren't out of here by the count of three . . . !" She's screaming with sufficient force to startle even Hersh, who seems just then to notice the guy.

"Oh, you, hello. Reverend Osbin."

The man remains completely unmoved by the outburst, perhaps waiting to hear the threat completed.

Mom doesn't finish. She scowls and absentmindedly picks a book off the shelf, compressing it between two flat palms, isometrically.

"I'll take care of this," Dad says, though he makes it sound like a question. He glances frantically from the reverend to Mom to Hersh (out of newspaper, now trying to tear the bed sheet) to Fred and back again. "Why don't we go downstairs, hmmm?"

Mom stares at the faith healer and begins kneading the book.

"Let no man deceive himself," Reverend Osbin recites. "I know, and am persuaded by the Lord Jesus, that there is nothing unclean of itself; but to him that esteemeth any thing unclean, to him it is unclean."

What the hell is he referring to?

Out of the mysterious pocketbook emerges a glow-in-the-dark rosary, which the reverend hangs upon Mary's rigid hands.

"This is a Jewish house," Mom snaps, belligerent. Her temple vein throbs on every *Jesus* spoken.

"Yes, ma'am! And the law was given by Moses, but grace and truth came by Christ."

Christ gets a wince.

"Charlotte," Dad warns, jiggling the change in his pocket.

"Don't you Charlotte me." She's seething. "*I want this man out of my sight by the count of three!*"

"The kingdom of God is . . ."

"*One!*"

". . . come nigh . . ."

"*Two!*"

". . . upon you."

"*Two!*" Two syllables.

"Maybe you'd better be leaving." Dad crumbles.

"And the God of peace shall bruise Satan under your feet shortly . . ."

Satan?

Satan gets a snort. "*Three!*"

"Please?" Dad gasps.

The stranger persists. His unwavering grin suggests that he's used to being despised, that he enjoys being despised, which incites Mom extra. She starts whacking at him with the book, oddly, *How to Solve Your Dog's Problems*. "I'll call the police if I have to. I'll get your ugly mug thrown in—"

"Stop that!" Dad begs her, not at all "in charge" now, looking wilted, in fact, ready to shake. His own father. Fred can't take it. "The reverend is leaving now," Dad lamely assures Mom. "Fred?" So now Fred's appointed bouncer. What next? Mom humphs.

"C'mon." Fred tries to make it sound as much like "Haul ass, buddy" as he can muster under the circumstances. He bends to grab the faith healer's hand, which looks unsettlingly delicate on top of Hersh's immense heaving shoulder.

"Let's go."

Fred expects an argument, fists; hocus-pocus from the pocketbook. Anything. But the reverend complies, follows Fred out with an awkward excess of movement—crossing himself, bobbing his head, lifting his legs higher than he needs to, scolding. "Knowledge puffeth up, but charity edifieth."

OUTSIDE on the stoop, the reverend jabs Fred's chest with his business card, then hands it to him. "I'm concerned about your mother." Oh, yeah? "She needs help." He says "help" like "God." "Son?" He says "son" like "wise guy or ingrate." "Son? I'm talking to you." Fred says nothing. He wonders whether it's against the Jewish religion to knock this guy out here and now. "When she pulls herself together, I want you to have her call me, see?" In your prayers, crackerhead. "I'll be at the Holiday Inn in town." Fred says nothing. "Will you do that?" Fred says nothing. "OK. Well, I tried, didn't I?" Semiapologetic now.

When the faith healer turns to go, Fred shoves the card in his back pocket and watches the inscrutable pocketbook as it swings blindly down the stoop, up the flagstones, onto Sidehill Avenue, which is well lit, warm tonight and deserted.

"Is he gone?" Mom, at the door, hugs herself.

"Yes." If it's true about bad things happening in threes, what next?

"Are you coming in?" Only a screen door between them, yet *in* and *Mom* seem incredibly remote. The hall light creates a little halo out of her artificial-yellow stray hairs.

"I don't think so. I might take a walk." And purposely by accident miss the next round—the real funeral parlor man—or, more likely, men: legitimate, faceless, swift, and uniformed workers with a van.

"Where is everyone?"

"Who?" Oscar, she means, but doesn't know it. Fred knows it.

"Maybe I'll hang out out here with you." The two clumsy "out"s in a row, on top of hearing her use the phrase "hang out" (a first, just like "ugly mug"), make it difficult for Fred to look at her. His realization—my mother is stronger than my father—churns up Fred's emotions but leads to no consequence. Only a matter of months before Dad turns the whole incident into another anecdote for his "usuals" at the parlor. Miming how Mom pounded the faith healer with a book.

Fred wishes she *would* come out here and sit with him. If she were rugged enough to do that, he might tell her the rumor about Oscar and Claire and the wild jealous feeling it gives him even as he misses his twin (alive) way more than Mary (dead). And maybe she could tell him things too, about Mary, things he never knew, or knew and forgot.

But Mom guesses she'll make some Sanka instead. She guesses she'd rather get re-busy getting busy.

"Mom? If you'd . . ." Fred begins. But she's gone.

Eight, nine, twelve o'clock at night. The funeral parlor men must get paid overtime for jobs like this. Fred calculates it'll take the reverend close to forty-five minutes to hoof it to the Holiday Inn, unless the self-proclaimed angel has genuine wings. Mary apparently thought so.

Mary. What epitaph will they give her? Mashed potatoes were her specialty. Smashed potatoes, she called them. Not a lump was there ever, not a spot, not a stray peel, never a dry patch or a watery portion, no two puffs alike. They were nothing like Mom's flake variety. Flawless they were, light, velvet-like, enticing. It's preposterous, of course, dwelling on mashed potatoes, but Fred's gripped by the sudden very real dread that he'll never stop craving them.

"We oughta be grieving like Jews." Fred hears Mom complain at Hersh from within. "Sitting shiva, not lolling around, not ripping up bits of paper. We should . . ."

Not be hungry, Fred thinks, guiltily.

"If Hersh wants to tear up the telephone book, he's entitled," Dad declares. "Hasn't he been through enough?"

"Too much," Mom thinks, accusingly.

Hersh himself repeats, "Much. Much." He's zombified, alarming.

"And why should he, a pious Jew"—let's not get carried away here, Ma—"send his own wife to a goyish funeral parlor, where they'll poke at her and whatever they do, pump in—"

"Spare us."

"Spare yourself, Lester."

Fred has heard enough of their arguments to know that this one has reached the disintegration point. From here on they'll only repeat themselves, on and on, meaninglessly. Anything, even a mashed-potato fantasy, seems more courteous to the deceased than this.

"We should be sitting shiva like—"

"You. We should all be you."

"Me." Hersh sobs out. "Mary."

Fred tries not to listen. Tries to inventory his limited memory of Miami, retrieving (aside from potatoes) only a couple of bad sunburns and good haircuts and this strange rotisserie thing that pulled out from the same wall on which hung the famous cherished signed photograph of Mary, Hersh, and Bette Davis. In the kitchen?

"All I know is in my family we sit shiva."

"Then go sit, Charlotte. Who's stopping you? You want I

should call in the neighborhood? You want bagels? What? I'll send Fred down for bagels."

"You've got a hide like a rhino, Lester."

"Rhino! Which rhino bullied that poor reverend out?"

"Much Mary," says Hersh.

"Go on, Char. Sit, sit."

"I always knew it. Ever since . . ." When? "You're ice, Lester."

Nothing like a crisis to bring the family together, hmmm? Silence, almost worse than fighting. Fred hears cars cruising Sidehill Avenue but can't see any. He looks in the few lit windows but sees only the dumb normal objects—sofa, plant, stove. He feels his butt on the brick stoop, but it doesn't feel like anything, not even hard. And he wonders whether he will always, from now on, associate Bette Davis with mashed potatoes.

IT'D BE DISRESPECTFUL to go up. It's disrespectful just loitering here, under the neon BILLIARDS sign, yet here he is. "The Roost," as Oscar calls it, the pool hall.

"No." Fred refuses himself out loud, the way he's told they make you do in Alcoholics/Overeaters/Smokers/Gamblers/Narcotics Anonymous. "No. No. No." If any of his friends could hear him now, they'd surely wonder. Fred surely wonders if he has any friends up there among the people he knows. "No?"

The stairwell smells like piss. Mary. Piss and potatoes. You can't get any less lofty than that. Fuck it, he's going up. He won't play, he just needs the noise to think. Noise and beer. He needs to hear some people who aren't grieving, arguing, preaching, giving him a blow job.

"Awww. Lookatdat, Tommy. Little Fred's crochetin his brow. How poignant." Sam looms over Fred's barstool, fake teary, musclebound, sticking the tip of his pool cue under the sleeveless, hooded, all-the-way-zipped-up sweatshirt, to touch his heart.

Tommy Eako merely shrugs and goes on picking his teeth with the bartender's pen cap.

"You'd think *his* lover had left," Sam continues, thrusting the pool cue underneath Fred's chin next. "Maybe it's true too. Ever ponder *twins*, Eako? That *special* relationship?"

Fred watches Tommy's blue pellet eyes and eternally hot pink lids for some small sign of old street-performer camaraderie. Nothing.

So Fred defends himself, meekly. "Scram. Or sit down." He's pretty sure what Sam intends is harmless, obtuse, rough-em-up kind of fun, and it's Fred's own problems that make this all seem blacker. Sam is Sam. Sam is a constant.

"Hey." Hairy Leroy, the sideburned bartender, talks with a mouth full of Cheez Doodles. "Where's ya friend at tonight, Sam, wild nine-ball woman? I was thinkin we might rustle up some bets. See, alls we need to do is have her play—"

Sam rams the pool cue across Fred's chest, winding him.

"Woo woo," Leroy says. "What's this?"

Fred says no silently, no no, and politely resists the pool stick. Going out brawling, real or play, seems more disrespectful to the dead than playing pool. And he says it aloud. "Cut it out."

"Say what, Bozo?"

"Stop, Sam. Please." Fred detests the whine in his own voice. "Fuck off." More authoritative.

But Sam loves it. The patchwork of scars that will one day dictate his wrinkles now veers into an inflexible grin; totally familiar. "Could I be disrupting something here?" he asks, reaching over with his free hand to stroke Tommy's receding hairline. "Two clowns havin a beer. Darling, ain't it, Leroy?"

Tommy easily flicks away Sam's hand. He always was tougher. While Fred would end his fire-juggling routine by dousing the flame with his tongue, Tommy'd slide the entire torch right down his throat, eating it. But, "I'm outta this," he says now, pausing to drink, not guzzle, an entire mug of beer at once. Which he knows begets an immediate audience. It's his trade, after all. "I'm on vacation here," Tommy adds. (In Queens?) What he's meaning is, *I've grown past this shit.*

"I always knew it," Sam tells Fred. "I always knew you'd get to me." Sam's hands are scarred up like the rest of him, cracked and white at the knuckles, trembling slightly as he slowly tightens the pool-stick hold on Fred. "You guys, constantly sabotaging each other's relationships . . . You"—Sam shoves Fred back against the bar again, hard—"pricks!" And gives a final push before letting the stick drop.

"Watch the property," says Leroy. Not watch Fred. "Watch those cues."

Sam laughs and doesn't look one bit amused. "You gonna stand up now?"

Although Fred takes the opportunity to do just that, he immediately turns away to stare at the old, frayed hanging moose's head. Apparently, Sam's heard the same rumor. Claire and Oscar, together, in the Yucatán. That doesn't necessarily make it true, but it certainly brings it closer to being true— truer. The only other decoration hanging behind the bar is a poster reproduction of Van Gogh's yellow flowers, which has had, as long as Fred's been coming here, a cardboard leprechaun Scotch-taped on top.

From behind, Sam has returned to paw Fred's head, to press Fred's cheek down onto the bar counter. To say, "Putty." If it were done gently, Fred'd want nothing more than to lay his face on some cool, dark surface. "Silly Putty." But not this way. "Like I been sayin for years, Tommy, one Arm's useless without the other."

"Cease, Lubin," commands Leroy. "Or I'm takin your table away." Not I'm kicking you out, I'm beating your brains in, but I'm taking your table. Some threat.

Still, Fred feels the hand let go. And when he slowly lifts his head off the bar, Sam's expression is a baffled stare, as if he's expecting to see Oscar. In that moment, it seems sure Sam is backing off, but then, wham! wham! wham! Sam administers three fast elbow jerks into Fred's hip region.

And that's it.

Fred gives in, gives it back. Pulse sparks, pores pump, tendons stretch, saliva gathers, and Fred pushes, is pushed, the beginning of virtually every male spar in history. Sam, Fred, Sam, pushing.

"Uh uh!" Leroy reaches over the bar and grabs Fred's arms, while Tommy rises from his stool to hold Sam.

They snarl and strain toward each other. "Where is Claire?" Fred taunts. "Where is that wild nine-ball girl?"

Which steams Sam enough so he breaks loose from Tommy. Which surprises no one so much as the fact that he doesn't plunge back at Fred but, rather, returns to his pool crew—Eliot Horowitz, cringing, and D.J. Gooch, fired up—for whose benefit Sam does think to yell back one last, "Yo, Leroy! Ya got Cheez Doodle crumbs in your mustache."

Yellow flowers.

And that's it.

Fred, watching now as if through a screen door, remote, could not care less, could not care more. Gooch—Deja Vu—waves at Fred as if he just walked in, while Eliot hangs his head and begins maniacally chalking his stick.

"Anyone have a lighter?" Tommy asks. It's the start-up line of one their favorite old street routines. Tommy mimes the way they used to pocket some sucker's Bic. "Does anyone have a watch?"

"Let this be an example to the rest of you." What you said when anyone gave you a five.

"Wait! Let's all take a moment to stare at that guy who saw the whole show and is sneaking away without paying anything."

"Help us to stay out of school and on the streets where we belong."

"Look, a fight!"

"Sex!"

These last two—desperate attempts to get people's attention—are, Fred suddenly perceives, miraculously working. A mini-crowd is forming.

"Drain your beer, Tommy." Fred laughs. He tosses his own bottle up over his back and across to Eako without warning, confident that it'll be caught, yes.

Tommy doesn't miss a beat. He flips his own bottle toward Fred, establishing the Rhythm. It's easy.

The response is a wealth of empty-bottle offerings from their audience.

"Three three ten!" Tommy calls, juggle talk for three passes every third catch, then three every second, then a barrage of ten continuous. Oscar and Fred used to practice this maneuver with taped knives for hours, days, weeks at a time to make it easy without seeming so.

The applause loosens up Fred's arms and shoulders the way Marci's massage could never begin to. He wants to rush home and get his Devil Sticks (two sticks you bounce a third back and forth between), his Bongo Board (a board the size of a skateboard, balanced on one wheel, that you stand atop, juggling—no simple trick), his machetes, pins, torches, cigar boxes (made to look gravity-defying if balance is applied properly), his Chinese Linking Rings. But the pool balls will have to do. They're ten times heavier than the bouncy lacrosse balls he's accustomed to, yet all of a sudden Fred's ten times stronger to accommodate.

Leroy yells for Fred to "put them down right now or . . ." He gets sidetracked watching the colorful popping circles, then doubly sidetracked watching Sam barrel through the mini-crowd, roaring and unintelligible, nearly getting beaned in the head. Sam wheels around and flounders in place as though he doesn't know how he got there. At all.

Crowd laughter. It's as if this were comfortably staged.

"Look," Tommy tells Sam. "I'm getting paid to make an ass outta myself. Could you go over there if you're willing to work free?" Tommy rifles a pool ball between his legs toward Fred with a goofy, glad expression as change, joints, subway tokens, and candy come clattering merrily down at their feet.

"I remember my first beer too, Sam," Tommy goes on heckling. Sam stumbles and brings his arm up to wipe his nose on his sleeve, then registers that he has no sleeve, then wipes his nose on his forearm anyhow.

"I remember I tried sniffing Coke once, almost drowned," Fred contributes. For Tommy's amusement and as a general comment. The runny-nose/energy-level combo is a dead give-away. Sam's speeded out of his mind.

"I hate girls who wear white all the time!" Sam's howling incoherently at a stranger. Her white dress is of tracing paper thickness. Next, Sam's charging her. Next, Leroy's hurdling over the bar. Next, the girl's on the floor beside Leroy, and Sam, once more the gentleman, is extending his hand to help them up.

With their audience diverted, Fred and Tommy take their final bows for one another.

"It's all right," the girl tells Sam, giggling. "I'll change."

STRESS MAKES some people (Fred, Oscar) confused; others aggressive (Hersh, Sam, Louette); others cranky and silent (Dad); but after any sort of conflict, Mom becomes sensible. She'll clean out the garage, organize junk drawers, label and date packages in the freezer, match caps to pens. Going through menopause, she made curtains, had a yard sale, retrieved the tie strings pushed into every pair of sweatpants in the house, and insisted the family eat off paper plates to save themselves valuable work time. There's a direct correlation between the rigor of the task and the depth of Mom's anxiety.

So when Fred finds her all alone in the kitchen, sorting coupons, he's relieved. He knows it could be much worse.

"Where is everyone?" Fred asks, just the way Mom did at the screen door earlier, as if to say, Where is Oscar?

"Your father and Hersh went down with her." Mom avoids three words in one short sentence: Mary. Funeral parlor. But not "Sad Sacks," apparently a reference to Fred's eyes, probably bulging bloodshot from the joint he smoked with Tommy Eako.

"So . . . And so when's the . . . thing." OK. He can avoid naming too.

"Monday," Mom says, instead of "tomorrow," arranging and rearranging the stacks of vibrantly colored coupons in some complicated system she's got involving paper clips and rubber bands.

Most of the products advertised boast of being "Quick" or, faster than quick, "Instant." "Boil-in-a-bag rice in ten minutes." "Seven minutes ago, this Sara Lee pie was frozen." Oats 'n' Fiber hot cereal, an all-time one-minute low. Not that Fred thinks muffin-mix muffins are bad, exactly; they just taste too much like pancake-mix pancakes, brownie-mix brownies, potato-flake potatoes. On the plus side, though, you know what to expect from, say, a can of soup, whereas the home-cooked variety (in this home anyway) is continually suspect. It's entirely unclear whether Mom is lured by one-minute food because she's such a gruesome cook or is such a gruesome cook owing to one-minute food. And when anyone else gets kitchen ambitious (Oscar's yoghurt chicken, for example), the response ranges from apprehension to alarm.

Fred tries joking. "Good thing Hersh left, or he'd be ripping these up too." Mom rubs hard at her freckly eyelids, unmoved. "Hey." For the first time Fred remembers something about Mary besides starchy foods and movie stars. "She"—he can't seem to say the name aloud either—"always used to warn me and Osc against rubbing our eyes, remember?"

"Hmmm." Is that a yes?

"She used to tell us about some TV program that showed a rubbed eye magnified like a billion times, all torn up, really disgusting." Not the most profound of recollections. Why'd he even have to mention it?

"So whataya do? When your eye itches?" Mom demands. "Just *let* it?" As if Fred were the parent, the one with all the supposed answers. "Everyone's got gripes galore, but do you ever hear suggestions? Solutions?" Again, Fred feels in the wrong for something that he doesn't recall doing or that Oscar did behind his back. "Take your father, for instance." This unhooks him. "Take Jane Fonda."

"Where?" He's still trying to get a laugh out of her.

"And Peaches."

"Won't fit." Fred's humor repeatedly bombs. I'd be funnier, he thinks, if I wasn't stoned, or else was more stoned.

Now that summer's encroaching, the rubber moms are always sitting around listing what they ate and which exercises on Jane's video they hate most. According to Latvia, the tapes fetch five hundred dollars on the black market in Romania.

"Peaches and her diet," Mom says. Peaches' new diet involves eating only green foods on Monday, red on Tuesday, yellow on Wednesday, like that. "Wanna bet she's gonna binge any minute?"

"And rainbow it, you mean?" Fred gives it one more shot.

After insulting the girl in white, Sam actually managed to pick her up and win money off her.

"We're all wasting time *not* doing things. Mary didn't rub her eyes, eh?" Mom's grappling. "But so what? Her vital statistics are nothin to write home about." She doesn't sound callous, though. Fred marvels at Mom's single tear as it slides out and drips on the nearest coupon. *"What a fantastic find! Scrumptious* describes the way everything looks in these 12 *metallic colored dessert cups* for only $2.99. Elegantly designed to look expensive."

"Oh, Ma." Embarrassed, Fred pretends to play the piano on her forearm, gently. "Whataya want these for?"

"I don't, particularly. I mean, I dunno. They're just . . ." She's sobbing now. It makes Fred fidget. "Only two ninety-nine." She's sobbing and laughing at the same time. "Oh, you." Fred goes to the bathroom and brings back a banner of toilet paper, still attached to the roller; it just reaches. "If only they'd stay out all night," she adds. "We could . . ."

But Fred knows she won't think of anything. Up to him, then. Eat. He's suddenly got the munchies for everything on the coupons. And mashed potatoes.

"I forgot," Mom says. "Marcia called."

"Marci." Luckily, there was no technical sex; otherwise, he'd have to call back.

"I heard Marcia."

"Really."

"She's a nice girl?"

"Guess so."

"So."

"Nice?"

"You're going to call her?"

"I don't know."

"Call. She's a nice girl."

"Ma . . ." Fred's certainly not in the mood for *this* conversation. He heads for the phone.

The patch of wood floor in the kitchen is still exposed, the way Hersh and Oscar left it two weeks ago. Fred stares at the irregular, scalloped grain as the phone rings in not Marcia's house but Claire's. Another thing he didn't plan but just did, calling information for her number in Beeswax? Beesville?— that's it: Beeslink, New Jersey.

"We'll mash some taters!" Fred calls to Mom. "You and me, we'll cook up some—"

On about the thirtieth ring, a man answers.

"Good evening."

Not once in his whole life has Fred ever heard that. A man answering a phone "Good evening."

"Uh, hello." Fred hasn't thought ahead to what he'll actually be saying. "Hi," he's saying.

"Hi," the voice returns. Not "Who is this?" as most voices would in the situation.

"I'm calling because . . . My name's Fred. Um, is Claire there? . . . Please. Fred Arm."

"No. I'm afraid she's away. May I take a message?"

Away away? Fred wants to ask, or just out? Are *you* afraid? *I am.* Message? Message? Get this straight. "Do you know, by any chance, where she . . . ?"

The man (butler or father) chuckles. "Mexico." It hits like a physical blow to the throat. Olé.

Fred hadn't expected verification. Shouldn't have called. Isn't clearheaded at all.

"It's a bit of a long story."

"Oh." But I have unlimited time. "Thanks. Bye." Fred hangs up.

"You can let go of the phone now." Mom laughs. "When you daydream like that I think your eyeballs are gonna capsize right back in your head. So. Tell, tell." She's newly uplifted either by the notion of Fred having a girlfriend or by the coupon she's holding: "*Save 30 cents*, and avoid the heartbreak of *wimpy* bags." The letters of *wimpy* are drawn in curvy lines to look wimpy.

"It's nothing," Fred lies. "She wants me to help clean out her fish tank." Mom's got enough to worry about without hearing her son's kidnapped Sam's fiancée.

"I see," Mom says, disappointed.

Which is when Fred notices, in double take, two slips of paper tacked to the corkboard. On one, "Marcia" is written in Mom's solid schoolteacherish script. On the second, "Emerson's Funeral Parlor," in Dad's abrupt block letters. Both slips feature *the very same phone number*.

Meaning?

The bachelor party hearse was Marci's dad's?

Sam's coffin is now Mary's?

AT THE FIRST SIGHT of Mary's hair, Hersh snaps. "Disgraced!" He rails at the funeral parlor styling job. "Wrong. All wrong. A horror show." He yanks his own few locks, works himself up to what Fred fears is some sort of seizure. "My Mary, poor Mary, my girl . . ." At the same time, Hersh seems more sane than he's been in a long time. "What happens to me when I die," he thunders, "I couldn't care less, but this is my Mary here. I will not, never, tolerate this butchery."

"Sir," Mr. Emerson interrupts. Marci's dad? He's wearing a sooty, dated, wide-lapeled tux. "Excuse me. I regret this had to happen, but . . ." His strained expression says otherwise, says, Who is this character causing a ruckus in my place? "I've been in this business thirty years." I've seen everything.

The Body is clothed in a black dress that Fred recognizes as Mom's. And shoes. He looks away. It seems cruel to have to wear shoes for eternity. Next, face. You can't see it under the hundred-layer pancake makeup, a little of which has brushed off onto the velvet casket lining. Fred will look only once more, at the hair, and only for Hersh's sake.

"Pickled," whispers one of the guests from Miami, but Fred knows for a fact that Hersh hasn't drunk since the moment Mary passed, when he ran out of the house and flung his bottle into the air (at God?) and waited in vain for it to come back down at him. Still up on the roof now. "Soused." Error, chum, this is grief. Great-Uncle Hersh leans against the grotesquely flowered wallpaper and all-out weeps.

The very least I can do, Fred tells himself, is look.

Instead of Mary's trademark hairstyle, the luxurious, polished swirl, dip, tuck, her hair has been manipulated into a do resembling a monstrous knit hat. Fred imagines someone sitting down to systematically, one by one, split each end, then furiously tease the finished strips (she can't feel it; she's dead), finally unloading an entire can of hairspray to get that final freeze-dry finish. It barely resembles hair. Tawdry, perplexing. It's all out of proportion to her head. And to the room.

Fred needs space. Floating out into the austere reception area, he finds Mom sitting straight-backed on the edge of a huge, gloomy pastel-green sofa, skidding her heart locket back and forth on its chain.

"Stop, please." That sound.

Mom obeys. "Guess who's here?" she asks with an almost imperceptible nostril flare, and Fred jump-thinks, Please not Marci. He scans the guests, all old-looking in this dismal setting. Strangers and neighbors. They came as friends, sure, good intentions (Lubins, Horowitzes, Freeds), but also as spectators and, to add to the paradox, as happenstance Jews. Which makes them intensely interested—what the hell is going on in here? They came ready to flee if necessary.

Fred spots among them a very distraught Shaky Bea. Not that Shaky's ever met Mary. She'd be this way at a wedding, or in front of the TV; probably bawls over corny long-distance ads. But what moves Fred is realizing that until now he's never once seen her minus the pink Chester's smock.

"You missed him," Mom says. She's crinkly-eyed and mean-looking from lack of sleep.

Him? Not Marci, then?

"Who him?" Perhaps it's Tommy Eako. Or *Oscar*, miraculously materializing. No. Fred would know. It occurs to him that Mom wouldn't recognize Marci if she saw her juggling bones. "Where?"

"In there." The Room.

Back in there, the thickly sweet flower smell mixes nauseatingly with the new-carpet smell, and with hospital-antiseptic smell which hides the death smell. No wonder Jews forbid flowers at funerals. It seems the equivalent of bringing children in, baby chicks, candy. You can't shut your nose.

The faith healer! ". . . last home, long home, narrow house, house of death . . ."

Sam! Sucking his class ring.

And Hersh. Suddenly lumbering toward the body, with his shoes wildly squeaking, breathing loudly, bending over the Body, touching it!

"Sir, please, you can't do that," Mr. Emerson yelps.

Hersh is fixing the hair on the corpse.

"Uh . . . uh, sir . . . uh."

"For behold, this selfsame thing, that ye sorrowed after a godly sort, what carefulness it wrought in you, yea, what clearing of yourselves," the reverend continues, ignoring Hersh.

"The d.t.'s," Fred hears someone whisper. Tsk. People make as if to leave. Can't they see how expertly those trembling old hands operate? Just a few quick, magic, and utterly controlled movements: a flick of the wrist—swirl—a fluid curve of the arm—dip—the soft pressure of devoted fingertips—tuck—and there it is, the familiar style, restored. Hersh stands taller, composed, tenderly puts his lips to the head, her face. "It's all right now," he says. "It's all right, Mary, everything is all right now."

Fred swallows. Sad Sacks he's not. "These twins aren't so identical as they look if you really look," he once heard Mary—or was it Bea?—say.

"Yea, what vehement desire, yea, what zeal, yea, what revenge! In all things . . ."

Someone's hugging him. Dad? No, Sam. Sam? "I love ya, man. I owe mega-apologies. Forgive me. It's just I was, ya know, *gone* last night, blicked. I had . . . no idea. I had . . . Yeah, and Claire sends condolences too. . . . She really really likes you."

So Fred ends up crying in Sam's arms (who would have guessed?). And not because Mary's dead, or Hersh is desolate, or Dad is ineffectual, or Sam's a problem liar, but because he does not want to have to be the sad one. Amen.

8

WAITING

TO EXPLODE

"I LIKE to jump into places I never see the bottom of. It's hard. Hard and beautiful. Sometimes you got lost fifteen times. *I* got lost once—no boat, no coast. Have to drop everything and swim back four, five hours. Have to drop my tank. First, no way, José, I'm not dropping *any*thing. You know, macho, pero I— was—scary. Un amigo, he was lost in Isla Mujeres *seventy-two* hours. We're working Japanese boats then. Thirty days—no coast to notice. Me, him, and the one Japanese diver. For the lobsters. You jump in and it's just blue, blue . . . beautiful. Two hundred sixty American dollars a day. Two hundred and ninety-nine feet down. Oh boy. Stupid crazy voice—squeak, squeak, like helium—and you don't know if this guy is watchin you or not, and you don't hear no motor, *no*thing. The Japanese guy just went freaked out, locura. In case of death—helicopters. Otherwise, no way, José. . . . Hey, how you say 'upness'?" Señor Fernando Jamón asks, with his mouth open and full of raw barracuda. He spear-gunned the creature himself—in one shot, fifteen minutes ago. "Like . . . upness? Como se dice?" One of his big toes grips the boat deck for balance, while the other lifts to indicate the—

"Sky?" Oscar guesses. He lowers his sunglasses to look up for clues. Seabirds (terns?) like black flying mustaches reel against a grandiose sunset. "Above? The top?" A V formation of pelicans breaks up in apparent response to some secret group Dinnertime signal. The birds begin singly to scan the surface shadows for fish. "Beyond." Plunging beak-first, the pelicans are as elegant as Claire's earlier streamlined dive off the side of the boat; while Oscar clomped down the ladder. Humiliating.

"Like that Bugs Bunny cartoon character," Claire says. " 'No way, José.' I never thought real Mexican people actually said that." But then Mr. Ham isn't exactly your average local. With his turquoise muscle T, tight Speedo swimsuit, good English, conquistador genes (blond, blue eyes), the most enormous chin Claire has ever seen, a boat and a dive shack (that's two homes), gold chains, this guy is somebody around here. A near idol in the eyes of his little Mayan helper, Paco.

"Overhead? Planets?" Oscar asks, free-associating. The sky is purple-red, salmon ribbons of light. Tomorrow's the big day, when he's supposed to go macaw-hunting, but Oscar's mind is still unmade, uneasy, uninformed. And Fernando won't "discuss no business en frente de la mujer." No way, José.

"What *is* that No way, José guy's name?" Claire is stuck on the subject. She watches Oscar nibble at his cuticles, restless. Each bleached hair on his too-long limbs, chin, eyebrows, eyelashes glints white gold, electrical in the sun.

"Cosmos?" Oscar asks. "Heaven?" He's worrying about how to tell Claire that he's leaving for the jungle. If he is leaving. After saving her from Sam, he can't just abandon her.

"Upness! Up!" Fernando shouts. Then to Paco, who has jumped to his feet in confusion, "Sientate." As usual, Fernando completely ignores Claire. He's sure she is Oscar's "woman"; he insists it and will not hear otherwise. And will not address her except indirectly, through Oscar. Does the señorita need a life preserver? Would the little lady like a drink? Fernando answers whatever questions Claire asks in this same third-party manner and without ever so much as glancing in her direction. Paco, on the other hand, constantly, blatantly stares at Claire's breasts, ass, crotch, the way only a nine-year-old who speaks no English can get away with.

"Miami?" Oscar shrieks. The sun-blistered skin of his neck stretches painfully.

Fernando pumps his Corona bottle in the air. "No! No! How . . . ? Peoples from another planet!"

"Martians?" Oscar tries. "Blue moons? Yellow stars? Green clovers?"

"UFOs?" Claire adds, unwise.

Fernando hisses a spray of fish spit, baring gray-filmed, widely spaced teeth. He is not familiar with that word—UFO—but he doesn't like it. "My English es very poor." And he violently jerks his head overboard, submerging it.

"Did I say something wrong?" Claire asks.

Rattled, little Paco leans his narrow chest over the water and watches the bubbling spectacle for uno, dos, tres—think he's OK?—cinco seconds, till Fernando swings back up and resumes angrily scarfing down his dinner. He drips salt water into his bowl of instant ceviche—barracuda, conch, lime juice, chili peppers.

"You speak very well," Claire says. "Don't underestimate. 'Helium,' you used. 'Helicopter.' Those are formidable words."

Fernando shrugs and accuses Oscar of "having me disremember what I tried to mention anyway!"

"Couldn't have been too important, then," adds Claire.

It's just what you add when someone forgets, Oscar knows, the same way you follow sneezes with God-bless-yous. But still he objects. These sorts of remarks always bug him. "Why couldn't it have been important?" Claire has no good answer, naturally. Just that mouth. Wily space between her front teeth. One of her few detectable defects. She has already whipped Oscar in pool, swimming races, staring contests, cards.

"My mother once said she saw a UFO," Claire reveals, somehow managing to translate unidentified flying object. Objeto volador no identificado. Big shot.

Fernando pretends not to care, but his eyes ignite instantly, while Paco, making no attempt to hide his fascination, lays his flat, vaguely triangular head on the deck near Claire's feet.

"One night she couldn't sleep—she couldn't sleep a lot—and

had a whim to get up and go outside. While out there, in the gazebo"—the gazebo, Oscar notes, as if every home came so equipped—"while still wearing her nightgown and a sweater, all of a sudden she looks up and sees, sitting not two yards back, right past the wall . . . this yellowish-greenish lit-up oval. A floating diner, is how she described it. A floating diner that went whoop whoop. Which is when she began getting the magnet feeling. She said it was as if the thing wanted her or she wanted it."

Here Claire breaks to translate the whole business for Paco, leaving Oscar to admire the view or, almost more interesting now that the boat is approaching the hotel dock, the view of people on the shore viewing the sunset.

Farthest back, on the porch of his bungalow, stands a sombreroed, very black Joe Watson, staring it down. As always, he's holding in his hands a can of Off! and a paperback copy of *Shōgun.*

Closest, in shallow water, the blond dancer is showing it up, or trying to, with her bidaily erotic yoga session. As always, she's attended by an audience of three fat, slitty-eyed Mayan dudes in polyester bell-bottoms.

In the middle ground, beside the honor-system beach bar (a thatched hut in which drinks are bought via pesos dropped into a slotted wooden box), is a pale, doughy tourist couple swooning at it. As always, her head rests on his shoulder.

Claire herself takes peeks at the view, small concentrated doses, as if all at once would be too much, and continues to relate the story of her mother's brush with outer space. "She resisted. She had to, she said, because she couldn't just leave us, her family, to go off into the unknown." A moral, as always. Doesn't it figure. "But turning away was difficult, like walking through 'mud, hip-deep mud,' she said."

"Sí!" Fernando interrupts, inspired. "The Japanese diver; he went weird too like that way. Waking us up each night on el barco with screaming of how he saw air pictures and itchy particles that come in to invade his brain. Just like that."

"Particles," Claire says. "Now, that's an excellent English word." For a Mexican or a Japanese man to use.

As for Fernando's method of sunset-viewing, he doesn't. Either too used to gorgeous sunsets to appreciate this one, or else too cool to act impressed with gorgeous sunsets—the way New Yorkers act around their skyscrapers, purposely never looking up so as not to be mistaken for a common tourista.

"She didn't even wake us after," Claire wraps up. "But called some UFO hot line to report it." Claire decides to forgo the epilogue—and, she realizes, the real point of the story—her mother's death that same week. It might spoil the barracuda, which is tasty, refreshing, slapped on crackers and eaten with your hands. Post-skin-diving-buzz has left her ravenous for the food. Pelican parade made her thirsty for air. Oscar, childishly rocking as he eats, taps a desire for—

"Música!" Fernando suddenly commands, which sends Paco racing into the boat cabin. Then, "Bueno," when Paco returns, just as swiftly, with an archaic-looking AM transistor radio in his fist, emitting a staticky, speeded-up Spanish-language female version of "Can't Buy Me Love," which Claire can tell Oscar almost recognizes but doesn't.

"Wait," Oscar says as if the song will halt for him, or as if he's afraid Claire will scream "Can't Buy Me Love" before he does. It's on the tip of his tongue, contorting his mouth, funny, and Claire wonders what it tastes like, his mouth. Barracuda-conch salsa? She tries and fails to ESP him the answer. The day they arrived, Oscar shaved off his beard tuft—becoming Fred exactly, until Claire produced the lucky half-dollar, clumsily, from his ear (the only belonging she brought with her besides the blue bathing suit and ripped dress, her purse with passport) and Oscar was not at all charmed.

Though now he is. "Mira!" he blurps in his experimental Spanish, which makes his voice rise an octave. Even cuter is his other method—English with a Spanish accent, randomly sticking a's and o's at the end of words. He points to where Paco can be half seen on the bow, dancing in private. The little guy's doing a lot of frantic pelvic thrusting and a pretty ac-

curate lip sync. No Puedes Comprar Mi Amor, the words
squished together fast to fit—that's it!

" 'Can't Buy Me Love.' We used to sing that song with . . ."
We again. Fred again. Constantly alluded to but never discussed. Oscar abruptly changes the topic. "When those bar-
racudas were following us," he whispers, looking down at his
food as if he expected it to do something. "When you could see
that eye moving around, following you. Oooh. I don't like that."

But Claire did . . . a lot. Jumping into the "blue blue," she
felt something happen. Jumping into a place she couldn't see
the bottom of, with fish eyes moving around her—something
snapped loose amidst the monstrous veiny man-of-wars, sea
urchins, parrot fish (you could hear them loudly crunching as
they grazed the sea bottom for food), red fire coral, burning
turquoise seaweed, stingrays. Claire saw Fernando choose his
target, take aim, and—suddenly she wasn't afraid—the fish
jolted dead. She was no longer afraid of Oscar. Rather, she
ogled him worse than Paco ogled her, scrutinized him more
thoroughly even than she had Russ, the gardener. Oscar's
smooth, loose limbs waved as gently as the most exceedingly
delicate sea plant. Claire was no longer afraid of anything. The
barracuda sank into Fernando's embrace like a sign-languaged
sigh.

"Sí, algo fresca." Fernando pronounces his verdict on the
catch now and crunches his final cracker, loudly, for emphasis.
Yes, it is a little fresh.

Oscar sympathizes with the hunter *and* the hunted, both. Sí,
algo fresca; Claire has translated: Yes, the fish is a little fresh,
yes. Señor Fernando Jamón, a man of understatement and exaggeration. Oscar would be more impressed if Claire were less
so. If Fernando would just admit that his perfect shot might
have involved luck. If at the moment before it was spear-
gunned, the fish hadn't looked straight at Oscar and so awfully
affronted.

And after two weeks of waiting . . . Fernando's coming mañana. Fernando, like Godot, mañana. Day after day, Oscar
waited out by the crummy locked shack, getting sun poisoning

all down his neck and back while a lot of strange hotel people—tourists, waiters, beach vendors, and little Paco—kept assuring him, "Fernando is coming mañana!" Señor Fernando Jamón, famous dive-snorkel-fish-and-party man, infamous playboy and parrot-smuggling connection. The man is more and less and different from what Oscar expected. He is nearly impossible to reconcile with Vladimir and the PetMart.

"Sss, Paco," Fernando says, picking his teeth with a fishing knife and laughing at the poor kid, a pesky, blaring laugh.

"When Paco visited me first, he had no shoes. He wants to work for shoes, he tells me. But no more. After he's been seeing many touristas, he wants watches now, sunglasses."

Naturally, all eyes turn to alight on Oscar's new, expensive, amber-tinted Ray-Bans, which makes Oscar too self-conscious to take them off and too embarrassed not to. "And he still has no shoes," Fernando says, not at all cynically but like, Thata boy! Like, Don't you dare mention the ironies of life, because there are none. Fernando holds up the fish carcass to lure the kid over. "Oye!"

Paco nods his small, flat head at his boss but creeps over to stand next to Claire. A definite crush.

"Hola, Paquito." Claire pulls a wet strand of hair out of her mouth. "Cómo estás?"

Paco nibbles at his fingers till he can get out a "Hola" back. A peep.

"Por tu mamá," Fernando tells the kid, waving what's left of the barracuda—three feet at least, head included. Paco takes it, gratefully and without bothering to wrap it up, without being bothered by the eyeballs at all. He simply hugs the fish under his armpit like a surfboard and sits waiting for shore, thirty feet away.

"Think I'll swim back," Claire says, climbing up on the side of the boat to dive. Since they arrived here two weeks ago, she's come out of the water only to eat and sleep. Like a bilingual infant. "Oscar?" Her abused blue bathing suit is stretched out to reveal where the two soft curves of her butt turn into legs—zigzag tan lines. "You don't think I'll get a cramp and drown since I just ate, do you?" she asks, flirtatiously. Claire? It couldn't be. It better not be. "That's silly, right?" Obviously wanting a no.

Oscar provides one. "And besides," he says, "I'd rescue you." He wishes she'd realize that he already has.

"There's always the lifeguard." Claire's new favorite absurdity. The hotel lifeguard wears long pants, a long-sleeved shirt, shoes and socks, glasses and binoculars. "But I'd prefer a strong Arm any evening." Claire giggles and dives—a high-arched, soundless swan.

"My future girlfriend," Fernando says, pointing not at Claire but to the blond dancer–yoga temptress on the shore. Sure. Señor Fernando Jamón would be the ideal tourist woman's dream fling—to screw an authentic macho blue-eyed Mexican diver, wow, exotic, but then not so exotic as to seem seedy. He's got blond hair, hasn't he? He can speak English despite his complex about it. He continually reminds Oscar of someone or something he can't quite and isn't sure he wants to place.

"We can talk now," Oscar says, thinking how it's probably better that Claire's excluded from this "business," however handy her Spanish would be. Will he actually go through with it? He'll just have to see. Wait and find out. Oscar studies Claire's refined and confident backstroke a steady yard or two behind the stern and is certain she won't need saving. A letdown. "Well?"

"Mañana." Fernando waves him off. "Like was said." In his conversations with Vladimir, does he mean? The duo is as incomprehensible as the rest of this scheme: going to the jungle *tomorrow* to catch endangered parrots worth ten thousand dollars apiece, with just a net and a box and some leather gloves, then concealing them on this boat, a pleasure cruiser, and heading north to Miami, to Vladimir. The entire escapade has an illusory, unfocused quality. Like looking at a TV screen up close and seeing a whole bunch of dots, no picture.

"But don't we have to ta—"

"Talk, talk, talk," Fernando mocks. He leans back lazily to

light a Delicado cigarette. "We will talk in the drive, mañana." He gestures with his elbow toward Paco—no business in front of women or children, got that?—but continues gazing at the blonde on shore. He adjusts his balls. "I hef a date this night."

"Does she know about it?" Now that they are nearer to her, Oscar's pleased to note that the blond has practically no chin. No chin, and Fernando too much of one. An optimal couple.

"Cómo?"

"The date. Does she know about this date?"

"Not yet."

Oscar suspected as much. And out of a faint homesickness, he adds, "She should tackle that blow-dry breakage."

OSCAR TRAILS Fernando into town. He is impatient to the point of discomfort. An American, he needs his information fast, clean, unabridged. Maybe he'll find it here.

The zócalo in Playa Alguna is virtually identical to every square on the Yucatán coast. Radiating out from the basketball-court center are church, post office, farmacia, el banco, Cervecería y Licores, Fud (food) store, and a row of stalls hawking repeats of the same itchy striped blanket. But Playa Alguna, slightly richer than the average town (owing to a ferryboat port, a bus station, and the occasional cruise ship stopover), also boasts its own Máscara's Casa de Langosta (lobster)—where a sign in the window says: I BUY DOLLAR WE SPOKE ENGLISH—and even a movie theater. This week's feature film, *Atrapados*.

"*Atrapados!*" Fernando exclaims, the way Sam would say, "*Rambo!*"

Oscar, too proud to so much as ask what the word means, is far from keen on a viewing. Not a chance of subtitles here, or of air-conditioning, or, as Oscar observes through the window, even popcorn. What the fly-ridden concession stand offers are little institutional plastic cups full of pus-like custard with raisins, or slices from a sweating, half-eaten flan, aswim in a greasy beige puddle. Luckily, though, the place is deserted, if you don't count the one toothless guy with a serf cut (long in back, short in front), kicking a cat around.

"I told ya we should have called for the movie times," Oscar jokes.

"Chingada," Fernando swears. Oscar follows him past the Mac Taco stand, across the square to where the whole town, looks like, is assembling for "church."

"On Friday night?" Time does loops here. It's possible that Oscar has lost two days. Which would mean—

Fernando nods. It is Friday, he says in condescendingly slowed Spanish, but in the Yucatán, church happens whenever the region's sole preacher gets around to your town. If it's Monday, it's Sunday Monday; if it's Tuesday, Sunday Tuesday; if it's Wednesday, Thursday . . .

"I get the drift," Oscar says. Even he remembers the names of the days of the week from high school Spanish class. At the moment it's the more important words he's concerned about missing. Parrot, jungle, and smuggling details, which might just be postponed again owing to this sudden religious development. "So what about this jungle—where is it exactly?"

"Momentito." *Again.* Mañana, momentito; a nice philosophy for a vacation, perhaps, but for Oscar it's a sour bowel. From the very morning they arrived (when it took Claire seven and a half hours to call New Jersey) up until today, it's been one perpetual wait—food, bank, Fernando, and now the jungle.

At the side of the church, a row of cute old ladies with slips hanging out of dresses that look like slips kneel in front of an open shrine for the Virgin Mary of Guadalupe. As Mexico's patron saint, she's as common as beans, to be found in every zócalo all the way up and down the coast; in every home, boat, store, stall; underwater!; on the dashboards of taxicabs; and, more subtle but no less real, in the faces of teenage boys employed to rake seaweed on the hotel beach, or straighten nails in the sun in long pants; in the daydreamy stance of young girls bathing with all their clothes on; in the women (many of them with five or six or twelve children, most of them with another on the way), waiting in tortilla lines or, as now, dressed up in spike heels for church on just a momentito's notice. And all because some Mexican peasant said he saw a vision ages and ages ago. The way Claire's mom said she saw a UFO in her backyard.

Fernando bows his head in deference to the plaster saint, which has, at its feet, offerings: rosaries, red flowers, baby clothes. It's Virgin mania. The whole country seems to share Sam's obsession.

"Soy forastero," Fernando says, slowly shaking his bowed head.

"What?" I am a forest? If anything, he looks more like a tropical plant. The only blond man around, besides Oscar; the only men without starched stiff white shirts on.

"I am a stranger," Fernando clarifies. "Of all these peoples, only *I* have been to America. Only *I* have been anywhere.... These people, forget it. These people ..."

Can't all fit in the tiny bright church. Whole families perch on car hoods or hang around in the street, rubbernecking for a view of the altar, which Oscar, being four or five inches taller than the tallest Mayan, manages to see without trouble through the open doors.

The Virgin is highlighted, alongside a much larger than life crucifix that looks straight out of some wax museum, as does El Padre himself—a wildly gesticulating figure in fluorescent green robes, a dead ringer for George Bush with a twitch.

"Put in a prayer for our birds," Oscar tells Fernando, who shakes his head at such foolishness.

Everybody knows: "Animals have their own gods."

CLAIRE SENSES its presence first. Then sees a crusty breathing fist of a spider in the soap dish. Ruining this already bogus shower. Like a Water Pik. No agua caliente to speak of. Think of *Charlotte's Web*, that's what Dad always said; spiders trap the bad bugs, and they're more scared of you than you are of them. Not this one, Dad, and let this be a lesson: an ordinary shower can be more dangerous than swimming on a full stomach.

When Claire called her father that first day, she was ready to have it out. The trip had prepared her. In stages. The leaving—when Claire still thought Sam was behind it all. The on-the-way—when she still thought Oscar was. The arriving—when (no luggage!) she discovered it was herself the whole time. She came of her own free will, didn't she?

I am calling to tell you . . . I am calling to tell you. Before this, Claire had never gone anywhere without Dad, and no place they went felt like anywhere. In a sense. Innocence.

A species dies out every fifteen minutes, Oscar told her. Claire's memory of this remark is the only obstacle coming between the spider on her soap and death. The creature, nothing like sweet Charlotte of the Web, looks everything like evil incarnate—crustaceous shell, eight legs, sand-colored head, and mean purply belly veins.

"Don't freak out. I am calling to tell you . . . in the Yucatán . . . what I mean is . . ." Within seconds Claire had flubbed, strayed, fumbled. Dad had the ball and no intention of using it. He didn't raise his voice. He didn't curse. He didn't interrupt or demand anything. He asked three questions.

"Are you all right?"

"More than."

"Are you with Sam?"

"No."

"Are you carrying a credit card?"

"Well, yeah."

And he was satisfied enough to fix a tequila sunrise in her honor right there on the other end.

The spider has stopped moving, but Claire's not about to take any chances—what if it's poisonous? fatal? She's not about to take a single breath until she comes up with a strategy. Where is the soap anyway? And what if the freak arachnid can hop? Eat soap and hop?

"You should visit the ruins," Dad had said. "Fabulous pyramids and things." "Go diving, you're a good swimmer; get your scuba license." This is the closest he'll come to saying, Do something with your life! now that he's recognized that she's a legal adult. "The bargains you can get on silver in that country will dissolve you, absolutely." He paused momentarily to gulp at his cocktail.

"You shouldn't drink, Dad; your heart."

"It isn't every day my daughter calls me from the Yucatán to say she's not marrying the wrong guy."

"Did I say that? *Wrong?* I thought you liked Sam. I thought you were getting him a job in commercials and—"

"Raised in a barn, that one."

"But you said—"

"A voice is not a son-in-law."

"Now you sound like Grandma Lillian."

"She's right, on occasion."

"Then you aren't going to yell at me?"

"I shouldn't yell, Claire. My heart."

"You aren't going to tell me to come back this instant or else?"

"*I* only want you to be happy."

Or, "I only want *you* to be happy."

Maybe, "I only want you to be *happy.*"

"NO TORTURE," Oscar insists after Fernando relates with relish several well-known horror stories. Birds smuggled between trailerloads of Mexican brick, inside hubcaps, car doors, air-conditioning systems, ice cream freezers, diaper pails, oil tanks, in hair curlers. As for hiding their own, on the boat, Fernando suggests, in an alarmingly offhand manner, shrimp. Underneath crates of shrimp.

"No way, José," says Oscar. "Think again." But think? How can Fernando possibly? He's nursing a bottle of tequila (two bucks as opposed to the five they would've charged Oscar). "Isn't that sort of sacrilegious?"

Now that church is over, most of the rest of the town is

drinking Cokes. The little kids out of straws stuck in plastic bags. The adults out of old-fashioned bottles, which are different shades of green according to how many times they've been recycled.

"You will pay me one hundred American dollar now," Fernando says. "Two fifty hundred after."

"Two hundred and fifty, you mean."

"Sí. Also for food, drink, and sleeping place in the jungle. I have found out a tree."

"One tree? You call that a jungle?"

"One tree in the jungle. Scarlet macaws come back each time."

"Their *roost?*"

"Shhh. Speak down."

"But roosting . . ."

"With paying nobody, we catch the birds straight from this tree."

"Macaws!" Oscar shouts, giddy now.

"So then," Fernando says. He wants to get this discussion over with and go on his supposed date. He likes to talk at Oscar, not with. In this way, he's really not different from Vladimir. "Shrimp would be good for pretending, and—"

"Not shrimp. Think." Not that Oscar can explain why he objects so strongly. But shrimp?

"To Miami, muy rápido. Finito."

"That's it?"

"You pay me one hundred American dollar now, two—"

"Yeah, I got that part." Not so different from Vladimir in that way either. "What if . . ." Oscar knows nothing about smuggling, true, but he knows everything about parrots. They have weak respiratory systems, and they stress out easily. They have to be checked for contagious diseases. When shoved into an uncomfortable place, they're gonna squawk. All in all, they're a lot like New Yorkers. "And how do you propose shutting them up if . . . ?"

Fernando closes his eyes and kisses the tequila bottle. "Con Cuervo. El anestésico nacional."

CLAIRE IMPROVISES. Get out of the shower. Find sheet for cover. Stalk the room and, quick, find something disposable to trap it in—the Off! can top. Next a flat something to keep it trapped—the Holy Bible. She grabs a towel too, added buffer between her and it.

It is alive. Waving one leg at her—hi, hi. Claire, armed with her gear, proceeds to close in on the monstrosity, slowly, muy importante, slowly.

It was decent of Dad to be so agreeable, but the fact is, he shouldn't have been. The fact is, coming here the way she did was a totally irresponsible/spoiled-brat/escapist-whim thing to do. And Claire at least deserves the satisfaction of denying it, defying him.

The spider lurches sideways one step. It shouldn't affect her so when mere hours ago she was swimming carefree amidst organisms confirmed to be venomous. But this life form is so *ugly*. Also, visiting *their* environment seems quite another matter from being *visited*. Under water is different. Under water, everything, even a slug, has grace.

"So how'd it go?" Oscar had asked about the phone call, after they were already in the rental car, speeding. Since he seemed to know where they were headed, Claire didn't ask.

"Terrible but OK, I guess. I can't explain it, really." Claire didn't know then not to say that. She didn't understand why Oscar was stopping the car, masticating the tip of his not yet shaved off semi-beard. She didn't get what that severe sucked-in face was about. And still doesn't.

"Please do not say that," Oscar implored her. "Ever again." He said it so seriously that Claire immediately promised. But still she didn't understand. "Say what?" She marveled at the flapping palm trees, a novelty that first day and a safer place to keep her eyes.

" 'I can't explain it.' Please promise you will not say 'I can't explain it' again. That's all."

"But I can't," Claire told him.

"Then don't! If you want to go home, just say so. I'll—"

"Are we fighting?" The prospect strangely excited her. Not as good as fighting Dad, but conflict at least.

Oscar got out of the car then, walked around it twice, and got back in. "Does your dad think I kidnapped you or what?" he sputtered.

"Kidnapping" hadn't occurred to Claire herself, but she welcomed the idea as glamorous. Like Patty Hearst.

"I . . ." Oscar said. "Well, I didn't." Sweep you off your feet—you're dreaming. "Fred was supposed to come and then Louette, and I thought . . ."

With one hand Claire carefully slides the towel under the Bible and the Bible under the soap dish, keeping her distance. She should have dried her hands first; everything's slippery. Get ready—she'll have to somehow scoot him out of the soap dish, then slam him in. Just do it. She lines up the Off! cap in the air. The can itself was a gift from Joe Watson, Off! fanatic, their neighbor in the next bungalow.

The spider clicks against the plastic top—*atrapado.* Claire bolts for the door, not certain the spider's even been trapped. But sure *she* is. Somehow her sheet gets caught in the sliding glass door while she tries to foot-push it open, carefully. She trips, saves herself, rips the sheet, lunges free. Finally, Claire dumps everything onto the nearest bush—red hibiscus. She issues a small shriek of relief.

"Son of a gun," a man's voice drawls, and Claire quickly straightens up to the spectacular sight of his hairdo—a truly glacial white pompadour, a welcome mirage in this night heat. "What the devil?" His cheeks have dimples deep as puncture marks.

"Well?" The man's much younger and apelier companion (lover?), who has a black eye, inquires, "Can we use it?" He's looking neither at the spider—an Off! can with legs—nor at the small calculator game—Golf!—in his fist but directly at Claire: cringing wet girl wrapped in bedding. Both men wear seasick patches—small round Band-Aids—behind their ears.

"Son of a gun," repeats the first one. His distinguished hair and dimples are offset by a hairy gut, which bubbles out beneath his T-shirt: KISS MY ASS I'M ON VACATION. "Son of a gun," he says again. " 'Animal Kingdom.' "

Meantime, Joe Watson, skinny black man with huge sombrero, shoots out of the adjoining bungalow door. He's carrying his copy of *Shōgun* and a can of Off!, cocked, aimed. "Issat . . . ? Whazat?" His voice trembles with elation.

Claire had assured Oscar that Dad knew nothing about his being with her. That Dad was thrilled to hear she split under pressure, the way *he* probably would have done. Maybe she can explain it to Oscar, after all. The key!

"You feverish?" Joe Watson asks. "You get bit? Don't she look blitzed? Let me handle this."

"May I seize the specimen?" Son of a Gun inquires. "For research?" Bowing, he introduces himself as "Señor Ducklander," leaving his Neanderthal sidekick unidentified.

"Be my guest." Claire is too involved with her own thoughts to be appalled. The key: simply not to tell Dad everything. She's backing up toward the door. "Nice meeting you all, but I think I'll be jumping back in the shower now." Even though Ducklander is lifting her only towel out of the dirt. His baby-blue Snoopy watch is a sharp contrast to the repulsive insect, which is now playing dead.

The key: to do something she would not tell Dad about. How about Oscar?

HE'S BEING FOLLOWED. By a dog. By the ghost of Nancy, who died in Sam's cake. Not really. It's just what Oscar conjures up to scare himself. A game he and Fred have mastered over the years—walking, then running home through Sidehill at night. An unnamed game. This dog following Oscar looks unnamed too, unowned, unfed, nothing like pampered Nancy, actually. Much bigger and spotted, with dark, versatile eyes rimmed in hot pink and a snout halved by a jagged line into black and white. A bitch. She sticks to Oscar's heels, shivering despite the heat. Rabid! Possibly. That's good. Oscar picks up the pace, hearing Claire's voice in his head telling everyone he's been mangled by a vicious frothing mutt at night alone in the depths of the Yucatán.

Or by lions and tigers and bears in the jungle (oh, Fred). Jungle. Jaguars, Oscar imagines, black screaming monkeys, and undiscovered Aztec civilizations still painting their victims blue, to rip their hearts right out from their chests, still pumping. It isn't working. Oscar knows what scares him really, and nothing compares. Federales.

A scream. He starts running, after all. The dog at his heels, Oscar races ahead onto the hotel grounds, which consist of a parking lot behind a line of beachfront bungalows and three ramshackle structures—office, dive shack, and do-it-yourself beach bar. The latter is where Oscar finds a man rolling on the sand, clutching his chest and a brochure.

"Don't move," Oscar tells him. "I'll get a doctor." He recognizes the man as the dandruffy half of the doughy newlywed couple.

"No, no. I'm just . . . it's just . . ." The guy is out of breath—tequila breath. "This dog sat on my foot, and I thought it was a scorpion."

What dog? Oscar sees only the mutt that's been shadowing him. Impossible for the animal to have been in two places at once, unless . . .

"Herb, Herbert." The man introduces himself, offering a handshake.

"Oscar," Oscar says, pulling him to a standing position. Male scorpions are cannibals, he informs Herb Herbert, for lack of anything else to say, and though the guy does not seem a likely participant in the fear game, he goes on to describe in detail a battle between scorpions. Each one tries to get at the opponent's head or mouth, the only places a stinger can be driven home.

"Sensational," Herbert says, chucking pineapple slices at the dog. "You're not one of those . . ." But deciding to drop whatever thought he had, he goes back to his brochure—"Mexico: Feel the Warmth!"—and reads aloud, slurring while Oscar slapdashes himself a margarita.

" 'Looking for pure magic?' " It makes one feel irrationally altruistic to slide pesos in the slot of the payment box. A great invention, the honor system, providing Oscar an easy karmic rush. " 'Looking for shopping and waterfun by day? By night, leisurely dining under a blanket of glittering starlight? Want to enjoy fresh, traditional dishes like the famous mole chicken—fifty ingredients! Only locals know how to make it! All at a very favorable exchange rate . . .' "

"Wait," Oscar says. "Lemme guess." He gulps at his already sweating margarita. "The Poconos." Ice in the tropics takes twenty-four hours to make and then doesn't even last the life of a drink. "Pineapple'll make him vomit," Oscar warns, after the fact, about the dog.

"Naah. It's only that bacteria. They throw the stuff in everything here, the way we put in MSG," Herbert jokes, his mushroom-shaped nostrils flaring. "He's used to it, see?" The dog is lying down at Herbert's feet, yawning. "But not me. Oh, no, I'm on the involuntary dysentery diet."

Oscar's mind gets working again. Maybe Herbert's actually the Ghost of Tourists Past come to revenge Montezuma for all the innocent vacation deaths before Lomotil was invented. But Oscar knows he's getting too old for this stuff. It's ridiculous. Herbert is just an ordinary fleshy American reeking of tequila and farts and suntan lotion.

"I'm worried about that neck, Oscar," Herbert says. "Looks real bad."

"It's just sun." Oscar lies down on the sand and balances his drink on his stomach. The well-advertised stars are all bunched up in cliques, leaving huge holes of unoccupied black. Oscar prefers these, real darkness, rarer than the stars. Like the horizon, neither exists in Queens. Both, for some reason, make him think guiltily of leaving Mary, of Mary leaving, then of jungles, jails, death. "They have Yum Kaak in that brochure, by any chance?"

Herbert consults the text but can't seem to decipher it, or loses interest, or simply spaces, goes back to harping about Oscar's neck. "Sun did that? Really? Looks bubbly. Looks like leprosy. You take anything for that?"

Oscar raises the dripping margarita and flaunts his newest Spanish. "El anestésico nacional." If it weren't for the sun poisoning, he'd sleep in the porch hammock like a real Mexican, or even right here on the beach; anything to avoid another round of nocturnal privacy measures with Claire. "Don't look." "Turn around." So far it's been antivacation for him—scheduled showers and having to sleep with his shorts on. It's extra excruciating now that their ceiling fan has died.

"What time is it?" Maybe Claire's already sleeping. It was she who insisted they "rough it" (with two beds, refrigerator, bathroom, beachfront porch) in the same room. Maybe a novelty for a rich girl, maybe she only insisted on the single room because Oscar insisted on paying—twenty bucks a night. Of course he had to—Mom's pride talking in his head. Of course it wasn't exactly a sacrifice—Vladimir's money blabbing in his wallet. Still, Claire didn't have to let him. If it weren't for her, he'd stay in town, for two dollars.

"What a time it is!" Herbert groans. "I feel like I look like I feel."

A MATTER OF LOGISTICS. How and when to seduce him. A matter of getting it over before her courage subsides. Before Oscar realizes why he's constantly flossing. In love with Louette. Anyone can see that, but Claire read it on a postcard, purposefully, because it was none of her business. The card said, "Lou—I want to kiss you." It said, "I am waiting to explode. You are waiting to explode. Sometimes we think we'll never explode." Claire's goal is to have a feeling even remotely like that before she's nineteen, then twenty, then fifty, before she's back in New Jersey, stranded again.

Not a big deal, probably. In the words of Louette herself: "Trust + Lust = True Love" and "Sex is just sex is just necessary." But that doesn't explain why it seems to underlie every gesture made, every question put, every joke, look, and conversation, like a secret everyone's in on except Claire, like a club, the us of Oscar and Fred, Oscar and Louette, even Oscar and Mr. Ham now, closed to her. Where is Oscar anyhow? I won't get in the way of your love affair, Claire will promise him. Purely clinical, this. Think of it as a teaching job. Afterward, I'll personally mail Louette your postcard; best wishes. I only want you to be happy. I only want you to be happy. I only want—

NATURE MAKES its a.m. racket. Claire sleeps. Each morning Oscar lies in bed, astonished to be conscious at six, six-thirty—too early—all because the birds are impersonating ratchets; while Claire, familiar with nature from New Jersey, perhaps, virginal of conscience too, sleeps on.

From Oscar's position, flat on his stomach (the only position he can be in without disturbing the sun poisoning), all he can see of Claire are legs—very tan, covered to the knees almost in his own blue Sidehill Y T-shirt—the skin there dried out, scaly at the calves, striped in the sun. The sun, coming through the wooden slats, illuminates a dead moth the size of a sparrow. Good morning.

The moth, unusually speckled, velvety to the touch, evidently took the fly-toward-the-light suicide route, same as any moth. Death by stupidity. A totally unimaginative creature. But in the jungle, Oscar has heard, they have a kind of stingless bee. Ambrosial honey.

"Good morning." Oscar sits partially on Claire's bed and blows in her face, the way he and Louette used to wake each other. Pleasant, except it doesn't work with Claire, and anyway the act makes him feel unreasonably adulterous. "Excuse me."

Unlike Louette, Claire is not one to reveal herself in sleep talk. Her lips, shut and chapped flaky, are void of expression. The only thing Oscar can glean for certain is the most basic: she's hot and she doesn't even know it yet. Sweat unaffected by gravity coats her face, which is not beaming pink the way Oscar's is but the same varnished color Claire is all over. She is lucky-skinned. What winds up waking her is Oscar's sneaker squeaking on the floor.

"Hi," Claire says, curiously genial. Her eyelashes blink in slow motion; otherwise, she doesn't budge.

"Hi," Oscar says. "I'm leaving for the jungle this morning for a few days. OK? Will you be OK?" He gazes out the back window toward the rental car, which at seven a.m. already looks able to burn skin on contact. "I'm sorry, but you can't ask to come. I've got this research to do and . . . I've got this thesis . . ." (But how ridiculous this sounds, considering that Oscar didn't even remember to bring a notebook on the trip.) "So, like, you'll be OK? There's just no way you can come. It's too . . . complicated. I mean—" He was about to say, *I can't explain it.*

"Good," is all Claire says anyway. She rolls over. "I hate sightseeing."

EATING in the Yucatán, Claire has discovered, requires a buddy system, someone to ask and be asked "Are you all right?" when you return from the bathroom or suddenly slump in your seat. So this morning she offers to treat Paco to breakfast. Like most locals, he orders pan dulce (coarse, ginger-flavored pastries shaped like pigs, roosters, pinwheels) and a Coke.

The pair of them attract attention. Frail, puzzled smiles from the other hotel guests suggest Claire's some kind of Peace Corps representative who reminds them of things they have come on vacation to forget. The waiters loiter nearby, moistening their lips. They coo, "Paquito have a new sweetheart, eh?" They rub their palms together or down the thighs and arms of polyester uniforms—like doctors' coats. "Paquito have a white girl for dancing partner?"

Turns out today is the holiday of Saint Carmen and a big deal. *Dancing.* It occurs to Claire that if she's really going to seduce Oscar, she should buy some sort of birth control, disease control, condoms. If they even sell them hereabouts. If they don't close stores on account of saints.

"Hola, spiderwoman," booms Joe Watson as he sits down at the next table, holding his trusty Off! can, felt sombrero, copy of *Shōgun*. "Buenos días."

"Buenos días," Oscar's note said too, written half in ink, half in scratches with an apparently dysfunctioning ballpoint on the back of a receipt for his sunglasses. "Don't know if you were conscious when I told you I'm jungle (Yum Kaak) bound. In search of research. Leaving you this gift. Look!" An arrow pointed toward a monsterish dead moth on the windowsill. "It's furry! Seriously, I'm sorry, but Ph.D. IOUs can't wait. Will be back pronto or in a few days. Things of science are never far from a table."

The dining palapa (hut) has wood tables with conch-shell centerpieces. A raucous unseen kitchen. Cats and dogs. A bar. Sand floors to keep your feet amused and a laminated typed menu in Spanglish: "Rosbif" (for breakfast?) and "Scramblin Eggs Rancheros." Each dish is served with a globule of refried-bean paste, a lime garnish, and an excess of paper napkins. The waiters scold if you don't order all the sauces and side dishes or don't eat all you've ordered or don't order more.

"This gal here personally prevailed over Spoooky Tarantula numero uno," Joe Watson announces to the room. "Let's hear a round." Thankfully, there is only some minor clapping, from the pasty couple at the next table and from Paco, who has no idea why he's applauding. Joe Watson eyes Claire's chest, sucks his lower lip white, and adds, "I sure was impressed." With the half-falling-off sheet, probably. "Bravavavavavado."

"It wasn't really a tarantula, I don't think. All I did was catch him in the Off! cap and—"

"Like I been tellin you—that shit is necessary." The man is obsessed with Off! Maybe he works for the company. Or else it's what he's chosen to talk about so that no one will know he hasn't actually read any of *Shōgun*.

"What I don't git is why didntcha blast the sucker outta commission?"

Claire laughs *at*, not *with*, her neighbor. "Can't explain it." But the cop-out answer doesn't bother him the way Claire intends it to, the way it would bother Oscar. Joe Watson takes up scanning the floor around his chair in search of zappable insects.

Paco, otherwise silent, orders seconds. His head is bobbing from the sugar buzz as if his neck were a spring. Buttery fingers drum a sheen onto his wide left cheek in time to the faint sputtering music, "No Me Encuentro Satisfecho." I Can't Get No . . .

At this rate, Claire tells the boy (now that Oscar's away, she can at least speak Spanish without feeling pretentious), all your teeth are gonna drop out before you hit puberty.

"Sí." Polite, sheepish, and factual. I know.

As for Claire's own appetite, she hasn't one, but that doesn't stop her. She has her usual plata de fruta, toast, and water, leaving the two sweet, runny oranges. Water costs more than Coke.

"You are right to emphasize nutrition," Joe Watson says as he douses his scramblin eggs with salsa ketchup. Huevos revueltos, a fitting name. There's a fly in them!

"Um . . ." Claire begins. Scramblin fly.

"You been to the ruins?"

"No." And if one more person asks her . . . Claire points to the black blot, and fearful that Joe Watson will either eat it up or douse it in Off! spray, she turns quickly back to Paco. "So where's your boss today, Mr. Ham?" Claire knows full well he's with Oscar, doing . . . research? And she's hoping Paco knows how to break into the dive shack.

"Not around."

"That so? Not around whe—?" But Claire is pleasantly interrupted by a sprinkle of wet from above. Through the bamboo lattice, she checks out three charcoal clouds. They are lining up offshore, dangling in the sun. They threaten to soak the six or ten comically swiveling butts: an odd contingent of walk-running uniformed adults led by that silver-bouffanted guy of the ducklike profile, who took Claire's spider home with him. His musclebound friend still clings to computer golf as he jogs along the seaweed-littered strip of shore. "Not around where, Paco?" Who are those people? "In Yum Kaak?"

"*Yum Kaak!* Is that *your* husband?" The obviously eavesdropping male half of the pasty couple leans over the table with his brochure, "Mexico: Feel the Warmth!" "I found that Yum Kaak. God of Maize."

"What?"

The man turns to a picture of a deity hugging a potted plant. "Pretty silly, huh? I—" But the guy breaks off then and there to bolt for the bathroom.

"You will meet my mother," Paco tells Claire. Like an order.

"OK, I guess; sure," Claire agrees. "But what about this Yum Kaak? It's a place too?"

Paco nods.

"And Fernando . . . ?"

"He will come . . ." Mañana.

Though Claire doesn't actually hear the word, owing to the sudden rupture of sky. The waiters jump into action, pulling green plastic sheeting over the crisscross tree limbs of the palapa while the guests mute their talk, awed by the force of the tropical rain gush.

"Wait five," Joe Watson says. "When those clouds peel, it'll be somethin."

"Do you like him?" Claire asks Paco. "Fernando?"

The kid squints, slightly cross-eyed. His neck has a very defined collar of dirt. Can you tell if it's raining when you're underwater? Claire wonders. When Paco finally answers, "I like him, yes," it sounds as if he's carefully weighed the pros and cons.

"How much does he pay you, a day?"

"Six hundred pesos."

"Six hundred pesos!" Joe Watson repeats. "Six hundred pesos!"

So negligible that Claire can barely do the math.

"Want anything else?" she asks the poor kid. "Still hungry?" Six hundred pesos—that's something like forty cents. Still, Paco's lucky compared with the dozens of other boys his age, out there right now in the rain scrounging for change, hailing taxis, selling Chiclets, hauling around beach chairs and luggage, competing with rats and juicy winged roaches for garbage from the Mac Taco stand.

"Herb?" the doughy bride bangs on the bathroom door. "What's going on in there?"

Claire continues to offer Paco "Grapefruit juice? Bacon? Anything?" peering down at his dark, fragile wrists from that uncomfortable altar of privilege first and indelibly revealed to her in the girls' locker room of Garth A. Battista Junior High by one Josephine Hadley. "No?" Though Claire could sign the breakfast bill to the room, to Oscar, she pays with her (Dad's) credit card.

This thoroughly enchants Paco. He fixes an intense gaze on the eagle hologram, cupping the card to turn it back and forth. "Muy bonita, Claire," he says, and very reluctantly returns the magic plastic. Is she famous from the television? he asks her. Would she sign his napkin? Then: Can he keep the pen?

"Herb?" Doughy bride still bangs on the bathroom door. "I need to get in there *baaad.*"

"Jesus." Joe Watson's grumbling. "Someone tell this lady we tryin a eat. What's the big idea servin up Scramblin Flies in any case? I'm sick. I wanna refund here. I'm soaked. Where's the manager. What kinda *re*sort is this? I asked for iced tea and they brought me an ashtray. I wanna . . ."

Claire pretends not to see Paco stuffing the leftover pan dulce down his pants.

Josephine Hadley was, for years, the invisible recipient of all Claire's old clothing, because Josephine's mother, Gloria Rose, who cleaned the Allswell house every Monday, Wednesday, and Friday, asked for the clothes outright. Gloria was a giggly woman from Trinidad. She had a husband and two boyfriends and dangerously high blood pressure and six fingers on each hand (little fleshy nubs with nails, jutting out from the side of her pinkies) and six toes per foot and no willpower. A bottle of Tabasco sauce was always hidden in her apron. She had a mouth that wouldn't stop.

So Claire eventually knew Josephine better than most people she'd actually met. She knew, for instance, that the girl was exactly seven months and seven days older than herself, that she had an unknown father, color blindness, musical aptitude, a job after school at Blimpie's, and a best friend named Princess, who had a "shoplifting problem."

Not that any of it really mattered much until Claire and Josephine were assigned adjoining gym lockers. While Josephine would silently pull on and off Claire's old clothes—the outgrown, thank god, dumb sailor's dress from Grandma Lillian (too small on Josephine, too, and just as geeky-looking), the outmoded white carpenter's overalls that Claire messed up trying to embroider, the red silk Chinese jacket she begged for and then never wore and then saw on this girl and wanted again—Claire would silently pull on and off *this year's* new ones.

"I seen this lady at the ruins didn't have no Off!," Joe Watson reports. "Man, her leg be all swelled up."

THE JUNGLE BELOW is like a loud, gusting steam room. After the downpour, the relief is minimal. Scalding heat returns, and the bug repellent on Oscar's face drip-stings into every orifice—an oily alcoholic taste. The dye from his new red gym shorts runs pink down his legs, splatters his white sneakers, dots and dissolves on the slippery stone steps of the pyramid that he and Fernando are climbing: 402, 403, 405 steps, they go on, 406, toward some measly little temple on top. Oscar cannot even see it.

"Four oh eight." In the bright mist Fernando's just a shape with a voice diligent about keeping count, since a bet rides on the number. Jamón's prediction: 646. Oscar's: "More." They're betting for who will carry the parrot box and knapsack when they set out for the macaws' roost, though guess who's been stuck with them so far.

"Four ten, four eleven." Fernando's disembodied prattle is more hypnotic than the rain and as heavy as Oscar's soaked-through sneakers. "As schoolchildren, here I was taken to see this temple"—the tallest, oldest (327 B.C.) pyramid on the whole Yucatán peninsula—"with machetes we had to have for cutting out a way in the brush. B.E."

"B.E?"

"Before Excavation. Then, I could run up."

There are as many sounds in the jungle as in the city, only different ones. Very few of which Oscar can even begin to identify. Machete wind through the lace haze of trees thick with birds giggling Spanish like . . . children on a school trip. Four fifteen.

"And *we* went to the Museum of Natural History."

"Sí, I heard of there. Four seventeen."

"With switchblades." City machetes.

"True?" Eighteen.

"Yeah." Till they installed metal detectors. "And brown paper bags sweating tuna fish." The Conservation Museum. The Brooklyn Botanic Garden. The Bronx Zoo. Which smelled worse than a Penn Station bathroom; nothing like the jungle. There are as many smells as in the city, only different ones.

"Twenty, twenty-one, twenty-two." Oscar feels encased in plastic, head to toe, like he's wearing one of those bags from the dry cleaner's kids are warned against. Yet it is through this suffocating blur that he spots the dog-size iguana disguised as a rock disguised as a cloud. Magnificent. The sighting outweighs the discomfort. He longs for a closer look. Still, Oscar doesn't stop, on account of another, unspoken competition: the real root of this pilgrimage is not Good Luck Power, as Fernando insists, but Machismo Test—who will need to rest.

It's not going to be me, Oscar assures himself. He'd collapse first. And it's not going to be Jamón. Four thirty-three. So it's simply not going to be.

Some people, Fernando tells Oscar, think this temple was

built by aliens who came down in UFOs. "Like your girlfriend visioned."

"What people? Japanese divers?"

Fernando says a lot of things, anything, Oscar suspects, to bring up the subject of "your girlfriend," and "T and A," an expression the guy obviously picked up in Estados Unidos. "Spicy T and A," he likes to say, and has said a few hundred times already today in reference to dance-yoga woman, Chicky Boom, whom Fernando claims to have "taken" on his boat last night. Five times around the harbor he "boomed" her. Afterward, they mutually applied moisturizer.

Four forty. One. Two. Oscar's breath sounds rusty. Claire would probably beat them both to the top, Oscar thinks, as the rain moves out the way it came, a swoop at their backs. Overripe fruit stink is released and a prickly sweat/repellent aftertaste. The heat and the bird chorus intensify.

"Some parrots," Oscar says, "can be heard as far as seven miles." Until this moment, he himself had never quite grasped the magnitude of the statistic. Mental field-notebook entry.

Fernando grinds on. "Four forty-four, forty-five ..." As if reciting an English lesson too easy for him. "Four forty-nine." His hand reaches down to "borrow" the sunglasses off Oscar's face.

"Hey." Momentarily blinded, Oscar sways and grabs at the air. "Gimme those." If Claire were here, she'd probably team up with Fernando and count in Spanish just to irritate Oscar. If Sam were here, he'd probably topple Oscar right back down all 453 steps. If Fred were here, Oscar probably wouldn't be, but then neither would Fred if Oscar weren't. The altitude dizzies. "I haven't eaten a thing but bug repellent all day." Four sixty-two. Three. Four hundred sixty-eight, who do we appreciate?

"You keep banging me," Fernando says, the shape of him now but a smudge in Oscar's spotted vision, a maze of mosquitoes having apparently passed up Mexican flesh for the more exotic processed American variety.

Leaves squeak as if miked.

THE HOLIDAY of Saint Carmen is being sponsored by Superior beer, or so all the signs around the zócalo seem to indicate. The red-and-black logo is emblazoned on everything from the half-erected band platform to the trucks full of folding chairs to the boxes of ready-made amusement park. The actual product is advertised by the men paid in beer to set up, one in each free hand, a dozen in each gut. Like the rain, the men work on and off today. When they feel like it.

Paco, less shy now that he's eaten, pulls Claire by her forearm confidently through town, past the Mac Taco stand, where he says he normally breakfasts, past the succession of booths, all with the same baskets, earrings, rugs, towels for sale, past el banco, the liquor store, Máscara's lobster house, toward his home, one of a row of cinder-block structures with steel rods left jutting up from the walls so that an extra story might be added on at any time. Mexico's continuous state of mishmash, no-rush construction (cement gets mixed in turquoise beach pails) only heightens Claire's inertia.

"I don't know," Claire says. "I don't think I should just march right in—"

"But I want to show you her," Paco whines, kicking up dirt (the yard), wringing Claire's arm. Show her his mother? What for? "Y mi casa?" he adds, a question, examining Claire's face to see what she sees, perhaps. No door, is what. *Something old.* The entrance is a gash in the hollowed-out slab of cement. Above it a sign stamped in metal like a license plate proclaims ESTE HOGAR ES CATÓLICO.

Claire balks. "I have errands . . ." In a nearby front yard, a whistling man with a hose and a bucket of suds simultaneously washes his car *and* his person. "At the farmacia. Before it closes." Condoms, maybe an alluring aphrodisiacal scent, coconut or passion fruit, *something new.* "At the post office too." Stamps for Oscar's card to Louette, and her own to Dad, Grandma Lillian, Peaches (an apology would be adult). "The best thing about postcards," Oscar remarked, in sharp contrast to Claire's own opinion, "is safety! You don't have to get anything back."

"But it's noon," Paco argues, pushing out his lower lip, which is too thin, too much the same beige color as his face, to achieve the pout effect he's after. "Es siesta. And you promised." In exchange Paco has agreed to show Claire how to break into the dive shack.

Paco ushers Claire inside with an air of control, his chin and the corners of his mouth raised. It's dark—no windows either. "Dónde está Mamá?"

It smells of garlic and wet feathers, mildew, pretzels, socks, pine air freshener, potent melting cheese. It feels sticky, the heat of something continuously cooking. It sounds noisy—TV spews in English, a baby's cries in chokes.

"I don't know." Claire can only picture a grown-up Josephine Hadley wearing the rejected engagement party dress Grandma Lillian purchased and brandishing a clothesline "to hang your rich ass." Absurd.

A big brass cross, a pink stuffed rabbit, a bunch of novelas (comics), and a turquoise bottle of bleach occupy the same rickety bookshelf.

"Paco?" a woman's voice *projects*. The kid becomes taller. "Paquiiito! Ven acá." The shelf trembles.

Paco tugs on two of Claire's fingers. "Come." Though scrunching up his forehead, he can get no wrinkles to happen. He is *that young*. His voice still high and smooth. "No problem." Canny, untamed, tar-ball eyes seem wired up to the rest of his body like two anxious muscles, unbearable holiday anticipation of—today anything might happen—free pan dulce, tourists become houseguests. The regular rules don't apply.

In the kitchen are women, one at the stove (gurgling so alive Claire can sense it five feet away), two, three, four more around a table (a bright mess of fabric, paper, yarn, ribbon, and fluffy whatnot). A boy stands with one cheek smushed up against the speaker of a small black-and-white RCA television—"Magnum, P.I."—which is crowned with a stack of tortillas. And above it all, suspended in an ingenious mini-hammock, squawls Baby.

"What is this?" a woman in curlers asks. What, not who. She reels Paco in by his belt loops, so that out pops the pan dulce—three pieces. *Something borrowed.* To everyone's amusement, a disk-shaped pastry goes skidding across the floor.

Paco strains against his pants to reach down for the remaining two pastries at his feet. But the woman in curlers—his mother?—pulls him back, tickles his armpits, grabs his chin, angles it toward her, asks, "Another?" grinning past him toward Claire with such a look of recognition that it seems entirely possible they could have met somewhere. The woman's long side ponytail is clinched with a child's elastic fastener, purple plastic orbs, and on one of her stocky upper arms there's a dark, intriguing perfect crescent birthmark. "An American?"

Paco nods, showing off the autographed napkin, while Claire flattens down her ripped blue dress, fingers Fred's half-dollar in her pocket.

"Just like his father," says a second, pretty woman, rocking the infant.

"It's true," says the woman in curlers, still keeping Paco harnessed, but semi-distracted by the TV and/or the boy up against it. Magnum, P.I. is creeping around in a warehouse filled with empty boxes. His shirt is red and flashy. His gun is cocked. "Think she knows how old he is?"

"Not ordinary, this one," notes a third, much more modern female. She wears jeans and lipstick and a "SUN YOUR BUNS IN ISLA MUJERES" tank top; she's chewing gum.

In turn, a fourth woman pipes up, or down at a ceramic bowl as if to sluggishly mash in her comment, "A blonde," along with its other contents. In her dusty black nightgown, she looks ancient, this one, two-dimensional, bleached out, like a painting that's been left in the sun too long.

Claire is certain the women are assuming she doesn't understand. And she wonders if she really does? Another? American? A blonde? And would they like her more or less if she was to speak? One thing Claire does register, however, is that their joking is without malice even if directed at her; it is surely a continuation of their holiday adrenaline.

"Hi?" Claire chances, but no one hears except maybe Paco, who breaks loose and gets tapped playfully on the butt with the long wooden spoon held by a fifth woman, the cook, hefty or pregnant, with an enormous, slightly graying, lopsided bun that looks sculpted out of papier-mâché or bread. Caught staring, Claire quickly turns and finds herself facing the boy with his ear to the TV.

"My brother Jesus," Paco whispers. *Hey-Zeus.* Paco picks up a piece of pan dulce and hands it to the kid. "Dumb y deaf, but vibrations he likes, comprende?"

"Sí." The simple acknowledgment rouses the woman in curlers to finally identify herself positively as Paco's mom.

"Consuela." Her gaze is a loaded mixture of friendliness and reproach, caution, mesmerism, perhaps a touch of indigestion.

Paco squeals, "Here's Claire." Customary? As if he's holding her up to the light for his mother's perusal. Claire shifts foot to foot, forward and back, wondering whether she should say something. "Don't feel nervous," says Paco. Nervous? That's not it. It's—

"Hello to you," Mother says, this time in English. "Will you eat?" She's probably no older than Claire, possibly younger.

"No; no, thank you. I'm sorry to—" Don't start up I'm sorrying again now.

The elderly woman in the black nightgown holds her bowl out as in offering. *Something blue.*

"Beetle wings," Mom explains, in English. Some are still intact, sticking to the sides of the bowl like flecks of tracing paper, the others are ground finely into a silky, iridescent powder.

"For makeup," the modern girl informs Claire. She pulls Claire by the elbow toward the bowl for a demonstration. Dipping in a carnation-pink fingertip, the girl then runs it across her own eyelids. "Oooh," she raptures. "Elegante!" She climbs on a chair to swivel her head back and forth and model the miracle dust—gold-green to tinselly gray-blue and back again. A quiet dazzle along the lines of the Arm eyes, opals of the Caribbean, happiness. Double Happiness.

"Sí, sí," the women affirm, and insist that Claire shadow her own lids. She does.

Then it's Mom's turn. She layers hers on extra thick. Next, the pretty lady rocking the hammock, who uses not her finger but an old toothbrush she whips out of her dress pocket. Lastly, bunhead, the cook, who has Claire apply the mixture, because her own hands are "limoso"—slimy. In return for the deed, she presents Paco with a bottle of vanilla extract with which to perfume "tu novia."

"Gracias, tía," Paco says, out of breath but with an air of new dignity, having wrapped himself in reams of the colored paper and fabric like a king with his harem. "See," he says, as the tip of his vanillaed pinkie approaches the space behind Claire's ear. "You fit."

This kitchen in Playa Alguna is no more alien than Chester's beauty parlor in Sidehill. Women primping are women primping. For the holiday of Saint Carmen, for the holiday of the All-for-Nothing Bridal Shower; no matter. Another constant seems to be Claire's role as the *guest* star, as the girl who's only and always passing through.

Paco squeezes Claire's thumb as if to inflate her. "You're the prettiest one," he murmurs, blinking up at the ceiling, to which he might expect she'll ascend when he lets go—leaving Claire to ponder whether it is necessary to be a virgin to be a saint.

WHEN OSCAR wakes up, or fades in, it is really hours later, or so Fernando says. They're on the second to the top step of the pyramid, with the disappointing little temple at their backs. The Mexican looks snooty in Oscar's sunglasses, reclining with his cigarettes all lined up beside him to dry in the sun. "And now, siesta's done. I've been thinking. . . ."

"Well, did I make it up myself?" To Oscar the answer seems

terribly important. What if this man had to carry him the "how many steps"? Besides the humiliation of it, Oscar would be indebted. Oh god.

The mosquitoes have bitten right through his shorts. Itchy ass and dehydration from the violent ultraviolet assault form a picture in Oscar's mind of a complete layer of his own skin, scaled off and lying there in one Oscar-shaped piece. He begins to ask the vital question again but is interrupted by an intense tickling in his right ear—beetle.

"Ah." Fernando beams as if he put the insect there. He gathers up his damp cigarettes in preparation for the descent. "I've been thinking that—"

"I just got here," Oscar says, not moving. "Answer me." There is nothing that can make you feel quite so vulnerable as passing out in front of a stranger and not remembering it.

"Six forty-six steps." Fernando flings out his arm like a deranged but inspired tour guide. "The temple of the Descending God: welcome. I win."

"You knew it all along. No fair." Oscar is not eager to pay up and continue carrying the heavy parrot box and knapsack.

"I did count." Fernando misunderstands, on purpose. "Six forty-six." He picks up the sack and drops it on Oscar's stomach for emphasis. "Exactamente."

Pretending not to notice, Oscar turns to reexamine the stone ruin. Good-luck power? The figure carved in its facade does indeed look as if it's tumbling down from heaven or the heavens, as the case may be for god plural. Then, trying to jerk up to a sit too fast, Oscar takes a clumsy slow spill and lands belly-down, four or five stairs lower, while the pack topples. Both he and Fernando watch as it picks up speed, bouncing in and out of sight, smaller and smaller.

From this height, walking down seems very high-risk, unless backward on your hands and knees. About as unmacho as it gets. The pack hits something—Oscar hopes not the iguana—pops vertically and stops.

Fernando shushes Oscar's curses in the name of "this temple."

The vantage point certainly is godworthy. Treetops like plush golden-green high-pile carpeting stretch farther than Oscar can see. A dense overgrowth has already begun erasing the recently excavated city of Yum Kaak. Ruins, each of which would seem gargantuan were Oscar at ground level, appear a bunch of scattered, puny rock piles, five or six miles apart, separated by the ghosts of maybe thirty roads. A definite step up from Temple Beth Israel overlooking Sidehill Avenue.

Oscar also counts one, two, three, four, five lakes edging the forest, and not ponds or swamps or any dinky alternative, but formidable lakes, five oases, the brisk blue of Claire's one and only dress. Of Fred's painted banjo. Of the beetle that crawled out of Oscar's own ear.

Fernando crouches to pray.

"Since when are you so pious, a-migo?" Oscar asks. "Slamming back tequila while the whole town's in church and then molesting an innocent tourist with tubs of aloe rub."

"How do you know how it is with me, anything?" Fernando fires off rapidly.

So Oscar gets up to touch the holy place. Can't hurt. Give Jamón time to cool. In direct sunlight, the stones look bluish, too, and somehow stubborn. "Am I allowed in?" Oscar asks the Descending God, discovering the deity will scowl if you squint one eye.

"Sí, if you fit," Fernando says, following.

"The doorway looks designed for midgets," says Oscar.

"No, to make you bow your head." Fernando pushes him. "Bow, Mr. Oscar." A dare.

Inside, there are only bats and moths, cobwebs, doors leading to stairs leading to more doors, more stairs, more bats, moths, cobwebs. "If I were a midget, it might be sort of cool for a clubhouse," Oscar says, emerging. To let Fernando know once and for all he isn't buying all the guy's explanations. "But I'm not only not a midget, I'm tall, taller than you, even with my head bowed, and this thing you call a temple is dank, claustrophobic. Frankly, Hambone, it's bleak."

"You insult me!" Fernando says. Time-release anger.

"It's not easy."

"And my religion."

"Which?"

"I believe . . . this." Fernando points at the Descending . . . bee, it looks like, actually. A big fat bee. "And this." And Fernando's suddenly yanking down his pants—to take a piss, make a pass?

"What the hell is *this?*" yelps Oscar. A blemished ugly butt with hair, tattooed. The Virgin of Guadalupe. So we meet again. The indelible Mary spans the full surface area of Fernando's left cheek—ever smiling. It strikes Oscar as particularly offensive in the midst of all this grandiose Nature.

"You like her?" Fernando laughs, making the Virgin perform a gruesome jiggly dance.

CLAIRE LINGERS among the cool, dusty shelves and glass cases of the farmacia, pretending to choose among the two shampoos in stock—Johnson's Baby and the generic brand, Champú—waiting to be the only customer, waiting for the Spanish words to come to her, as they always have before. Condoma? No concepción? Por no birth? Wrong, wrong.

The farmacia doubles as a clothing store of sorts, and so Claire rummages through the elaborately embroidered guayaberas, the shapeless sleeveless dresses, the Italian-type T-shirts, the sandals, for something . . . something seductive, or at least with a waist, or at least above the knee, or at least that she could imagine wearing. Nada.

"What do you want in here?" the woman behind the counter hollers. So much for customer service.

"Ice cream," Claire says, in hopes of getting a smile. But instead the woman winces, as if the unexpected gringa Spanish physically pained her. She grinds her teeth and folds her arms and glares out of eyes like deep incisions.

"Not here," the sourpuss says, clearly not one to be moved by any holiday spirit. She has that used-to-be-beautiful-but-now-bitter-because-old look. Justifiably or not, she obviously despises all tourists, outright, and has despised them so strenuously for so long that she's even forgotten how to enjoy it. Willing to forgo cash, anything, to let this be known. Her bark—"Not for sale"—is in fast-forward to throw Claire off and is extra loud to scare her.

"In that case, I'll take this," Claire blares back, not only in English but with a Queens accent. She pulls a dress at random off the rack. "And condoms, please. And some vanilla extract. And this Champú."

The woman bristles but rings up the items. Claire bristles, waiting, or tries, interrupted by the curious ragged bruise on the storekeeper's throat. Maybe she's an abused wife. Maybe I should pity her. Until Claire hears the price—nearly quadruple what it should be. "And you forgot the condoms."

"Qué?" Claire's used to this, bored with this, furious and fed up with this. A local habit—not understanding on purpose. Claire notices that her new dress is blue too, slightly darker than her old one.

"Anticoncepción?" Claire says. Not right, but closer. The woman shrugs, busies herself rearranging dusty gauze and hydrogen peroxide. "For sex," Claire goes on, shamelessly. "To lose my virginity." She is not sure why she's divulging this information. To hear herself say it out loud, perhaps. And for its shock value. There are virgin places still.

The woman reaches under the counter for the rubbers. No, a papaya. The woman holds the yellow fruit and begins fiercely punching holes in it with her fingernails. Bizarre. She hisses, "This store is Catholic, miss."

So Claire stoops to being a lowlife American, holding out ten thousand pesos—roughly seven bucks. So her opponent stoops to being a lowlife Mexican, taking it—enough to buy beans and tortillas for a month. The two of them can no longer look eye-to-eye at one another. Or at the suddenly materialized box of ribbed Azteca sheaths. Papaya drools.

DEEP IN the rain forest, the green canopy makes a perpetual twilight in which luminous orchids, snakes, parrots thrive, but which kills any sense of time or of north, south, east, west. The flies are relentless. Oscar's hip becomes bruised by the steady banging of the parrot box as he forges on. This is *forging on*, he thinks, and if Vladimir has not sent me to have some sort of religious experience, then Fernando must have the ability to smell his way to a single tree in all these acres and acres of them.

"Rubber, almond, banana, sapodilla—gum," Fernando tells Oscar, but not which tree is which in the tangle of exposed, easily-tripped-over roots like fat meshed fingers, and Tarzan vines that require a machete Oscar and Fernando don't have.

It'd be a complete drag if it weren't so phenomenal. Thick masses of lemon butterflies; fluorescent rainbow blurs of birds; a lone toucan putting around, munching on fruit with its big beak, bright as plastic; a processional of dark giggling Indian women with plantains on their heads, taking care not to step on three-foot-wide columns of ants, each creature the size of a thumb. It's like one of those rides at Disneyland where things pop out of the dark at you—terrible and terrific things—except here Oscar and Fernando are simultaneously on the ride and part of it.

THE "UPNESS" fades to night with a cloud parade like chalk blurred out by hand in a rush—no, like only the shadows of clouds done in apricot—no, no, ice cream soda? Floating babies? That's it! *Floating babies*. Now for the "downness." It is equally indescribable—pink rocky sand, scrubby beach plants, a lightning lizard running past on its hind legs, swim mask prism.

Drip-drying on the sand, Claire is happily making sense of things, when she is besieged by the *friendly people*.

"Hi."

Ramona and Herbert from Oklahoma. Who asked them to sit? A speech pathologist and a meteorologist respectively.

"Really."

Ages twenty-five, twenty-nine.

"How about that?"

They corner Claire with their good cheer and cloying introductions. They back her right up against the dive shack.

Paco did keep his promise and get her inside, but Claire found no incriminating evidence there. No drugs. No weapons other than spear guns. No leads whatsoever as to what Oscar's up to. So she borrowed some equipment and jumped in, went mermaiding. Maybe she should never have surfaced.

These sorts of *friendly* couples chatter with the aggressiveness most people reserve for tennis, office, driving. Vital statistics out of the way, they proceed to jam on their room, the "Luna de Miel Suite"—not what they saw in the brochure. "Someone's gonna have some explaining to do" to their three unborn children—two boys and a girl, all three years apart. They plan to get started right away—*after* the honeymoon? Then on to Ramona's bothersome hammertoes, the Cuban missile crisis—Herbert's hobby—until Claire yawns, quite unintentionally, and finds herself answering a string of droll and predictable questions. Where did she get that great tan? From the sun. Where does she "hail" from? France—not really; New Jersey. How long has she been here? Long enough not to know exactly. And the sobering but inevitable What do you do?

"Oh . . . let's see. I would say . . . in transition."

"Transmissions?" Herbert asks, impressed.

"Transition. Flux." Somewhere between beer-testing and swimming again.

THE INDIANS FREEZE as the two white men—one decidedly whiter—step out onto the hillside and espy the small, crooked clearing obviously hacked out of the jungle. Slash and burn. Instantaneous farmland.

Fernando, blinking in the sudden light, lets out a satisfied exhalation before hurrying down the incline to the desolate plot, where maize is being cultivated. Yum Kaak. The sparsely planted corn stalks are offset by the precision of the laborers themselves, all wrapped in identical white sheets wound tightly around their chests and flowing loose to the ground. A scene that has, to Oscar's limited experience, the look of a motion picture epic. The sort of movie that never fails to put him to sleep.

Oscar's so tired it's all he can do to keep up with Fernando's wildly flapping pants, looser by the hour, looser by the stride, and now so low-riding that Oscar can see the crack of the guy's butt and part of that hideous Virgin halo. Oscar's so hungry not even *that* sight can dissuade his stomach from considering grabbing a fistful of the raw green plant to stuff in his mouth. Oscar's so muddy and cut up and irritable that it takes him much longer than normal to realize that the workers surrounding him are women—all of them women, with shoulders wider and more powerful than his own.

But short. The girl who stands to greet them barely reaches Fernando's chest. She answers his question with stagnant, averted eyes and a fiercely docile expression that seems bred into her bone structure. Appearing oblivious to Fernando's attempts to get his shirt tucked in for her, she raises one slim, muscled charcoal elbow in a follow-me gesture. Oscar is overcome with the desire to touch her.

She glides ahead, an apparition in the white sheet (how does she keep it so white, kneeling in the dirt all day?), her long, dark neck tilted forward slightly as she maneuvers with no excess motion around the larger tree trunks sticking up like fangs out of the burned earth, toward a group of thatched huts twenty or so yards off. Oscar's struck with the odd idea that if he were to touch her, she would vanish.

The other workers whisper and point. Oscar must look demented to them, scary, with his blistered neck and muddy pink scraped legs, with his hulking, unshaven companion.

"Here is the home of my friend," says Fernando.

Oscar is slow to process this information, lost in the coils of the woman's dark hair. What friend? All around them, the towering trees of the jungle lean in, ready to reclaim this grubby clearing. One year? Perhaps two. The incredible futility of it seems somehow to echo Oscar's own ever-trickling Fredsickness. To be with him again. To be rid of him.

"What friend?" Near the huts, turkeys and hairless dogs run wild; bees dance in the humidity.

"Mi amigo who owns the parrot tree."

"Owns?" Oscar's getting suspicious. "How do you go about buying one tree in an entire rain forest?"

"Not like buying." Fernando groans, exasperated, sorry he ever took up with such a novice. "It is passed down in a family like houses, like furniture." Furniture?

The houses don't look built to last more than one man's lifetime, if that. Outside the hut closest to them, a bunch of kids share their mud puddle with an apparently tamed and delighted black pig.

"You will pay my friend money for the birds in his tree." Oscar has suspected something of the sort. "And pay me."

"Money, money. What can you buy with money right now? What can you ever buy?"

"Teeth," Fernando says. "Visas." They have reached the entranceway. No door. A string of bells signals their arrival.

"Wait a second. His birds or his tree?" And, "Who is he?" And, "What happened to doing this ourselves without a middleman?" And, "Did you tell Vladimir about this?"

Fernando pretends not to hear.

The woman steps aside, allowing the men to enter first. Oh, money is evil, Oscar thinks, if only because it has pull enough to divert me from this. Of course the woman's allure has nothing to do with who she is—who is she?—and everything to do with how much of her Oscar cannot see beneath the sheet.

Fernando snaps his fingers and motions Oscar inside.

"How much money?" Oscar asks. "Why not just mug me and get it over with?" Three men—one jolly, one dapper, one caved in—look up at him from around a small scratched and stabbed wooden table. Pretty much the extent of the heirloom furniture.

Fernando bows and seats himself in the only extra chair,

next to Jolly, who immediately points to the sunglasses—his arm has a big pink gash—and nods, approvingly, admiringly, obsessively. Belatedly, Oscar bows too, but no one seems to notice him. The woman fires up the stove.

Food. Women. Oscar thinks dreamily of Louette's chicken cutlets, crisp but tender. A dozen steamers and a plate of potato skins from Lil's Fish Fry Palace. *"Que es por food?"* Oscar asks, but the woman doesn't seem to hear or chooses not to answer. It doesn't matter anyhow. He will eat anything. Then again, since he has not been offered so much as a seat, perhaps not.

Jolly dons the sunglasses, and his feet spring up onto the table; he makes a peace sign. Dapper tries them on and whips out a comb, slides his hair back, stands to play some air guitar. Concave man merely looks out from behind the Ray-Bans, incredulous, sits up almost straight, then proceeds to have a snort attack, as if seeing his friends for the first time in 3-D. Beyond them, in the bedroom, lie a shovel, seven or eight hammocks, and a television, unconnected.

When each man has had his turn trying on the glasses, Fernando puts them back on and launches into what sounds like a speech. Every so often he points toward Oscar. Who understands none of it.

This mysterious woman could be married, for all Oscar knows, could be pregnant under her drapery, could be mistress to all three of the men and to Fernando on occasion. Growing increasingly inattentive to Jamón's long-winded remarks, the men twist around in their seats, fan themselves with baseball caps that advertise Coca-Cola, Superior, Chevy Truck, and occasionally interrupt in arguing tones or bursts of uproarious chuckling. Displays of sparkling gold teeth.

At one point, even the woman at the stove—cooking mud patties?—creaks out a little giggle, making Oscar want to laugh too, but there's always the possibility that they are all laughing at him. In any case, he's physically unable to so much as smile. Between the foreign language and the heat, Oscar feels so thoroughly sapped it's an effort not to fall asleep right here, standing up. It'd be so easy, too easy, dangerous.

"What is it? What's going on?" Oscar asks Fernando's ear. "Tell me. Now."

"Whispering es not necessary for you," says Fernando. "These people, no habla español. Y inglés? More never."

"What then?"

"Just Mayan."

Is that something like speaking Brooklynese or Jewish? In any case, it cheers Oscar slightly. Even Claire wouldn't know Mayan, would she? He moves back over to check on the mud patties.

A mistake. Larvae are slowly wriggling out of the dirt clods and onto the smoking pan and into the woman's bare, unwashed hands and onto a plate. Do they eat the mud part or the larvae? Will Oscar be expected to eat either? He's not *that* hungry. He's relieved to be beckoned away by the summit members.

"Mira," Fernando says. "Beautiful, sí?" On the table now are necklaces of black coral and ivory. The same schlock sold in stalls all up and down the coast. "You will buy some." This is not a question. Fernando vigorously nods yes, as does Jolly, scratching his pink gash, eyes rolling.

"But why?"

"For the use of his tree."

"But why can't we just pay him off, like you said?" Oscar cannot believe he is making such a suggestion.

"We do not offend."

"I don't understand. Are you getting a cut? Is that it?"

Oscar picks up one of the necklaces. The black coral, cool on his skin, is studded with highly polished silver balls.

"Mí amigo made these jewelry," Fernando goes on. "You will like it for your girlfriend, ah huh."

Louette would maybe, in extreme desperation, wear them as part of some tropical Halloween ensemble. Claire (who Fernando means), there's no telling. Oscar's mother is the one who'd love them, who'd call them "kooky" and/or "primitive art" and tell everyone in Chesty's they were a gift from her son, bless his generous heart, who brought them back for her all the way from Mexico, where he went on his research trip. And all the ladies would say they wished *their* sons were as thoughtful and studious, or else bring up examples of how and when their sons were. Then they'd ogle the thing, and those without wet nail polish would pass it around to cop a feel.

"How much?"

"Fifty-six." The men nod. They understand this English word fine. Concave man even rubs his fingertips and makes an ugly slurping sound. "Special for your girlfriend." The men mmm and hiss; they understand this English too. But maybe Oscar's mistaken, because it comes to his attention then that the food has been served. Larvae and Cokes. The men dig in happily.

"Thirty-five," Oscar says, though the necklace is not worth nearly that much. "On one condition." But Fernando doesn't comprehend the expression, so Oscar puts it plain. "I am not eating this . . ."

Fernando pops one of the hors d'oeuvres in his mouth with exaggerated relish. "Mud wasp?"

"Yeah, whatever."

"No es necesario."

Not wanting to watch them eat the things, Oscar turns and notices the woman floating back out the door. Her white sheet remains on his retina long after she's disappeared, like a light stain from having your picture taken.

CLAIRE AVOIDS the packs of young men who roam the bug-infested amusement park or hang out of slowly cruising VW vans with their doors open, with funky moving lights outlining back windshields. She probably couldn't stand the embarrassment were they to call out, as she's heard them do to other girls, "Baby. Blondie." She also couldn't stand the embarrassment if they didn't. In the circumstances, even if Herbert is geeky, Claire's finding him here seems more lucky than not.

"Where's Ramona?"

"Oh, off looking for earrings with character." Herbert illustrates his contempt by executing a cruel imitation of his wife. He bunches up his chins and whines, " 'These have character but they're too blobby.' "

"I lost all my money on the picture roulette," Claire confesses. On the Langosta. "And Paco—lost him too."

"Saint Carmen works in unexpected ways," Herbert says. "I lost my patience. Hence this jaunt." He tries to take Claire's arm, but she wriggles free. "I like your dress," he says.

The new blue dress. Claire decides she doesn't like it. Definitely not. She walks a little ahead of Herbert now, through the seedy, unappealing fairground—testimony to Mexico's constant fascination with low-budget glitz. Foozeball and pork rinds, whistles and fortunes, puppets. A shooting gallery where pink plastic donkeys trot around hubcaps. Like Coney Island in some warped, bilingual nightmare. Each time the band takes a break, a voice over the loudspeakers encourages you to drink some more Superior. But all Claire's toy money is gone.

"Wanna go for a spin?" Herbert proposes in front of the carousel. A flimsy, loose-looking apparatus. It makes short, lonely metal sounds and sheds rust. Claire laughs, a fake laugh. She feels fluttery in her abdomen, a little dizzy, a little reckless, continuing on past the game stalls, which exhibit prizes you couldn't pay her to take: heavy deer statuettes and Virgin of Guadalupe bumper stickers. Herbert buys a helium balloon to suck in and make his voice funny. Not funny. Next he asks Claire to dance with him, under the disco lights. No, thank you. Cotton candy? Had some already, thanks. A stroll on the beach? Uh uh. No way, José. When they stop to examine the fluorescent painted hermit crabs set to race, a voice from out of a prowling pack of boys calls Herbert amigo and asks, most politely, "How much for your sister?"

THE HUGE-HEADED watchbirds screech deafeningly, "Predator! Predator!" as Oscar and Fernando approach the roost. Majestic hooked beaks open wide to emit the monotonous, headachy warning cry, exciting the flock to rise up and halo the tree in scarlet. Only the sentinels remain posed on their high perches, glowing red; tails spread wide, yellow; agitated blue neck and rump feathers: glorious. "Scarlet macaws!" No mistaking them. Nor the holes in the trees. "Nests." It is mating season.

Oscar feels his heart go messy.

"Ruidoso!" Fernando shouts. He holds his hands over his ears. Still, Oscar could kiss the señor for bringing them here. Better than fifty-yard line seats at the Super Bowl. "My tequila maybe will not have strength enough."

"And us?" The macaws, a whirling nimbus containing at least a hundred birds, now seem to know they are endangered, in danger. "You said yourself, animals have their own gods." An idea Oscar likes even if he doesn't agree. He doesn't not agree. Wait and see is his philosophy. Not for proof but for belief, and for the parrots to reassemble on the still-quivering branches.

Fernando and Oscar put on their gloves slowly and slowly move closer. Oscar's having trouble standing still in this state—expectancy and insects chewing on his face, elation and ticklish sweat dripping, apprehension and thoughts of It's still not too late just to watch now, act later. There is some sense to mañana. And he can't miss a thing. Commit all of it to photographic memory. If only he were equipped with pen and camera instead of box and gloves. If only it were Fred here with him and not Fernando.

Roosts, like any other place, have their rules. Without fading out, the live sirens halt abruptly. Birds grow calm, a hundred red bellies descend in unison, each member keeping exactly the right distance from his neighbor.

Then again, roosts have their rules broken too, like any other place. A deviant parrot lands too close to another bird and is met with an open beak that issues a low, hostile growl. But the intruder does not budge. This starts the whole community

squawking. Look! Look! Look! The bird on the defensive proceeds to make threatening gestures, hacking at the air yet never
actually touching his opponent.

"Wooo, wooo," Fernando says as he catches his first glimpse
of the female the defensive bird is protecting. She's practically
lying on the branch to signal her readiness. "I'd guard that
babe too," he whispers. And quietly Fernando roots for the
rightful stud, who is now raising his foot and pointing it toward the enemy's abdomen.

I have no intention of vacating this perch, ya hear? You tell
him, get him, tell him. The outlaw, stubborn, raises his foot
also, which starts a foot-boxing match! Oscar has never felt so
privileged.

"I think we've found our couple."

Fernando wants to jump in and help. "Who is this big shot?"

But Oscar knows they will not injure each other, even if given
the chance. If they do, well, that'd be publishable research.

Fernando suggests that they save themselves all this trouble
and just knock a nest from the tree. "Easy."

"You're not serious," says Oscar. Cruel. There could be eggs.

"Sí, very. If we—"

"Forget it. That is not the plan." Oscar would despise Fernando now if the birds weren't so fine, if he had time to afford
that luxury, if he weren't waiting to see . . .

"So what, then, the plan; tell me."

"Me?" A distinct communication problem. "What do you
mean, me?"

"You want birds, right? I want money. So I have showed you
to find the trees here. Like was said. Mi amigo—"

"But . . . you've done this before."

Fernando sighs. The intruding bird has at last retreated,
leaving the lovers to huddle. Lovers, naturally, are exceptions
to the "space" rule; a mixture of more freedom and less. A gap
Oscar hasn't had the guts officially to cross yet with Louette
(hence, holding on to his crummy apartment) but which he has
unintentionally crossed with Claire (sharing their room).

"Yes, sure, I come to this tree before many times." Oh, good. "But taking parrots and bringing them to America? Not a time." Oh god. "I am a diver."

"Well, why didntcha say that in the first place?" Oscar whines. He kicks a mammoth oozing slug off his sneaker. No experience? All day he's been following a complete buffoon.

"I am the diver," Fernando repeats. "You—"

"Just shut the hell up." Oscar is snapping more at Vladimir than at Fernando, though in his mind the two have melded into one and the same.

"You are the smuggler." Oh, no. "I have just a good idea of taking nests, easy—"

Damn Vladimir and his bargain connections. Oscar the smuggler? This is too too too much.

"No. I'm—" But Oscar realizes he can't set Fernando straight or he might raise the already thrice-raised price. And his voice; he might scare off the parrots, and then what? Wait and see no longer seems a working philosophy; Oscar's got to think *now.* "OK. Forget it. Just be quiet, all right? It's under control." Hah.

"Forget what?"

At least Oscar has the upper hand for once, for the moment. "If you promise not to suggest any more horrendous . . ."

"Qué es . . . horrendous?"

"Just put on your gloves."

"We did that."

"Yeah . . . of course. Well . . ." What's the worst thing that could happen? Getting an eye gouged out? Lip bit off? Pecked through the head? Not getting the birds at all? Getting them, then getting busted?

"Well?" Fernando asks. He takes another swig of tequila.

"Right. First put that shit away and listen. This is how we'll . . ." How? He'll just have to teach Fernando the way parrots are caught in aviaries. "Now memorize this: You're gonna have to move and reach very swiftly. I'll let you get the female; she'll be weaker."

Fernando chuckles. "Puta." Whore. That is one word he's taught Oscar.

"Serious. What did I say?"

"De prisa le atrapo la puta."

Atrapo? Atrapados? There it is, that word again. "In English, bonehead."

"Hurry up and trap the whore, you said, right?"

"Yeah. You're gonna hold her head—"

"Bonehead?"

"—like this, see." Oscar clasps an invisible bird skull between his thumb and index finger, and Fernando imitates correctly, obediently; amazing. "Bueno. Now restrain the wings with the rest of your hand . . . OK. Otherwise, she's gonna go wild fluttering and hurt herself. You got that?"

"Simpleness."

"I doubt it. We're gonna count to three and reach at the same time. Ready?"

"I am."

"You sure?"

"Uh huh." Oscar could still back out now. The victims-to-be are happily scratching each other's red heads with gentle, careless abandon. It's appalling to think of yanking them away and shoving them into that little box. "Got any handy prayers?" he asks Fernando, stalling, desperate. "To those animal gods or your ass; whatever."

"You the boss now." Fernando smiles. "Say one of yours. In Jewish." But that seems useless. The Jewish God unfortunately doesn't forgive trespassing. Oscar decides to direct his silent apologies to the birds themselves.

Just remember, kids, this is for the good of your species. Your babies will have more babies. Oscar tries to clear his mind of Vladimir and of the at least ten thousand dollars apiece that these beauties are worth. You'll be together. Cooperate and you won't be hurt. You have the right to remain silent. . . .

"One," Oscar says, slowly opening the door of the box with his foot and pushing it a little closer to the tree. "Two . . ."

"Wait!" Fernando stops him. "When you say 'three' or when you say 'go'?"

"Three."

Fernando dives at the tree, tripping the bird sirens. *"Cawww!"* Oscar has no choice but to grab at random—the leg—all he can catch and just in time. Hold on. The male macaw is startlingly strong and warm in the struggle, using his free claw to dig into and through the leather glove at Oscar's wrist while Oscar attempts to follow his own instructions and work swiftly to right the furious pecking head, cup the blue rump firmly. It's not working. The leg in his hand is palpitating in time to the deafening wing-slapping bluster that sends leaves and feathers spinning, blows Oscar's hair in his eyes so he can't see where the box is till he sort of falls over it because something swipes at his neck in what feels like slow motion, nearly knocking loose his hold, the bird or another bird or three, hacking at his shoulder like a can opener. "Fernando!" No answer, although the captured female screeches and trembles from inside the grating as Oscar pushes her mate in and runs with it.

And keeps running through the thick, hot, dripping growth, a network of snapping branches, trick vines that wrap around Oscar's legs and get dragged along with him as he runs through the field of huge slapping wet leaves, like those slatted plastic drapes in a car wash, stumbling over swollen corkscrew roots, on and on until all at once the bird screams stop. Silence.

Oscar goes down. A sick sensation swells like the blood seeping through the leather glove in a dark wet stain—puncture holes in the shape of a panda—and dripping in dots down his arm the way the dye of his shorts did, only thicker, redder. Oscar thinks, oddly, of the one time he really beat Fred up good, even though now he's the one beat up, lying on the itchy ground with the sense of watching himself tear off a piece of his shirt for a tourniquet, which he may or may not really be doing, all the while aware of the ominously silent box that he hasn't the guts to look into or touch, and well aware of just how lost he is but not of the more obvious—that it is night—

until Fernando appears, or the hovering outline of Fernando in the dark, taking on a significance he shouldn't have as he sniggers with satisfaction at finding Oscar like this—a pathetic, writhing mess on the ground. "How did you find me?" Too numb to feel relieved, Oscar wonders whether he is hallucinating.

"Find you where?" The presence, sitting right beside Oscar now, reeks of tequila and sweat. He's real, all right, Oscar decides. If I were going to have a vision, my mind would do better, would conjure up the woman in the white sheet, Fred or Louette, Marci, Claire, on down the line; even Sam would be more welcome than this guy—my fellow murderer, who has to show me that the Tree is *right* there, and full of birds again, that I did not run more than thirty yards! Asshole. "You dropped the jewelry of tu novia," Fernando adds, whipping the black coral necklace at Oscar and then reaching for the Box.

"Don't! . . . I mean, I should do that."

Fernando shrugs—go ahead—so Oscar follows his eyes to where the birds—alive!—are pushing their fluffy red heads against the mesh. How did this happen? Divine intervention? Just then all the birds begin to wail, perhaps in anticipation of the drizzle that starts up in the next instant.

Fernando is cursing. "Shit, wet, wet." But he assures Oscar it is nothing to cry over.

THE LEAD SINGER of Grupa Música wears a conch shell tucked into his belt, over his crotch. The bass player wears some kind of ceremonial cape. The drummer has on platform shoes circa 1972. They play a rocking version of "Feliz Cumpleaños" for Saint Carmen.

"And how old are you now?" roars Herbert. He picks the lobster off Ramona's plate and makes it dance.

Joe Watson waves his sombrero as if to swish away a bad smell. "Feeeedback," he says. His face flashes on and off in the candlelight, spotlight, firework light—loops of dusty gold and pink sparklers streaming from the church. A wedding just happens to be in progress. The bride ascends the steps with a bowed, veiled head and a huge familial entourage. Little girls with curlered hair hold fistfuls of her train. Little boys throw lemon rinds at tourists. The Mayan couples walk arm in arm. Not smiling but not not smiling either.

"Sure," says Mr. Ducklander, the expert, consulting his Snoopy watch. He's been coming here, he boasts, "for the better part of a decade now." He should know. "They feel sorry for the little bride. See, tonight is the night of rape. Then she spends the rest of her life in tortilla lines."

"That's not nice," Ramona says. She shakes her head at two kids standing on a nearby table, taping a live gecko to the ceiling fan.

"*Nice?*" Mr. Ducklander scoffs. "What's *nice* got to do with the truth?" But he seems to be asking Claire alone this. "What's *nice* got to do with money, sex, anything?"

"Well, I don't know. Nothing, I guess." Claire is sidetracked by the word "sex," by a renewed anticipation of more than just sex, of nice sex, by the pocket in her new dress, where Fred's half-dollar mingles with Oscar's condom, its strange foil package like some not yet invented space food.

"Nice has its benefits," Joe Watson argues. Claire thinks that if she were to describe Oscar, she probably wouldn't use that particular word. "Nice at least helps." Fred's the nice one. "What's wrong with nice? Spiderwoman? You like nice?"

"I like jumping into places I've never seen the bottom of."

"Nicely said," Herbert compliments.

The kids serve up the gecko's last supper, chili pepper with salt.

But Ramona's shaking her head at Claire now. "You'll see. Jumping in is just the beginning."

9

PLEASURE'S MINE

"THEY DON'T COME IN for a decent haircut. They come in for magic. They have dark skin, they want fair. They think a haircut's gonna give them blue eyes and a promotion. And if they pay more, they figure they'll get better magic," Hersh says, with his I-know—I've-been-on-Fifth Avenue air. The proof of this has, in fact, just arrived express mail from Miami—his beloved movie star photographs.

Already Great-Uncle is measuring to hang the pictures on the long wall that meets the window. It is here that his own haircutting station is now established. Soon any passerby will be able to have a "look-see" back in time to those good old days "when I had hair," Hersh says, though his green eyes make clear that what he means is "when I had Mary." "And backstage passes every night of the week, from Bette Davis herself sometimes: fact. Not that *she* was beyond expecting from me magic. But *her* I gave."

Point made. Still, it won't help the hysterical red-frizz-headed teenager—Fred's two o'clock appointment—who's now swerving out the door. Fred watches her take four or five steps onto the pavement before crumpling against a parking meter. He moans, "Some great advertising she is," as the girl's sunburned shoulders heave to the beat of his headache. "I warned her a blow dryer would make that hair explode. I warned her a bob wouldn't work on that hair."

Hersh howls, a feat considering he's holding a dozen nails in his mouth. "Whataya say we redo these walls white." Fred's in agreement—anything would improve upon the existing dirty salmon gloss. "Or cream." Fred's all for it. "Bone maybe it should be." Fine.

But why hang the photographs now, before painting? Fred doesn't ask, spooked by Hersh's next brainstorm.

"A coupla nice birds we'll get when Osc comes back."

What made him think of that?

Hersh is a changed man. A changed man making changes. Because of Hersh, Chester's now has piped-in jazz and fica trees. Customers eat complimentary Danish. New signs advertise: HAIR MASTER HERSH IS WITH US! FROM 5TH AVE.; MANLY MALE MANICURES ONLY $4. Taking advantage of the recent retro craze, Hersh has slowly begun a gold-mine enterprise—Bob Mania. Everyone in town wants one. Unfortunately, though, the bob does not suit everyone.

"She's in misery," Fred says, still gazing out the window at the teenager. One of her pink bra straps has slid into view. "Look at her—the Bride of Bozo. She hates me."

Hersh shrugs and spits a nail into his palm. "Get used to it." His hands still shake some after five weeks of widowerhood and the detox, but he looks healthy and comfortable in red Bermuda shorts and a Chester's T-shirt. Another of his recent innovations. "Get over it. They're all gonna hate you till you can give them straight hair, nose jobs, and a cellulite cure. You're paid to provide a service, not a miracle."

But Fred is used to performing on the street, where the service is all about providing miracles, or at least momentary illusions.

"Only one thing stands between a haircutter and a stylist, Fred, between a beauty parlor and a salon, and that's *attitude*, got that? Think like a professional, and you are one."

Fred is not used to Hersh making sense. And revived as the old man suddenly is, he keeps reminding Fred of that dead goldfish Oscar once brought back to life by sticking the Electric Thriller, an old science toy, in the aquarium tank. Dead for hours, and then, just like that, the fish was up and swimming around, even eating. The ultimate in miracle work—resurrection.

"Beyond that, bear in mind: Good styles look good wet too. Any style looks good on an oval face. When you look in that mirror you should see nothing but the customer . . . like Dracula."

The teenager finally extricates herself from the meter with a clumsy sort of backward skip. She had no choice. Peaches' station wagon is bulldozing into the parking spot.

"Hey," Hersh asks, "did I tell ya the one about the Catholic school?" He takes his time hammering—attitude—even though his three forty-five bob-to-be is all washed and waiting.

"Yeah," Fred says, "a few times." Immediately he regrets it. Hersh has a bad habit lately of repeating himself. "It's a funny one, though." Hersh brings back some surprisingly good jokes from those AA meetings at the high school.

The girl reaches up to try and flatten her hair—a huge orb of dull orange lint. Compounding the horror is Peaches' emergence from the car—gold-sandaled foot followed by log thigh in white stretch pants, gold belt, white blouse, folds of breast/neck, and so on. Finally, the distraught teen breaks into a sprint, heading off to kill herself in private.

"Get used to it," Hersh repeats.

"I HAVE shed thirteen pounds," Peaches announces before she's all the way through the door of Chester's. And another three times before she puts away her car keys. She's proud of herself, probably also afraid no one will notice unless she mentions it. They wouldn't. Which, Fred decides, is exactly where the distinction between just overweight and *fat* lies.

Mom speeds over to greet Peaches with the "bad news." "Sorry. We're busy, busy, all booked up." Her clipped, no-nonsense manner, bordering on bossy, is intensified by freshly plucked eyebrows (two ant lines of single hairs) and the big leather appointment tome (the object Fred used to picture whenever he heard the phrase "Book of Life") in her arms. "Looks like my son'll have to do you."

"You're not serious." Peaches' first reaction. Denial. "I could have been done yesterday, but I was testing the new perm solution!" She thrusts her arm out to show: no reaction this time. Disbelief. "Lester's been doing me for going on fifteen years!" Indignation. "You're not the only hairdresser in town, Charlotte. You're not going to get away with this." Belligerence. "This is two strikes here. I have a mind to take this up with the Better Business Bureau."

"But business couldn't be better," Hersh calls, stressing all the *b* words with mouth farts and winking at Fred, who isn't exactly thrilled to hear his service being volunteered.

Mom, in her old pink smock and her new bob haircut, still appears mystified by the new scene. She, too, has changed a lot since Mary died. But unlike Hersh, the updated Charlotte is not a favorite around the workplace. She's turned Honest. Not that she was ever Dishonest. But six months ago, in this same situation, she would have been oiling Peaches right up. Saying how "slimsy" Peaches looks after losing thirteen pounds. "Like a thread." Asking for Peaches' diet secret and begging her forgiveness for the mix-up. Customer service.

Now Mom says instead, "Lester's out." Out head-hunting for salon-level stylists by getting his own hair cut and recut in scattered establishments across the five boroughs. A method with certain obvious limitations. "If you would like to make an appointment with him . . ."

Peaches makes herself taller. "I haven't made an appointment in—"

"Fifteen years," Mom supplies. "Believe me, I'm aware of that." She pats the back of her thigh.

"And after all these years that I've been patronizing you—"

"I'm aware of that too," Mom says, perhaps a smidgen sadistically.

"I don't think you quite understand," Peaches begins to explain. In less than a whisper: "My son . . ." Up squeak the whole row of bonnet dryers. Sandrine and her regular, Mrs. Friday Henna Treatment, angle their heads to lip-read in the mirror. "My son . . ." Shaky Bea sashays into earshot. "It's an emergency. My son . . ." Could be anything, really, that Peaches says then. My son is getting carried away, friend; wary from seeking; buried, pretend. Many things can rhyme with or sound like "My son is getting married this weekend."

"Again!?" asks Mom.

THE CUSHION gasps and slowly hisses flat when Peaches plops herself into Fred's chair. Just as he feared, she wants a bob. A *permed* bob, no less. ". . . Medium length, smart-looking, like that Nancy Goldfarb got, but no tint; I'm in a rush. Use the *tested* chemical, don't forget, but no hairspray; I think I'm allergic. And you better not botch it, Fred, or there'll be real hell to pay. I'm warning . . . Oh, yeah—and don't touch the wisps; the wisps stay."

Act like a professional, Fred thinks, brushing out Peaches' hair, pushing aside the news that Sam is getting married to ponder Peaches' head from all angles, the way Hersh taught him. Anyone can, with practice, cut a straight line; the real craft is balancing hair shape with face shape and head shape.

Fred's not that bad at this job. The chemical stuff can get tricky occasionally, what with keeping track of all the various processes. But cuts he has down pat. The quintessential bob is snipped straight above the chin and may have bangs.

"I don't think a bob is *you.*" Fred breaks it to Peaches. A no-no. Remember: Never speak in the negative. Rather, *explore* other options. Trust your instincts. "How do you feel about layers?" Fred tries. *Who* could Sam be marrying, he wonders, and what for, and when did this happen and why? Focus on the good features. "Layers would frame your face marvelously." Show, don't tell; gently. Fred feathers the wisps with a comb. "Layers would blend more with your . . . teeth and—"

Peaches flares up pink as the walls. "I don't recall asking

your opinion, Fred." She rifles through the pocketbook kept securely guarded on her lap and pulls out a pack of appetite-suppressant gum. "Mr. Big Shot! A few months ago you were out in the gutter, standing on your head for loose change." Low blow, but not entirely false. "Besides, now that my face is thinning, I happen to think a bob would be just the thing. A little lift. Something sprightly, bouncyish. I'm far too young to be going around looking like an old fogy." She dabs her eye makeup with a Kleenex. "Nancy Goldfarb said—"

"Certainly." Fred gives in, arming himself with scissors and comb. You asked for it. He's read Peaches her rights; he can no longer be held responsible. And the last thing he wants to hear is what other pseudo-enlightening things buck-toothed Nancy Goldfarb had to say. Only old fogies use expressions like "old fogy." "O . . . K." Fred flexes the scissors. "We only want our customers to be happy."

Peaches laughs then, probably starting to dose on the gum, which has a kind of beery/peppermint smell and which, chain-chomped forever, would still never give Peaches the frighteningly high cheekbones of Nancy Goldfarb, a woman who's been working on the same butterfly hook rug for years.

"So how is he? Sam?" Fred decides to out-and-out ask, though it occurs to him that Peaches must be pretty embarrassed having her son betrothed twice in less than six months.

"Would ya watch it?" Peaches squeals repeatedly from first snip onward, in that lockjawed way people have of talking during haircuts. "This is my head here."

"I mean, he must be really busy," Fred says. The I-know-already tack. If it weren't for all the renovation and apprenticing at Chester's, and the hanging with Marci—a semi-lively because still unconsummated romance—Fred would have heard on his own by now. If he could just get to a phone, he'd call Tommy or Eliot and find—Shit. Fred remembers he forgot to call her, Marci. Again.

Peaches raises a single eyebrow, one of those genetic skills, like double jointedness or tubing your tongue, that unduly impress Fred, since he has none of them. But all Peaches will spill about Sam is "He's a doll," for taking Peaches out to Lil's Fish Fry Palace in celebration of her milestone weight loss.

"Your hair has a lovely . . . texture," Fred manages to eke out.

"You really think so?"

Like lettuce texture actually; romaine.

"A lot like Sam's." One last attempt: "Sam doin any gigs these days?" Marriage probably is like a gig, to Sam's way of thinking. Wife as permanent groupie.

"You're his friend?" Peaches says. She probably still holds it against Fred that he declined the post of second-string best man. And who's it gonna be this time? Deja Vu Gooch again? "I'm just his mother." She chomps savagely on the speed gum. "Who ever tells their poor old mother anything?"

Really, Fred thinks, I should feel sorry for this miserable woman, finding out her son is planning another wedding after all that's happened. She wore the same dress as a Mrs. Doody to the New Jersey bash, then vomited champagne and escargots on the lawn. She threw Claire—a shiksa even!—a bridal shower, then broke out in hideous boils from the untested perm solution. She's generally mortified is what she is. Or if she's not, she should be.

"What do you think of all Hersh's improvements?" Fred asks, partly as a last-ditch effort for info, partly to be nice, partly because Peaches' question—You're his friend?—has him stopped. It depends. Is this new wedding the cause or result of Claire's leaving? Is Oscar to be blamed or congratulated?

"Hmmm," Peaches says. "It's . . ." She whips her head around without warning—dangerous—and takes in the room with those oversize varicose eyeballs. ". . . subtle." Then she asks, "Has your mother been feeling well? I'm concerned," in a tone Fred recognizes from Reverend Osbin. *Your mother needs help.* Just last week, Fred found that charlatan's card († Faith Healing † Bereavement Counseling †) in his pants pocket after the pants had been through the washer and two dryer cycles. "I mean, what with your aunt passing right there in the house and all." In other words: You want dirt on my family, we'll swap.

Fuck that.

Fred's done with the cut anyhow. The bob, naturally, looks ridiculous. Like she's wearing a wig too small for her, crooked.

Peaches rips off the rubber apron and regards herself in the mirror with the sour mouth, sucked-in cheeks, and widening nostrils of a cover-girl parody.

"Like it?" Fred ventures. "Of course, with the curl from the perm, it'll look ten times . . ." worse.

"What? Oh. It'll do."

He certainly didn't expect that. But Fred sees it's her body that Peaches is distracted by—perhaps, like Hersh said, having expected the haircut to give her a waist.

"I might get a new outfit," Peaches says, eyeing Sandrine. "Pink lacyish strapless, maybe. Or backless, something evening."

"Why not?" Sandrine yells over the blow dryer, encouraging. "Go for it."

" 'Scuse," Bea says, plowing her big push broom between Peaches and Fred, then around the chair, tilting to get at the tight spots, brisk.

Fred, donning rubber gloves for the perm, watches the pile of hair on the floor enlarge—the yellow child curls wadded with grape Bubblicious he cut out first thing this morning, the teen's nearly weightless orangish frizz balls, Peaches' wavy, still damp brown clippings sticking to the broom, and a couple of coarse black snips from a man's head—all nudged toward each other, mixing, suddenly strange to him, as if a completely new substance. And Fred thinks of Mary—how people allege that your hair and nails keep growing after you're dead, but how Marci taught him that really they only appear to get longer, since your flesh shrinks.

MARCI WAITS, engine idling, in her dad's pale-yellow Mercedes for Fred to wrap up. Her lacquered fuchsia lips clash with the car's upholstery.

When Fred ran out to see what she'd come for, he didn't expect her to pull him in through the window and kiss-kiss— little sucks on his lower lip that made him feel as if he was being siphoned. "I know," he said, pulling away. "I didn't call again." Not apologizing exactly, but casually setting up what he was expecting—a chew-out. Marci hasn't chewed him out yet.

"In those days, we didn't know so much," Hersh is in the middle of telling his own perm victim when Fred walks up.

"Night, Unc."

"In the late forties, I'da been hooking up your hair to electrical wires and burning off the fly-aways with a candle. Haw haw. Even Bette Davis—"

Bette Davis. She's the only star Fred can recognize in the photographs. "See ya tomorrow," he interrupts again.

"Righto." Hersh holds out his rubber-gloved hand, but then, realizing it's covered with perm solution, holds out an elbow. "Promise you'll do all the things I can't." He nods toward the showy car out front. Marci is watching herself sip a can of orange soda in the rearview mirror.

Hersh's client flags Fred down with her smile. Stained teeth like popcorn kernels. "You're Charlotte's son, I bet?" She doesn't bother to mention who she might be. "Oscar—am I right?"

"Yes," Fred lies. For convenience, he tells himself. "Hello." Hersh licks his lips, letting it go. "Well, see ya tomorrow, then."

"Bye."

"Bye."

Mom says, "Do me a favor. Do your laundry for a change, please. I love you."

Latvia says, "Put your towels in the hamper and your brushes in the sink, thanks."

Sandrine says, "Hot date?"

Bea says, "Be careful."

The various heads say variations on the same. The sole exception is Peaches, who screams, *My hair is smoking!*

THEY TAKE TURNS driving the car fast. Fred, with two feet—one on gas, one on brake, the way Dad taught him and Oscar. Marci, with one hand, using the other to massage Fred's leg and thereabouts. Her hair snaps and flickers generously in the wind. Like a fire catching and that hypnotic. She, for one, has not, hallelujah, succumbed to the bob fad.

Only when they find themselves cruising through a strange Haitian neighborhood in Brooklyn, where all the movie theaters have been turned into churches-marquees quoting Scripture in French—are they able to speak without having to yell over expressway and radio grumble. And only then do Fred and Marci find they have nothing to say. Nice night. Yeah. (It's sticky hot and disgustingly muggy.) Nice car. Yeah. (More upbeat than the hearse she picked him up in last time.)

Peaches is the obvious conversation starter here. Though Fred leaves out the part about Sam getting married, he goes into some detail when it comes to the smoking hair. Already cranky from Weight Watchers, when the poor woman discovers Lester's stood her up, Charlotte aims to snub her, Fred has been designated stylist du jour. Already tested the new perm chemical and everything, but Peaches happens to sit under the leaky air conditioner and . . ."

"And?" Marci's hooked.

"Put it this way. Freon doesn't jive with sodium hydroxide."

"Jive?" Marci's confused.

"Combustion." Sound effects by Fred's cheek.

The neighborhood turns Puerto Rican or Dominican. Streets chock full of big women wearing expressions of indigestion and bright, chaotic-patterned housedresses. They straddle the bent aluminum piping of lawn chairs that have been dragged out onto the sidewalk by their undershirted husbands, who are busying themselves with beer, dominoes, beer, Los Metropolitanos (Fred strains but fails to catch the score out the car window) on scratchy transistor radios.

Marci says she got a free lunch out of Vlad for finally selling Memo, the blabbermouth parrot, to the newly elected city councilman Aldo Tate. "Liverwurst," Marci says. She threw the sandwich out in secret, in the warehouse, where she found Nip and Tuck, the Mexican yellow-cheeks, commanding some puppies to Sit, with results.

To the younger crowds, on every corner, the transistors of their fathers must seem antique, silly. Their own state-of-the-art boom boxes thunder with bass-heavy music to hang out by. The kids look haggard from so much hanging out, even though it's only the beginning of July—the whole slow, hot summer still to go. The boys, shiny-foreheaded, moussed, restless, playing—who can flick a beer top, spit, throw garbage, fart the farthest—praying for a fight. The girls, shiny-foreheaded, moussed, restless, not playing—who can shove a bright chunky plastic bracelet up her forearm the farthest—praying to be fought over. Fred never wants to be that age again.

"I see pizza," Marci says, and slams on the brakes, causing a canister to shoot forward on the car floor and ricochet between Fred's ankles. "You want pizza?"

Fred shrugs an I-guess-so and picks up the can, which is curiously heavy, maybe lead. Plain brown paper wrapper, Magic Markered with a name, Bertha Doyle. He shakes the can, but it feels and sounds empty. "Do you know a Bertha Doyle?"

Marci pulls into a metered space. "Think the car'll be safe here?"

"Does this belong to her?"

Marci remote-controls all the windows shut.

"Who is Bertha Doyle?"

Marci locks the empty glove compartment. Fred, noticing the tiny embossed *Emerson's Funeral Parlor* on the can, finally puts two and infinity together. "*Is* this Bertha Doyle?" Fred's so unnerved he loses his grip. Bertha Doyle bounces on the lemon carpeting.

"Ashes. Yup. To ashes. You guessed it."

Fred feels terrible for letting her drop like that. Picks it, her, up again and places the canister carefully, ceremoniously, on the carseat.

Marci shrugs, leans her head on the steering wheel, reaches over to feel Fred's forehead as if she suspects fever, then lets her hand—long nails—trail down his face, neck, chest, arm, and settle near the wrist, slowly tightening her grip. "I'm starving." For attention, apparently. "Shall we?"

"But what about ..." Fred gestures with his chin toward the can. "Shouldn't we do something with ..." Chin again. "The family ... We can't just leave ..." Chin again.

"She's dead, Freddy. She can wait another five minutes."

"We can't just leave when ..."

"So bring her. What do I care?"

"We can't ..."

"Then leave her."

"We can't ..."

Stalemate. Marci looks as if she wants to laugh but is too polite. She gets out of the car. "We for yourself," she says.

THE HAIRY MAN behind the counter flaunts a gold pizza medallion—silver crust, gold cheese, and ruby pepperoni. It has Marci reaching for her cross on reflex. Bertha Doyle sits on the grimy countertop.

"It's your lucky day," the man says. "Special for the ladies— free soda with yo order. Sprite, Diet Sprite, Coke, Diet Coke, No Caffeine Coke, No Caffeine Diet, ginger ale, or orange." His eyes drool down Marci's neckline and stick there.

Fred spots a pay phone across the room.

"Orange. No, Diet Coke. No, Orange?" Marci says, demurely indecisive.

Fred wonders who's the best person to call for an accurate Sam update. The worst person doubtless being Sam himself.

"Take all the time you need, sweetness." The man licks at his mustache.

"Orange, for sure," Marci purrs, amused or, worse, faking amusement.

Fred thrusts an itchy fist into his pocket to search for phone change and says, "Coke. To go."

Both statements are immediately vetoed. "Sorry; special for the ladies only," the man informs Fred.

"We can't eat in the car, Freddy. My father'd die," Marci adds.

"All right," Fred says, walking off toward the phone but turning back in the next second to collect forgotten Bertha off that sticky counter.

"You can *buy* a soda, Freddy," Marci tells him then, looking toward the pizza guy for confirmation.

"Sure, Freddy," the man says.

JERRY'S NOT HOME. Eliot's showering. Tommy Eako has run off with the circus, or at least that's what his father says. Big Apple. So Fred calls Louette.

"This is Fred," he says, before she can mistake his voice for Oscar's. Or not.

"Hey, Fred!" Louette sounds scary-ecstatic, or maybe she drank too much coffee. "You get one too?"

"One?"

"Postcard."

Fred's whole insides shift left. "Uh . . ." And farther left. "No. . . . What did he say?"

"Well . . . that's sorta personal." Winsome. On Louette's end, what sounds like a refrigerator door suctioning open suctions all the air out of the phone booth somehow too.

"When?"

"Day before yesterday."

"And . . . so. How's he doin?"

"Oh, just great. It's his thing, all the birds and stuff, right?"

Right. What exactly does she know about the birds and *stuff?* "No," Fred says, shaking his head at the blurry image of Marci balancing three paper plates sealed together with pizza cheese.

"No?" Louette asks, differently. "Whatayamean no?"

Fred doesn't recall meaning anything, ever.

"*Claire*, that's what you're thinking." Bingo. "There is that . . . Claire. But"—here Louette's voice surges into fast-forward— "I don't know if he knows I know she's there or if she's there with him or just there, ya know, or what there is I don't know or what."

"We'll talk later." Fred presses the receiver against his ear, creating pain.

"We'll wait and see, I guess."

And it is not till he's out of the booth that Fred remembers why he called.

"YOU'RE SWEATING up a lather like a horse," Marci says. "Also, your pizza's cold."

"That's OK."

"Can I have it, then?" asks Marci.

"What?"

"Your pizza."

"Why not."

Marci leans over and picks just the cheese off the slice on his plate, announcing, "I'm going to Miami in a couple of days for a couple days."

"Bertha!" Fred left Bertha Doyle in the phone booth. He rushes to retrieve her.

Back at the table, Marci eyes the canister, asks, "Should I be jealous?"

On the way out, Mr. Pizza Man eyes Marci, asks, "Marry me?" He makes Fred wait for his three dollar bills change, using them to wipe crumbs off the counter.

At the car, they discover that someone has rear-ended the Mercedes hard and sped off, not realizing that they've left their license plate attached to the fender.

After extracting it, Marci uses Fred's shirttail to carefully wipe the license plate clean.

THE COUCH AGAIN. Marci offers a massage, back scratch, story. She tells Fred he looks tired, he should lie down, rest. She comes over to the apartment more and more often, wearing less and less. There, she enthrones herself on his butt like a conqueror.

"Go call the police," Fred tells her despite his erection. He yells into the couch cushion. "You have the guy's license plate—"

"Guy? I like that. Most men would assume it was a woman—women drivers, ya know. That's just what I like about you."

"What about your dad? And what about Bertha?" Now a houseguest. Fred could not leave her there to roll around forgotten in the car like Louette's diaphragm.

"My father's working," Marci says. She always calls her dad "father." A curtain of her hair swipes down over the back of Fred's neck, soft, slightly ticklish, but chilling him as Marci's hands make that subtle but significant transition from above to underneath his T-shirt, scratching all the right spots with psychic accuracy. The more she scratches, the more he itches.

"The Mercedes is wrecked. Phone now!" Fred says. He flips himself over. But now she's sitting on his stomach. Leaning toward him. "Please." Fred tries standing. Why is she giggling? Her legs slide halfway off the couch, but still she hangs on, wrestling him; she's strong or he's weak, or both, maybe.

"C'mon, Marci. I gotta pee. Get off." Fred pushes her, this time too hard, perhaps. It works. "Just make the call to the cops, wouldya?" he says, fed up at having to go stand in the bathroom now even though he doesn't have to urinate. Oscar's gonna hear all of this, first chance Fred gets. For instance, Marci puts the toilet seat up for him after she finishes using it. Beyond considerate. Marci insists on picking the seeds out of his grapes. Beyond servile.

"Freddy?" That name! Marci knocks on the bathroom door. "Freddy? . . . Fred? Do you think it matters that I don't have a driver's license?"

Figures. "No. Just call, would you?"

"OK. After, I'll go down and get you some beer?"

"No! No, thanks." Fred can hear Marci pick up the phone, dial, speak.

Sir: she calls the cop sir. She reads the number off the license plate. Fred should sleep with her already. Or do his laundry.

Laundry. It's his face that decides it, catching his face in the medicine cabinet mirror, the weave of the couch cushion imprinted all across his left cheek and down his chin, a shaming deep-red plaid that's unrub- or unwashoffable; he tries. "I'm sorry, Marci. We have to cut this out," Fred says as he storms out of the bathroom with his face dripping.

"Cut what?" Marci laughs nervously—at Fred's face, perhaps.

"I just want to . . ." fuck you already. "That's it, that's all." The whole problem. He could say, *Let's be friends*, but not honestly. If he thought they could be friends, he would fuck her. But fucking would be the wrong word if they were true friends. If they were any sort of friends at all, he'd be sorry she was going to Miami. And, "Why Miami, of all places?"

"Business. . . . Aren't you even gonna ask what the policeman said?" She glares, cradling the license plate as if Fred were threatening to rip it from her arms. The phone rings.

"How about those Mets?" Dad responds to Fred's hello. "Yeah, but barely. Come collect. Yeah. . . . Oh, Peaches'll be OK. Excuse me, it's not funny, Charlotte. It's not your fault, Fred; don't sweat it. . . . Don't mention it."

"Can I call you later?"

"Hey, guess what? A card from Osc we got."

"We?"

"Your mom and me. Says he shaved."

"And I didn't get one?"

"Well, this is for all of us, I'm sure. Says he—"

"Yes or no. Does it have my name on it?"

"Well, you know how screwed up the mail down there is. I'm sure he's written. I'm sure—"

"I'm hanging up, Dad."

"You're hanging up on a bald man. I haven't even told you what my head-hunting dug up. Antoine from—"

"Gotta go, Padre. I mean it. Adios."

"This license plate is from a stolen car," Marci says as Fred slips out the door and flies down the stairs for the mailbox. Of course, of course, and yes.

Oh ho. Knew you'd be camping here—there. Evolution begins at home, comprende? But why haven't you tried getting my car too (hint: airport). I know. You need a car to get to the car. Oh ho. I was just about to ask you to check my mail. The Toyota, though, is most likely towed by now anyhow. You should have never—but that's not fair. You aren't mad still, are you? or holding against me whatever you might be hearing? Under a microscope small creatures begin to feel uneasy.

As you can see, this business business is getting to me. Also heat. Also awesome local color. Mexico is like gua-camole served with not enough chips. I feel more like I do now than I did when I first got here. Yes I miss you. O.

Oh. Fred reads the postcard a second time, still standing by the mailbox. Then a third time, hearing Marci coming down the stairs, license plate clunking. As far as information goes, the postcard clears up absolutely zero.

"OK. I'm blowing the whistle," Marci says, as if it were all her idea. "Before we get too gluey here." As if Fred were trying to convince her otherwise. "Watch me evacuate."

"No. Watch *me*." What Fred means for himself is: Either I go to Mexico now or I go crazy.

"Then you can hold this on the way out," Marci says, dropping the license plate into Fred's arms. And, "By the way, I knew all along that this was Oscar's place. So don't you try giving me any gibberish about bullshit."

"Wouldn't dream of it." Fred follows Marci and her hair—swinging left, right, left—onto the street. "Long farewells suck."

The catch with Oscar's goldfish, resurrected by the Electric Thriller, was that it lived only two days more and could not be revived a second time.

"Thanks," Marci says.

And Fred, "Pleasure's mine."

WITH ALL his newly earned wages withdrawn from the bank (plus two months advance on his paycheck), with newly cleaned clothes from the laundromat, gum and Life Savers, Oscar's old sunglasses, with the postcard (the Playa Alguna postmark is all he's got to go on) and last-minute orders from Mom—hammocks, please—Fred was off.

Or so he thought.

He'd forgotten Bertha Doyle. Bertha Doyle waited patiently for him on the kitchen counter. It wasn't, as Fred likes to pretend, Marci's many latent peculiarities (a few of which could still enthrall him) that doomed their otherwise promising relationship. It was instead . . . But how could Fred have possibly told her: So sorry, Marci, but you remind me of death.

If anyone had come by as Fred stood with his luggage in the doorway of the funeral parlor, CLOSED, said a sign, going over his options, and asked him what the matter was, he would have said it aloud: I'm terrified, holding a woman in a can. The dead are so goddamn helpless.

Fred couldn't very well leave Bertha with his parents to return for him, like a library book, after all they'd been through. Or on the funeral parlor doorstep, like a baby (but the opposite). Or in the mail—inhumane, possibly illegal. He seriously considered bringing her along to Mexico and scattering her neglected remains somewhere clean, peaceful, still. If Customs hadn't occurred to him, Bertha would be with him at this very moment.

On Aeroméxico. Circling bumpily over Cancún in a tropical storm.

"So there was this girls' Catholic school," Fred says to try and calm the drunk but gentle man next to him, who has miniature-liquor-bottle empties set up like chess pieces on his fold-down tray. The glass tinkles during turbulence, sometimes a bottle topples, but the fellow takes care always to right them again.

"Because these teeny vessels prove," the man has interrupted Fred to say, "there *is* a parallel world of tiny alcoholics." The man's squeezing his armrest, chewing ice, fidgeting worse than a kid getting his hair cut. The wrong analogy, since he's toupeed, badly.

Fred had eventually gone to the pool hall to look for someone he knew, someone responsible, someone he could trust to return Bertha Doyle. And there he'd found Sam, with his fiancée, Candy—the girl in white! The girl Sam had both started a fight with and picked up in the same night (passion?). The night Marci sampled Fred, and Mary died, and the faith healer came disguised as the funeral parlor man, who later turned out to be Marci's father. The night Fred and Tommy Eako juggled flawlessly together, until Sam screamed "I hate girls who wear white all the time!" to the girl in white, who's also wearing white tonight, as well as the white-gold diamond ring that Sam purchased for Claire. The night Fred and Mom and Dad and Hersh ripped up the kitchen floor. For Oscar.

The pilot makes an announcement not to worry.

"I knew there was something screwy right away," the man says. "What kinda flight has only stewards?" Five of them, all with receding hairlines and fake epaulets on their uniforms and plane tie clips. "Do you have anything I could take? Valium, Librium, Tylenol with codeine?"

"Just the joke," Fred starts in, though the man has begun having some noisy problem with his nasal passages. "And one day, see, this nun teacher was going around the classroom asking all the girls what they wanted to be, and one girl, Marci, she said, 'I'd like to work in a pet store,' and the nun said, 'Very good; animals are friends to man and cute.' And then the nun asked a second student, who—"

"What fruits are in Juicy Fruit?" the man wants to know. An Oscar question. A non sequitur Fred admires too much to cheapen with a response.

"So the second student, Louette, she said, 'A dental hygienist, sister.' 'Oh, good, very good. Cleanliness is next to . . .' "

The pilot announces that they're about to start the descent.

"Oh god," the man says. "Oh god. No god." In a bumble, he or Fred clasp hands but wind up with only a few fingers. They hold fingers.

"Moving on down to Claire," Fred resumes, "who looked down at the floor and said, 'When I grow up? I don't know, sister. Let's see. How about just a kind, curious, well-adjusted person?' So the nun skipped her."

The man laughs at that.

"And the nun finally gets down to the last row and to this girl Sandrine, chewing gum, with her feet up on the desk and makeup on, real sassy like. Sandrine says, 'I'm planning on becoming a prostitute, sis.' The nun is instantly winded and turning a pukey greenish-ocher then hot pink then navy on her way toward spontaneously combusting. 'What did you say to me, Sandrine Neapolitana?' 'A prostitute.' 'Oh, thank Jesus.' The nun sighs, so relieved she crosses herself. 'I thought you said *Protestant*.' "

The man doesn't laugh now. He looks at Fred. "If I die," the man says over the landing squeal, "I wanna be cremated."

FRED'S A MINORITY on the second-class bus out of Cancún. Humans are a minority, actually. Fred—American, white, Jewish, the only creature taller than five feet five, the only person carrying inanimate luggage—is invisible. Or the opposite.

To his left, a scalp-psoriatic, squashed-nosed girl, fifteen years old, maybe, with an infant slung around her neck, holds a turkey upside down by its feet. The bird, its neck craning upward in a effort to defy gravity, intimidates Fred by delivering sporadic beak jabs to his shoulder.

Meanwhile, the ponytailed child to Fred's right tends a baby goat on a rope, a piglet strapped with a handle like a briefcase, and a bulging tortilla, whose innards, vaguely tomatoish, splatter Fred's arm en route to the floor. Down there, dozens of chickens run loose in the aisles. Every so often someone throws water on the animals, and Fred wants to shout, *Me me;* it's that sweltering. On and off raining, rank, highly unpleasant; hell bus.

The shag-haired driver wears purple velour. He cackles as he takes the curves—the road is all curves—fiendishly fast, blasting through a continuous series of water mirages, past flimsy huts, seat bouncing. He sits within a makeshift shrine of fringe and Virgin paraphernalia—tattered religious illustrations torn from books taped to the windshield, flapping, a big plastic crucifix dangling from the not-yet-used, perhaps busted, horn.

"Hola," Fred says to the turkey girl every so often, unsuccessfully.

The rain starts up again—big, hot, wet drops that spray in off the palm fronds licking the side of the bus, sometimes getting stuck, snapping off in the windows. And the odor: old oranges/boiling tar/lime juice/man and beast secretions/ sweet pot/mildew/tequila, and a steady brown haze of exhaust that leaks through the burning grate Fred has the singular misfortune of sitting above, knees folded to his chest, chest folded over his knees. Only marginally uncomfortable, though, thanks to the numerous afternoons Fred has spent performing Pretzelman at Columbus Circle.

What does bother him is this state of being both unable to blend in here and ignored. Maybe every second-class bus has its token scruffy tourist.

"Hola." No response again. But Fred's afraid that if he startles the girl with anything more drastic, she might drop the turkey on him. The child holding the goat seems to be asleep with his eyes open. The bus slows, belching smoke.

Fred rereads Oscar's postcard for clues. It features a picture of the Spanish hogfish. *"Bodianus rufus,"* says the byline, "adopts an aggressive territorial stance when confronted with an intruder." What if Oscar doesn't want Fred barging in with bad news (Mary's dead), with good news (Hersh is alive), with possibly bad, possibly good news (Sam's getting married)? What if Fred ends up feeling like the tag-along again, the way it's been from day one in the delivery room onward?

All of the women wear dresses. All of the men wear pants and long sleeves. None of the kids wear shoes. The driver evidences no surprise whatsoever when the bus sputters to a halt mid-lane-change. He simply stands, crosses himself, and pronounces it "muerto."

WHEREVER THEY ARE, it's stunning. Emerging from the vehicle—a gray and still ticking beat-up chunk of steel—into a nacreous zone. Dusk or sunrise? Dorothy after the house lands. And there's water! Fred can taste the salt in the breeze. There's a breeze! He has arrived.

Kicking his knapsack like a soccer ball, Fred breaks into a trot. The blue line ahead thickens. Ah, swimming. He picks up the knapsack and charges.

The Factory of the Black Coral springs into the picture. A windowless cinder-block structure, and above it, vultures. Vultures also afeast on the dump out back. Excepting these big, reeling birds, it's actually quite an appealing little place: a lot of turquoise garbage—pails, bottles, wrappers—a lot of margarine-yellow butterflies and green, green lightning bugs that hover and ignite. Not three hundred yards away, the last of the rotten-peach sunset can be viewed fuzzing down into the sea. What Fred needs is a swim.

What Fred sees undoes him. A vulture plunging its head and neck into the bloated belly of a chased-down dog. Talk about fear of death.

Dozens of birds go at the poor puppy. Lustily. Their black, oily-feathered wings span five or six feet, making for that weird hump-necked vulture posture. Their delicate wrinkly pink heads are like obscene, alien genitalia with beaks. Bertha Doyle doesn't really have it so bad, relatively speaking.

In the pool hall, the girl in white, Candy, came right out and volunteered to take the ashes. To Fred this was both worrisome and relieving. Here was this person she'd never met before, Fred, trying to unload the remains of a person she'd also never met before, Bertha, in a pool hall, for god sakes, in front of another person she's just met, whom she's marrying, Sam. And none of it lit the girl's curiosity a tad. No, this one, this Candy (perky ribbons in limp hair), was pure sugar, nothing at all like Claire. Though probably also in that gray area between jail bait and virginal.

"Armless is hurtin worse than I thought without his better half," Sam said. "Lookin for friends in ashtrays. Well, I never."

"That's mean," scolded Candy. And to Fred, she said, "I'll take it. I pass the parlor every morning on my way to work. It's no prob—"

"Oh, yes it is," Sam said. "We ain't takin some dead woman home with us."

"No, *we* ain't," said Candy. "I am."

Then Sam pulled Bertha out of her hands and threw her to Fred. Then Candy pulled Bertha out of Fred's hands and fled.

Sam took a slug of his drink and pushed up his shirt to ask, "Do you think I'm gettin love handles?"

"Hola," Fred calls across the dump to a greasy-headed, stocky figure emerging from a wrecked pickup. Recently wrecked it must be—the butterflies stuck in the windshield wipers have still not fully decomposed. "Hola," Fred calls again. The guy has severe acne covering features that look sketched in finger paint, and his arms are full of corrugated metal. He lifts one foot, then the other, examining his thong soles for vulture shit. "Hola," Fred repeats. Three times, his limit. "Whatchyou got there?" The stranger could be twelve or thirty. Deaf or unfriendly. Homeless or already at home. "You live around here?" On "here," an unidentifiable rodent suddenly darts, squealing, across Fred's foot. "Ugggh!" A remote smile blooms on the dude's face. The *thing*, which resembles a Chihuahua, burrows into a mound of bleach bottles.

"Nasty," Fred chokes out, trying to keep cool. "What the hell was that?"

No answer.

"Do you happen to know how I can get to Playa Alguna? . . . Por favor?"

Then the boy-man detonates. "Haaheechhaaheechhaa." "Poderoso caballero es Don Dinero," he whispers, moving closer and closer to Fred's face.

"What?"

"A powerful man," he translates, letting the armload of garbage drop, "es Mr. Money. Haaheechhaaheechhaa."

FOR A DOLLAR (1500 pesos), Fred is directed toward a rotting pier that he would have found himself pronto had he just kept on walking. For five dollars, he is on a ferry, which he thought for a long while would never appear. The stars, like those glossy specks you see when you stand up too fast, give the impression of sliding around recklessly in the dark sky, which is some serious dark, dark as black coral, dark as the water, excepting the single revolving curl that faithfully trails the ferry. Finally snailing toward Playa Alguna (what if Claire and Oscar have moved on since that postcard?), Fred is ravenous.

He has half a pack of Juicy Fruit and a melted-to-a-stain chocolate bar in his shirt pocket. The former he chews all in one wad till the flavor runs out. The latter he takes his shirt off to lick, bare-chested, ashamed.

TRIPPING OVER a man in a cardboard box, Fred skids off the pier and into town—Oscar's town! "I'm sorry," Fred says, wondering whether he's twisted an ankle. "Really mucho . . . shit." Did I crack the guy's ribs? In his anxiety, Fred immediately coughs up all his change. A weak man is Sir Money.

But Boxguy's fine, distracted in fact, chewing gum with the

intensity of an insane person. Like Peaches. He lightly moni-
tors his jaw movements with his fingertips. Looks related to
the other guy, back at the dump. But less like a bum. Probably
five bucks of Fred's hard-earned change lie on Boxguy's stomach, unacknowledged. No Gracias, nothing. In Manhattan,
there is absolutely nothing anyone on the street could do to be
so handsomely rewarded by Fred as that.

Oscar's town. Kids are playing catch with sucked-out lime
rinds, and basketball barefoot. There's been a party or an elec-
tion. Smack at center court (also the center of town) stands a
partially disassembled or collapsed stage that's ringed by a
torn and drooping banner skirt advertising Superior beer.
Puddles of the stuff are dyed colors from dissolving crepe-
paper streamers. The logical solution would have been a simple half-court game. But these kids have developed a hybrid
form of hoops. Under lights, they run around the stage, alternating directions. No nets.

Fred is not about to start asking a man in a cardboard box
where the nearest hotel is. Bad manners, too, to ask about food
during the guy's meal of gum. Everything becomes an offense
when you've just stepped on someone. Thus, Fred walks toward the first sign he sees: I BUY DOLLAR WE SPOKE ENGLISH.
Máscara's Casa de Langosta! Langosta! Langosta!

Dying balloons are underfoot everywhere.

"Bubble Bubble yo kitten," Boxguy calls after Fred.

MÁSCARA'S IS HOPPING. With old ladies nursing Cokes, Italian hipsters in skimpy clothing, American military guys from
some Central American outpost in Belize. All lit flatteringly by
candles inside glass globes and a massive central wood-burning
stove.

Fred sits at the bar with his Superior, feeling inferior, a new
and he's sure unoriginal joke. A lot of people in this dive apparently know each other to the point where there seems to
be random hugging. But when Fred ventures to ask a beefy-
armed, overbrushed blonde, Chicky Boom ("I don't know why;

they just call me that"), on the next stool, "Where's a good hotel nearby?" she looks appalled, accused, insulted; her hardly existent chin disappears in on itself. She slams down her white wine spritzer and bolts for the bathroom.

"That was fast," Fred says when she returns a moment later, calmer, with her blood-red lipstick freshened.

"The toilet is on a pedestal," she says, drunkenly latching on to Fred. How is it possible to get drunk on white wine spritzers?

"So where's the hotel?" Fred tries again. "I need to find someone. It's urgent. I—"

"Hold ya hawses." She might even be from Westchester, judging by those r's. "Ya no betta than them"—the military table. "Can't sit regula like a human fa one iota? Has it been that laaawng?" How could she tell? Could be an import whore.

Unraveling her from his arm, Fred looks around for somewhere else he can inquire. What a dunce he is not to have noticed this pick-up fiesta in the first place. "No one's even eating!"

"It's not lobster season," Chicky Boom says. "For another two weeks. Do you think they carry guns?" She means the army guys again, an obsession. They look shy and too young, too uncertain, to be really bored or really jolly either; their wallets are all out on the table in front of them. Walk along the beach a ways, thataways, they assure Fred; you can't miss her. Her? Hotels, it seems, are feminine.

ON THE BEACH, it's surprisingly noisy—the water sloshing in and dogs barking themselves hoarse at the stars. Stars and distant lightning. Fred's journey seems to be turning farcically arduous. He goes plunging over an expanse of sharp creeper weed before it dawns on him to walk along the waterline. He trudges another few hundred yards, to where he's in sight of the row of stucco hotel bungalows, before thinking to remove his shoes. And a couple of giant steps farther before he gets his feet wet.

But all along, This is top drawer, Fred's thinking, the Yucatán. He must jump in. Water's warm and seaweedy, very still. The Atlantic or the Pacific? He's privately vague on this, the way he used to confuse steak, pork chops, lamb chops, and roast beef, and is now confusing shadows for people, a shadow for a person, for a girl. The girl for Claire.

"You're here," she says. What are the odds? Mostly teeth in the dark, then a tangy, clean, distinctly human smell mixed with vanilla, then a swash and feet pushing up from the shiny surface, finally the glint of slick shoulders and iridescently powdered eyelids; the flash of whites—just right.

"You're here," Fred says too, very faintly aware that Oscar isn't, of an elbow, his or Claire's, of their knees bumping as all the watery space between them thins. Soft pushes. Rib meets rib. Thighs slide together. They are hip to hip beneath the . . .

"Caribbean," Claire supplies in giggles, with splashes. She seems silly, calling Fred "Jungleman." She seems adamant and almost as hungry as he is. "Me llama Jane." Seductive. If she could see how she seems, she'd be shy.

10

QUICK INVENTION

PSYCHIC ABNORMALITIES are not uncommon in parrots. Or in any creatures ripped harshly from their home, doubled up in a cage, force-fed tequila by the dropperful, and hauled aboard Fernando's roach-infested boat.

"Still," Oscar insists, for the trillionth time, now inside an airless cabin, Jamón's bedroom, "even if we hadn't done all that karmically rotten stuff to them, they wouldn't mimic. Only some parrots do that, and only single tame ones, period."

"Mimic? Mimic?" Fernando whines. "Period. Pero *why?*" He sounds like one of the many unhappy customers Vlad has ripped off and left for Oscar and Marci to tranquilize. Unfazed by the sneezing, pacing, shivering, and all manner of mental disturbance going down in that honeymoon cage, Fernando waffles his mug right up against the wire mesh, begging, "Mimic me, Puta, por favor. Qué es tu problema, sweetheart? Mi Puta loca. Mi Puta bonita." Like he owns her. Since he personally stuffed her in a box, perhaps.

Fernando's porky hand digs for a cigarette in the pocket of his shirt—an avocado-green polyester guayabera. He recently untacked the garment from a wall-size corkboard, where his whole wardrobe hangs, full of tiny holes but unrumpled. Completing the *look*, he's fashioned himself a mild ducktail, using lard.

"Don't you dare light—"

"Callate!" Fernando bangs his head on the low ceiling. But his hand remains pressed over his heart, the pack of Delicados.

After forty-eight hours of this agonizing involuntary intimacy, Oscar's tolerance for Fernando has shriveled. The man's been warned repeatedly: These birds are stressing—no loud noise, smoke, or sudden movement. These birds are for breeding—no allowing them to form attachments to humans. "Or to subhumans like you."

Fernando's convinced that parrots speak. It's their purpose. And he's waiting. He claims some Guatemalan cousin, uncle, nephew of his had a pair that could not only sing rounds of all the local ditties but hold actual political debates, for which democratic outspokenness they became famous and were eventually assassinated alongside this cousin, uncle, nephew.

A true story, Fernando swears, on Jesus, Mary, Joseph, and the whole pantheon of Mayan gods, roughly one hundred sixty-six of them. The point is, Fernando believes it. He insists that were it not for this tragic family miracle, he'd be nowhere near these parrots right now. He does "no favors to no one." He neither desires money nor needs fame. "Everyone has heard of Fernando the diver." He's in it for the talk is all, a nice long chat, man to bird.

"C'mon, Puta baby, talk to me," Fernando pleads, never tiring. For three hours, they've been on this boat, still tied to Playa Alguna dock, waiting.

"For what?" Oscar keeps asking. "What are you waiting for?" The too-small cage sits atop the mini-fridge, which rests on the ugly green shag area rug with its telltale bong water reek. The bug-eaten paneling is plastered with discolored posters—Cybill Shepherd next to Divers Do It Deeper and Deeper. "Can't we get out of here?" Oscar is very aware that nighttime, the cover of darkness and all that, has just about passed them by.

"Relax," Fernando says again and again. "We relax." His courtship of the skittish, runny-nosed girl bird has driven the macaw to start gnawing on her own skin. Her husband (aka

Homeboy) seems more adaptable but will only allow his human rivals a certain proximity before he waggles his foot in threat—Keep back. Then Homeboy's long ruby tail splays, his wings lift slightly, puffing, his feathers stand on end to provide the illusion of largeness for his enemies, and for Puta, of raging studliness.

"Just look at them." Oscar sighs, penitent. Despite rapidly deteriorating health and the poor cabin lighting, they are still some of the most striking creatures he's ever had the chance to view. Indelible reds, yellows, blues, in such sharp contrast. "Look at *me*. Who would have ever imagined? Me, a guy who uses Humane Society return-address stickers." He gestures toward the tray full of distressing, watery-greenish droppings. The intention: to *disgust* Fernando into caring. Or out of the room.

No chance. Jamón's brilliant diagnosis: "Jus hangover." It's true that they did tequila-spike the birds' water dish, they had to, but Oscar made sure it was not with any cheap swill. Only más fina for these lovelies.

And, "Look at you," Oscar continues. Fernando's hairdo has crusted over, helmetized. "Look at this place." Scummy bunk bed, beanbag chair, bachelor-pad hull in hell.

"Hey. You are the smuggler in charge aquí." Fernando retaliates yet again. His chin seems to elongate with each boast of "I am a di—"

"Yawn." Oscar cannot take it. He's starting to pace just like the nervous female macaw. The proportion of man to cabin is roughly the same as that of bird to cage. Oscar has to turn around every third step. And hobble to avoid the low ceiling.

From the very start, this whole thing has reeked of amateur hour. "What am I even doing here?" There's no seed or fruit for bird food, nothing to boil water in. The cage is junk, not to mention this boat! "I had no idea we'd be going in this boat." The same hot-wired boat Fernando takes tourists out snorkeling in. "Stop drooling and yammering all over my birds, will ya? And if you don't gimme a break from your face, I'm—"

Ranting. Oscar realizes that. Getting himself all worked up

over something he has already seen to be beyond Fernando's skewed comprehension. And further upsetting the birds: the male wakes with a shiver, as though from a nightmare of stupid people stalking him, while Puta continues her neurotic behavior—scratching imaginary itches, slamming herself against the cage to fray and batter her feathers. Oscar groans.

"Cerveza?" Fernando asks. Truce?

"All right." Oscar's hardly the type who would insist on being sober in order to witness his own demise.

Usually, when he tries to picture what's ahead for them in Miami, Oscar's mind fills with images of Mary and Hersh's house, the white wicker chairs and seashell place mats. Hersh's movie star photos. Mary's mashed potatoes.

But this time Oscar tries consciously to envision Vladimir meeting them—palm trees, a dock, etc.—and nothing comes. Unlocking the mini-fridge, Fernando, oddly enough, resembles the Russian. The way he makes sure to block the precious combination from Oscar's view brings to mind Vladimir shielding his liverwurst sandwich.

It smells like liverwurst, Oscar thinks, but quickly realizes it's worse, much worse: it's the opened icebox—such a whopping concentrated sour curdling stink that even the groggy parrots begin howling for mercy.

"What the hell is in there?" Oscar asks. "Your mother?" The wrong thing to say. Fernando's nostrils contort, his cheeks flare, his eyes go mucky. He slams the fridge door and draws from his pocket a long, jagged fishing knife. "It's just an expression we use a lot back in—" Fernando pushes past Oscar and grabs a tackle box from the shelf behind the birdcage. He wouldn't hurt the birds, would he? "Shhh." Oscar tries quieting them. He communes silently for a moment with Cybill Shepherd, who's smirking as if she, too, could smell this revolting odor. She's looking progressively homelier by the hour.

"You like?" Fernando asks. He seizes Oscar's arm from behind and yanks it up, back. "You want?"

"No." On the damp and dirty paper, Cybill's white lipstick looks like epoxy.

But Fernando doesn't mean Cybill or the knife, Oscar realizes, as the sweet, slightly skunky aroma of pot cuts through the stench. Fernando is holding the pried-open tackle box under his nose and mmming.

"Es muy malo, sí?" Fernando says, finally releasing Oscar's arm and moving again for the fridge.

"Don't open that again!" Oscar begs. "Please. Don't—" Too late. The smell again. Like a blast of sewage; worse, like sewage and rancid cheese; worse, add mildew, add disease, diesel fuel, enchilada farts, and vomit. In search of relief, Homeboy dunks his whole red head in the water dish, then shrieks.

"Mi madre es muerta," Fernando says, sadly, lighting a bong load. "Of a lump."

"My aunt, of pride," Oscar says. And having said it, is sure that it's true.

THE TACKLE BOX is decorated with archaic hippie stickers. One depicts a sexy black woman in red genie clothes, smoking out of a chillum. The other shows a blond girl in a fringe vest, playing bongo drums.

"Rap with me, girlie, Puta, missss. Eh-low there," Fernando jabbers as he cleans the weed on a Jimi Hendrix silver rock mirror. It reminds Oscar of the Beatles mirror Sam and the guys all chipped in one birthday long ago to buy Oscar and Fred, now relegated to the closet. "Eh-low. I lof you." Fernando breaks into song. "Want you tell me of your name." Oscar looks away in horror.

He might have guessed that Fernando, stoned, would launch into song, and having butchered that, now into another one of his diving babbalogues. Eyeball blood vessels ablaze, the big larded head wagging, Jamón boasts of buried treasure—coins rusted together, ancient jars of olives, smooth skulls in reef-encrusted clipper ships. Each hit of pot slows him down a little more, which appears to improve his English.

It's because he's used to getting high with American chicks,

Oscar deduces. Jaded young white ones who'll screw him for pot. Jaded old white ones who'll smoke pot to screw him. Incredible as it seems at a time like this, Oscar's actually bored. And not just with Fernando but with himself, with the Yucatán, Superior beer, Cybill Shepherd. Though not necessarily in that order.

"No," Oscar says to the bong when Fernando gets around to offering it to him. He's bothered by the thought of Claire, all alone in the bungalow at the mercy of finks, rapists, druggies, horny tourists, and other Fernando types. She can take care of herself anywhere, sure. But it was Oscar who brought her here. Who left her there.

"Tasty," Fernando assures Oscar, flaunting his ever expanding vocabulary. The pot, he means.

"No, thanks." Oscar could run down right now, quick, just a hundred yards or so along the beach, and check on Claire. At this hour, she'd still be asleep. He wouldn't even have to say anything. "No, really, no." But he can't leave the birds alone with Fernando. "I said no, thank you." Neither can he get stoned, no matter how great the temptation. If he did, total chaos would no doubt erupt. They'd get lost on the way to Miami, accidentally on purpose set free the birds, fall asleep, or wind up best buddies, high-fiving.

Quieter now, the ill-fated lover birds preen, drawing each other's colored feathers one by one, for the entire length, through their bills. Each bird's neck can twist one hundred eighty degrees without effort. Finally, to rearrange the fussed plumage, they bristle it up, give one vigorous shake apiece, and lay the feathers down again, orderly, smooth.

"Ahh. They feels better?" Fernando says. Because he does. "They es allll right now." Because he is.

Do I look all right, Mr. Bully? Puta breathes against congestion. *Do I sound all right?* Her nostrils are wet and clogged still. Not good.

Hush up, squawks Homeboy, giving her armpit a couple of scratches with his beak. Returning then to his own ablutions, he raises his foot to his mouth to go at the dirt and bits of hard skin there. *Ain't no use sorrowin over things those human beans do when—*

"You're slipping asleep," Fernando warns, loudly.

Oscar jerks awake on his feet, to catch Jamón untacking a sports jacket from the corkboard, rummaging through the pockets, and flinging their contents to the floor. They are: half a pack of stale smokes, an IUD-shaped piece of coral, comb, and condoms, but "no dinero." Fernando sulks awhile and does some preening of his own. With open palms, he flattens jacket, cheeks, then hairdo.

"All dressed up to get arrested?"

Fernando smacks his chops, signaling cottonmouth. He announces, "We are readied."

BACK OUT on deck, air. With the boxed parrots between his knees, Oscar bends over the rail near the stern and listens. Surrounding him, in sad contrast to the sneezes and squawks of trapped macaws, is the loud morning din of free birds—operatic throat clearings, flourishes and hiccup riffs, power-tool imitations. The water glares white, its surface glinting with long-snouted silver fish, pocked with water striders, clotted with trash. The sky is like a continuous camera flash. It's 6:30 a.m. at the latest, but already Oscar desperately misses his sunglasses.

"Cross your fingertips," Fernando calls down from the control console and the half-booth that houses it. While he dives beneath the throttle to wind together those life-giving wires, nerves of the boat, Oscar waits by the double outboards and anxiously toys with the starter rope. What if it doesn't start? What if it does?

Ahead, Playa Alguna sits in the dregs of what has clearly been a celebration. "The party they had when they heard you were leaving town," Oscar tells Fernando, who comes flying down the ladder two rungs at a time.

Correction. "La Fiesta de Carmen." Fernando barrels past

to get at the outboards and deny Oscar that small but momentous cord-yanking privilege. The engine catches, it feels, on Oscar's heart.

The boat, spinning to face seaward, reduces the whole town of Playa Alguna—dock, stalls, bank; drug, liquor, fud stores; post office, church, movie; Mac Taco, Máscara's lobster house—to a not even very colorful smear.

The box in Oscar's hand grows heavier. Miami. Soon he'll be either temporarily rich or in big trouble. Major birds, these. Birds that need an aviary if not a jungle if not a planet to themselves. Oscar swallows, smiles, flips open the box's hatch . . .

But no go. The macaws won't budge or even peep. They're that freaked. And Oscar has nothing, no fud, with which to coax them.

"Shit you," Fernando says, reaching over to slam the cage shut. The door rips off Oscar's pinkie nail.

"*Yow!*" It is then, throwing his head back in pain, that Oscar first notices her. Anchored two hundred yards offshore and growing fast. A highest-tech deluxe power yacht.

"Dreamboat," Fernando says, showing off, charging it. But she's more, bigger. A vision in sleek pearlescent fiberglass. Happenstantially showcased in a rinse of nectarine-bluish dawn light like an advertisement for Getaway vacations—with the Texas Lone Star flag waving, a beatific captain waving. This spectacular vessel has been christened *Roundup*.

"*Roundup?*" As in that nauseating amusement park ride where they strap you standing up?

Fernando cuts the engine. The remaining putt-putt sound soothes Oscar, who shuts up. He likes the thought of how little these two boats have in common. He likes bouncing along and gently ramming up against the pristine yacht, where rubber tires have been hung for just such pleasures.

"Holaaa," Fernando calls, buffoonish. "Holaaa." A surge of fifteen or twenty crisply uniformed Mayans—Oscar half expects them to break into song—rush out to moor Fernando's boat.

"Move it, buttheads!" says a man with a monstrous silver

pompadour who comes barreling through their chorus line. "Wheeeel . . ."

He's wearing deck shoes without socks, gym shorts without underwear, no shirt but a whistle that glints against the mass of tangly white chest hairs. His neck is bull-muscled, no doubt from years of holding up that giant shiny coif. From this angle, below, he could be mistaken for a low-floating cumulus.

"Howwwdy!" That voice can really project—as authoritative as Sam's, if not so melodious, reaching all the way to shore; as authoritative as a . . . *cop's!* Oscar is suddenly plucked up by his right bicep. He panics: Fernando's turned on me, turned me in! With one arm, one grunt, in one continuous motion, the man has hoisted him, birds, and "All aboard." There, Oscar finds himself in the midst of a handshake. The man—"Me llamo Elmer"—looks awfully familiar, though Oscar focuses mostly on his disconcertingly friendly sky-blue plastic Snoopy watch. "Welcome. Mr.—"

"Arm."

"Right. Caught us in the midst of our stretchies, didya?" Elmer fingers the whistle necklace with a lewd rubbing gesture. The crew, standing by "at ease" all in a row, actually do appear rather overheated, but Oscar might have attributed it to their outfits. Ghastly synthetic steward wear. "Repose awhile, amigo, then I'll give ya our grand tour, worth waitin for, sure as death."

Oscar steps back. The man's face is spacious to the point of being difficult to survey in one take, and excepting a cone nose, flat as a platter. In profile, the guy looks a lot like a woodshop project. Something to hang towels on.

What is going on? A string of muffled pings—Puta sneezing in the box, four, five, six times—are little digs reminding Oscar of his recent irredeemable trespasses.

"Hmmm?" the man asks. His intense sapphire eyes are surrounded by the sort of laugh crinkles that inspire trust, no matter how well you know they are merely the result of sun abuse, opportunity, leisure. He sizes Oscar up. And down. "Have we met?" Very uncoplike.

"I think it's possible, sir, but—"

Puta: seven, eight.

"Gad bless ya, scarlet." Elmer apparently knows his birds. Licking thin, colorless lips, he regards Oscar's full length for the second rude time—up, down, up—before peering into the box. "Only one pair?" He shrugs it off immediately. "Better get these babies under an infrared quick. . . . Jit!" This Elmer definitely—

"*Elmer!*" Oscar's astonished. This is "*The* Elmer R. Ducklander?" owner of the PetMart chain, head honcho, big cheese, kingpin of the whole nationwide shebang.

"The same." Elmer nods, adding, "*Esquire.*" And, "Aw, don't be looking so vexed, son. A touch a glucose-laced chamomile, the birdies'll be right as pain, you observe. . . . Jiiit!"

This could mean only one thing.

"Jit!"

Oscar and the parrots will be traveling to Miami in style.

"Where is that idiot? *Jiiit!* Where the—"

"I'm right hair behin ya." Lumbering into view are major abdominal muscles, glistening like cooked chicken livers.

Oscar gasps. Jit's wearing a loincloth. He has purple acned arms and legs, waxy black spiked hair, and sin-ugly slit eyes, one swollen. A pocket calculator game bleeps in his fist: Pro Golf 2000. Even Fernando, stoned smiley, winces at the sight. The unmistakable aroma of coffee, eggs, bacon, drifts toward them on a sudden shift in the breeze.

"Smell bueno, amigo?" Ducklander asks, pumping Fernando's hand. They've apparently met before.

"Señor Ducklander," Fernando says with a deferential bow.

"Lookin good," Ducklander tells him. Jamón does manage to achieve a certain suaveness in his ratty jacket.

Reluctantly, Oscar surrenders the parrot box to Jit, whose sullen mouth is jammed with yellow plastic braces. If only Louette could see this, Oscar thinks, as he's led inside the cabin to a living room, nicer than his parents' in Sidehill, bigger too, with wooden beaded drapes, corduroy couches, bamboo bookshelves, halogen track lighting, a central spiral staircase leading downward. In there, the uniformed Mayans lounge about the plush red carpeting.

"Arm, say hello to my hands," Ducklander says, clicking on a boom box to no effect. "Hidalgo, Manuel, Frank." He smacks at the tape deck between each name. Nothing. "Juan, Jesus, Juan, Pedro, y Peevo, el capitán." Ducklander flings the machine—"Dang thang"—on the ground and then kneels down to retry it.

"Hola," Oscar says. What else is there? "I'm Oscar."

"Arm," Jit corrects. He's only about seventeen, with hardly any forehead. And on closer examination, Oscar decides that what he originally took for pimples are actually tiny mountain ranges of bug bites, inflamed. "Arm? What in heck kinda name is that? Armmm?" Jit hums cracking his neck, "Armmmm."

"That's right. Arms up time, y'all!" Ducklander interrupts. "Let's go! No jumping jacks, no flapjacks, fellas."

That snaps the crew to it. In no time, the floor's screeking underneath the weight of so much jumping and flailing. Seven in the morning. To the tune of "Go, You Chicken Fat, Go," sung by Elmer himself on account of the busted tape deck.

After the aerobics section, they do shoulder rolls and hip gyrations, pelvic thrusts and ankle circles, then get down on the floor for thigh scissors, stomach curls, doggy-style butt squeezes.

Absentmindedly, Oscar has reached down to the coffee table to lift a ship-in-a-bottle, but it won't come up. It is then that he looks around and notices that *everything has been nailed down*—the coatrack, the footrest, the TV/VCR unit. Even the drinking glasses, equipped with straws, have been bolted to their places. Ducklander must be a sensible man. A man who plans ahead. Oscar's almost feeling safe enough to yawn.

BREAKFAST FOR twenty-five. From what Jit calls "the hot seat of honor"—flanking Ducklander on one side—Oscar looks down at the tablecloth and forgives Fernando with his eyebrows, asks to be forgiven with his chin. Thus ringing out his face muscles, Oscar suddenly realizes that everyone but Fernando has been watching him.

"You an entertainer, boy?" Ducklander asks. "One a them street clowns?"

Oscar shakes his head, too deeply amused by the coincidence to laugh.

"That ain't exactly po-lite, Duck, now is it?" drawls Jit, sarcastic. "What if Arm's face is suffering a real-life ailment, a tic, say, ur a spasm." But Jit's the one who's rubbing maniacally at the lumpy welts on his forearm and throat, then disappearing under the table to get at his feet and ankles. The wretched scraping sound makes Oscar actually wonder whether the guy's using his knife and fork.

"That right?" Ducklander sounds impressed. "You got a spasm, Arm?"

"No," Oscar says.

"Speak up, son!"

"No, sir!" Oscar notices that the handwoven tablecloth, sea colors, has a deceptively simple pattern that changes depths with the slightest tilt of his head. "Just tired."

Decent coffee for a change, though heavily disguised under the local cinnamon, sugarcane, and clove flavor. Café de olla, they call it. Oscar finds it a wimpy drink, too complicated for the morning, too hot for the climate.

He'd prefer instant Nescafé on ice. And instead of the fine china service, a thermos, better yet a vat, or an intravenous time-release caffeine patch to wear behind his ear, like the patches sported by cast and crew of *Roundup* for motion sickness. Of course, they might also be like the tags used for tracking wild animals. Under observation by Claire's mom's extraterrestrial friends. Oscar *is* tired.

The warmed cream, though, is comforting, the Sweet'n Low a reminder of home, home and the view of DoNuTs! from Louette's futon, a view that has permanently linked the smell of frying dough, the taste of sweet icing, the texture of oozing jelly, the ever-festive sight of colored sprinkles on wax paper, with sex, mysterious donut holedom, the universal—

"Oscar agrees, I see," says Ducklander.

Oscar looks up from the tablecloth to find that the plates of food have arrived: blindingly yellow eggs, blood-red chili peppers, fat fuchsia slabs of jamón (ham), and a psychedelic array of tropical frutas.

"No need to be embarrassed, son. I see ya noddin over there. And I say, o-pine a-way."

Then it's silent while they all cram their faces and wait to hear Oscar's view on some subject completely unknown to him.

"Well." The tablecloth again. Fernando laughs knowingly. Oscar thinks he hears a noise like breathing from behind. "Why not?'"

"Why not is right!" Ducklander's fist comes down on his saucer. "Hear that, Peeve? Why not!"

"Sí, Ducky." Eggs stream from the mouth of el capitán.

"Hell, yeah. Why not?" Ducklander licks those horribly thin, flaking lips excitedly. "So the next question becomes . . . Arm?"

"Who knows?" Oscar tries this time. Who knows what he just endorsed. Who cares? He's feeling the coffee kick in, feeling good. He's a valuable employee, isn't he?

Ducklander nods. "I'll say." Positively misty-eyed, looking at Oscar. Jit snorts.

"And what the hell for?" Oscar throws in, unsolicited, caught up in and flexing this newly discovered flair for bullshit. Fred is not the only one so gifted.

". . . my kinda guy . . . that's the kind of initiative . . ." Ducklander says. "You'll see . . . Grand tour . . . Lemme be honest with ya. . . ." He wags a folded corn tortilla with a bite taken out of it. "I didn't for shit sure get here, remotely, by sittin on my buns." He grins. His teeth, bent way in and way out, in a more or less alternating pattern, disappoint the rest of his handsome, if overexpansive, face. "I wanna hear what you've got to say regardin this Mr. . . . uh . . . the Russki character."

"Vladimir Petroff?" A subject that can and does instantly douse Oscar's relatively good mood.

"I never *act*ually met the feller," confesses Ducklander.

"Never? Why this favor, then? Transporting the birds?" Though if he had met Vlad it would be even more unfathomable.

"My way is democratics," Duck goes on explaining to Oscar. "*All* my peoples get a shot." A shot? "Let's call it a holiday bonus equivalent." Let's. "I, however, happen to prefer partyin down here where it's warm . . . swingin. La Fiesta de Santa Carmen. Dos días a Miami. A cruise, eh? What better way to show appreciation to my dedicated workers than two days—"

"Two days!" Two hours, Oscar thought. "To Miami?" He could swear something's breathing inside the vent behind his head.

"Two, three. Depending."

"And the parrots?" Oscar is stunned.

"Yours. Your papers, your parrots."

Papers? Does Ducklander think this is legal?

"How bout the animals? Does the Commie keep em healthy? Good turnover? Does he—?"

"Let the boy eat, Ducky," el capitán interrupts, sounding vaguely Yiddish.

But Oscar is no longer hungry. The myriad minor wounds he's sustained in the past few days all flare up at once, a symphony of affliction. Plus, after four cups of coffee, he too is turning Jit, jit, jittery.

Jit's computer game bleeps crazily. Hole in one.

"You were saying," Ducklander insists, addressing Oscar. "Vladimir."

Hesitantly, Oscar says, "Well. Vlad's a loner, I guess. His wife"—who he married just to get five hundred bucks—"comes and goes. His feet hurt a lot." Oscar's making the guy sound pitiable. "He gets pissed at the customers because they don't speak Russian, and . . ."

"Yes?"

He paints fish and dyes birds to make them look exotic, trains retrievers to pickpocket, breeds pit bulls to kill—a venture Ducklander supposedly commended, Oscar recalls. The man's a spiteful, sadistically nasty, money-grubbing bigot. But Oscar says, "Nothing." Because Vladimir *is* pitiable, he realizes. From a distance anyway.

"OK." Ducklander lets Oscar off the hook, but not without adding, cryptically, "Your loss," followed by a lascivious twinkly-eyed wink that bears no resemblance to Lester's paternal variety.

Homesick, Oscar studies his food to avoid further eye contact. He's got to be careful of the tablecloth.

THE GRAND TOUR at last. Down in the hold: not two parrots, but two hundred. Hidden on the far side of an enormous revolving Naugahyde sectional couch. Parakeets too, and doves, cockatoos, toucans. A few bats, even, stuck inside the heating/air-conditioning system, and four stingless-bee hives concealed in artificial floral arrangements under domes of plexiglass. And that's just the winged creatures.

"Who does he think he is?" Oscar whispers to Fernando, who lifts his chin, imperious, then slumps down on the sofa, weary.

His perception: "Jus another conquistador."

In the engine room, iguanas inhabit the crawl space of wide, unused lengths of pipe and empty water tanks. Crocodile, snake, and leopard skins have been stashed beneath the liftable staircase that leads to the bar/dining area, where tropical fish swim concealed in kegs of salt water lining the wall to the pantry, which boasts buckets of black beans cut with black coral, jars of rice mixed with shark teeth and pearls. On to the kitchen with its tower of muffins "a-cooling." Chunks of gold, silver, and platinum have been baked inside. Under plastic wrap, in the fridge, three enormous jade salads keep.

"And oh, yes," says Ducklander. Radiant with ego, he leads Oscar down a little hall and back out on deck. "Can't forget my trusty wetback crew. They pay me to smuggle them; now, that's some twist, huh? But swell people, lemme assure ya. Amigos míos. My kinda people. Sí?"

Oscar holds up a hand, sí, affirmative.

"You all right, son?"

Fine, just gulping. Just swilling some air here. Oscar leans over the rail and contemplates leaping. Before Ducklander knows what's happened, he could hightail it back to shore, over to Claire, into the car, down to Cancún Airport, and be flying home.

In theory.

Oscar's emotions stop him, surprise him, partially disgust him. The very idea of leaving here without the macaws has him all choked up.

"Arm," Ducklander says. A hot, revolting blast of jalapeño breath. Oscar's eyes water. "Now, first thing, we gonna learn ya some Spanish." Hand slips down to the small of Oscar's back. "Not to speak, a course, just to comprende, comprende?" Hand begins rubbing, a slow, insidious spiral. The down-home simple-folk crap turns Oscar's stomach gassy.

Goose pimples sprout. But Oscar remains still, staring into Ducklander's dimples. They look poked in.

"Don't give another thought to those birds. She'll be knocked up by the time we hit Fla. Guarantee it." Fla? Even the blue plastic Snoopy watch has turned sinister.

And when Oscar risks a "Where is everyone?"—there's not a deckhand in sight—trying to make it sound as if he's making small talk, Ducklander hoots and throws himself into a chaise longue. *Face it, dolt,* his expression communicates, *you're an accomplice now.* Ducklander smacks the chair next to him: Sit. *You're a full-blown criminal now, and there ain't a dang thing you can do about it.*

So, "Let's fish."

Gingerly Oscar approaches the chair. It looks comfortable. The place on his back where the man's hand just was still burns.

"Rods!" Ducklander shouts. King of the boat.

The chair has an adjustable mattress, like a Craftmatic bed, a place in the arm for your drink and another for an umbrella.

"Plush, huh?"

"Yeah."

"Anything ya need, just holler Jit."

Right, sure.

Deck creakings announce the five deckhands before they round the bend with fishing gear.

"About time. You run like women." Ducklander takes the rods and waves the crew gone, whispering, "They ever fix to mutiny, I'd love it, I tell ya. Make em all *walk the plank* with . . . Jit?"

Iron boy has appeared too instantly to have not been eavesdropping. He's carrying a pail of chum, his own rod, his calculator golf, plus a tackle box.

Pot? Where *did* Fernando go? What did or does Fernando know? The Maya, he told Oscar, used to catch fish by just drugging the water.

"And their women," Ducklander continues. "They look like toenails."

"No, turtles," Jit corrects him. "It was turtles without the shells."

"Yeah, OK. . . . Thanks. Now scram."

"Bu . . ." Jit holds up his rod, already baited.

"Give Arm your rod."

"Bu . . . He's got one, an—"

"*Wha?* Ya run outta batteries or somethin? Go throw some knives inna wall." Jit's hobby?

"Bu . . ."

"Bu . . . bu . . . bu . . ." Ducklander mocks. "Ya have ta act like Popeye your whole life?" One shake of his pompadour completely paralyzes Jit. Oscar wouldn't be surprised to see him burst into tears, or curtsy. He's almost but not quite able to feel sorry for the guy. Until Jit's fishing rod comes flying at his face to sober him, a snarl attached.

"Oh," Oscar says, shook up. It's hot. Probably nine o'clock, by the sun's position, and he's sweat-soaked. Used to it and not. Longing for his sunglasses, and hardly able to keep up with Ducklander's incessant chatter.

"More than an ordinary hobby, Jit's knife-throwin; well, it's been goin on long e-nough to be termed a bona fide forte. Comes in handy too. Why, I remember an instance where . . ." Ducklander loops Oscar's fishing line twice around the deck rail, so the two of them can relax in their wonder chaises. The grand tour is apparently over, or to be continued at some later time. "You look beat." And again, Ducklander's Herculean hand descends on Oscar's knee and slides.

"I haven't showered in quite a while," Oscar says, for lack of anything better, failing to knock Ducklander's hand away accidentally. Oscar wonders, Is this an act to intimidate me, or is he really . . .

"Them Mayans," Ducklander resumes. "Ya know what their problem was?"

"They got invaded and killed off by Aztecs and Spaniards?" Oscar guesses. He realizes in a flash that Fernando taught him this. He didn't use to know it.

"Naah. That was in-evitable. Let me set ya straight: the Mayans, them people were dim-bulbs, plain and regular."

"Yeah?" Oscar says. His eyes are trained on the tinselly-haired knuckles on his kneecap. "I didn't know that."

"They failed to preciate the value of the wheel, see." Ducklander licks his lips with a swiping tongue motion every couple of words. "Addin to the problem, they got no horses or any kinda otha beasts a burden. Leavin em where? Carryin all that shit on their backs. It's downright mental. Secondly, they never could figure how to build a simple arch. And for ma personal specialty interest, *guess*, now jus take one conjecture what you reckon they did with all that gold a theirs?"

"Made muffins?"

Ducklander reaches in his tackle box and holds up a string of fishing hooks—golden, sure enough. But real?

"Priceless."

"Where'd you get those?"

"Oh, grave robbers, archaeologists. Same as anythin—connections, investments."

Oscar gazes longingly toward the dock and the wakening town, which, though still the same one hundred yards away, seems to have moved into the far distance, a place he can no longer easily get to. Not without a plan anyway. "Where did Fernando go?"

"Fly bridge. Last I saw. Betchyou wasn't aware Fernando and maself is old divin buddies. Oooh, we been down a ways. Hell, bout—"

"Three hundred meters?!" Oscar explodes. And now that he's begun, begins. "You know Vlad too, I bet, don't you?" Ducklander, licking those lips again, inadvertently confirms it. "So whataya need me for, with all these friends? Me and my two parrots. Holiday bonus, my ass. Who caught the others you got shoved in the wall down there? Jit? Aren't you even a sliver ashamed of yourself?" But looking at who's talking winds Oscar down. "What about carrying diseases in? *If* you can get through Customs." Oscar's anger is simmering to crankiness. "What the hell is a fly bridge anyway?" And fatigue. "Purely out of professional curiosity: Where is the market for bats?"

The boat bobs and rocks. "Are you free-associating on me?" Ducklander laughs softly. The water blip-blips. A wisp-size breeze glances by Oscar's throat. "All I'm doin is helpin out Mother Nature some." Ducklander's hand finally leaves Oscar's knee and resettles on the yellow floral plastic chaise arm. "Don't see no better way. Export ban is one load of bureaucratic manure, you know that. The rain forests'll be Benettons year after next; the macaws . . . history. You got better suggestions? Listen up. I'm lots older than I look and lots smarter than I sound, and one thing I know for certainly is the squeaky palm *always* gets the grease."

A long drink of a pause; nice. The boat swings. Go/stay, on/off, in/out. The water pawing the hull—salty plus, bottle green, inviting. Cranked-up midmorning heat penetrates Oscar's skin to counteract all that coffee. Vision tricks make a row of life preservers behind Ducklander's chair grow fur.

Oscar dreams: He gets his sunglasses back by just walking up to Fernando and—

Yanking. On the line, something major. Oscar quickly finds himself on his feet, reeling like a madman, reeling in . . . "A monster, damn, that's a merman bitin! Move over." Ducklander helps out, pulling back on the pole. "Easy. Slow now, don't lose that googly-eyed sucker, whoa. *Jiiit!*"

Soon Jit is leaning over with a gaff to stab the massive fish through the gills.

A grouper. It frightens Oscar with its slimy scaliness and its tail-thumping, hysterical wiggle-to-live. The word is shouted round. *Mero.* Everyone crowds in to be witness.

But no one listens when Oscar decides to "Throw it back." The fish's gripless, watery tap dance too much for him.

"Muy grande!" el capitán commends, sucking his starch-white teeth.

"El pescador magnífico!" shout the deckhands. And other garbled compliments.

Ducklander pushes two fingers deep down in his mouth to whistle.

"Bravo!" Jit sneers. "Bravissimo!"

All the red and white and blue uniforms mash in close around the big dying fish while Oscar stammers, like Jit, "Bu ... bu ... bu ..." Partly out of frustration, partly shy in the spotlight, partly curious how much this big fish weighs, and so generally caught up in the event that for a moment he forgets this isn't a fishing trip. That he doesn't like these people. Isn't amused. Doesn't approve.

"Excuse me for a sec," Oscar says. "Bathroom," recognizing the moment as his chance to take control and let loose the whole wildlife arsenal. Chaos? Why not? Heroics? Yes, yes. After he takes a piss. All that coffee, he's—

Awakened by something nibbling on his line, Oscar realizes he was asleep that whole time. Whoa. There was no big catch. Talk about vivid wish-fulfillment dreams: catching big fish and freeing birds. Oscar's embarrassed. Talk about self-righteousness.

"Ain't nothin," Ducklander says now, reaching over to feel the rod. Just a light, insistent tugging. Like a kid's hand at your pants leg. "Garbage," he speculates, "or a jelly."

Wrong. "Sand." Oscar lifts the line and detaches from the

bolt sinker: "Wet sand in a plastic bag." Gee. He's some sportsman.

Oscar puts down his rod and lifts a life preserver off the peg behind Ducklander's head, casually, and casually dons it. He asks, "Is this some new sort of material?"

"That's the fillin inside the President's head," Ducklander says, unsuspecting, inspiring Oscar to make his move.

"Excuse me. I need a john."

"Oh ho. I got your number," Ducklander says, pausing to allow Oscar his moment of terror. *My number?* Then, "Mexicali breakfast. Do it to ya every time."

Relieved, Oscar saunters into the bar/dining area. "Ahoy." He nods to a few of the crew on Delicado break. Above them, a huge grouper is mounted on the wall. Oscar hadn't noticed it earlier, at least consciously.

One of the fellows is nosy or friendly enough to inquire, "No puedes nadar?" Can't you swim? or so Oscar infers since the guy's pointing with his cigarette at his life preserver.

"Nope." He'd learn Spanish pronto if he stuck around here, but already he's hastened the saunter to a trot, managing to reach the banister without having to answer another question. Next, down the stairs to the hold, glitchlessly. He goes straight for the ottoman from whose hollowed-out insides he recalls he can extract a parrot box, yes. Momentum is beautiful.

But Fernando, with gelatinized hairdo, is there to screw it up, snoring on the Naugahyde couch, still wearing Oscar's sunglasses. Fernando is so annoying, he's even annoying in his sleep. Of all places to nap, he chooses *the* decoy sectional that Oscar needs to spin back into the wall in order to get at the parrots.

"Hasta luego, señor." Oscar is cautious not to wake Fernando as he pushes the couch. "Pleasant grouper dreams, Mr. deep, deep, deep, please be a deep sleeper, deep-sea diver." Though trying for a soothing stream of lullaby-like burble, Oscar is out of breath and sweat-soaked by the time Ducklander's menagerie has finally slid into view.

In a curious high-tech mixture of cruelty and humanitarianism, the man has fashioned an aviary-in-the-wall. A generous space made of tough material; ordinary wire grating wouldn't stand up to the macaws' destructive bills for long. An *environment* complete with simulation dusk, dawn lighting, proper perches, ample seeds and greens, the same plata de fruta—kiwis, oranges, bananas, mangoes—that Oscar was served for breakfast. Everything's been planned, right down to the sand on the floor (aids digestion). Toys are plentiful—wooden spools, ends of rope, bells, chains, and branches. A real nice setup. Considering.

It's in the wall. Artificial light. The double water dishes (plain and spiked) are what keep the birds dazed, mute and reeling. It's better this way, Oscar tries to convince himself. Pain dulled, consciousness altered, the world without edges. We humans certainly like it.

But in Oscar's personal belief system, animals are above all that. Cats above even catnip.

And as he gazes at more and more stupefied birds, he makes a second, even more depressing, detection.

All their wing feathers have been trimmed. Expertly.

There has been a mass operation to assure that no bird will try any stunts. Like flying.

It wasn't at all like this in Oscar's dream on deck. They were going to be OK. He was going to free, save, heal every one of them. The blue and gold macaws, the great green-wings, with five rows of small dark feathers under their eyes like lash liner. The hyacinths and militarys, birds that remind him of Fred, because they're the kind that can learn to ride miniature bikes, play Ping-Pong, or roller-skate on talk shows.

Two hundred birds. And, Oscar realizes, every one of them is a type the scarlet macaws would and do mate with in the wild. A wild experiment. This Ducklander may be demented, but he is not dumb.

And when Oscar locates his own birds, which have been kept in a separate enclosure, he sees . . . they are flirting. Prattling softly to each other, pushing their bright-red fluffy heads together. The sight makes his cheeks hot with wonder. Beaks entwine in a passionate kiss. They're happy!? Tequila-induced, perhaps, but ... Homeboy is regurgitating into her mouth. Practice for feeding the babies. Maybe they've even done the deed already—in the wall! Completely illogical and beyond any adaptability Oscar's ever seen; it's preposterous, frankly. Overwhelming and comical. Sort of like, well, love.

Oscar slips a gloveless hand in and takes them. No retaliation. Interesting. The tipsy birds come easily, though once back inside that torture box, Puta takes up her wheezing again, and sneezing, ping, ping. Oscar's own breathing seems to take place in his veins, as he wraps the box in the life preserver and makes a run for it. He's halfway up the stairs before he remembers Fernando, still in the wall. Oscar can't just leave him there. He backtracks, sets the bird box down. He works up a second sweat, pushing the cages back. And by the time the couch is restored to its former place—Fernando still fast asleep—a spooky amount of time seems to have elapsed.

Remain calm, Oscar coaches himself, keep cool, doin fine. He climbs back up the stairs and cuts quickly through the living room. "Hi," Oscar says to the now thankfully empty space. "Hi," a second time, saluting the mounted grouper. Pushing on at a crisp clip into the pantry, Oscar eyes those muffins again and, what the hell, snatches one, he's no moralist, then breaks into a run, down the hall, out the side door, where—

Jit, the punster, is waiting to "snap some Arm" and find out whether the hot muffin is "Bran, corn, or blueberry?" He sprays the little cake with spittle, barricading Oscar's every attempt at movement. His purply face gleams like something about to split open and ooze.

"Let's see," Oscar says, trying to keep the attention on the muffin, which he holds toward Jit, and not on the bird box, held behind his back.

"Yeah," Jit says. "Let's see what y'all got there." He snatches at the life preserver. Oscar head-butts him in the stomach. Jit tears at the life preserver. Oscar bites his wrist. Jit rips the life preserver off and tries to muscle the bird box away. Oscar brings down the muffin on Jit's head, hard.

Corn. Jit drops. So does the muffin. Jit stays slumped, but the lump of platinum rolls and rolls, trailing its tasty-looking crumbs right up to the edge of the boat, where it pauses strangely, then plops overboard, with a meager but exceedingly final-sounding splash.

Oscar looks around and realizes that he's fast being surrounded by uniforms. Some move toward him, some hover above Jit, some still gape overboard where the muffin sunk. Oscar wildly throws pesos, coins, wads of bills, gum wrappers, and scraps of whatever he finds inside his pockets. "*Shhh*, por favor," he sings, hurrying to refasten the life jacket around the bird box. "*Shhh*, por favor, amigos, *Shhhhhh!*" till he's slipped himself under the rail and begun swimming the short but excruciating distance to shore.

Go go go go go. A two-hundred-meter sprint to the pilings. Quick invention—a one-armed butterfly/frog stroke—accommodates the bird box, which finally gets into a rhythm and lopes there along the surface beside him.

The water's passive, bathtub temp, puddled with motor oil. Closer in, Oscar find himself kicking beer trash—aluminum, sea glass to be, soggy cartons. Near the dock ladder, a school of translucent, shifty-eyed fish swarm around a bobbing can of Easy Cheese.

When he's doubled over and dripping on the pier, Oscar realizes he's still got his high-tops on. (Duct tape held!) The tourists seem to think he's dangerous. They clasp their pink, peeling, hysterical children out of harm's way. The Mexican boys swear at him for scaring off their morning's livelihood—diving for coins. But no one taps him on the shoulder or shoots him in the back.

At the end of the pier, Oscar trips over a man lying in a box. "Sorry. You OK?"

"Juicy Fruita, amigo?" The man addresses Oscar as if they were old friends. Maybe he likes being stepped on; it must happen often enough. There are actual footprints in dust on his clothes. "Juicy Fruita," he repeats.

But Oscar's pockets are cleaned out. "Sorry, no gum."

"Chicles?"

Oscar races on. He will tell Claire everything, and she'll pay the hotel bill. He will lie down in the backseat of the car while she drives away. Once on hotel property, Oscar slows down to a mere out-of-control sprint.

Midday, and everything routine in resortland. The sun. The seaweed getting raked. A man sighs and turns over the tape in his Walkman. Towels and chairs. The sun. Random splashing. A kid dips his ice cream cone in the sand for topping and eats— bite, dip, bite, like that. Joe Watson is conked out with his hat on, clutching *Shōgun;* binding still uncracked. Snorkelers wait by the dive shack for Fernando, mañana.

Oscar cradles the bird box to his ribs for bounce resistance and to press down on a cramp there. He's aware of himself as a sopping, dirty, crazed-looking individual when, exhausted, he finally reaches his bungalow and throws open the door.

"Fred?" In midair over the bed, in his underwear, then spazzily falling floorward on his ankle, a clapping sound. And *"Claire?"* Even worse, wearing only Oscar's T-shirt, trying to freeze but knocked down by the springing bed. She suffers the remaining small bounces, on her knees, hand over her mouth, mouth saying:

"Wait a minute, wait a minute."

"No, wait," Oscar says. "Wait a minute."

"I'm waiting," Fred says.

They all scratch their heads, figuratively.

"Fred?" Claire says. "Oh my god. I thought—"

"You thought—" Fred says. "Oh my god, but we—"

"You—oh my god," Oscar says. "But—"

Someone is knocking.

11

KISS OUT

Oscar blenches. Fight or flight? "Don't move. Get dressed. Keep quiet. Hurry." Oscar chomps down on the tender spot where his pinkie nail recently used to be, and blurts out a Spanish obscenity that he didn't even know he knew.

"*Abre! Abre la puerta!*" Jamón shouts as he beats the door. "*Dame la Puta.*"

The she-parrot sneezes.

"Gesundheit, Oscar," Claire says.

Fred asks, "That guy a friend of yours?"

"Move it," Oscar pleads.

But Fred remains on the floor, massaging his little ankle boo-boo. He demands that Oscar tell him "just what sort of machete-wielding maniac we're dealing with here."

"Oh, just my dad," Claire jokes. Not funny. The boys' indignant, identical, fiercely bony pink faces make that doubly clear. "Excuse me." Forever, she could watch them watch her. In duplicate, wincing. Oscar's nerves fire on the downbeat of each rap-rap-rap at the door. Fred's, like Claire's own, on the more menacing, crescendoing silences between whacks. Yes! It's just further evidence of this giddifyingly berserk hunch Claire's been having about somehow being the audience for whom all this has been staged. "Gesundheit," she says again. Even these sneezes she's hearing sound stylized, quirky. "Oscar? Are you allergic to . . . what is that smell?"

"*Ladrón! Abre now por payment!*" Each syllable is accompanied by a slightly different sort of blow to the door. Sometimes what seems like foot meeting door. Sometimes an elbow. Sometimes the porch chair.

"It's like a chicken odor or—"

"Oscar," Fred says, still dazed and furious about the mixup. Claire thought she was seducing *Oscar?* The ultimate insult. Fred feels it viscerally. His heart wallops in his ankle. "The guy just wants to pay you. Why don't you save us the—"

"Shhh." Oscar shudders, along with the flimsy doorframe.

So Fred makes a point of yelling. "You could've knocked too, ya know." He kneads his ankle, hard, amplifying pain. "Like announced yourself, maybe."

More commotion at the door. "I heared you! You don't fool Señor Fernando Jamón, never!"

"And look who's talking!" Claire wails at Fred. "Why didn't you announce yourself ? Before you—"

"Spare me the details," says Oscar.

"Tell you I'm me?" Fred asks Claire. "I don't usually have to."

"Do too; we always do," Oscar says. He notices that the door is warping inward. *Flight.* Oscar races into the bathroom to find—no window! He races out of the bathroom. *Fight.*

"*Las warning! O I rupture esta puerta, hear ok? To mean you pay double time, me y hotel.*"

And what other Ducklandian element might be awaiting them? Oscar wonders. Jit the Revenge-thirsty, wearing a ghoulishly blood-soaked head bandage?

"I hear chirping!" Claire realizes. "That smell is coming from—"

"*Abra!*"

"Shut up, Ham." She hasn't forgiven Fernando for the way he—a snorkeling guide—ignored her on his boat. Hard to believe that Oscar would be green enough to buy birds from an obvious ass like him. "You need money?" Claire asks Oscar. Her bag is on the night table. "I have money."

Yes. "No." Maybe later. "Thanks." All I want is my brother to—

Puta sneezes.

—look at me.

The doorjamb explodes. Fred ducks, deflecting scraps of soaring molding with his forearm. Next, Fernando's bare foot punctures the door, and it's raining wood splinters, the entire thing buckling in one terrible, skeletal crunch.

"*Hide!*" Oscar shouts.

Through the sweaty, threadbare sheet, everything looks altered. The brothers seem ghostly, vaporous. As if their bodies could pass clear through one another or through her. Claire scoots down toward the foot of the mattress, lower.

Fred rolls under the bed.

Oscar stashes the birds behind drapes and turns to confront . . . The door! Coming fast! Jamón attached! The door and Oscar slam together, bounce apart, slam. Fernando breaks his fall by grabbing a handful of Oscar's curls, regaining his balance as the hair wrenches right out of the scalp. An appalling sound, like carpet shredding. Fred, from his hiding place beneath the bed, can feel it in his teeth. Also in commiserative agony, Claire stuffs sheet down her throat. Oscar, in tears, fumes. Fragments of his beloved sunglasses lie scattered here and there when the scuffle is over.

"*Dónde está la Puta?!*" Fernando checks behind the door he's still holding, which now resembles a piece of driftwood with a knob.

Don't sneeze, Puta. An unspoken wish that immediately backfires. Atchichoo.

Hee hee. Fernando pounces on the drapes. Hee hee. "Muy inteligente hiding spot, Oscar." He removes the life preserver and is greeting Puta with the usual "Cómo está, baby?" drivel, when a jangling sound startles him.

Claire's hands rifling through her bag. Oscar watches Fernando watch Claire's tongue play in the space between her front teeth. And she squints. Wallet's gone! With the drapes pulled, the sun blasts straight into one eye and out the side of her head. Her temples pound. The wallet can't just be gone.

"Otra Puta tuya?" Fernando asks Oscar. He rearranges his balls and, addressing Oscar, orders Claire "*Out* of here so I can kill you."

From under the bed, Fred chances, "Don't you ever *ever* dare talk to her that way again."

"*Qué?!*" Fernando looks at the mattress—did it speak? He is totally clueless. Then he glances from Oscar to Claire (smiling) to Oscar to Claire (glaring). "Dónde está this money you are owing me?"

"Don't have it."

"Americano sin cash, no es posible."

Oscar fumbles for his wallet. "See." Proof. "Poof! All gone."

"Mine too," Claire says. Her whole bag's emptied out now. "Did Paco . . . ?"

Who's Paco? Fred wonders. Paco? Ham? They need a plan. Right now.

Fernando's gleeful. "That little bandido!" Hee hee hee again.

Oscar grabs for the bird box, but it eludes him, swished out of reach, like a bullfighter's cape, at the last possible moment.

"Two hundred plus fifty dollars. And I am keep Puta."

Two hundred fifty dollars? That's about all Fred has.

"The hell you are."

Tell him, bro.

"You have some more hair, sí?" Fernando lunges for another clump.

No.

"No!" Claire jumps to her feet, brandishing the room key.

"*I said out, woman, so I can kill him!*"

Don't let him yell at her like that, Fred bristles.

"Out!" Fernando tugs on Claire's shirttail.

Claire doesn't wait to be told a fourth time. She runs into the bathroom and starts ransacking the toiletries for something weaponesque.

"Enough." Oscar's playing it tough, finally.

Thata boy.

"Now gimme the box nice, Jamón, or you might have to explain some things to the federales."

Yes, Osc! Fred grinds his fist into the carpet. Way to go!

"Or maybe to those friends a mine down at the American embassy?"

Kickass! In his excitement, Fred bangs his head on the frame.

"Money," Fernando says, monotone.

"Give—me—the—box."

"Other way, silly man."

Sillyman? Sillyman! Oscar squares off for a battle but is interrupted by Claire, who blasts Off! toward Fernando as a slice of light from the window meets a fish scale slowly twirling down from the tip of Jamón's gutting knife.

Claire screams.

Fred pops out.

Fernando screams and drops the box.

The birds scream on the way down, and then one stops.

Oscar drops down and screams.

12

SOMETHING

TOASTABLE

"Toast!" Sam shouts, swinging his mike cord, as he rallies the wedding bash at Chester's. "Best man Osc!" Sam pumps his hips. "Come *on* up, you twin, annnd . . ." Sam pulses his scar-flecked chin in syncopation with Peaches' "Hava Nagila" snare solo. "To-oast!"

To a new beauty in the family. Good goin, bro. I love ya, man, don't ever change. Oscar crouches in the door shadows, Homeboy perched atop his left shoulder. *Fred and Claire sitting in a tree. K-i-s-s-i-n-g.* It's useless. He sees nothing remotely toastable in the idea of Fred with a wife, even Claire. It's stupid, how his only thought is that it's Sam's fault. *He* brought her here. If it were God, He'd have brought one for me too.

"Yo! Heave ho!" says D.J. Gooch, self-designated leader of the Traditional Chair Lifting. "With your legs," he reminds his boys, "not your backs!" as they elevate the newlyweds in beauty parlor swivel stools, which Hersh himself unscrewed from the floor. Also "on the up and up" are groomfolk Lester and "Ups-a-daisy" Charlotte Arm, and bridekin No One and Arthur Allswell.

"I like it, this . . . Judaism thing," Mr. Allswell says, and reaches down to pat Eliot Horowitz's spiny neck. "Hell, Clara, why don't we convert!"

"Why not is right!" Charlotte's tipsy, clutching her champagne glass as she joins in calling for a "Toast." To her two firsts—daughter-in-law, and, if it's no scam, a winning entry form, redeemable for one brand-new Japanese four-stroke water-cooled motorcycle.

"In or out?" Down below, at reality level, Louette has "had it up to here" with Oscar's indecisiveness. Still skirting around in that doorway like a stray. And her feet hurt. When's *her* turn to be levitated? she'd like to know. When's *she* going to be prized and paraded? She waves a miniature tuxedo, a gift for Homeboy. "Just try it on, pleeease, for me. That bird's so unsightly, he—Hey, look at Hersh!"

But Oscar's got his eye back on Sam, who's in rare form, sliding slo-mo down the mike stand as Peaches plies the high hat. "Do it, Mama!" Kneeling, Sam takes a pull off a hairwash hose (flowing with champagne for the occasion) before reprising "Hava Nagila." "Hersh, my man. World-Class Hair and Hora Master!"

The old man, slowly raising his good right knee, winks mischievously and stamps. He snakes his arms upward, stylish, and snaps. He kicks first left, flick of the ankle, then right, and claps.

A red alert goes out among the dancing circle. Rubbergrandmom eyebrows shoot toward hairlines:

"I knew it!"

"I told you!"

"Did I tell you?"

"It's that Lillian Allswell wallflower."

"Bowing to her, yet."

"I thought he had disk problems."

"I thought he had a bum leg."

"I think he has ideas."

And when Lillian, completely attired in plum, from "heeled moccasins" to tinted bun (freebie by Fred), bows back, Hersh kisses her hand.

"Look, Ida! Are you looking? Ida!"

"And he only widowed six months; it's not right."

As Hersh leads her across the beauty parlor, Lillian flirts in little peeping glimpses, her head thrown back.

"She's meshuggener."

Hersh plucks her a rose from a passing bouquet.

"Poor Shaky Bea. She had her eye on him first, ya know."

Lillian has placed the flower between her teeth and now merges into the circle without missing a step.

"A hora natural."

"Dance at every wedding and you'll cry at every funeral."

UP NEAR the ceiling, the chair under Claire "feels like Gilbert!"

Her shriek startles Fred out of visions of decapitation by track lighting. "Who?"

"Close your eyes," Claire says soothingly. The frothy white wedding dress, her mother's, so obscures the chair that it appears she is gliding on bubbles. "A sensation." The new hair—Mary's swirl, dip, tuck—so suits her, it inspired Hersh to quote the Midrash on Genesis: When God created Eve, he decided to give her a pleasing coiffure before presenting her to Adam.

But Fred would rather watch his bride than bounce around with his eyes shut. Like Sam's no-headlight game. "Who's Gilbert?"

"You know. The storm." Claire refers to the hurricane that blew into Cancún a mere six days after she and the Arm brothers blew out. Now she covers her head with her hands—no hands!

"Careful." Fred's in a constant state of fear that Claire will fall.

"Wasn't it our stinky luck to miss Gilberto, though? Drama! And glamour and danger and wet! All my favorites!"

What about underwater sex? Fred wants to ask. That was dramatic, wasn't it? Semi-dangerous. Wet. She couldn't get enough of the mermaid life, seafood soup and body surfing. She loved those mariachi costumes with gold piping, the tiny red-eyed tree frogs, jumping up and down on the bed. And, "If you had to choose between the two, hurricane and honeymoon, what then?"

"Hmmm. I've never been to Brooklyn," Claire hints. "Or the Bronx, or Staten Island for that matter."

"I'll take you," Fred says, blushing. Sweet cheeks. "We can do all the boroughs."

Below, the circle of guests contracts and expands. Supra-cleaved Constance Dufour tries to scream up at Claire, something about lucky garters and bouquets, but the mass swallows her up. Tommy Eako horas handstanding. The band applauds. A relief crew of chair operators—mostly Sam's friends, ex-Binghamton-frat guys—causes some heavy turbulence.

"I offered knee pads." Lester shrugs. Along with this protective gear, he wears rainbow suspenders, a wooden bow tie, sneakers, and the eight-hundred-dollar tux that Charlotte made him purchase to impress "their people"—Claire's family and friends. "No one wanted knee pads."

Charlotte's ignoring him. "At least *their* people aren't put off by the beauty parlor reception." She sips the last of her champagne. Indeed, "Lillian proclaimed it 'an absolute hoot.' I heard her." Ironically, the Sidehill snobs are the ones abuzz.

"So why the bargain reception?"

They're spreading the horrendous untruth that imminent bankruptcy must be facing Allswell Cap N Gown. A speculation derived from a sidebar to the recently much televised Hurricane Gilbert story: the scandalous fall of zillionaire Elmer J. Ducklander's famed PetMart empire.

Being an ex-employee naturally doesn't hurt Oscar's renown any. And the fact that it was he, not his twin, the groom, who originally went off gallivanting with Claire, who at the time was set to marry Sam Lubin, just about qualifies Oscar for a spot in Sidehill gossipdom's hall of infamy.

"Toast! Toast!"

The chant reaches Oscar, now all the way out the door. *He could keep going too—across the street, behind Hardware and Pain, through the overgrown softball lot, hop the fence and van-*

ish. Here, on the sidewalk in front of Chester's, pockets of guests enjoy a smoke or the reverse, fresh air. The bird, Homeboy, enjoys an apple snack and a head scratch. Oscar and Louette: part two of their quotidian argument.

"Since when did you start using words like quotidian?" Louette asks.

"Since the intro of your fall collection." Oscar sneers at the micro-tux, hanging on a miniature plastic hanger.

"It's Wedding Ken apparel actually, but—"

"Weddingk En, WeddingK En," Homeboy mimics. The macaw is unsightly, like a stewed chicken with wads of dyed feathers glued on willy-nilly. He sits on Oscar's left shoulder, such a frequented perch these days that he's forged himself a callous there. "WeddingK En." A podium. "WeddingK En." Out to get himself a toy, he pecks Louette's big wooden lightning-bolt-shaped earring.

"See, he likes you," Oscar says.

Louette snorts, fussing with the dangling zigzags. Her preposterous outfit—orange crushed-velvet pantaloons, white steel-toed pumps, handmade licorice jewelry, big cherry-red bow barrette on top—is, frankly, irritating. Only the new cranberry-rinsed bob flatters her. Fred's creation.

"So he's a little moth-eaten," Oscar grants. He's alive at least. "If he'll stoop to talk human talk after all he's—"

"Deranged," Louette insists. You can't blame her. "Say it."

Oscar won't comply, but Homeboy dutifully mimics, "Say it. Say it. Say it."

"He's no slouch," Oscar sighs. "Give him that." Every day there are improvements. Feathers around his neck are beginning to grow back. Every day brings a new addition to Homeboy's already extensive vocabulary, which includes names: Oscar, Lou, Fred. Ordinary words: Hello, Yeah, Shit, What?, OK. An occasional impersonation: Crazy Eddie, Morton Downey, Peaches. Every day Oscar has a new "my pet" anecdote.

Louette scrapes her steel-toed pump along the asphalt. "Crappy new discount shoes," she says.

"*Me* of all people, a pet person," Oscar continues. Lately, he finds himself loitering in bird shops. As ironic as Sam's new role on radio as The Voice of Conscience. ("Don't drip N.Y. dry." "Hugs are better than drugs." "Before you fall for a line like this, call . . .") Oscar's even made a couple of new friends— parrot people.

"Maybe he *wants* to wear a tux," Louette says. "Maybe he's cold, what with all those rubbery bald spots he's got from plucking and chewing through his skin." Louette's face scrunches. "That's muscle tissue, isn't it?"

Oscar kisses her. Or doesn't. Misses her mouth entirely as Louette flinches over "that bird's neck, it's creased." Then she tries to kiss Oscar back but can't reach. They squeeze limbs, rub heads, but something's wrong. She chins his chest, hard.

"Say it!" Homeboy squawks.

Louette explodes. "I hate him!"

They polarize. Oscar has the distinct feeling that this is it. And he's not sorry so much as amazed that a pet finally finished them off.

Would things be different if Louette had been in the Yucatán to see Homeboy just after the box dropped? "All twisted weird, unconscious on the bungalow floor." Or later, on the plane home, "bandaged, drunk on tequila, hidden inside my shirt." Perhaps if she had felt "that puny heart beating against my belly . . ."

"My feet hurt," Louette drones yet again. Meaning *I heard* it. Meaning *What would you like me to say?* You can't blame her. "Oh, Osc, why don't we—"

"Say it. Say it," Homeboy repeats. "Say it."

"Make him stop!" Louette pleads, squeezing her temples.

"He seems to really like that one." Oscar's at a loss. "It's interesting"—seeing as Homeboy was actually mute for more than a month after arriving in Queens. Trauma, Oscar's zoology professor diagnosed. He recommended a vet, who also said Trauma and who recommended a pet shrink in SoHo, who said Trauma and recommended three two-hundred-seventy-five-dollar-a-month speech therapy sessions to start.

Oscar picks a banana off a low branch of the sycamore in

front of Chester's. Lester's touch. In honor of the wedding, Dad dragged out a ladder and personally tied fruit onto the tree. Too gorgeous a display to disrupt, people must think, or that it's plastic, though a light from below illuminates the very real bunches, oranges too, apples, pears, even a few pineapples, all attached with invisible string (fishing line).

"Gifts to the god of passersby," Lester claims. "My personal deity. The source of all our clients over the years, and many friends."

Mr. Allswell nods, and strokes his mustache. Like a misplaced eyebrow. "Akin to revelation, was it, Lester?"

"Indeed. A light blinking on in the fridge."

THE CHAIR beneath Claire bucks and jerks as the crowd gets wild, pushing in.

Fred marvels at "All those scalps." Claire at the upturned faces, smiling ferociously.

Lillian dances the music faster. Her rose sheds petals, her hairdo shoots out bobby pins, her plum satin sleeve issues tissues and tissues and tissues. Like one of Fred's favorite old magic tricks. The hora circle orbits and counterorbits, rotating in ever smaller paths with ever larger kicks.

"Can you tell them to put me down now?" Claire asks, but her voice gets sucked into the funneling celebration—this hunger to congratulate, hora, light candles, break bread, make blessings, raise chairs and glasses, "Toast!" throw rice, toss birdseed, hand out check-stuffed envelopes—and evaporates. In the voracious ritual, all is consumed.

No one is exempt.

Except, sadly, Shaky Bea, envious of Lillian and pretending now to mind the food table.

"For a woman like that, a buffet is a weapon."

Except, of course, The Bouncetones. Sid (on bass), Sam (keyboards and guitar), Peaches (rocking the skins), the geriatric brass section, and, wearing a white spandex unitard, Sam's new fiancée, Candy (on the tambourine).

And, naturally, except Oscar, twin brother, best man—Toast! Toast! Toastmaster—who is still missing, along with his newly reinstated girlfriend, Loonette, as the mouths have tagged her for being so senseless as to take Oscar back after everything they've heard.

"And does he have any intention of finding a new job?"

"He's back in school."

"School schmool. Tell me, does he carry that shmata of a bird everywhere?"

"God forbid something should happen where it flies off."

"Or she does."

"A resemblance not to miss: the way she squawks at him, always some new meshugge hair color."

"And skinny as a gutted herring."

"I should be so lucky. A ton I musta gained over those mashed potatoes."

"Uh. Did you ever? Cream-y, it's obscene. Not a lump in there."

"Eggs, I bet. Eggs, milk, paprika, butter, let's not discuss it. Mmm, not another word. Well, maybe just one more little taste."

Fred was as stunned and delighted only last night in his parents' kitchen—the newly exposed hardwood floors freshly sanded, waxed, polished—to discover that all along he'd been mourning Mary's mashed potatoes unnecessarily, because *Hersh* makes them. Turns out that those famous mashed potatoes are, and always have been, Hersh's specialty, a fact that everyone but Fred seems already to have known.

He might never have found out had they let Arthur Allswell have the reception catered. They might right now be on the Allswells' lawn eating escargots instead, in a hotel ballroom choosing salmon or chicken, at a restaurant, in "Hawaii, or up in a fleet of hot-air balloons over the Grand Canyon." The man gave them every option. "Anything to make you happy. I only want you kids happy." He insists on it. He's gone so far as to offer to give Claire and Fred his house. "The old galoot. Too big for one guy. If it'll make you happy . . ."

Happy. Happy. The prospect puts Fred on edge. This much goodwill, however genuine, makes him feel like a lab rat given sudden massive doses of Nice. Will he absorb it and glow some back?

Claire speaks up where Fred cannot. She hopes to "start small," "scale down," "simplify" for a while, "for a change." More than anything, she hopes she and Fred can live right here near Chester's, "like regular people."

"Which is all well and good: modesty." The gabhounds endorse it.

"Adorable."

"But what exactly is the fascination this shiksa has with poverty, tell me?" Clearly unaware that the champagne they've all been guzzling costs a hundred fifty dollars a pop.

Sam announces that the chair bearers have decided to hold the airborne wedding party hostage. "Ransom set at a toast from Oscar."

"What do I care!" says Charlotte. "Give yaselves hernias. It's not every day I'm swept off my feet by a team of strong young lookers." Blowing kisses, she reclines in her chair, legs resting on an imaginary ottoman, her control-top panty hose exposed clear up to the crotch.

"Ma!" It's not like her. It's the alcohol. It's overexcitement. It's Claire.

Oh, eventually Charlotte'll get to know her—not as "poor Claire," motherless teenager and goy high school dropout, nor as "that Claire," the already hot, thoroughly chewed-up piece of yak around Chesty's, where some tongues even maintain she is Sam Lubin's leftovers: for shame!—and will learn to love her, Fred has faith.

Though he's pretty much given up hope of having the prize motorcycle forked over to him, them—new them!—for a wedding present. Hersh, too, has made it known he'd appreciate the bike as a gift for the six-month anniversary of his sobriety. Lester also, for his coming fifty-seventh birthday. And Oscar, as a sort of general consolation prize. Though yet to arrive, the machine already has its own space cleared in the garage, a lock, cover, insurance.

"A motorcycle! At her age?"

"Next thing she'll fly off like her son to do *research.*"

"Fathom when Fred showed up and saw that. Oscar researching the girl, my."

"With good intentions Fred's loaded."

"But too late. He most certainly missed the boat. Oh, stop with that look, Ida. I'm not livin in the dark ages. It's a different world. Today they—"

"Ladies," Hersh interrupts, voice booming. "Sure, it's a different world, but isn't it incredible? Mousse we have. Press-on nails! The astronauts go into space to take pictures."

"Humph!" exclaims a woman Fred recognizes as the one who's always ripping stuff out of the magazines in the waiting area. Humph. "If you have money, you travel."

Out of patience or breath, Hersh breaks free from the dancers, turns and waves up at Fred: "How's the view?" At Claire: "Delighted to hear you registered at Chester's." At Lester: "Where's Oscar? He's no deserter. Used to wake up every night to check whether Fred was breathing. Recall that?"

"No." Dad can sleep through anything.

"I do!" says Charlotte. "The saying goes: When a son weds, he divorces his mom. But in this case, it's twin split."

"What?" Fred looks forward to sleeping with Claire forever.

"I wish *your* ma could be here, Claire." Mr. Allswell's teary. "Toast! Toast!"

The spinning has accelerated to the point where it can no longer accommodate footwork. Sandrine, in stocking feet, trips when she attempts a kick. The pinwheel of dancers keeps going, dragging her around, around, while she laughs painfully, raucously.

"She likes it!?"

The chairs, held aloft, careen even more precipitously when their third set of operators takes over. Chester's big picture window is completely steamed. The mood changes the music, or the music the mood, as The Bouncetones offer their version of "Psycho Killer." Absolute proof you can hora to anything.

And even Charlotte's had "Enough! I'm the hostess. If you don't put us down by the count of three . . ."

"Uh oh. Thar she blows," Lester says. "Be grateful they can still lift ya, Char." Ha ha.

"One." Charlotte is not laughing. To the contrary, she's bawling. The reception's ruined. Makeup drooling, she looks like one of her students from Makeup for the Blind.

Fred's relieved to see his mother back to her old self. "Two and a half" sounds to him like a lullaby. "Two and three quarters."

But it upsets Claire. "Isn't somebody gonna help her?!"

She might just as well be referring to Sandrine, who's now not enjoying the ride. Her arm, no longer properly attached to her shoulder, reminds Claire of that poor scarlet macaw in Playa Alguna, the way her head flopped loose from her neck socket at such an unusual angle. The widower, Homeboy, got injured trying to flee the scene. Forgetting his missing wing feathers, he nose-dived. Luckily, Oscar had studied Advanced Pet CPR and began resuscitation. Fred muscled the fishing knife from Fernando, who, mourning the dead female, tried to light his cigarette with the faucet.

In the quest to lose her virginity, Claire saw her desire focus less and less on sex per se and more and more on Fred. "Will you marry me?" she asked, appalled with herself.

Until he said, "Yes, sí."

Until *they* said, "Yes, sí." Twins will be twins.

Until Fernando said, "Bigamy?" He knew that word. And tried igniting a second Delicado with a hotel sewing kit. Finally, he gave up, fell to his knees, and picked the dead bird off the carpet.

"Stop! Really!" Sandrine's begging.

Someone's got to help her.

Charlotte's hysterical. "Two and seven eighths! . . . Keep this up, I'll have you all arrested. Lester? Lester!"

"Go ahead, Fred. Do something," Dad says.

"Claire," Fred says.

Claire says, "Dad?"

Mr. Allswell buffs his head, narrows his shoulders, and even seems to ice up some regarding Fred. Gone is his enchantment with "these shenanigans."

"Two and nine tenths."

"I'm constricting," Mr. Allswell announces, ominously.

"Clear out!" Fred leaps, managing to land on two feet without twisting his ankle, but far from suavely catlike.

On the ground, he hears snickering, shouts, one belch. Standing, he sees pink dots, then "Claire!?"

"You said jump."

"Not aloud I didn't."

A sudden hush falls over the dance floor, then, "Oooh."

"So cute."

"I see that special look."

"A groom and a bride have glass eyes."

"Whataya bet it's that space between her teeth that gets him? Just like whatshername's."

"Ida says she's got one in the oven."

"What's that? You hear that?"

"Sirens?"

"Ice cream?"

"Are we on fire?"

Outside, the EMS vehicle arrives, one of its wheels hopping the curb. Two men hurl themselves out of a sliding side door, do a double take at the fruit hanging on the sycamore, then rush into Chester's.

"Hersh!?" Oscar, panicking, takes off after the uniforms. But there he is, "Uncle Great," animatedly directing a flurry of leave-taking, exhibiting no sign of ill health whatsoever.

"Fore ya go, grab an eyeful of our famous Bette Davis photo. The star at a tender age poses with Yours Truly, Hersh T. Arm from Fifth Avenue. Have a look. It's free."

"I'd love to," says a laughing woman Oscar recognizes. "But I'm blind." It's the dogless pretty one.

The EMS guys shove past to exit, empty-handed. Sandrine

traipses after them like a tail. "Stop." She sobs, clutching her shoulder. Sob. She demands a stretcher. "I made the phone call. Wait, *I'm* the patient."

Louette, unconsciously sympathetic, clutches her own shoulder and follows. Tommy Eako—trailing Louette trailing Sandrine trailing the EMS guys—clutches the blind woman's shoulder.

"What the hell *is* this?" Oscar's pissed.

"Later, Fred," Tommy says, with a quick flutter of his ever-fuchsia lids. Of course, that wouldn't matter to a blind pickup. "Eternal congrats."

Oscar momentarily considers "Eternal congrats" as a possible toast overture. The impending duty is not without honor, he's decided. "To the engagees," is how Mr. Allswell began *his* salutations at the engagement party. But then what? "One bone, one flesh" is all Oscar and Fred truly share.

Scanning the room, Oscar glimpses Claire's dad, standing with Lester by the sinks. He could go ask for advice. But the sight of the two men, arms interlocked to drink from each other's hoses, subdues Oscar, impresses him, makes him sad.

"*You're* not Sad Sacks," Hersh walks up to say. "What is it? Is the bride too beautiful?"

"Too beautiful?" Oscar shrugs. "I'm sure that's relative." He's about to tell Hersh how he, too, said yes when Claire proposed, but Fred pounces.

"Where the . . . ?" Pounces and springs back, as if Oscar's arm had scalded him. So this is how it feels to feel shy in front of your own twin.

"Outside," Oscar explains, though they've clicked in to where speaking is unnecessary. He bumbles, "Outside, just right out . . ." It's not so easy letting go of words. The vagaries of meaning they afford are more pleasant than most people can appreciate.

Without speaking, Fred is saying, "Look, Mom's become a bouncer." She's ousting Deja Vu Gooch and his "morons" by force. "This is the way she banished the faith healer from his/their/Mary's room. You weren't there, of course, but . . ."

Two minds communicate clearly the same way two mouths do—one at a time. And Fred's hogging.

Am not. Fred's fidgeting with his bow tie. This telepathic flow has only happened to them so full blown once before. Fourteen years old, walking home from school. No special occasion that time.

"Half day." Oscar pushes his way in. Untying Fred from the black tie noose, he gently flicks his cheek with one end of the tie. Then, loosening his own tie, Oscar flicks himself for balance. "Snow."

"Sandrine insists her shoulder unsocketed and resocketed, and no one will believe her," Louette has come back to report. "Horaing."

"Whoring?" says Sam, taking a break from his emcee duties.

"Where'd *you* come from?" Louette holds her heart.

"Originally, Flushing . . . Hey, guy?" Sam slaps Oscar's shoulders. "Cómo está?" But in his voice, he's tentative.

"Bien. Bien." Homeboy responds.

"No!" Oscar isn't finished yet. "What I mean is . . ." Or maybe he is. "Is . . ." Or maybe . . . "But I don't know what I mean."

Only Fred does. "Yes." That is, "No." Fred doesn't "know either what he means too."

"What is going on with you guys?" Louette says, marching off theatrically for the bathroom. But after three or four steps, she slips and crashes nose-first into the dessert cart (a converted manicure table with wheels), sending her shoe flying into the wedding cake, the cake careening toward a tower of gifts, the gifts toppling with the smothered-explosion sound of wrapped-up fragile things shattering.

"Whoa," Oscar calls, running to help Louette up. "Really jonesing for the spotlight, aren't you?" He collects the stray shoe off the cake on his way.

"Yes."

Oscar didn't expect that. As he lifts her by the elbow, he refrains from mentioning that he's discovered why her feet hurt. Instead, Oscar licks some whipped cream/raspberry goop off her eyelash. It tastes black (mascara), along with the creamy sweet (frosting), and damp (tears).

"Can I ask a gigantuan favor?" Louette pleads as Oscar steers her through the tittering crowd toward the bathroom, shoes in hand. "Osc?" She forgot to take out the cardboard insoles.

"Why not?"

"Would you, like, how would you like to maybe, would you, like, marry me?"

FIN. Señor Fernando Jamón lifted Puta off the carpet, said, "Antes que te cases, mira lo que haces," and departed. Nothing else. No adiós, nada, just this advice (untranslated, Oscar suspects, for that final obnoxious last impression). Just the sight of Jamón, cradling the dead bird. Fin. He walked off into the sunset.

"It was more like a glare," Fred amends. "High noon. A scorcher."

They are all piled into the bathroom, guarding Claire's stuff while she throws up. Something old: the veil, which Oscar's now wearing. Something new: the hairdo—Fred's pulling the strands out of vomit's way. Something borrowed: Louette habitually claps together the shoes—her pair against Claire's. "The something blue," Claire says, trying not to think about toilet bowl cleaner. "That's between the bride and groom."

"I wish you'd a let me waste that guy," Fred says, referring to Fernando. He will repeat his wish at this point in the story forevermore, Oscar knows. The thought is somehow comforting.

"I got one squirt in with the Off!" That's Claire's refrain. Feeling shaky but better, she stands to wash her face. "Ham was just trying to be authentic. 'Antes que te cases, mira lo que haces' sounds a whole lot snazzier in Spanish."

By the time she got a chance to interpret, it was much later. It was after things had more or less been settled for better or for worse, till death "do you Clara Bride take this manly man

to be your awful wedded hus-band?" After it had been established that Homeboy would not die, or probably be the same
ever again. After Fred had effectively taken charge—paying the
hotel bill and damages, insisting on a Jewish wedding. After
their cash was halved, buying bandages and bird food, then
halved again, bringing the car back to the rental office in Cancún. After roaming in search of a rabbi, all those streets,
beaches, hotel lobbies. After feeling collectively queasy from
the profusion of tropical metropolis smells: diesel fuel, salt,
boiling asphalt. After they finally settled on a drunk ship captain who claimed to have once been to Israel and who agreed
to marry them there and then, at four a.m., for the price of a
pitcher of margaritas. Still, it was not until after Fred stomped
the ritual glass, forgetting to wrap it in a napkin, and Oscar
stopped the bleeding, that Claire, picking shards from her new
husband's ankle, recalled Fernando's parting counsel, "Antes
que te cases, mira lo que haces."

Before you marry, watch what you're doing.

" 'Before you marry a second time' would be more precise,"
says Claire now. "Today" being, "well . . ."

"Sickening," Fred agrees, already nostalgiatizing their real
wedding day. He remembers how, with Claire as their barker,
Fred and Oscar became once again the Arm Twin Juggling
Team, rusty but not uncoordinated. They worked the hotel-
row beach lots instead of street corners, threw papayas in
place of beanbags, pocketed restaurant knives for daggers,
burned matchbooks shoved into empty Tehuacán water bottles
in place of torches. They performed for three hours, which
stretched into four, six, before they finally raised the necessary ten bucks apiece departure fee. They even had a few pesos
extra for cerveza and hammock rentals.

Then they slept and didn't sleep, guarding Homeboy in shifts.
During Oscar's watch, Fred awoke and found his brother actually juggling more, juggling balled-up dirty T-shirts, smiling,
juggling. During Fred's watch, Oscar awoke to catch his
brother experimenting with Claire's neck. Any spot Fred would
kiss, Claire would scratch in her sleep. Kiss, scratch, kiss,

scratch. During Claire's watch, Fred and Oscar both awoke to catch her asleep, asnore.

"I'm still not in any of my dreams," Claire informed them happily the next morning. "But last night I was at least mentioned."

Oscar then presented Claire with the black coral necklace and explained how anytime she could also "claim a platinum muffin down on the bottom of the Caribbean." Just ask.

Seems it's the year for redeemable wedding gifts. Louette has offered Two Free Years of Dental Hygiene. Latvia presented Claire with a Certificate for One (too many) Free Waxing(s). And Sam's gift, The Bouncetones, are out there right now, deep into "I Can't Give You Anything But Love."

While Fred, he provided affection, life, a chance to lose her pristinity in the right way after all, underwater with snorkels and giggles, and with parrotfish for witnesses. Their extraordinarily clueless expressions were another sort of gift entirely.

"TREATS!" Oscar dispenses palm nuts to Homeboy to demonstrate the strength of the bird's enormous beak. "Watch. It can crush things that a man'd need a hammer for. Wooden lightning-bolt earrings, say."

"Sure," Louette says, bewildered. "Fine. He can have em. Fair trade. He wears the tux, he gets one. He wears the little top hat accessory, I'll give him the pair."

Homeboy peels the inner nut skin with his tongue and beak. His head is constantly turning, turning. Eyes on the sides of his head like a fish; straight on, you can hardly see them. Bare skin around eyes.

Are the earrings birdproof? Oscar's concerned. Will Homeboy choke on the metal hook part? Wood's all right, but cut in a zigzag? "To be safe, I think you'll have to keep them on."

"On?"

"He's sat on your shoulder before."

"Don't remind me."

As long as Louette shared her jewelry, Homeboy would have

no problem with Oscar marrying her. Think of it. In some ways, it seems right. Oscar could save Louette from ants. Louette could save Oscar from gingivitis. They could save each other from terminal loneliness.

Only, Homeboy has beat her to it. What Oscar needs next is a job, not a wife. And—

"I gotta go." Louette knows it.

"No." Claire tries to help. "I haven't told you the rest. Our breakfast scam and . . ."

They gorged themselves on the hotel buffet and charged it to a fake room number.

"Oscar already did; thanks; good one. See you guys some—"

"Did he mention who thought it up?"

"You." Louette tries to hand back the shoes, but Claire appears not to notice. "I'm proud of you."

"*Toast! Toast! Toast!*" Homeboy picks up the chant after all.

"To my new sister-in-trouble-with-the-law," Oscar improvised the first time, in the Yucatán, raising a tortilla. At that posh place tortillas came in shades from beige to blue. "The poorest rich girl I know . . . And the most beautiful." Within arm's reach of their table, a kid was painting the palm trees white. The palm trees came in all shades too. The kid couldn't say why. To match the hotels, he guessed.

Which put Claire in mind of the breakfast she had bought Paco. How he had asked for her signature, then stolen her credit card. "Oops."

"Oops," Fred repeated. "Yikes." But sweetly. His heart fed, still feeds, on these her interjections. And on the subject of Claire's stolen wallet. "If we're really strapped for funds," he also teased Oscar, "there's always the platinum muffin." Still not totally convinced the thing exists but fond of the mythic image.

Fred also has to take Oscar's word for what Oscar claims he saw aboard the now notorious and demolished Ducklander yacht. Ironically, it was what Oscar didn't see that saved the man—*pot. Roundup*'s crew and human passengers, including Marci, were found scattered atop seven bales of Mexican bud.

A miracle. The marijuana rafts survived the storm, floating on long after the sinking of all that sleek fiberglass. A feature on "60 Minutes." Marci was interviewed, looking swell, swearing she hadn't "an inkling." She had come aboard the yacht at Miami "for work" and clung to the drifting drugs "for survival." Once out of jail, she intends to do volunteer work for Greenpeace.

"Toast! Toast!"

"Here's to salsa ketchup in your eye" also worked well in Mexico, but you had to be there. Oscar smooths his unsmoothable hair and beelines it toward the stage, stopping only to deposit Homeboy with Louette. "He's not ready to make any commitments, but for now yours is the only shoulder he wants to be on."

"Why?"

"He doesn't know."

"If you can't figure out what you want, you'll never know which things you should feel bad about not having."

"That a warning?"

"You bet."

"TESTING ... Testing ... Toasting." Oscar's voice sounds fuzzed with his mouth too close to the mike. He sticks his finger in his ear; why?

"Chill," Sam whispers. "Breathe deep, from the diaphragm. Concentrate on a point across the room and ... forgive me."

"My stomach's bubbling."

"Don't move." Sam disappears and reappears with two shots of something golden. "How you gonna make a toast without the antifogmatic?" He rubs at Oscar's shoulder kinks. Their first contact in months.

"How's Nancy Poodle?" Oscar asks.

"The bitch ate two hundred sixty-five dollars."

"Haven't you heard of mint doggy bones?"

"It's no joke. I UPS'd her to my sis, Lynn, in Maryland." Sam's face droops. "Actually, I miss her guts. But we ... but

Candy . . . it was her paycheck that Nance scarfed. Big blow-out, ya know. She threatened to call off the wedding if—''

Oscar shakes his head. "Well, congratulations anyway, I guess." Sam thumb-twirls his class ring in inconsolable circles. "About the wedding."

"Yeah . . . Ya know, I still got those chicks ya gave us. Claire's and mine."

"Yeah?"

"Yeah. Keep em in the bathtub. They're startin to look edible. Well, you'd better go spew. This toast shit is beginning to alterate my heartbeat."

Oscar has accidently already drunk his shot.

"You peckerhead." But Sam relinquishes his, offering "background music" and turning to cue Peaches for a drum-roll. "Listen. How bout you bein my best man?"

"What?" Peaches, arms in the air, incredulous.

"Stay outta this, Ma. He's about to say yes."

"Am I?" Oscar smiles, lifting the shot glass. This could turn into a full-time career. Professional best man. Surprised to be smiling, Oscar scans the much-diminished party.

"To a most unlikely couple, Clara and Frederick, newly spliced and bound for happiness, drink!" Oscar's raised arm begins to ache. His free one begins to rise. He throws a kiss. And that's the extent of it.

"Them are toastin' words," Sam yells.

"To Sam!" then. Oscar has not forgotten that it was Sam "Who made this all possible!"

Once the liquid's gone down, they'll strike a deal. Oscar'll agree to be best man as soon as the jerk retrieves his dog.

A NOTE ABOUT THE AUTHOR

Jill Eisenstadt grew up in Rockaway Beach, New York. She was educated at Bennington College and Columbia University. She lives in New York City.

A NOTE ON THE TYPE

The text of this book was set in Aster, a typeface designed by Francesco Simoncini (born 1912 in Bologna,
Italy) for Ludwig and Mayer, the German type foundry.
Aster was introduced in 1958, and has since enjoyed wide
popularity as a newspaper and book type.

Composed by Creative Graphics, Inc.,
Allentown, Pennsylvania

Printed and bound by Arcata Graphics,
Martinsburg, West Virginia

Designed by Peter A. Andersen